Catherine's Heart

Catherine's Heart

LAWANA BLACKWELL

BETHANYHOUSE
www.bethanyhouse.com

Catherine's Heart
Copyright © 2002
Lawana Blackwell

Cover illustration by Paul Casale
Cover design by Becky Noyes/Dan Thornberg

Published by Bethany House Publishers
A Ministry of Bethany Fellowship International
11400 Hampshire Avenue South
Bloomington, Minnesota 55438
www.bethanyhouse.com

Printed in the United States of America by
Bethany Press International, Bloomington, Minnesota 55438

Library of Congress Cataloging-in-Publication Data

Blackwell, Lawana, 1952–
    Catherine's heart / by Lawana Blackwell.
      p.   cm. — (Tales of London ; 2)
    ISBN 0-7642-2259-7
    1. Women college students—Fiction. 2. Girton College (University of Cambridge)—
Fiction. 3. Cambridge (England)—Fiction. I. Title.
    PS3552.L3429 C38   2002
    813'.54—dc21   2002010130

LAWANA BLACKWELL is a full-time writer with nine published books, including the bestselling GRESHAM CHRONICLES. She and her husband live in Baton Rouge, Louisiana and have three sons.

This book is dedicated to my brother,

Robert Chandler,

who is loved by so many
for his tender heart and gentle soul.

One

On the fourth of October, 1880, something besides coal smoke tinged the morning air under the arched iron-and-glass train shed at King's Cross Station. It was an atmosphere of anticipation, evident in the flushed cheeks of the "freshers" going off to University for the first time.

Students heading up for a second year could be identified by their bored, almost scornful expressions, maintained so as not to be confused with the newcomers. Third-year and fourth-year students, along with those returning for advanced degrees, wore the look of someone simply waiting for a train.

Those differences were pointed out to eighteen-year-old Catherine Rayborn by her Uncle Daniel as she waited to board the Great Northern Railway Express between London and Cambridge. "It'll be the same at Paddington with the Oxford lot," her father's brother said, humor creasing the corners of his green eyes.

For the fourth time since leaving the house on Berkeley Square, Catherine felt for loose pins in the chignon beneath the brim of her claret-colored felt hat. Her fawn gloves were spotless and black boots polished to a luster. Beneath her grey wool outer coat she wore a black Eton jacket and bustled skirt of soft brown serge. Eight other outfits were folded in tissue in her trunk, along with a tennis costume, nightgowns and wrapper, underclothing, stockings, and shoes. She had helped the chambermaids pack, and slept only fitfully last night from the excitement of it all.

"Do I look like a fresher?" she asked.

Aunt Naomi's bottle-blue eyes appraised her. "I'm afraid you do, dear."

Sarah Doyle, Catherine's cousin, nodded. "One would think you just stepped off the farm."

"Now stop that, you two," Uncle Daniel ordered his wife and daughter.

"You'll have her too intimidated to leave."

"Not at all, Uncle Daniel," Catherine said, returning the women's smiles. Their light banter was intended to put her at ease, and she appreciated it.

Even more, she appreciated their not insisting on accompanying her for the ninety-minute journey. The two women had already visited Girton College with her in August to help order linens and draperies, lamps and carpets for her rooms. Addressing Sarah, Catherine said, "I can never thank you and William enough for inviting me to stay with you."

William Doyle was Sarah's husband, who had wished her a pleasant journey this morning with a peck on the cheek before heading off to work.

"It has been our pleasure, Catherine," Sarah replied. She possessed a quiet strength that belied her waifish green eyes, delicate features, and hair the color of cornsilk. The fingerless left hand did not detract from her beauty. *Better a diamond with a flaw than a pebble without,* Catherine's mother, Virginia, had once said of her.

"Yoo-hoo! Catherine?"

Catherine turned. About ten feet away, a woman was weaving through the crowd with a young girl in tow.

"Why, Aunt Phyllis . . . Muriel," Catherine said, closing the gap between them. "How good of you to come."

"I feared we were too late!"

Catherine was caught up in a *Jardin de Coeur*-scented embrace. Then her mother's younger sister seized her shoulders and stepped back. "How smart you look!"

"Thank you, Aunt Phyllis. So do you."

And it was so. Time had only slightly eroded the beauty that shone from the portrait that had hung in Catherine's late grandparents' parlor, of a slender young woman with alabaster cheeks and ethereal-looking brown eyes, under an enormous chignon of auburn hair.

"And Muriel," Catherine said to the girl, who hung back timidly, "I thought you would be in school."

"She begged to see you off, so I'll drop her by afterward," her aunt said, taking the girl's hand again. She blew out a breath. "We had a little difficulty."

"Difficulty, Mrs. Pearce?" Uncle Daniel said as he and Sarah and Aunt Naomi approached. "Are you all ri—"

"I said I WANT some lemonade!" Muriel cried, jerking her hand from her mother's.

The seven-year-old reminded Catherine of those little English girls whose images graced biscuit tins or jars of lemon curd. But a scowl ruined the effect of the violet eyes, rosebud lips, and heart-shaped face bordered by golden waves and ringlets. "All you had to do was stop for a minute!"

"Just a little misunderstanding, Mr. Rayborn." Aunt Phyllis offered a hand to Naomi. "Mrs. Rayborn, Mrs. Doyle . . . how long has it—"

"Mum-mee, my throat is DRY! I NEED some—"

"EX-press to CAM-bridge," a guard singsonged over the whistle of the *Jenny Lind* locomotive. "PLEASE take your SEATS!"

"Oh dear! Not a minute too soon!" Aunt Phyllis turned to her daughter, and in a voice wavering between soothing and shrill said, "Catherine has to go now, dear. We'll get the drink as soon as the train has left."

"I like lemonade too," Catherine said, stepping toward the girl with outstretched arms. She was met with a violet glare and folded arms and had to settle for giving the girl a pat upon the shoulder. But by then, she was not inclined to embrace her anyway.

"She's just overtired from the rush to get here," Aunt Phyllis explained. "But she was so excited over seeing you off . . ."

Again she attempted to placate the girl. "Weren't you, dear?"

"I wish you weren't my mother!"

Aunt Phyllis gaped at her. "You don't mean that!"

Feeling a touch upon her shoulder, Catherine turned. Aunt Naomi sent a pointed glance toward the steam hissing from the locomotive's smokestack. "You really should be finding a seat, dear."

Uncle Daniel nodded. "And your ticket and trunk tag are—"

"—safely in here," Catherine finished, raising her hand to show the dark olive brocade reticule hanging from her wrist. She embraced him first, then Sarah, Aunt Phyllis, and Aunt Naomi. Another shoulder pat for the scowling child, with the thought, *At least her brothers didn't come along*.

"Thank you all for seeing me off. I'll write very soon."

In the nearest first-class coach, a middle-aged man in a black suit sat at the opposite window, across from a woman wearing a taupe grey velvet hat with matching ribbons and ostrich plumes. Catherine exchanged shy *good-mornings* with the two and settled herself just inside in the front-facing seat. She smiled from the window at her relations, who had stepped back to leave room for boarders and the porters hurrying by with luggage upon handcarts. Another wave of gratitude swept through her as she returned Sarah's wave. Had the Doyles not offered her a place to stay between terms, her father would never have allowed her to enroll at Girton.

"Pardon me, Miss, but are those seats available?"

Catherine shifted her eyes from the window to the open door. A tall young man stared back, handsome in a continental sort of way with his dark hair and eyes. At his elbow waited a fair-haired young man. Their navy blue coats were embroidered with the crest of Saint John's, one of the seventeen men's colleges that made up the University of Cambridge. Girton and Newnham, the two women's colleges, were not officially connected with the University.

"They are available," the gentleman at the window replied before Catherine could answer. He picked up his folded newspaper from the middle seat.

"Thank you." The two took the two remaining rear-facing spaces, stashing gripsacks beneath and hanging their straw boater hats on overhead brass hooks. A shrill whistle rent the air.

"EX-press to Cam-BRIDGE, LAST call for BOARD-ing!"

"Room for three?" a harried woman asked, peeking inside the open doorway, but she frowned and disappeared before anyone could reply.

Then an older gentleman with a growth of coppery mustache and beard eyed the empty space next to Catherine. "Peggy! Here!" He called over his shoulder, then stood aside to assist a young woman into the coach.

"Do mind that someone feeds Pete every day, Father," she said, turning to brush a kiss against his cheek.

"I'm surprised you haven't packed that bird in your trunk," the man said, but affectionately, and handed over a violin case. With a quick pat to her cheek, the man stepped out of the coach. The young woman dropped into the empty seat next to Catherine and let out a stream of breath.

"I still feel like we're rushing through traffic!" she exclaimed to Catherine, clutching her violin case to her bosom.

"That's why my father despises London," Catherine said sympathetically.

"My father's just the opposite. He's a tailor, and so more traffic means more customers. It's just a tribulation when you have to be somewhere in a hurry."

Freckles besprinkled the girl from collar to widow's peak, and coppery curls strayed from beneath the brim of a black straw hat. Her lips were thin, yet her mouth appeared to be almost too wide for her face. Her hazel eyes gave Catherine an appraising look. "Girton or Newnham?"

"Girton." And it was fortunate that Girton College was Catherine's first choice, for Newnham was located too close to the men's colleges for

Father's comfort. The fact that Girton students were not allowed to wander into Cambridge, two and a half miles away, without an adult chaperone, meant more to him than its reputation for excellent academics. "And you?"

"Girton!" the girl replied with a broad smile.

A guard stuck his head through the doorway to ask for tickets. "I'm Peggy Somerset," she said when the door closed behind him.

"Catherine Rayborn. I'm pleased to make your acquaintance, Miss Somerset."

"Please call me Peggy. After all, we're going to be schoolmates."

"Thank you. And do call me Catherine."

The wheels started moving. Quickly Catherine resumed her watch at the window, this time pressing herself against the back of the seat so that Peggy could lean close to the glass. On the platform, the woman standing with Peggy's father fluttered a handkerchief. Aunt Naomi, Sarah, and Uncle Daniel waved, and Aunt Phyllis, kneeling with Muriel sobbing into her shoulder, lifted a hand from her daughter's back.

"The girl is your sister?" Peggy asked.

"Cousin," Catherine corrected, a hand raised in front of her chin to return the waves.

"How touching. You must be very close."

"She wants some lemonade."

"Oh."

When the train had left the shed, Peggy moved back to the middle and asked, "Where is your apartment?"

"Second corridor downstairs," Catherine replied. "And yours?"

"Main corridor downstairs. Pity we can't be neighbors. Where do you live in London?"

"Berkeley Square."

The hazel eyes widened. "Indeed?"

"But only since August," Catherine explained. "It's the home of my cousin Sarah and her husband. She was the woman with the brown hat and blond hair. My uncle and aunt live there too, and their two children."

"Those weren't your parents?"

Catherine shook her head. "My father is headmaster at Victoria School in Byculla."

"Byculla? Is that in Africa?"

"Bombay." The James Rayborn family never settled in one place for too long, for Catherine's parents were fond of travel. The only reason the family had moved from Malta to London in 1875 was so that Catherine and her sister, Jewel, could be close to their only remaining grandparents. But when the position at Victoria School was offered two years ago, Grandfather and Grandmother Lorimer had already passed on within six months of each other.

"We live over my father's shop on Saville Row," Peggy said. "Very cramped until my brothers married. Now their old room is mine."

They chatted with voices raised barely above the hum of the wheels, out of consideration for the other passengers and partly from shyness, at least on Catherine's part, for she had spent scant time in the company of boys her own age. She didn't even have a brother. Peggy had three, she learned, all older, and partners with her father at Somerset and Sons, Fine Tailoring.

"I should have liked to have had brothers," Catherine told her.

"And I've always thought it would be nice to have a sister. Sometimes I think I have four fa—"

She paused and gave Catherine an odd look.

"What is it?" Catherine asked, instinctively dropping her voice to a whisper.

Peggy raised a shielding hand to her cheek and leaned closer. "That fellow . . . he's been staring at you ever since we left the station."

"At me?"

She nodded.

They moved apart then as if guided by the same impulse. Catherine turned her face, pretending to study the cottages and hedgerows of Enfield while the corner of her eye took in the young man with the blond hair. Sure enough he was staring, a little smile at his lips. Chills ran up her back. Her arm felt a nudge through the layers of wool and serge, and she turned again.

"Say something!" Peggy whispered.

"I can't," Catherine whispered back.

"Then *I'll* tell—"

Catherine clutched her sleeve. "No . . . please. I don't want a scene." Not on this first day of college, and her first occasion to travel without a chaperone.

Why me? she asked herself.

True, she happened to be directly in his line of vision, but there was also a window on his right, and a friend on his left who would surely look up from his copy of *Punch* magazine for a chat if prompted.

Peripheral vision told her he still stared. Indignation swelled in her chest. *You're a college student,* she reminded herself. *You can't give him the satisfaction of simpering like a helpless female.* She swiveled her head to send him a severe look. He merely stared back with that maddening half smile. Averting her eyes again, she thought, *You wouldn't be doing that if my father were here!*

"You know . . ." Peggy said abruptly, ". . . I wish I could trade places with the Queen for just a day."

Catherine blinked at her. "The Queen?"

"Yes. For starters, I would have all boors shot. *Especially* boors who stare at people."

"Hear, hear!" came acidly from Peggy's other side.

Leaning forward a bit, Catherine gave the woman in the feathered hat an appreciative nod.

"I'm afraid the Queen has no authority to command such a thing, Miss." The older gentleman turned from the window, eyes filled with amusement. "And surely a gentle young lady as yourself doesn't really advocate capital punishment for lack of manners."

"No, of course not." Peggy shot the starer a withering glance. "But I would certainly banish them all from England."

"Send them to France," said the woman.

"Too late for that!" the gentleman in the window seat chortled.

The dark-haired young man in the center raised his eyes from his magazine to give Peggy a curious look. And then he turned to his companion.

"Hugh . . ."

"Yes, Neville?"

"I wish you could see this cartoon in this magazine."

The young man named Hugh leaned his head in a listening posture, but did not turn his face nor blink his eyes. "Describe it to me."

Catherine's breath caught in her throat. She turned to Peggy, who nodded back with eyes wide.

"Oh dear," said the woman by the window.

"I beg your pardon?" asked the older gentleman.

"Nothing," she murmured.

". . . and the doctor," explained Neville, "watching the boy leap from desk to table in the surgery, is scratching his head and asking, 'Have there been any major changes in his diet lately?' And the woman is saying, 'Why, naught to speak of, Sir, other than beef off the boat.' "

After a second Hugh chuckled. "Australian beef."

"At least we're *told* it's beef," his friend said.

What if you had said something? Catherine asked herself as she and

Peggy sat in guilty silence. The very thought caused queasiness in her stomach.

When Neville returned to his magazine, Catherine darted several circumspect peeks at his companion, until she could convince herself that she was not being rude by studying him. While not classically handsome like his dark-haired friend, he was rather nice looking. The straight, wheat-colored hair looked freshly washed and fell untidily over his forehead. Thick brown brows and lashes were set over unblinking brown eyes flecked with tiny bits of amber, and the tan in his clean-shaven cheeks suggested much time spent out in the sun. His smile was slightly crooked, asymmetrical, but in an interesting way.

Again Catherine chided herself. If she had looked more closely—not merely stolen glances like a coy schoolgirl—she would have noticed the absence of expression in the brown eyes. *What a tragedy,* she thought, her pity mixed with admiration that one with such an obstacle as blindness would attempt University.

How fortunate he is, having a friend to watch over him like that. She could imagine the two of them walking down Regent Street. Neville would hold Hugh by the elbow—no, it would be safer if Hugh had a hand up on Neville's shoulder and walked just a bit behind him. Neville's image faded in her mind's picture, and she stepped into his place.

"It's so kind of you to guide me back to Saint John's," Hugh was saying. *"I can't imagine what happened to Neville."*

"I'm happy to be of assistance," Catherine replied, and slowed her steps a bit. *"A delivery cart is blocking the pavement just ahead, so we'll have to step out on the street when the traffic clears."*

"Just lead the way, Miss Rayborn. I have perfect confidence in you."

"I feel just wretched, Catherine."

The scene evaporated and Catherine looked at Peggy, who was leaning close.

"Saying all that rot about shooting people," Peggy whispered.

"I'm sure he didn't realize you meant him," Catherine consoled, albeit with a surge of relief that *she* had not been the one to speak out.

But now that it was brought to light that he had *not* behaved rudely, it didn't seem decent to sit there chatting over him—even though she was certain he couldn't hear them over the wheels. So to steer the subject in another direction—and because she was curious—she said, "May I see your violin?"

"Yes, of course," Peggy replied, unfastening the case and raising the lid.

She drew out an instrument of polished mellow wood inscribed with a small cross. The other sighted passengers looked on.

"It was made by Giuseppe," Peggy said, beaming like a doting mother. "They're very valuable. An earl in reduced circumstances traded it to my great grandfather for a cloak and two suits of—"

"Oh!" she exclaimed, grabbing for the case as the coach made a teeth-jarring lurch. Catherine bounced an inch off her seat. A boater hat sprang from the overhead hook and was snatched in midair by the young man across from Catherine.

All eyes went to him. Sheepishly he balanced the hat upon his knees.

Neville's chortle pierced the stunned silence. "I'll take that fiver now, Hugh!"

"It was a *wager*?" Peggy said with eyes narrowed.

Hugh grimaced. "We meant no disres—"

"Have you both taken leave of your senses?" demanded the woman at the opposite window.

"Or had you any to begin with?" added Peggy.

The older gentleman appeared to be struggling to suppress a smile, causing Catherine to wonder if most males were lacking in sensitivity. Anger pushed aside her shyness, and she frowned. "And have you *any* idea what it's like to be blind?"

"I never—"

"My Grandfather Lorimer was stricken blind weeks before he died. He didn't find it so amusing."

Both young men shrank in their seats. "It was a spur-of-the-moment thing," explained the dark-haired one. "You know . . . impulse."

Hugh nodded remorsefully. "I played Gloucester in a production of *King Lear* at St. John's last term, and Neville here wagered I couldn't pull it off in real life. If we would have taken time to think it over . . ."

"I believe the young ladies would have preferred you had chosen the death scene instead," the gentleman said.

"There is still time," Peggy said tightly, putting her violin back in its case.

Neville chuckled, but then glanced at Peggy and turned it into a cough. Hugh just sat wearing a look of misery. For the half hour that followed, Catherine and Peggy studiously ignored the young men, who took to ignoring them just as studiously by passing the magazine back and forth and commenting on various cartoons and articles.

It wasn't having been deceived that piqued Catherine the most, or even so much the bad taste of pretending to have a disability. Most mortifying was that he had sat there—probably struggling to hold in the laughter—and allowed her to study his face as if he were a portrait in a museum. Was there any approval showing in her expression? Her face burned again at the realization that there probably was.

"It was a hateful thing to do," Peggy whispered, affirming Catherine's right to a grudge. "I've a good mind to write to the head of—"

A whistle drowned out the rest as the wheels started slowing. When the guard opened the door, Catherine and Peggy hesitated only long enough to bid good-day to their seatmate before stepping onto the platform of Cambridge Station.

"We should keep our eyes out for a porter," Catherine said, then realized she was taking something for granted. They had gotten on splendidly during the journey. Was it presumptuous of her to assume that meant the beginning of a friendship?

"That is, if you would care to share a cab," she added.

"But of course." Peggy's hazel eyes shone above her wide smile. "We're going to be good friends, aren't we?"

Having brothers must make a girl bolder, Catherine thought with a little envy. She smiled back. "Yes, good friends."

Two

*O*ne of the many conveniences of being a fourth-year student, Hugh Sedgwick thought, sidestepping a porter and handcart, was that one could simply leave most of his belongings at college for the duration.

Besides, he needed them during the summer days not devoted to rowing in the Henley Regatta or cheering Cambridge on against Oxford during the cricket matches at Lords. Hugh was of the third or so of Cambridge students who chose to stay in residence at their colleges during most of the long vacation, from mid-June to early October. He convinced himself it was to study ahead for the next year, though he did not open the books as much as he knew he should. Truth was, his father was not overjoyed at his choosing University over coming to work at Sedgwick Tea Company straight out of secondary school, and Hugh knew that his idling summers at home would only serve to irritate him.

"Over here!" Neville called, tossing his gripsack into the first available carriage in queue on Station Road.

Hugh did the same but stopped short of hopping into the seat.

"What is it?" asked Neville.

"Somethin' the matter, Sir?" asked the driver from the box.

You certainly gave their first year a great start, Hugh told himself, turning toward the station. *How would you like someone treating your sisters that way?*

He glanced over his shoulder. "Wait, please."

A male voice came from Catherine's right. "May I beg just a moment of your time?"

She and Peggy turned to face Hugh-from-the-train, who looked even more miserable than when under their tongue-lashings. The brim of the hat that had betrayed him was clutched in his hands. Standing, he was not overly tall, perhaps just four inches above Catherine's five-feet-four.

"Well, what is it?" Peggy demanded.

"It was beastly of me . . . the way I behaved."

"Yes, beastly," Catherine told him, folding her arms. "You should be ashamed."

"I *am*, terribly." The young man's frown was as asymmetrical as his smile had been. "But have you never done anything that you profoundly regret?"

The question gave Catherine pause. *What a sheltered life you've lived*, she told herself when the most serious recollection that surfaced was of disobeying her mother at age fourteen by slipping out to cycle during a summer rain. The one-inch scar on the underside of her chin was a reminder of that folly.

"Perhaps," she replied.

"But nothing so tasteless as your performance," Peggy said.

He winced. "Yes. And I do beg your forgiveness."

Catherine was moved by the misery in his expression in spite of herself, and more than a little awed that they possessed the power to increase or lessen it. But she was not quite ready to make him feel better. "My grandfather suffered terribly."

"If I had only known . . ."

"But you couldn't have, could you?" Peggy said. "That's why such subjects are inappropriate for humor."

"Indeed," he agreed, the frown deepening. "I know my word means nothing to you, but please be assured I shall never do anything like that again—to anyone."

He had proved his acting ability on the train. Still, Catherine found herself believing him. "Should we forgive him, Peggy?"

Peggy leaned her head to give him an appraising look. "Yes, I suppose we should."

Catherine nodded. "Very well."

"Thank you!" He blew out his cheeks. "Now I'll be able to sleep tonight."

"Miss Rayborn?"

Catherine looked off to her right. Through the crowd she caught a glimpse of Miss Scott, the resident assistant lecturer in Mathematics, whom she had met in August. It wouldn't do to have one of the Girton staff assuming they had come to Cambridge to flirt with young men. She looked at Peggy, who nodded.

"We have to go now," they said in unison.

"Of course," he replied. Before turning to blend into the crowd, he smiled crookedly. "Again, I thank you for the absolution."

Miss Scott was a frazzled-looking woman of about twenty-five, who nonetheless wore a welcoming smile and explained that she and two other assistant lecturers were out there to provide assistance if needed. "We've a porter available, and a wagon is just about to leave with luggage. Give me your tags, and we'll see to your trunks."

"Thank you," Catherine said, and handed over hers. As Peggy dug into a faded green reticule, Catherine could not restrain herself from glancing over her shoulder. She saw no sign of Hugh.

He must have made an outstanding Gloucester, she thought.

They followed the porter—just to be sure he had the right trunks on his handcart—then left the platform and exited the station. Cambridge gleamed like a jewel in the noonday sun, a pleasing amalgamation of Saxon, and Norman Romanesque, Gothic, Georgian, and Greek Revival. A cabby waved them over to a hackney hitched to a team of bored-looking dray horses. "Girton or Newnham?" he asked, a smile parted over teeth as grey as the hair overlapping his collar.

"I can see we're going to be asked that a lot over the next four years," Peggy murmured.

"Girton, please," Catherine replied.

"Very good, Misses!" He assisted them inside, then hopped into the box and snapped the reins. The team snorted in unison and set out toward Regent Street with hooves ringing against paving stones.

It was slow going, for the town was an anthill of activity. They passed the yellow neo-classical buildings of Downing and then Emmanuel College, followed by Christ's College with its mellow tan stone and several connected shops and cafés with flats above. A trio of young men standing under the awning of The Bulldog Pub nudged each other. One broke ranks to trot along Catherine's side of the carriage.

"Good day, fair damsels!" he called, lifting a boater hat while his companions hooted out encouragements. "Care to join us for lunch?"

"You'll leave them ladies be, elst I'll have th' police on you!" the driver scolded, twisting in his seat.

Laughter rolled from the pub, but the grinning young man gave up his sport. Peggy rolled her eyes at Catherine. "First time away from home, I'd wager my last shilling."

The pounding against Catherine's rib cage eased. "And I thought Father was being overprotective when he warned me about University men."

"My father warned me too. But I believed him."

"You did? But wouldn't you assume they would behave more . . ."

"Scholarly?"

Catherine was going to say *dignified,* but *scholarly* served just as well. "Yes."

"The amount of education doesn't matter," Peggy said knowingly. "Did you study algebra?"

"Algebra?" Catherine echoed, giving her an odd look.

Peggy smiled. "Young men behave according to an algebraic formula. When they're together, the quantity of restraint each possesses is inversely proportional to the number of men in the group. Just like Hugh-from-St. John's. He would have been a perfect gentleman had he traveled alone, but as he was with a male friend, his capacity for restraint was divided by half. Had he two more friends present, there would have been a belching contest or some such nonsense."

When Catherine finally absorbed all that, she shook her head in awe. "You learned that from having brothers?"

"And from their friends. *And* five years at Burlington Street Grammar School."

"I've only been to girls' schools," Catherine confessed. "And my sister and I shared a governess in Bombay."

"I don't think I would have cared for that. Males can be exasperating, but they do make life a lot more colorful."

"They've certainly added color to our trip."

"And yet you wanted to come to Girton?" Peggy said. "I should think you would be sick of girls."

"Oh, quite the contrary." A little shiver went through Catherine. "This is the most exciting day of my life."

"Yes, mine as well."

"What will you be reading?" Catherine asked.

"Natural Sciences. I'm particularly interested in chemistry, and have been ever since I first set eyes upon the Periodic Table."

"My cousin's husband, William Doyle, is an analytical chemist for the Hassall Commission. They investigate—"

"Adulterated foods and medicines!" Peggy finished for her. "I've read all about them. How fulfilling to be involved in something so noble."

"He does enjoy his work. You can't imagine what people will put into food to save a penny."

"I hope I may meet him sometime," Peggy said. "What will you be studying?"

"Classics," Catherine replied. But her smile faded at the thought that had nagged at her for weeks. "I only hope I can keep up."

"But why wouldn't you?"

"I'm not much of a reader."

"Really! Not even for pleasure?"

"Well . . . on occasion." She could become absorbed to the point of shutting out her surroundings with adventures such as Marryat's *The Phantom Ship* and Collins' *The Moonstone*, and even the occasional "penny dreadful." But her limited exposure to Greek and Roman myths had left her with no thirst for more.

"You must have done well in other subjects or you wouldn't be here."

Catherine gave her an appreciative look. "Yes," she replied, simply because to say otherwise out of modesty would be to lie. But all one had to do to master Mathematics, Science, and even Grammar was to memorize certain laws, rules, and formulas and apply them. Finding which particular key would unlock each problem was therefore like a game, vastly interesting. But when a subject did not capture her attention, her mind frequently detoured down other paths.

"It may not be too late to sign up for something else," Peggy advised. "That's what I appreciate about college—it's like dining *a la francaise*. You can put only the foods you like on your plate."

"But sometimes you have to put broccoli on your plate for your own good. My father says that no academically advanced school will hire a schoolmistress who isn't well-versed in the Classics."

Peggy pursed her lips. "I'm sure I don't know about that. But it seems to me that you ought to study that at which you're most competent, and which you enjoy. The world is changing from how it was when our mothers were our ages. You can become a scientist, an architect . . . almost anything."

"But I've wanted to teach children ever since I was a little girl. I know I would enjoy it. It's just the getting there that may be difficult."

"Then we'll help each other stay on track. Be accountable to each other. Make sure we spend enough time in the books."

"I'd like that," Catherine told her.

"And, if you'll forgive my immodesty, I'm fairly good at Latin." Peggy shrugged. "With so much of it used in chemistry. So if you should ever need help . . ."

"God must have led you to my coach." The sentiment surprised

Catherine even as she spoke it, for while her family had faithfully attended church since her earliest memories, they did not speak of God as if He were intimately involved in the goings-on of their days. That was more like Uncle Daniel's side of the family. Having just spent three weeks with them, she reckoned some of their devoutness had rubbed off on her.

"Why, I think He did," Peggy returned.

Their shared smiles melded into a companionable silence, just as limestone buildings began melding into neat cottages soon after they crossed the Great Bridge over the River Cam.

The old name for Girton was Gretton, meaning "village on the gravel," said the college pamphlet Catherine received upon her first visit. It was given the name because the settlement grew up along a gravel ridge. Traffic lightened, and the breeze from the horses' quickened pace cooled her face. Already she had a friend here. The four years stretching out before her seemed filled with promise.

Presently they stopped several yards short of Girton College's wooden gates, in queue behind two other carriages. The living and lecture rooms of the seven-year-old terra-cotta brick building in their sights formed an inverted *L,* leaving room for future growth on a quadrangle plan. Miss Bernard, the mistress, stood with a young woman at the main entrance under the clock.

"Well . . . this is it," Peggy said, hugging her violin case closer.

"This is it," Catherine echoed.

"Do go on ahead, Misses," the driver said, offering an assisting hand. "Miss Bernard there hasn't bit anybody yet."

When they put heads together to divide the fare, Catherine resisted the temptation to offer to pay the entire five shillings. She could recall the years when money was tight in her own family, before Grandmother and Grandfather Lorimer finally forgave her mother for marrying a lowly schoolmaster. She would have been mortified to have anyone assume that she needed charity.

But she did fish an extra florin from her reticule, out of appreciation for the driver's having scolded the young man in town. Even though the student had posed no threat, it was a good feeling to have someone champion them.

"Can you afford to do that?" Peggy whispered uneasily.

"Yes," Catherine assured her. The three hundred pounds per annum willed to her by Grandfather Lorimer made that possible. And Father had always tipped generously during the highs and lows of family finances over the years, so it seemed only natural to do so.

"Why, thank you, Misses!" the driver said, giving his palm an appreciative look before pocketing the coins. "And may th' good Lord smile down upon you today."

"Misses Somerset and Rayborn," Miss Bernard said with a glance at the notebook in her hands as they approached her. She was an elegant, slender woman appearing to be in her thirties. Moving her pencil to her left hand, she offered her right to Catherine, and then Peggy. "Welcome to Girton. I trust your journey was pleasant?"

"Most pleasant, Miss Bernard," Catherine replied.

"We discovered each other in the same railway coach," Peggy told her.

"And you weren't acquainted before? What lovely happenstance." The mistress took up her pencil again, checked their names from her notebook, then introduced them to Miss Howard, a tall fourth-year student with a white streak running through her brown hair to the coiled braids in back. "Will you need Miss Howard to show you about?"

Peggy thanked her anyway, saying, "We were given tours in August."

"Very good," Miss Bernard said. "Then feel free to explore on your own. There are sandwiches in the dining room, where you'll see notices for an assembly after supper. Welcome to Girton."

From the entrance hall they turned left into the long main corridor, airy and light from sunlight pouring in from east-facing windows. Doors to sitting rooms and bedrooms and the lecture rooms ran along the left side, each sitting room adjoining another so that their fireplaces could share the same chimney. On the right, several feet apart, were a bathroom and then a chemistry laboratory. Peggy stopped at the sitting room door to number four, turned the knob, and looked back at Catherine. "Would you care to come in?"

"In a little while?"

Peggy smiled understanding. "You can't wait either?"

"No." And it was fitting that each should see her apartment for the first time alone. "I just wish we could be neighbors."

"We'll ask permission to move next year."

If I last that long popped into Catherine's mind as she looked back to send Peggy a wave. She squashed the thought. *Confident thoughts from now on!* she told herself, turning left into the south corridor. Number twelve, the next-to-the-last apartment, opened into a sitting room furnished with a study table and four chairs, bookshelves, two plush upholstered chairs, a rug, and a small table and lamp. Coals glowed in the gate of the fireplace. The paneling was painted a restful pale green. A folding doorway led to a bedroom with wardrobe, bed, chair, and chest of drawers with a mirror. Long windows filtered sunlight through lace curtains. The curtains, bed linens, and rug that Naomi and Sarah had helped her select from Selby's Quality Drapers in Cambridge lent a homelike feeling.

My own apartment! she thought, unfastening her coat. If only her parents and Jewel could see it. *I'll have to sketch it for them.* She hung her coat over the cane chair by her bed and pressed her back against the far wall. *Or perhaps there's enough room for a photograph.* Surely Girton or Cambridge had a photographer for hire. She could send her family a photograph of her apartment, and even of Peggy, so they could envision her surroundings and new friend as they read her letters. *Wouldn't that be something!* she thought as she removed gloves and hat and put them atop her chest of drawers.

A knock sounded at her bedroom door.

My first visitor!

"Your trunk, Miss . . . Rayborn?" said a balding man in his late forties or so, with a sheen across his forehead and a stoop as both hands held the handle behind his back. He introduced himself as Mr. Willingham, groundskeeper, and the thickset man who followed him into the room at the other end of the trunk as Mr. Hearn, husband to the cook.

"Beside my bed, please," she said, and thanked them as they hurried out. She opened the lid, then knelt to unwind the towels from the silver-framed portraits of her parents and Jewel, relieved that the glass plates had not cracked. *The chimneypiece,* she told herself, rising again to her feet. But she stopped in the doorway to the sitting room. Voices were coming from the bedroom adjoining hers. She held her breath to listen. The conversation was too muffled to decipher but was obviously a heated one. There seemed to be three participants, one male and two female. Catherine stepped into the space between her bedside table and cane chair and pressed her ear to the wall.

". . . have to grow up sometime . . ." came through in a man's voice.

". . . would behoove you to show some gratitude . . ." in a woman's.

What are you doing? Catherine asked herself. Seconds later she was out in the corridor and knocking at number four. Peggy answered straightaway.

"Why, I was just going to nip over for a look at your place. But you can see mine first."

Catherine walked through the two rooms, pausing to finger the fine cotton lace at the hem of the coverlet. "How lovely."

"My mother made the coverlet—curtains too."

"Your mother sews?"

"Why, yes." Peggy peered into her mirror and started removing pins from her hat. "She was piecing army uniforms in an attic factory in Cheapside when she met Father at a May Day festival. They were fifteen and got married three months later."

"Three years younger than us." Catherine shook her head. "Two of my cousins were married at sixteen, but I just don't think I could . . ." She stopped herself. "Oh dear. I wasn't criticizing your parents."

"Of course you weren't." The hat came off, and Peggy started tucking stray red curls into her chignon. "But I agree with you—that's too young. But my father's of the mind that, because it was good for them, everyone should do it that way."

"He wishes you were married?"

"Dear me, yes. To our neighbor's son, Oliver Piggott. He stands to inherit his father's haberdashery, and Father says he's a 'decent hardworking sort who knows how to treat his patrons.' "

She shook her head, loosening a curl from her chignon. "Thank heaven for Aunt Mabel. If she hadn't insisted upon paying my tuition and board, Father would never have agreed to college. She even pays for my railway tickets, or I would have been in third-class. Would you like to see what she gave me when I graduated from grammar school?"

"Why, yes."

Peggy removed a key from the pocket of the coat draped over the footboard of her bed. She unlatched her trunk and fished about in the bottom. Handing a narrow velvet-covered box up to Catherine, she said, "I've never bothered with jewelry, but I do wear these to church every Sunday, in her honor."

Catherine raised the hinged lid. Atop the black velvet lining lay a strand of seed pearls. She touched one. "They're exquisite."

"Thank you," said her new friend, beaming as she reached again for the box. "But I've shown off enough. Shall we tour your place now?"

"Why don't we lunch first?" Catherine said. "I'm famished."

Which was the truth. Still, Peggy gave her an odd look. "Is there something the matter?"

"I'm not sure." Catherine told her about the voices.

"I'm impressed with your restraint," Peggy said as they walked down the corridor. "I would have been tempted to eavesdrop."

"Oh, I was tempted, mind you."

Sociable laughter drifted down from upstairs, and Misters Willingham and Hearn lugged another trunk past. A trio of young women ambled toward them, older students, judging by the ease of their bearings. They paused from conversing to send smiles and say, "Welcome to Girton."

"Thank you," Peggy replied.

"We're glad to be here," Catherine told them before continuing on. They were several feet from the dining room entrance when she said to Peggy, "May I ask you a question?"

"Certainly."

"This Oliver . . ."

"What about him?"

"May I assume you're not fond of him?"

"Oliver?" Peggy shrugged. "Fondness is one thing, picturing him seriously as a husband is another. To me, he'll ever be the gangly boy who once slipped a toad into my pocket and was always saying I reminded him of a matchstick. Besides, can you imagine going through the rest of your life with the name Peggy Piggott?"

Catherine had to smile. "He sounds rather fun."

"Not you too!" Peggy groaned. "Then you may have him. I'll be sure to introduce you some time."

"Hmm." Linking her arm through Peggy's, Catherine said, "Just remind me not to wear anything with pockets."

Three

I boxed up Catherine's macaroons this morning," Naomi Rayborn said to Sarah in London five days later. "I should write and thank the postmaster general. When William was at Oxford, I had to ask Stanley to deliver his packages to Paddington, and it cost twice as much to send them as what parcel post costs now."

An unseasonable sixty-five degrees had drawn the two to a bench in Berkeley Square. Bethia, almost four years old, was seated between them, and two-year-old Danny sat upon Naomi's lap. Guy Russell, the coach-man's son, sat at the base of a nearby plane tree.

"I wonder how she's adjusting to Girton," Sarah said.

"Oh, very well, I expect. James's family thrives upon travel. And to be able to walk just down the hall to so many interesting lectures . . ."

Sarah pictured herself doing the same, until she realized a seed of discontent was attempting to take root in her mind. She reminded herself that, had she also gone away to college, she would not have been reunited with her father when the late Mrs. Blake hired him as her tutor almost six years ago. She could see his shadowy form in the third-storey window, where he kept his desk while writing a history of Saint Paul's Cathedral. He would probably still be living alone in the little Surrey Street cottage, still believing his daughter had perished in the Thames as an infant. Naomi would probably still be a cook, unmarried, and Bethia and Danny would not be here in the Square with them.

And William and I may not have even married, she realized, taking the vein of thought even further. *He's worth more than all the college memories in the world.* And the degree granted her by London University after last year's examinations was just as valid as if she had gone away. Being that it was impossible to travel two life-roads at the same time, she told herself that the one God had set her upon suited her just fine. Especially considering her humble beginnings.

All she could ask for was one more thing, and as Doctor Raine advised, she just had to be patient. Three years was not an alarmingly long time to pass without conceiving a child.

She drew in a deep breath, held it, and eased it out again. "I wish I could box up some of this weather."

"But if it were in a box, how would you enjoy it?" Bethia asked, bottle-blue eyes serious.

Sarah smiled at her half sister. "Well, that bears some thought. It would have to be a very *big* box."

"As big as an apple crate?"

"Oh, much bigger. Roomy enough for me to sit inside. With a book."

"You would need a candle, too," Bethia suggested. "And matches."

"That's a good idea, Bethia."

"And would there be room for us? Me and Mother and Father and Danny and William?"

Sarah's and Naomi's smiles met over the girl's head.

"But of course," Sarah replied.

Looking at the boy seated on the ground, Bethia said, "Guy?"

Guy Russell stopped turning over in his hands the harmonica Mr. Duffy had given him last year. Though his six-year-old eyes indicated that he did not believe such a box would be fashioned, he smiled. "Thank you, Bethia. But I shouldn't wish to be without Mother and Father and Lottie."

Lottie was his sister, born just one week ago. "Sarah . . . ." Bethia began.

"Anyone you would care to invite could join us inside," Sarah reassured her with a pat on the back. "We'll just build a bigger box."

Two-year-old Danny, in Naomi's lap, showed more interest in passers-by than in the warm breezes of Berkeley Square. "Who's he, Mummy?" he asked of every stroller who passed, regardless of gender.

"She's Mrs. Gregory," Naomi replied, returning the neighbors' house-keeper's wave.

"Would you like me to play a song?" Guy asked hopefully.

He was clearly Stanley's son, with sapphire-blue eyes and sprouts of dark brown hair. From his mother, Penny, alto in the choir at Saint George's, he had inherited an ear for music, which had prompted Sarah and William to bring the boy along to a matinee performance of Gilbert and Sullivan's *H.M.S. Pinafore* at the Opera Comique two months ago. Any misgivings over doing such were put to rest even before Buttercup came onstage with her basket of goods, for little Guy sat as still as Lot's wife, soaking in the music through every pore.

"Yes, Guy," Sarah told him. "Play something for us."

With hands cupped behind the harmonica, he began coaxing out the notes from the musical, *As I Walked Through the Meadows.*

"Do it agin!" Danny exclaimed after one stanza. And so Guy complied. This time Naomi kissed the back of her son's fair head and sang along softly,

> *"As I walked through the meadows to take the fresh air,*
> *The flowers were blooming and gay;*
> *I heard a fair damsel so sweetly a-singing*
> *Her cheeks like the blossom in May . . ."*

An elderly couple strolling along past a stand of trees smiled, the gentleman touching the brim of his top hat. Sarah smiled and nodded back, marveling to herself at how her stepmother could sing so comfortably in the presence of others. Whether it was from having been married to Father for the past five years, or just that reaching forty-two years of age caused one to shed some abashment, she was glad Naomi no longer hid her talent under a bushel. Her clear, soothing voice was a perfect accompaniment to such a fine day.

When the song ended, little Danny's fickle attention was captured by the approach of two women sheathed in rustling silks and carrying frilled parasols. Mmes. Beale and Archer, formerly Misses Fowler and Welch. Neither had spoken to Sarah since selling her tickets to a charity luncheon outside Saint George's years ago. Nonetheless, when they glanced her way, Sarah smiled and greeted them.

"Good afternoon, Mrs. Beale . . . Mrs. Archer."

The two pushed out simultaneous "Good afternoons" through tight smiles before hurrying past without a glance to spare for Naomi or the children.

"Who's he, Mummy?" Danny asked.

"Two ladies, Danny," his mother replied.

Not ladies, Sarah thought, watching the two parasols meet over whispers and giggles. At least not by her definition. A true lady did not measure a person's social status before deciding which degree of courtesy to extend.

But she was used to such treatment, having endured it since her arrival at 14 Berkeley Square as a spindly orphan girl with a crippled left hand. Being made legal ward of the late Mrs. Blake, whom she had addressed as Grandmother, and then inheriting Blake Shipping, only brought out the fortune hunters and opportunists. The remainder of Mayfair, with the exception of a few dear souls such as Vicar Sharp, clearly resented that a daughter of the slums had the audacity to live better than most of them.

If they only knew it all, she thought. Drawing room conversations could be fueled for years over the account of how she was pulled from the Thames as an infant by a drunken fisherman after her insane mother jumped with her from Waterloo Bridge.

Naomi's high crime was being a cook before marrying Father. Marrying above one's station was considered bad form, for it blurred the dividing line between the classes, giving other servants romantic notions toward sons and daughters of households.

"I'm sorry, Naomi," Sarah told her.

"Sorry?"

"For the way they behaved."

Naomi waved a hand. "They can't make the afternoon any less lovely, can they?"

But they had done just that for Sarah. Until the thought struck her that the breezes stirring Danny's cherubic curls were not confined to Mayfair. She asked herself, *Why do we cling to this place?*

"Because Mrs. Blake wanted you to have this house," William said after stepping out of the little runabout he took to and from the laboratory of the Hassall Commission.

Stanley came out of the carriage house wiping his hands upon a rag, and took Belle's reins. "I'll stable her, Mr. Doyle."

"Thank you, Stanley," William told him, then turned again to Sarah. "Say, is Trudy still planning fried soles for supper?"

"Yes, fried sole."

"Very good! I thought of little else all the way home. We had to work through lunch with that court date breathing upon our necks. But we've enough evidence now to send those Sleepy-Tot Soothing Tonic rascals to jail."

They passed the stable yard, where Comet and Daisy pitched and snorted and hung their heads over the top railing at the sight of William. But Sarah's spirits were not as high as those of the pair of Cleveland bays. In fact, they were heavier than when she had come through the gate earlier to wait for her husband.

Once alone in the garden, William stopped to switch his leather satchel and umbrella to his left hand. Twenty-six years had not taken the hint of boyishness from him; dimpled clean-shaven cheeks and unruly brown hair still balanced out a masculine square jaw and contemplative smoke-colored eyes. Resting his hand upon her shoulder, he studied her face. "I thought you would be happy to hear it."

"Oh, but I am," she assured him. People who caused infants to become addicted to opium were among the lowest on earth, in her opinion.

Awareness entered the dark eyes. "Forgive me, Sarah. You were speaking of moving, and I blazed on past you. You were serious?"

"There's nothing for us here anymore," she said as they walked the shaded stone path. "As for Grandmother . . . as much as I loved her, she's gone."

"And have you a specific place in mind?"

Sarah took a quick breath. "Hampstead."

"Hampstead?"

"Grandmother once wanted to move us there. Every time I visit Saint Matthew's I fall in love with the countryside."

Saint Matthew's Foundling Home for Girls was where Sarah had spent most of her childhood, only in those earlier days it was located in the slums of Drury Lane. Months before she died, Mrs. Blake donated a fine Hampstead mansion to the institution.

"Then let's move," William said. "We can ask Mr. Mitchell to recommend a good architect. Or would you rather we hire a house agent to see what's available now?"

"We could move sooner if we didn't have to have a house built," Sarah replied, but a little uneasily. All that mental labor put to organizing and steeling her arguments, only to have him agree so readily?

"But what about your work?" she asked. "It's farther out."

"Not prohibitively so. I'll simply leave earlier."

"We wouldn't have a telephone."

"Just for a few months until the lines are extended."

"What if Father and Naomi don't care for the idea? It was difficult enough to coax them to move here."

"You have only to ask them," William said. "But I should think they'll be agreeable. And a bigger house would allow each family more privacy. We're practically bursting at the seams here."

"Yes, more privacy."

"And we'll need more room for our own children one day."

She smiled at him. "Yes."

They passed the green wire arch that William had been painting when Sarah first set eyes upon him ten years ago. "Oh dear," she said. "But what of the servants? Marie's sisters are employed here in Mayfair, and—"

"We'll help those who want to stay find new positions." He stopped at the edge of the terrace to study her face. "Are you certain *you* want this, Sarah?"

In the space of Sarah's hesitation, she realized it was fear of the unknown facing her now that the barrier of William's protest had proved nonexistent. And she had to tell herself that fear was a silly reason for stagnating in one place. "Yes, William, I want this."

Father and Naomi did not protest when the subject was broached during supper, and indeed, Naomi wore an expression of quiet relief.

"Are you sure you haven't grown weary of our company?" Father asked. He wore his fifty-one years well, still having very little grey in his light brown hair, though his trim beard was liberally sprinkled with it.

"Never," Sarah replied, and William agreed.

The following evening Sarah and William walked downstairs just as the servants were finishing supper. The hall just off the kitchen was as familiar to them as any other room in the house, for both had taken many meals there in their youth. All were present save the Russells, who took their meals in the apartment over the stables while Penny was still confined to bed with the infant Lottie.

"Please, don't get up," William said, raising a hand as chairs started scraping against the wooden floor. To Trudy and Brenda, cook and kitchen maid, he said, "Those were outstanding cutlets."

"Why, thank you, Mr. Doyle," Trudy said. She was a plump woman with coarse blond hair, several moles on clear cheeks, and eyes as brown and moist as a spaniel's. She nodded toward a pedestal dish, where one slice of chocolate listed to the side amidst dark crumbs. "Would be a shame to waste that last slice . . ."

"You know very well he had two upstairs, Trudy," said Sarah, accompanying William to the head of the table.

"Only two?" housekeeper Mrs. Bacon teased, her bespectacled eyes crinkling at the corners. Because almost everyone at the table could recall when William was a servant and Sarah just a spindly girl with her crippled hand and shorn hair, they treated both with a respect born more of maternal and paternal camaraderie than subjugation.

"Now, you'll leave Mr. Doyle to his chocolate," Mr. Duffy said, turning his chair around to face them. Humor softened the gardener's fierce countenance. "There's worser vices a man could have."

Lady's maid Marie let out an audible huff of breath. "I do not believe

Monsieur and Madame are here to make talk over cake."

William nodded. "Yes, that's so, Marie." Without further preamble he announced the plans to leave Berkeley Square when an adequate house could be found. "We wanted to inform you as soon as possible so you can make plans."

Silence became thick in the room as questioning sets of eyes met each other across the table.

"We would very much like you all to come with us," Sarah hastened to assure them. "But if that's not possible, we'll help you find other positions."

That dissolved only some of the tension.

"Have you questions?" William asked.

"Leave my garden?" Mr. Duffy said in the tone of one who has been asked to abandon his children. "But the potatoes ain't even in."

"I'm sure it'll take us months to find the right place," William told him. "And when we do, you'll have a new garden to tend."

The gardener rubbed his grizzled cheek thoughtfully. "A bigger one, do you think?"

"I should imagine. A bigger house usually means a larger garden."

"Meanin' more room for my vegetable patch?"

"The household is growing. We'll need more vegetables."

Mr. Duffy raised eyebrows at his wife, parlormaid Claire, who smiled and nodded.

"Then we'll come along!" he said with a slap on his knee.

Trudy had other concerns. "Four burners ain't enough, with more people in the house to cook for now. But there ain't room in this kitchen for another stove or even a bigger one. And we've been needin' another maid down here, but there's not room enough in the attic for one to board."

"We'll look for a larger kitchen, too," Sarah promised. "And more servants' rooms."

"With a bigger hot water tank?" Brenda asked meekly. "So's it don't run out when I'm halfway through the dishes?"

William nodded. "Sounds reasonable."

"Please check the fireplace flues before you buy any house" was Avis's only request. "The rooms on the east side wouldn't collect so much soot if the flues worked better."

"Yes, we'll do that," William agreed with the gentling of tone that every adult in the house used when addressing the parlormaid.

She had been hurt, and no one wished to rub salt into the wounds. Spindly thin, with owlish grey eyes, Avis had expected to marry an army corporal with whom she had corresponded for several years, even sending him bits of her wages for tobacco. But it so happened that, once he was discharged, he married another woman with whom he had also corresponded. Avis never mentioned him in conversation anymore and devoted her spare time to her watercolors. Some were beginning to sell, mostly to servants from the neighborhood seeking gifts.

Minutes later on the staircase, William said to Sarah with low voice, "Perhaps we should take them all house hunting with us."

"They were very good suggestions," Sarah said, giving his arm a squeeze. "After all, their home is their workplace. But did you notice how quiet Marie was?"

"Hmph! For how long?"

And sure enough, the lady's maid had obviously required some time to think this over, for she said while laying out Sarah's bedclothes an hour later, "If I make this move with you, I shall be allowed to leave thirty minutes earlier on Thursdays, yes?"

The voluptuous Frenchwoman had ceased plastering little curls across her forehead upon turning forty, in favor of drawing back her dark hair into a simple knot. For over a decade, she had spent her half day off on Thursday afternoons going on outings with her three sisters, two who worked in Mayfair and one who had married a milliner widower and lived over Beaufort's Fine Hats and Bonnets on Bond Street.

"Yes, of course," Sarah told her.

"*And* . . . will you pay cab fare for the extra distance?"

Sarah pretended to think it over for a second or two, even though both knew that the request would be granted. And indeed, Marie showed no surprise, but gave her a knowing little smile, when Sarah replied, "Yes, we'll pay extra."

Four

*T*he order of Girton's days was a pleasant surprise for Catherine, who had feared high academic standards would mean a Spartan routine.

Mornings were ushered in at seven o'clock with footsteps and the creaking of hinges, as college servants entered sitting rooms to lay fires. Soon afterward, yawning students in dressing gowns and slippers began drifting up the corridors. Queues were not a hardship, with only four or five sharing each bathroom. The eight o'clock bell signaled prayers in the morning room, led by Miss Bernard. Attendance was not required, but most of the sixty students took part, including Catherine and Peggy.

Breakfast was laid out in the dining room from eight-fifteen until nine o'clock. Private or group study followed. Some of the classes were conducted by the four Girton graduates who were resident assistant lecturers. Catherine attended one morning lecture every Monday, Wednesday, and Friday: Greek and Roman Society, taught by Miss Welsh, the vice-mistress.

After lunch, some form of exercise was encouraged. When fields were dry, many students paired off for an hour's rapid walk through hedge and ditch. They were warned to shut any gate they passed through, for part of Girton's sixteen acres was leased to a farmer—a fact that amused Catherine greatly when recalling Sarah's quip over her stepping off a farm. Lawn tennis was popular too, and sometimes even cricket matches were held. During inclement weather the girls dressed in blue Bloomer suits and assembled under the covered court to play "fives," a game resembling tennis with a bat and ball.

Afternoon lectures were conducted by professors from Cambridge colleges, men dedicated enough to the ideal of women's higher education to extend their working days. Dr. Precor, of St. Catherine's College, lectured Catherine in Latin I on Mondays, Wednesdays, and Fridays, and in Age of the Scipios on Tuesdays, Thursdays, and Saturdays. Tea was taken round by the servants at four o'clock, and the dinner bell rang at six.

Various meetings followed dinner, depending on the day of the week— the Debating Society, Dramatic Society, Choral Society, Lawn Tennis Club, Chess Club, and even Fire Brigade, among others. Catherine signed up for the Lawn Tennis Club, and Peggy, the Girton Chamber Music Society and the Chess Club.

There was also study in rooms until nine, after which dressing gowns were donned, tresses unpinned, and most of the evening amusements began. Maids brought around hot chocolate, students visited in friends' parlors or gathered with a larger group in the reading room for poetry readings, charades, or singing around the piano. Half-past ten was the unofficial, but mostly observed, bedtime.

Catherine got along splendidly with the majority of the students, though she spent most of her free time either studying alone or with Peggy. The one student with whom she had not formed even the most tenuous friendship was her neighbor on the bedroom side, Millicent Turner. Tall and slender and yet buxom and robust, Millicent had indigo-colored eyes and ash blond hair rippling to her narrow waist like the moon's reflection upon water. She made the other girls feel like dusty house sparrows in the company of a swan, mud huts in the shadow of the Taj Mahal. All questions put to her were answered with an economy of words. Millicent joined no clubs or societies, dined alone at the end of a table with a book propped in front of her, and spent her free time in her apartment.

Thus she became the object of speculation and gossip, especially among the freshers, who felt as a rule that she cast all of them in a bad light. Two weeks into term, the discussion among six girls seated at one end of the breakfast table revolved around how Millicent had snubbed Elizabeth Macleod from Nottinghamshire during a tennis match the previous afternoon.

"I only asked her to play out of pity," Elizabeth said, blue eyes wide as if she still could not believe yesterday's turn of events.

Catherine glanced over her shoulder. She felt no guilt for joining the gossip, for Millicent had brought it upon herself. But the thought of Millicent walking by and overhearing made her uneasy. The memory of the angry voices on that first day still caused her to wonder if her neighbor might have a reason for her standoffishness.

Beatrice Lindsay, Peggy's neighbor, shook her blond head. "I would have thought winning would have made her more sociable."

"Sociable?" Elizabeth snorted. "When I turned around after fetching the ball from out of bounds, she was walking away! 'Congratulations!' I called after her, and she merely sent me a backwards wave."

"How rude!" exclaimed Emily Perrin, a second-year student.

"Rude," Catherine agreed after another guilty glance about.

That evening she had her first actual conversation with Millicent. It was not a cordial one.

"Pardon me, but I neglected to copy our Latin assignment," she said to Millicent's impassive face after her knock on the sitting room door was answered. Raising the small paper bundle in her hand, she smiled and said, "And I brought you some macaroons for your trouble. My aunt bakes the best—"

"No, thank you," Millicent said before disappearing. But she had not closed the door. Upon her return she widened the opening only enough to allow Catherine to peer at an open notebook.

Catherine slipped the bundle into the pocket of her dressing gown so that she could balance her own notebook upon her splayed hand. Regret oozed through her as she penciled the information. Mary Dereham, her neighbor on the sitting room side, took the same lectures and would not have left her standing in the corridor like an unwashed *Sudra*.

What were you thinking? she asked herself. That Millicent would be so grateful for being needed, that they would at least be able to look each other in the eyes? That here was merely a troubled soul who needed someone to go the second mile and extend the hand of friendship?

Still, she made one last effort, using self-effacing humor. While her hand moved the pencil, Catherine sighed and said, "You would think a college student would know better. I didn't even realize my mind had left the room until everyone started rising from their chairs."

Smiling, she looked up.

The indigo eyes staring back at her were flat with boredom. "Have you finished there?"

Heat rose from Catherine's collar and diffused through her cheeks. She scrawled the last two words, snapped her notebook shut, and murmured, "Thank—" The door clicked shut as she finished "you."

She paced her bedroom floor while her heart hammered as if trying to escape her chest. Sounds of moving about came from next door. Glaring at the wall as if her eyes could burn a hole in it, she muttered, "Very well, your Royal Highness. You can rot over there for all I care!"

The anger turned inward as Catherine dropped into her cane chair. *Brave words,* she told herself, when said from the safety of her apartment.

Like a small dog barking threateningly from behind a gate. *Why did you just stand there and swallow such abuse?*

It was with great restraint that she did not relate the incident to those seated about her at the breakfast table the following morning. She would have certainly done so had Millicent not been within hearing range at the next table. But she poured out the whole scene in Peggy's sitting room afterward.

"Nothing I hear about her surprises me any more," Peggy said, shaking her head. "But it's her loss, if she wishes to spend her time here friendless. Just don't allow her behavior to distract you from what's important."

On the study table before Catherine lay her open notebook and the Latin verbs she had painstakingly conjugated. Peggy, at her right, was balancing chemical equations. At length Peggy put down her pencil and said, "Now, read to me what you have there."

Catherine nodded, holding her notebook a little closer:

"*Mittere,* 'to send,' " she read aloud. "*Mitto,* 'I send,' *mittes,* 'you send,' *mittor,* 'I am sent,' *mittuntur,* 'they are sent.' *Capere,* 'to seize,' *capio,* 'I seize,' *capis,* 'you seize,' *capior,* 'I am seized,' *capiuntur,* 'they are seized' . . ."

"Well done," Peggy said ten minutes later when Catherine had finished.

"Thank you." Catherine lay down her notebook and brought up again the issue that troubled her more than Latin stems, tenses, and moods. "I could hardly sleep; I just berated myself over and over for not just turning on my heel and walking away. Why did I stand there prattling on like that?"

"Anyone else would have done the same," Peggy assured her.

"*You* wouldn't have."

"Perhaps not," she said with a shrug. "A compensation for having older brothers. One learns to assert her rights. I'm just thankful you're not like Millicent, or we should never have become friends."

"Thank you," Catherine said, then gave her a curious look when the last statement sank in. "But why do you compare me with her?"

"Well, you know . . ."

"No, I don't."

Peggy rolled her eyes. "I admire your modesty, Catherine, but you don't have to be coy with me."

"Truly, I don't know what you mean."

"Hasn't anyone ever told you how becoming you are?"

"Becoming?" Catherine shook her head. "My parents never discuss appearances unless it's to tell us to wash our faces or trim our fingernails.

Jewel looks like an angel, but whenever I tell her so, Mother says 'Beauty is vain, Catherine.' They praise her more for her character than anything else."

"But you have a mirror."

"I don't exactly hover over it like Snow White's stepmother. My mother did once say she liked the color of my hair. But it's not half as magnificent as yours, Peggy. Why, it turns so many lovely shades in the sunlight."

Peggy gave her a grateful smile, even as she shook her head. "The whole is equal to the sum of its parts, remember?"

"Meaning . . . ?"

"You have more becoming parts." She touched one of the curls at her own temple, already sprung loose from its chignon. "I only have magnificent hair."

When Catherine opened her mouth to protest, Peggy raised a halting hand. "*And* a natural talent for Latin, which will do you no good if you don't finish conjugating verbs."

On Friday evening at eight, Catherine attended the first meeting of the Lawn Tennis Club in one of the lecture rooms.

"Weather permitting, we will play doubles every Monday, Wednesday, and Friday after lunch," said the elected chairwoman, third-year student Susan Martin, to the eleven students present. "In inclement weather we'll conduct serving and backhand drills in the gymnasium. We'll need every bit of practice we can squeeze in before the tournament against Newnham in May."

It's only every other day, Catherine rehearsed mentally on the way down the corridor. Surely Peggy would easily find someone else with whom to spend those alternating afternoon exercise breaks.

"It'll be good for both of us to cultivate closer friendships with the other girls," Catherine could hear herself explaining ever so gently, as her mind pictured the two of them in Peggy's sitting room.

Peggy bit her lip. "But I'm afraid you'll decide you'd rather be with them than me."

"Never," Catherine said, patting her shoulder. "You're my best friend here. Nothing will change that."

The scene was still taking place on her mind's stage when she reached Peggy's door. She did not hear the voices inside the apartment until after she had knocked.

"Why, I was just down at your door a minute ago," Peggy said with traces of white sugar on the side of her mouth. "Eileen brought over the most marvelous lemon biscuits. You *must* join us."

"Thank you, but there were refreshments at the mee—"

"Then come in for a chat."

Against her better inclination, for she felt very much an intruder, Catherine allowed herself to be persuaded inside. The three other freshers who were in the Chamber Orchestra were seated around the study table—Ann Purdy from Birmingham; Helene Coates, at twenty the oldest first-year student; and Eileen Stocker, who wore wire spectacles and was a niece of Miss Welsh. After practically pushing Catherine into the only empty chair at the study table, Peggy dragged her upholstered chair close.

"Peggy has had us in stitches," Helene caroled, passing the plate of biscuits toward Catherine. "Telling us about those cheeky St. John's men on the train."

"I would pay a pound to have seen 'Gloucester's' face when he caught the hat," Ann said. She was a thin young woman, not much taller than Jewel, with dimples in each pale cheek.

Though she politely declined a biscuit, Catherine laughed along with the others. She didn't mind Peggy's retelling the incident—in fact she had written all about it in her first letter to her parents.

"We've discovered that we all began music lessons at the age of six," said Eileen from the head of the table. "There must be some sort of musical awakening at that age."

"Not in my case," said Ann. "A doctor told my parents that taking up the flute would strengthen my lungs. I wasn't interested at all in those days and had to be forced to practice."

"She has asthma," Helene explained to Catherine.

Ann nodded and held up a red tin with *Gee's Lobelline Lozenges* captioned in white letters on a blue background. "I carry these everywhere."

"Does the flute help?" Catherine asked her.

"Quite so. Did you know that it takes more breath power to play the flute than the tuba?"

"Fortunate for you," Peggy said. "You're not much bigger than a tuba yourself."

That led to more talk having to do with music and instruments, and so when she felt able to do so without offending, Catherine rose and excused herself. "I've some letters to write," she explained, truthfully.

They all bade her good-evening, Peggy even rising to see her the few feet to the door. "You'll tell me all about the Tennis Club in the morning, won't you?" her friend said, freckled face glowing from the warmth of shared hospitality.

"I will," Catherine promised. An odd little pang struck her while she walked alone down the corridor. *You were going to suggest that you both make other friends,* she reminded herself. She just hadn't expected Peggy to do so *before* she gave her little speech, and in such great quantity at once.

But she felt much better when she touched her doorknob and felt definite traces of sugar.

After changing into nightgown and dressing gown she sat at her table and wrote a three-page letter to her parents and Jewel, another letter to her relatives at Berkeley Square, and a third to Aunt Phyllis. She read in bed from the translated Latin lines in her notebook for an hour or so, until her eyes grew weary. Turning off her lamp, she lay on her left side, shoved the pillow under her neck, and pulled the covers around her shoulder. Her thoughts grew less and less crisp, blurring together as the words had begun blurring on the page. She dreamt of lawn tennis matches, the ball thumping against one racket, then an opposite one, back and forth; until her thoughts sharpened enough to discern that she was hearing knocking on the wall at the head of her bed.

They came again, a series of five knocks, a pause, and five more. She raised herself on an elbow, reached over her headboard, and knocked back five times.

The knocking came again, this time more rapidly. Pushing back the covers, she lit a candle and slipped on her dressing gown and slippers. Goose bumps crawled up her back in the dark corridor. She paused at Millicent's bedroom door to consider whether she should fetch one of the resident lecturers first. *But what if she is choking,* she asked herself, *or seriously ill?*

"Millicent?" she said, walking into the bedroom with candle aloft. The ungracious thought struck her that she was probably the first student to enter this apartment since its current lodger moved in.

"Is that you, Catherine?" came a small muffled voice.

"It is." All Catherine could see of Millicent above the covers was her forehead and wide eyes. "Shall I fetch Miss Scott?"

"No . . . please." Easing down the covers so that her face was visible in the amber light, she said, "Will you come closer?"

"Of course." Catherine moved on over to the side of the bed. "What's the matter? Did you have a nightmare?"

"Yes," the girl said thickly, then whispered, "It was so real."

"Well, it's over now, isn't it?" Catherine said, lifting the globe to the lamp on the bedside table. "You know now it was just a dream."

"Not over yet. I still feel sick inside from it."

Catherine lit the wick with the candle and replaced the globe, then set the candlestand upon the table. "Is that better?"

"Yes." Millicent's indigo eyes drank in the light. "Thank you."

"Do you have them often?"

"Yes. But this is my first one here."

Catherine wasn't sure what to do next, until she recalled how her own mother had handled her childhood nightmares. "Why don't you tell it to me?"

"I couldn't," Millicent said with a visible shudder.

"Very well." Reaching for the lamp, Catherine said, "I'll put this on your study table, so there's no danger of fire, and leave the door—"

A hand shot out from the covers and grabbed her sleeve. "Do you think that would help? Telling you?"

"Yes." Catherine straightened. "It's what my mother always had us do. She says if you bring your fears out into the light—"

"Your mother . . ." A sob broke her voice. "If only mine were still alive!"

There was no time to wonder what her own mother would do. Catherine hefted herself on the side of the bed and put a hand upon Millicent's shoulder. "There, there now," she soothed. "Cry it out."

Cry she did, pressing the bedsheet to her eyes. When the sobs died down to rasping breaths, Catherine rose to pour water from a carafe into a glass beaker. Millicent had to sit higher upon her pillows to drink.

"Thank you," she said, wiping her mouth as she handed over the empty mug.

"More?"

When she shook her head, Catherine put the beaker on the table and sat again on the side of the bed. She was leery of asking bereaved people about lost loved ones, under the assumption that it would cause a person to remember that loss and become sad. But Millicent's late mother was clearly heavy in her thoughts this evening. Cautiously she asked, "How did your mother pass on?"

"A tumor in her breast," Millicent replied. The indigo of her eyes was all the more striking because of the redness rimming them. "The best surgeon in Huntingdon attended her, but she lived only weeks after that."

"I'm sorry."

Millicent blinked, nodded, and wiped her eyes. "Do you know where St. Ives is?"

From the poem? Catherine wondered. She had skipped rope to it countless times as a girl.

As I was going to St. Ives
I met a man with seven wives . . .

But she could not ask for fear of sounding flippant in the wake of Millicent's sad news. Instead, she said, "I wasn't sure if there was really such a place."

"It's where we live—only fifteen miles northwest of here and a stone's throw from Huntingdon. My father founded a newspaper, *The Huntingdon Mercury*. He married our neighbor's cousin in April. Her name is . . . was . . . Evelyn Singers." She drew another breath. "She's only seven years older than I. They honeymooned on the Continent for six weeks, but Father spends most of his time in Huntingdon anyway, so our lives went on about the same."

"*Our* lives?"

"Constance, Harriet, and Justin—my two younger sisters and brother. Only we address Constance as Connie. They call me Milly."

She swallowed audibly and continued. "But when Father and . . . his wife returned, she declared that our education was lacking and our lack of discipline appalling. And so she persuaded Father to enroll the girls in Cheltenham—even though there is a day school in Huntingdon. They sent Justin to Rugby, with us begging them not to, for he has a stammer and the other boys will make sport of him. They even sent away our governess, Miss Pierce. After her being with us since I was seven!"

It was a horrific story to Catherine's ears, worse than any bad dream. At least one eventually woke up from a dream. "And so you didn't want to come here."

Millicent drew a breath. "I actually took the examinations in the spring with that in mind. It seemed a grand adventure, and home would stay the same. Now all I can think about are my sisters and brother, how wretched they must feel."

She gave Catherine an earnest look. "I would never knowingly cause a child to be unhappy. Evelyn is what she is, but our own father? How can he live with himself?"

"What will you do?" Catherine asked.

Millicent pulled up her knees under the covers and wrapped her arms around them. "I don't know. My first plan was to lay about idle and skip lectures so I'd be sent down at the end of term. I even threatened that when they brought me here. But to what end?" The red-rimmed eyes narrowed. "Evelyn isn't going to put up with my being about, and I certainly don't wish for her company. Besides, it wouldn't be the same without the others. So I rise every day and go through the motions, wishing I were dead."

"Don't say that, Millicent."

"Why? What difference would it make to you?"

Catherine had to search her mind for an honest reply. In good conscience she could not gush over how fond she was of Millicent. "I would miss seeing your beautiful hair."

"My hair."

It was a weak lob, Catherine told herself, but now that it was in motion she had to play it. "It's like looking at a painting, especially when you take it down in the evenings."

The tiniest hint of a smile curled Millicent's lips. "It's kind of you to say that. Especially after I've behaved so badly toward you."

Catherine shrugged. "All in the past."

"It's even kinder of you to say that."

"Will you be all right?"

She sighed. "I'll never be so until my family's all right. But I suppose bearing a grudge against the whole world isn't going to make that happen."

"I should think it would make the term seem even longer," Catherine told her. "At least being involved with people makes the time pass more quickly."

"Hmm. I never thought of it that way."

An idea popped into Catherine's head. "Do you play tennis? It's probably not too late to join the club."

"We have a court at home." Millicent mulled over it for another second. "Perhaps I shall. May I tell you the nightmare now? I think you're right—I should speak of it."

"But of course."

"A monster was after me, and I couldn't run fast enough. My feet felt like lead and my scream wouldn't leave my throat."

"A monster?"

"Yes. Like Doctor Frankenstein's monster."

It was almost winsome, hearing an eighteen-year-old speak so. Monsters had not visited any of Catherine's infrequent nightmares since she was a small girl. As she grew older they were replaced by more definite threatening forms—wild dogs, mad people, snakes.

"You know, it seems almost funny now," Millicent said, rubbing her eyes.

"At least he didn't catch you," Catherine told her. "Perhaps his feet felt like lead too."

That made her smile. "It was so good of you to come. But you must be terribly sleepy."

"That's all right," Catherine said, covering a sudden yawn.

Millicent covered one as well. "I think I can sleep now."

"Very good." Motioning for her to lie back down, Catherine tucked the covers about her shoulders. She then smoothed Millicent's forehead with her fingertips. "May you have pleasant dreams for the rest of the night."

"Mmm. Thank you. No one's done that since Mother."

"What shall I do about the lamp?"

"You can extinguish it." Millicent smiled again. "Now that I know you're just a knock away."

"Very good." Catherine took up her candle, extinguished the lamp, and walked back to her room. On impulse she went into her sitting room where the letters she had written earlier lay, yet unsealed, on the table. She sat, opened her jar of ink, and in the candlelight added a postscript to one. *Thank you for being the kind of parents you are.*

At breakfast the flow of conversation at the table shared by Catherine, Peggy, Helene Coates from the Chamber Music Society, and Jane Stretten of the Tennis Club was hampered by Eileen Stocker's reading aloud from her notebook:

> "*. . . they are also known as preganglionic fibers of the sympathetic system; the axons of others pass into the anterior and lateral funiculi, where they—*"

"Please, Eileen," Helene interrupted. "Not at the table."

Eileen raised bespectacled eyes from her notes on Henry Gray's *Anatomy of the Human Body.* "You shouldn't be so concerned over having your delicate sensibilities offended, Helene. You know Mr. Foster will ask about this."

Professor Foster, M.A., LL.D., F.R.S. from Trinity College, indeed was reputed to be the most thorough lecturer at Girton, even among those who, like Catherine and Jane, did not attend lectures in Physiology.

"It's not my delicate sensibilities that are offended," Helene argued, "but the universal notion of common courtesy. Meals are reserved for pleasant conversation, not frantic last-minute study. Remember?"

"Very well." Eileen sighed, setting her notes aside to send a forkful of buttered eggs to her mouth. Her brows raised over her spectacles. "Mmm . . . these are good."

The others laughed, for half of the eggs on her plate had already been consumed while her mind was preoccupied.

"*Lateral funiculi?*" Jane pursed her lips in thought. Thickly proportioned, she had a powerful backhand upon the tennis court. "That reminds me of a song. What are they, pray tell?"

"Don't get her started again," Peggy groaned.

"Nerve fibers," Eileen replied after another forkful of eggs.

"Surely the song's not about nerve fibers!"

"What song?" Catherine asked.

"The Italian one. I heard an organ grinder singing it last May Day. I'm not sure of all the words." Jane cleared her throat, sang softly, "La-la-la-la-la . . . *Funicu-li, Funicu-la.*"

"It's about fun and frolic and music," came a voice from above. "It translates into 'Joy is everywhere, *funiculi, funicula.*' "

Everyone looked up. Peggy and Helene twisted in their chairs. Millicent stood with plate and cup in hand, hair tied with a ribbon at the nape of her neck, and shadows beneath her indigo eyes. She wrinkled her nose. "Only . . . I'm not sure of the translation for those last two words. I suspect they're just nonsense, like abracadabra or jabberwocky."

Still gaping, Jane nodded. "Uh, thank you."

Four students at the next table had quieted to stare. Millicent glanced at them, then explained, "Our former governess was proficient in Italian."

Rousing to her senses, Catherine motioned toward an empty chair. "Will you join us, Millicent?" She had to smile at the curious look Peggy sent her, for they had not yet had opportunity to speak privately this morning.

Her admiration for her friend multiplied when Peggy turned again to the newcomer and said, "Yes, Millicent. Do join us."

"Thank you." Millicent put down her dish and cup to pull out the chair. Unfolding her napkin, she said, "The bacon looks good, doesn't it?"

"Then have the rest of mine, too," Helene offered. "I took more than I have appetite for."

"Why, thank you."

"Millicent is considering the Tennis Club," Catherine told Jane.

"Indeed?"

"Please . . ." Millicent smiled at the faces turned to her. "Will you pay me the honor of calling me Milly?"

Five

*I*n London, Sarah spent the morning of the twenty-fifth of October at the Cannon Street offices of Blake Shipping, looking over ledgers with Mr. Mitchell and his son, Harold, formerly the senior accountant and now his father's aide. Sarah visited the company two or three times weekly, but she had no interest in spending most of her time at the office, nor did William wish to leave his position at the Commission. Thus she left the day-to-day running of the company to the Mitchells but still made the major decisions herself, after poring over research and seeking the counsel of the two men.

She referred to them as "the younger Mr. Mitchell" and "the elder Mr. Mitchell," unless speaking directly to one or the other, in which case "Mr. Mitchell" applied to both. The younger, Harold Mitchell, at thirty years of age, was actually six years Sarah's senior. Back in his accounting days, he proved himself to be of sterling character and brought to the company an appreciation for new innovations to balance out his more conservative father. Steel-hulled ships was the topic of their discussion today.

". . . double hull, and a dozen transverse bulkheads," Harold declared, having spent six weeks in Liverpool observing construction of the Cunard Line's S.S. *Servia*. "I tell you, steel will be the wave of the future." He smiled. "Forgive the play on words."

"What about the cost?" Sarah asked.

"Eighteen percent higher than iron. But with the reduced weight, Cunard will save that and more on fuel."

"We should wait to see how the *Servia* proves herself next year" was his father's advice. "Profits remain healthy, so there is no call to rush into change."

Sarah agreed with the cautious route. To soften Harold's disappointment, and because it made good business sense, she said, "If you'd care to investigate further, we'll put you on the *Servia* when she makes her maiden voyage."

"You're right to make him keep his feet on the ground," the elder Mr. Mitchell said as he accompanied Sarah downstairs. His shoulders were still broad and straight, but the grey hair, cane, and limp gave evidence of his almost sixty years.

"But we're a shipping company," she reminded him with a smile. "And so we can't afford to keep our feet on the ground all the time, can we?"

He chuckled. "Well said, Mrs. Doyle. I'll try to be more patient with him."

In the entrance hall, she spoke with him again of the plans to move from Mayfair. They had made the decision with such haste that second thoughts were beginning to plague her. Mr. Mitchell had known Mrs. Blake longer than anyone still living. Sarah hoped he could put her misgivings to rest.

"Why do I feel so disloyal?" she asked.

Switching his cane to his left hand, he took hers in a fatherly gesture. "Because you loved her. But if Mrs. Blake could speak to us today, she would remind you that you once had to talk her out of leaving Mayfair because of her physical frailties."

Sarah's eyes clouded at the memory. "She was willing to make that sacrifice for me. There is so much of her in that house."

"There is more of her in your memories. You'll be taking those with you." He let go of her hand and touched her cheek. "Don't you think your happiness would be more important to her than the notion of hanging on to a piece of property? After all, she's in a place where material things down here are of no interest to her."

It was what she needed to hear. She raised herself on tiptoe to kiss his bearded cheek. "You're such a comfort."

"It's only the truth," he told her, smiling. He also promised to keep his ears open for any quality Hampstead houses for sale. A brisk northwestern wind rushed in when the doorman swung open the door. Mr. Mitchell escorted her out to Cannon Street, where Comet and Daisy stood hitched to the coach.

"Where is your driver?" asked the solicitor.

"Perhaps he went for coffee," Sarah said, raising her voice over the wind.

"Didn't you tell me he has a newborn?"

"Why, yes."

Mr. Mitchell smiled. "Look at the windows."

Sarah looked. They were silvery with condensation.

"He must have ducked out of the wind and fallen asleep," Mr. Mitchell said, reaching for the coach's door handle. "I almost hate to wake—"

"Then don't, please." Sarah touched his sleeve. "I wanted to stop by Loft's on the way home."

"Shall I flag you a hansom?"

"It's only a block. The walk will be refreshing." She touched the brim of her ecru felt hat with burgundy trimming. "And Marie put in extra pins."

With a wave she set out down the busy pavement. Just a decade ago she would have been an oddity, an unescorted woman walking in the heart of London's business section. But those of her gender were finding more and more places in the work force as secretaries, shop assistants, and operators at the one-year-old Telephone Exchange on nearby Coleman Street.

Aromas of leather bindings and paneling wax and pipe tobacco greeted her inside Loft's Booksellers, an old establishment that boasted Prime Minister Gladstone as a frequent patron. She moved among the oak shelves and was delighted to find for her father a copy of *Ben Hur, A Tale of the Christ*, by the American writer Lew Wallace, and for Bethia, the latest adventure of The Parker Twins. She was looking through a collection of poetry by new author Cecil Talbot when a man's voice cut through her concentration.

"Judging by your smile, Mrs. Doyle, that's either very good or very bad poetry."

Sarah looked up into a pair of sharp blue eyes. "Lord . . . Holt," she said.

She hoped awkwardness wasn't evident upon her face. She had made the man's acquaintance five years ago while viewing the diving bell exhibition at the Polytechnic Institution with Naomi and William. He had seemed pleasant enough that evening, even gallant. But when he suggested visiting her at Berkeley Square, William threatened to reveal his licentious past. That was not a memory she enjoyed revisiting, not with the man standing there staring down at her.

Neither was it pleasant to recall how she had sent his card back downstairs on two occasions when he attempted to pay calls after Grandmother's death—though she did not regret doing so.

He was straight-backed and consciously elegant, with wavy auburn hair and brows that arched in a slightly quizzical manner. A pencil-thin mustache ran along his full lips, and a dimple was centered in his chin. His six-foot frame was clothed in a finely cut double-breasted jacket of mist-grey wool and striped trousers. She would have thought him exceedingly hand-some had William not informed her—after they were married—of his mis-deeds at Oxford.

But no matter what thoughts ran through her mind, she could not bring herself to be discourteous. Fortunately, logistics would not allow her to extend her gloved hand, which was required to balance the open book resting between her left wrist and its fingerless left hand, while *Ben Hur* and *The Parker Twins at the Circus* were anchored in the crook of her arm.

"How do you do?" she said.

"Very well, thank you," he replied with a polite little inclination of his head. He nodded toward the book she held. "May I?"

"Yes, of course." Robbed of her right hand's excuse, she caught up the other two books into her arms as if they were in danger of falling. Lord Holt seemed not to notice her discomfort, or else he was a very good actor.

"Catechism of Nature," he read from the black clothbound cover, then began turning pages with careless ease. A ring, made of a large diamond set into a gold claw, flashed reflected light with every movement.

"I was only curious," Catherine told him. "I'm not familiar with Mr. Talbot's work."

"Hmm. And neither will be most of England, I predict."

Even the clearing of his throat sounded elegant. Softly he read:

> *"O thou Aspen on the village green,*
> *so lovely to the unjaded eye,*
> *with whispered songs of love abandoned*
> *yet mine own despair gives thine the lie.*
> *For every breeze, thy leaves do quiver*
> *yet my trembling brings thine own to shame*
> *mine very heart is made to shiver*
> *by the sound of but her name."*

He winced as if swallowing quinine. "Mine very stomach is made to retch, if you'll forgive my ungentlemanly language."

In spite of herself, Sarah smiled. *People can change,* she thought, drowning out the warnings in her head. Indeed, there seemed no trace of arrogance about him. "Perhaps that wasn't his best work."

"One would hope not," he replied, blue eyes merry. He closed the book and offered it to her.

"I was just about to replace it," she said with a glance at the gap between books on the shelf. If she freed her right hand, she would have to shake his.

And she still wasn't certain about that. "Would you . . . ?"

"But of course," he said, shelving the book. "And might I suggest that you try Matthew Arnold, if you're fond of poetry?"

"Thank you. And I pray you have a pleasant—"

"That's a Parker book, isn't it?" he said with a glance toward the two books remaining in her arms.

"Why, yes." Moving *The Parker Twins at the Circus* with its distinctive sky-blue cloth cover to the top, she said, "How did you know?"

"My mother happens to be the author."

Sarah's eyes widened. "Your mother is Harriet Godfrey?"

Smiling at her puzzlement, he said, "Formerly Lady Holt. She remarried some years after my father passed on."

"Oh, I'm sorry. Not that she remarried, but . . ."

He waved an elegant hand. "I understand your meaning. And we're all very proud of her."

Tempting as it was to mention that her father also wrote books, Sarah said, "My sister has every one of the stories." She glanced at the one in her arms and smiled. "Or at least she will very shortly."

"Mother will be pleased to hear that."

While the subject of conversation interested her, Sarah had not expected to stand under the gaze of those blue eyes for so long. Awkwardness pushed words out of her mouth almost as fast as she could form them. "I've read *The Parker Twins at Hadrian's Wall* to her a dozen times. It's good for children to develop an appreciation for reading early, my father says."

"Absolutely," he agreed. "I've told Mother I wish she had started writing them when I was a boy. But even at my age, I've read every one, just because . . ." He shrugged self-consciously. "Well, you know."

It was very sweet, the notion of a grown man reading children's books because his mother wrote them. This time Sarah shifted the books willingly and offered her hand. "It was a pleasure to chat with you, Lord Holt," she said with some truth, for he had been nothing but courteous. "But I must beg your leave now. I'm expected home for lunch."

"I'm rather hungry myself." His hand closed over hers. "Have you a telephone at Berkeley Square?"

"Why, yes," she replied, and then wished she hadn't spoken so quickly. The box telephone attached to the sitting room wall for the past two months was the marvel of the household. But if he was planning to suggest any further contact, she would have to demur. Whether or not Lord Holt had mended his ways, William would not be willing to socialize with him. Some past acquaintances were better left in the past.

The pressure of his hand increased slightly, so that she could not pull hers away without jerking it. "Lambert's is just up the street," he said with a little smile. "Very cozy private dining salons. And the chef is ten times the artist of our nature poet Mr. Talbot."

He's inviting me to lunch, Sarah realized, while cold clamminess spread up her neck.

But he had addressed her as Mrs. Doyle, meaning he was aware of her marital status. And his countenance was as benign as if he had commented on the weather. Surely he was only paying a courtesy by suggesting she might care to sample Lambert's cuisine instead of hurrying home. And an unaccompanied woman alone would naturally desire a private salon, for eyebrows would be raised should she enter a main dining room.

"My husband and I must visit there sometime," she replied. Just in case.

"Do sample the *Saumon Fumé et Roti.*" While he released her hand as soon as she eased it back, there was a hint of knowing in his blue eyes. Or was she imagining it?

You sadistic rake! Sidney, Lord Holt told himself. Still, he could not help but smile at the sight of Mrs. Doyle hurrying past the bow window outside. She reminded him of a fox fleeing the hounds.

One of the wealthiest foxes in Britain, he thought. And it didn't hurt that she was beautiful. Had he thought for a minute that there was the possibility of a liaison with Sarah Doyle, he would have bade his time and never been so transparent. But women such as she were tediously faithful to their husbands.

Which was why he had extended the not-quite-subtle invitation to Lambert's. Five years ago William Doyle, former stable boy and college servant, had dared to insult him at the Polytechnic Institution. While Sidney was too practical to allow the memory of such an affront to smolder in his chest and sap his intellect for five years, he could not pass up the opportunity to cause Mr. Doyle some discomfort. *He'll be livid when she tells him.* Which she would, of course.

"*La vengeance est un plat qui se mange froid,* Mrs. Doyle," he said softly, quoting French author de la Clos', century-old sentiment. Revenge was indeed a dish best served cold. Yes, the portion he had served William Doyle was relatively small, but still enough to lodge in his throat.

Smiling again, he reached for the copy of *Catechism of Nature,* with all its purple prose. He would give it to Leona as a lark.

"Thank you, Sir," said the proprietor, a wizened old man, as he closed bony fingers over the half crown dropped into his palm.

Sidney nodded and left the shop, tucking the book into his coat pocket so he could hold his bowler hat against the wind. His coachman, Jerry, hopped down to open the door. Even though Sidney had just an easy walk up the street, the rig might as well wait in front of Lambert's as in front of the book-shop. As the team of Welsh Cobs eased into traffic, he mused idly over what he would have done had Mrs. Doyle taken him up on his invitation. *A comedy of errors,* he thought with a glance at his watch. For a familiar crested coach was probably already waiting outside the restaurant with its stunning—and highly jealous—passenger.

"Why, that snake!" William exclaimed, pounding a fist into his hand. "If only I had been—"

"Sh-h-h," Sarah warned with a glance at the terrace door. Fearing that very reaction, she had suggested they sit outside, for sounds flowed more freely through a house bedded down for the night. "I'm not entirely positive he was suggesting I go there with him."

"Sarah . . ." He shook his head. "Then why did he mention the private salons?"

That was a point she had not considered. Private salons were standard in most elegant restaurants, so pointing out that Lambert's had them was as unnecessary as mentioning that they had tablecloths. Unless that fact was wrapped around a subtle hint. She could still feel the pressure of Lord Holt's hand clasping the one she had so foolishly offered.

"You're right," she whispered. "He's a snake."

William shot up from the wicker chair. "Surely he's in the directory."

"William!" This time she forgot to whisper. Rising, she clutched his arm and lowered her voice. "You can't go to his home!"

"I'm not. At least not tonight. But I'm going to telephone His Lordship and arrange to meet—"

"Please! Don't!"

Anger showed clearly in his face, even in the feeble light of a half-moon. "Sarah, he treated you like a common—"

"And what if I'm mistaken?"

Now that she thought about it, the pressure of Lord Holt's hand was no more intense than when Mr. Mitchell, who was never less than a gentleman, had held her hand earlier. "He never suggested accompanying me."

Uncertainty and helplessness mingled with the anger in William's expression. He looked at the door, then back at her.

"Please, William," she said. She could feel the muscle knotted under his sleeve, the tenseness of his posture. "He's not worth this. And how often do our paths cross with his?"

Her husband blew out his cheeks. "What I don't understand is why you allowed him to chat with you in the first place."

The accusation in his tone stung. "I didn't realize . . ."

"Sarah . . . are you crying?"

"No." Just because one's eyes burned a little didn't mean one was on the verge of sobbing. But when his fingertips brushed her wet cheeks, she could not hold back a sniff.

"He caught me by surprise," she said thickly.

"Now, now." William pulled her close, resting her head upon his shoulder. Her arms automatically went around him. "Forgive me, Precious," he murmured into her hair. "I know it's not within you to be rude. Even to such a blackguard."

"He could have mended his ways, for all I knew," she said, still needing to defend herself. "Like Ethan."

They corresponded regularly with Ethan Knight, a former curate sent to work in a leprosy mission after being caught stealing from the tithes. Married now to an Indian nurse, Ethan had recently founded a mission in the Rajasthan Desert, where William shipped crates of purified Gynocardia oils to aid in treatment.

"Yes, he could have," William agreed.

"And he *was* extremely polite. He even spoke highly of his mother."

"Well, no wonder you were deceived. Bad men aren't allowed to speak highly of their—"

"Ouch!" he exclaimed when she pinched him in the side.

"Good men aren't allowed to mock their wives," Sarah said, smiling against his shoulder.

❧ Six ❧

"Mind you hang on to that umbrella, Eileen," Catherine said, wringing salt water from the hem of her gown as she noticed the dark clouds on the sea's horizon. "We'll use the underside to collect rainwater."

"Perhaps there's a brook or creek?" Mary Dereham said with a tentative nod toward the dense plant life meeting the sand.

That was a possibility. Along with the possibility of creatures of all sorts. Catherine had read of carnivorous lizards the size of ponies . . .

Don't think that! she ordered herself. She had to be strong for the others. And she felt partially responsible for their plight, for it was she who had chartered the boat meant to carry the whole freshman class to Bombay for the long vacation.

"Tomorrow we'll explore," she told the others. "But our first priority must be shelter." She pointed off toward the craggy cliffs rising above the cove. "I spotted a cave just before we hit the rocks."

"A cave!" Eileen Stocker exclaimed in a dismal tone.

Ann Purdy broke into sobs. "We're never going to get—"

Catherine moved over to the girl and took hold of her narrow heaving shoulders. "We'll get through this," she said firmly, and not just for Ann's benefit, for other faces were beginning to crumble. She dipped into her pocket and brought out a red tin. "And look what almost floated past me."

"My lozenges!"

Expressions lightened. In keeping with the more optimistic spirit, Peggy pulled a handful of long grass from a clump pushing out of the sand. "We should gather some on the way, don't you think? For bedding?"

"Excellent idea, Peggy," Catherine told her. "But quickly. And I'll pull some bamboo."

"What for?" Helene's voice came from behind as Catherine started toward a stand of stalks at the jungle's edge.

"You never know what may come in handy," Catherine replied over her shoulder. Best to wait until they were sheltered to inform them that they would have to spend most of the evening using rocks to file sharp points to make spears.

We should collect hairpins, too, she told herself. She could feel one against her damp scalp, so surely the sea had not snatched all of them. They could be fashioned into crude hooks. Fishing line would be a problem, she thought, until she glanced back and caught sight of a certain head of long ashen hair. She could only hope that Milly's philanthropy outweighed her vanity . . .

"Miss Rayborn?"

Catherine blinked and drew in a quick breath. The deserted island gave way to Lecture Room Two, her summer vacation turned back into the first of November. And staring down at her stood Dr. Precor of Saint Catherine's College.

"Yes, Dr. Precor?" she said with cheeks aflame.

He clasped his hands behind his back during a silence that stretched out forever. "I said, Miss Rayborn . . . for what reason did Cato the Elder, who so fervently despised Carthage that he closed every speech to the Senate with *Karthago delenda est,* oppose Scipio Africanus's consulship and plan to crush Carthage?"

She cleared her throat, shifted in her chair. "Cato . . ."

". . . the elder," the professor supplied.

Think, think! she ordered herself, mentally racing through the corridors of her mind for whichever corner held the information she had absently tossed there after last night's study session with Milly and Peggy. Easily she recalled the meaning of Cato the Elder's closing words: *Carthage must be destroyed.* So why would he not support Scipio Africanus's endeavors to do just that?

Dr. Precor was still staring, waiting, which made her all the more nervous. The fact that she could not remember the answer was not as shameful to her as the fact that she had been caught spinning wool during lecture. Finally she had to admit, "I don't know, Sir."

Mercifully, he allowed his eyes to linger upon her only a fraction of a second before moving on. "Miss Turner?"

Catherine looked over at Milly in the second row on her left. She could read in her friend's expression that she knew the answer. *Go ahead, tell him,* she urged silently, though Milly was still looking at Dr. Precor and not at her.

"I don't know, Sir," Milly replied. It was obvious in her tone, at least to Catherine, that she had had to force out the words.

Dr. Precor closed his eyes, sighed, opened them, and moved on. "Miss Dereham?"

Catherine's neighbor on the sitting room side answered, "Cato the Elder detested the extravagance of the Scipios and their adoration of Greek culture. And he may have envied Scipio Africanus's popularity."

"Well said, Miss Dereham."

As Dr. Precor walked back to the lectern, Mary Dereham sent Catherine an apologetic look. Catherine smiled back, shook her head slightly. She couldn't expect the whole class to fall on their swords to spare her embarrassment. But in the corridor after lecture, she put an arm around Milly and gave her a squeeze. "Thank you," she said just under the hum of conversations going on about them. "But please, never do that again."

Milly's face was all innocence. "Do what?"

"You knew that answer." Catherine lowered her voice. "I don't want you to lie for me, just because I wasn't paying attention. It's not right, and it's not fair to you."

"Oh, very well. But do try to save your grand adventures for night. Where were you this time—Paris?"

Catherine shook her head and gave Milly a sheepish look. "A deserted island."

Her friend, who was her enemy until ten days ago, slanted her indigo eyes at her and laughed.

And I should have never doubted you, Catherine thought, smiling. *You would have sacrificed your hair without a second thought.*

One discipline mastered by every Girton student, no matter what her lecture schedule, was to check the mantelpiece of the reading room in the short space of time between breakfast and penciling her initials on the marking roll for the first of three times daily. On Tuesday, the second of November, Catherine, Peggy, and Milly each had a letter.

"Justin!" Milly said, breaking the seal after the three stood aside so others could check for mail.

Catherine recognized her cousin Sarah's precise script and slid her thumb under the flap.

Peggy grumbled under her breath and tucked hers unopened into her waistband.

Oh dear, Catherine thought, restraining a smile. This wasn't her first letter from Oliver Piggot. When Peggy glanced at her, she assumed a blank expression and turned her attention to the words on the page before her.

> *Dearest Catherine,*
> *William has asked me to accompany him to Cambridge on the seventeenth of November so that I might visit with you while he observes a new microscope at Pembroke College. Are you allowed to lunch away from Girton? If so, will you ask permission for me to call for you—*

Peggy's voice cut into her concentration. "What is it, Milly?"

Catherine looked at Milly, who was holding a page to her bosom. "Justin and Adam Croft, the headmaster's son, have become close friends. Adam has a stammering problem as well. But no one dares make sport of either of them, for fear of Mr. Croft hearing of it."

"Why Milly, that's wonderful!" Catherine said.

Milly swiped her fingertips under her eyes. "It's good to know there are still some people in this world who treat children kindly."

"Yes, it is," Peggy agreed, resting a hand upon her shoulder.

Smiling appreciatively, Milly said, "And your letters?"

"My cousin Sarah," Catherine replied. "She's to visit Cambridge in a fortnight."

"And you, Peggy?"

"Just a neighbor," Peggy muttered.

Sundays at Girton were altogether different from the rest of the weekly routine. Services at Saint Andrew's in Girton Village had the unfortunate reputation of being as lifeless as its churchyard, so all but a few students and staff went to Cambridge for the day. There were always fine sermons in the University Church, many conducted by distinguished visiting preachers. A leisurely lunch followed at Mrs. Golden's Reading Room for Ladies, and then afternoon choral services at King's College Chapel.

Such became the Sunday ritual for Catherine, Peggy, and Milly. But on the seventh of November, Catherine blinked at her reflection in the mirror above her chest of drawers and prodded her murky mind to make a decision. *Girton or Cambridge?*

While concentrating on the sermon would be far more difficult in Saint Andrew's, she could be back in bed in less than two hours. Not so if she chose Cambridge, even if she left directly after morning services. Lunch was not a factor either way—during the night hours she had nibbled away a tin of Temperley's Tempting Chocolate Biscuits and a wedge of cheese saved from supper, and her body craved sleep more than food.

At the light knocking on the sitting room door, she left the bedroom and padded around the study table, still strewn with books and papers and crumbled waxed biscuit wrappers. "Yes," she yawned, staring at the knob as if it would turn itself. "Come in."

Milly came through the door, ash blond braids coiled upon her head like a silver crown, a forest-green-and-black striped silk lengthening her five-foot-seven frame.

"Catherine . . ." Milly's eyes traveled from the uncombed hair falling to Catherine's waist to the bare toes peeking out from the hem of her dressing gown. She took a step closer, brushed a finger against Catherine's chin, and stared at the black speck that came off on her fingertip.

"Chocolate biscuit," Catherine explained, too sleepy to be embarrassed.

"Breakfast is laid," Milly said. "Why haven't you dressed?"

Taking a step backwards, Catherine nodded toward the table. "The Hellenistic Age."

"But the composition isn't due until Tuesday."

"Yes, Tuesday," Catherine sighed. And if she burned the midnight oil again tonight, perhaps she would be able to explain competently to Miss Welsh, lecturer in Greek and Roman Society, the effect of Greek culture upon the known world in fourth-century B.C.

"Did you go to bed at all?"

"Uh . . . no." Catherine blinked at her and smiled. "But I'll make up for it after church. I'm going to join the Girton group, so you shouldn't wait."

But wait she did, Peggy as well. While Milly brought toast, quince jelly, and tea from the dining hall, Peggy chose from Catherine's wardrobe a costume of blue India cashmere with an overdress of a grey-blue shade called *nuit de France.*

After Catherine finished her toast and tea, sponge bathed, and brushed her teeth, both helped her into her clothes. Peggy gathered the sides of Catherine's chestnut brown hair into a comb at her crown, over which she pinned a blue velvet hat. And the two went the second mile by declaring they would accompany her to the village church.

"Please, you've done enough," Catherine protested.

"We three musketeers have to stick together," Peggy said.

"Stick together," Milly echoed. "All for one and one for all."

"That's so . . . sweet," Catherine said, touched to tears by their self-sacrifice. She yawned, then said, "I love you both."

"We love you, too." Milly exchanged sage looks with Peggy. "But don't go pinning medals on us just yet. We plan to enjoy lunch and the afternoon service in Cambridge once we've put you back to bed."

The three walked up Cambridge Road with seven Girton students and Miss Scott. Chatter was kept to a minimum, everyone either preparing hearts for worship or being hushed by Miss Scott for not doing so. Other groups of parishioners strolled in the same direction, turning onto the lane leading through the churchyard to the south entrance. On either side, old and not-so-old gravestones were shaded by lime trees.

Twelfth-century Saint Andrew's was a squat, solid structure of light brown fieldstone, with parapets and a range of Gothic perpendicular windows situated below a handsome clock tower. In the pew Catherine was flanked by Peggy and Milly—just in case. Reverend Murray's soft-spoken sermon on *The Milestones of Life* did not help Catherine's state of semi-attentiveness; but then, it would have been the same had he thundered out the story of Gideon and the Midianites.

Less than an hour later she lay in her chemise, sandwiched between sheets and covers, listening to the bedroom door easing closed. From far outside the window drifted the lowing of cattle. The sound was always a comfort to her urban ears. *How serene they are,* she thought. *They're content to munch on grass and don't care a pin about Ancient Greece.*

————

The study was smaller than Hugh would have expected, considering Reverend Leigh's positions as vicar of Saint John's Chapel as well as head of the History Department. An oak desk took up most of the space. The shelves groaned with worn-looking books with titles such as *The Marrow of Modern Divinity* and *Hebrew and English Lexicon of the Old Testament.* Stuck in a space between books was an odd item for one who lived an ecclesiastical life, a mottled cricket ball with frayed lacings.

"From the winning game against Eton when I was in sixth form," the heavyset man explained from the opposite side of the desk, after a glance in the direction Hugh was looking. "I was fielder for a little school in Sutton, so it was quite a victory."

His sentimental smile gave Hugh just a fraction of hope. Obviously Reverend Leigh, whose blond hair and beard had no traces of grey, had not yet forgotten what it was like to be young. Perhaps he had even laughed privately at the prank, and had only sent for him out of a clerical obligation to set him back upon the straight and narrow.

But hope faded when the somber expression resumed itself. The minister laced thick fingers together atop the folded handkerchief upon his desk and fastened brown eyes upon Hugh's face. "You have attended chapel faithfully for almost four years now, Mr. Sedgwick. Thus, I have labored under the assumption that you are a Christian . . ."

That stung. "But I am, Sir," Hugh mumbled.

"And you believe what you did was Christlike?"

"No, Sir." The fresh memory of Reverend Leigh turning his back to the congregation to offer prayer burned into his mind. "I beg your forgiveness for my . . . humiliating you."

"Is that why you think I'm angry?" The minister sighed, shaking his head. "I am only too aware that obesity inspires levity among weak-minded individuals. What you did was far more serious than humiliate me. You made a mockery of worship, the awesome privilege of communing with a holy God. He had Moses take off his sandals when He appeared in the burning bush. We may not take off our shoes, Mr. Sedgwick, but He is still to be reverenced."

Shame washed through Hugh with feverish chill.

"I will not ask why you did it, Mr. Sedgwick. Of course it was to win some wager. No doubt the laughter was music to your ears."

It was indeed, but now the memory sickened him. And he had thought himself so clever! He wiped his forehead. "I wish I had never done it."

"Wishes cannot alter the past, young man." Slowly Reverend Leigh unfolded the handkerchief and spread it upon the desk. Bold black painted letters spelled out *Exitus acta probat*. Not a humorous phrase *per se*, but when pinned to a certain area of the back of a minister's vestment, could cause a nave filled with college men to double over in their pews.

"The end justifies the means," Reverend Leigh translated flatly. "For someone with such mediocre marks, at least you've learned your Latin."

Hugh winced. The temperature of the room had jumped ten degrees, and the walls were closing in on him like the torture chamber in Poe's "The Pit and the Pendulum."

"How did you get your hands upon my vestment?"

"I slipped into the vestry late last night, Sir."

"Alone?"

"Yes, Sir."

"Then I would like the names of everyone involved in the wager."

There was no wager, rose to Hugh's lips. But he could not bring himself to compound his sin with a lie. Yet he could not turn in his friends—even though one had so obviously broken his vow of secrecy. "I can't tell you that, Sir."

"And why not?"

Hugh decided to risk appealing to the vicar's not-too-distant youth. "Sir, would you turn in your friends, if you were me?"

The brown eyes narrowed. "You know I could have you sent down."

"Please don't," Hugh said, moving to the edge of the chair. "I'll do anything."

In a silence that seemed palpable, save the pulse pounding in his neck, Hugh sat under the minister's scrutiny. Finally Reverend Leigh sighed.

"Very well."

Hugh let out a breath, only then aware that he had been holding it. "Thank you, Sir! I'll never forget this."

"Nor shall I, Mr. Sedgwick. And now to your penance."

"Penance?"

"You did just say you would do anything, yes?"

"Oh yes, Sir. Anything."

"First, you will put every shilling you won in the parish poor box. Can I trust you to do that?"

"I'll put it in your very hands, Sir."

"That will not be necessary. The box will do." The vicar sat back in his chair and folded his arms. "During your slipping about last night, you must have noticed crates of hymnals. They arrived Wednesday, but must be inscribed before we can set them in the pews."

"Inscribed, Sir?"

"Inside the cover, with 'Saint John's College Chapel.' "

"And you want me to do the inscribing?" That didn't seem such a difficult penance.

"In your neatest hand. There are two hundred. I'll not assign work on Sunday, so you will begin tomorrow."

Two hundred? Hugh was careful not to allow panic to creep into his expression. *Better than being sent home,* he reminded himself. "Of course, Sir. But if I may beg your pardon . . . I've rehearsals every evening this week. May I wai—"

"Then mornings before breakfast will have to do, won't they? The vestry is never locked—as you are well aware. If you pace yourself at forty a day, your task will be completed by Friday. And if you will not share the responsibility for this prank, you will not share the work. I want every one done in your hand."

Hugh swallowed. "Yes, Sir."

The vicar nodded. "You may go."

"Yes, Sir." He rose from the chair. "Thank you for not sending me home."

"You're welcome, Mr. Sedgwick."

Hugh was turning again for the door when the vicar's voice stopped him. "Oh, and Mr. Sedgwick?"

"Yes, Sir?"

The vicar quirked an eyebrow. "I plan to continue hanging my vestments in that room. If you happen to be tempted—"

"I'll not be tempted, Sir."

Neville Broughton was waiting in the sitting room of Hugh's apartment. He sprang from the armchair. "Will you be sent down?"

"No." Hugh hung his hat on the rack by the door. "But I'll be inscribing hymnals all week."

"You don't say! He wasn't angry?"

"Oh, he was angry all right."

They had been friends since boarding school at Harrow, and joked that they could read each other's thoughts. Hugh could clearly read self-preservation in Neville's. His friend proved just that a moment later by saying, "Did he ask if anyone else was involved?"

"I didn't tell."

"But of course you wouldn't." Neville smiled at him. "Well, at least the best part remains."

"What do you mean?"

He pulled a stack of pound sterling notes from his trouser pocket. "Twenty-five! Everyone paid up."

"Good." Hugh took the money and slipped it into his coat pocket.

He had been beckoned to Reverend Leigh's study just before lunch, and his frayed nerves had his stomach demanding food. But when he took the Gregor's Scottish Shortbread tin from the mantelpiece, it rattled with loose crumbs.

Neville shrugged at his questioning look. "I didn't finish lunch, for worry over what would happen to you."

Hugh tossed the tin onto his study table. His nerves jumped at the clatter it made. "I'd rather have a sandwich anyway. No, some soup would be better."

"Then let's make way to Boswell's." His friend clapped him on the shoulder. "You'll treat, of course, now that you're suddenly wealthy."

"You'll be buying," Hugh said, taking up his hat again. He thought about the morning hours he would be spending alone with hymnals. "You're getting off cheap. And we have to make a stop in the chapel first."

He had to chuckle at the mock whimpering noises Neville made as pound notes began slipping through the slot in the poor box. It wasn't as if either of them even needed the money, for both received more than generous allowances from wealthy fathers. There was just something about ill-gotten gains that made them more attractive. But in this particular instance, he was glad when that last pound disappeared.

A woman was exiting Boswell's Student Café on Petty Curry just as Hugh and Neville arrived. Hugh stepped up to hold the door. "Thank you," she said, and was followed out by three younger women who also thanked him. Hugh smiled at the sight of some red curls beneath the brim of a brown hat. The Girton girls from the train had visited his thoughts more than once since the beginning of term. *Perhaps God has forgiven me after all,* he thought.

Catherine's next conscious thought was to wonder why no one was answering the door. She opened the eye not pressed into the pillow and stared at vaguely familiar pink flowered wallpaper. *School,* she remembered, raising her head and pushing away the covers.

The knob turned, and then Peggy stuck her head inside. "Catherine?"

"You're back?" Catherine asked, still stupefied by sleep.

"Oh dear. I woke you? It's half-past five, so I assumed . . ."

"I'm glad you did. I didn't want to sleep the night through. Do come in."

Peggy had apparently not stopped at her own room, for her wrap of black knitted yarn was still about her shoulders, and she still wore the hat that matched her brown faille gown. Her cheeks were so flushed that her freckles seemed to fuse together. "You'll never guess who we met in Cambridge."

"Don't make me guess, Peggy," Catherine pleaded, slipping out of bed and scooping her dressing gown from the back of her chair. "My mind's not ready for work."

"Oh, you poor dear. But don't put that on. You need to dress for supper. You can't live on biscuits and toast."

Catherine nodded and took the gown she had worn to church from her wardrobe. "Whom did you meet?"

"Hugh-from-Saint John's! After church, Milly talked Helene and me into steaks instead of tea room dainties. She bribed Miss Scott into chaperoning us by insisting on paying for her meal. Well, Miss Scott said a place called Boswell's was reputed to have the best in town." She wrinkled her nose.

"Between the two of us, mine was overcooked. But guess who should happen by as we were leaving?"

"Hmm. Hugh-from-Saint John's?"

Peggy laughed. "His surname is Sedgwick. Like the Tea Company, which his family owns, by the way. He was with his friend Mr. Broughton. You know, Neville-from-the-train. We chatted for some five minutes. Miss Scott didn't raise an eyebrow, as it was obvious we were acquainted. He, Mr. Sedgwick, that is, asked how we were adjusting to college. He also said that St. John's is staging a production of *The Man of Mode* on the thirteenth, and that we should see it. Bellair is his part—don't you think he fits it perfectly?"

"I wouldn't know," Catherine replied after pulling the dress over her head. "I've never read *The Man of Mode*."

Peggy rolled her eyes. "Heaven forbid you should read something without high adventure. Mr. Broughton may be the more handsome, but he has the personality of moldy cheese—he jabbed Mr. Sedgwick in the ribs, hinting of some prank they had played, until Mr. Sedgwick told him to stop. Then he— Mr. Broughton, that is—boasted to Milly of his father's horse-breeding farm in Hammersmith."

"Yes? Was she impressed?"

"Hardly. She looked at him as if he were something she scraped from the bottom of her shoe. You know that look, don't you?"

Catherine grimaced. "I do."

Absently Peggy picked up Catherine's comb from the top of the chest of drawers, then put it back again. "As good as it was of Miss Scott to allow us to chat, I wish she hadn't been there. Perhaps Hugh would have asked permission to write me."

"You would really wish that?"

"Insofar as it's against the rules for him to visit, it's better than nothing. You've fastened the wrong button there."

Pressing chin against bodice, Catherine pushed the button through the loop. "But you've ridiculed him for the train prank to anyone who would listen."

"Not ridiculed . . . *related*. It's an amusing story." She sighed. "I wish he weren't a senior. He'll be gone by summer."

"But he surely lives in London if he took the train at King's Cross. Perhaps we'll happen upon him again sometime, and he can pretend to be Hamlet."

"Hamlet." Peggy smiled. She stepped close enough to seize Catherine's hands. "Miss Scott said she would chaperone a group to see *The Man of Mode*. You'll come too, won't you? I won't be so nervous if you're there. And if we have a small group, it won't seem as if I've set my cap for him."

"Then I'll come," Catherine told her.

"Thank you!" Peggy gave her a quick embrace, her face glowing again. But by the time Catherine finished combing her hair, Peggy had stalked into the sitting room to drop into the cushions of the upholstered chair. "What good will it do? I'm not the sort of girl men of that sort are interested in anyway. No doubt he would have been interested in Milly, had his friend not laid claim to her right away."

"What do you mean . . . not the sort of girl?" Catherine moved over to kneel by her side. "You're a lovely young woman, bright and witty." She thought it best not to remind her of a certain Londoner who wrote every week.

Peggy's hazel eyes glistened. "You don't read about bright and witty girls in fairy tales, Catherine. The prince fell in love with the sleeping beauty before he knew if she even had a mind. Before he heard her speak. She could have believed the earth was flat and had a grating voice for all he knew."

"Then he was a simpleton, wasn't he? If I had a brother, I just know he would be terribly in love with you after an hour in your company."

Her friend made a face. "You're just saying that to cheer me. I appreciate your kindness, but—"

"But it's true. And who knows? Perhaps when Mr. Sedgwick sees you at the performance, he'll reflect upon how much he enjoyed the encounter and write to you."

"I doubt that." Still, Peggy gave her a grateful look. "But it doesn't cost anything to hope, does it?"

Catherine patted her arm. "Not a penny."

Seven

*T*hey should starve out every last one," Sidney, Lord Holt muttered the following day, halfway through the *Times* account of how the Irish Land League was inciting tenant farmers not to harvest crops for absentee landlords. All the London newspapers were shrill with the tension in Ireland. Fortunately, in 1877 he had discerned the scent of trouble in the wind and sold off the Kilmaine estates that William III had awarded one of the Holt ancestors almost two centuries earlier.

There are enough sound businesses to invest in, he was fond of telling fellow members of the Brookes' Club. *I'll not be subject to the whims of potato diggers.*

This astuteness in financial matters came as naturally as his talent for sketching, his ear for fine music, and eye for fine poetry. Unlike his late father, who had entrusted his financial holdings to a solicitor, Sidney studied daily, educating himself over new innovations and trade opportunities. Such as the London Telephone Company, in which he owned ninety shares of stock. There were little more than two hundred telephones in London to date, but he was confident that one day in the future even the meanest cottage in England would boast one.

He could even foresee the time when houses such as his, in the aristocratic neighborhood of Belgravia, would have two, perhaps three. Why not? If men could stretch a cable across the Atlantic, they could do anything.

At the sound of a soft *click* he lowered the newspaper. Incredibly, a maid walked into the room, closed the door behind her, and walked over to the fireplace. She began moving bric-a-brac about on the chimneypiece without so much as a glance in the direction of the sofa. A coal ignited in Sidney's chest, burning hotter with every twitch of the feather duster in her hand.

Finally, deliberately, he cleared his throat. The girl jumped, glass tinkled against hearthstone.

"Oh, m'Lord!" she cried, hand to throat as she gaped at him. She fell to her knees and began picking up shards of what once was a statuette of Venus, as if by hastening she could make the damage undo itself. "Oy didn't know you was back!"

He had indeed just returned last night from a week of fox hunting on the family estate in Northamptonshire. Still, rules were rules.

"Abigail," he said.

"It's . . . Alice, beggin' yer pardin, m'Lord," she corrected meekly, the cockney accent so thick that he could almost imagine the smell of eel pie and mash in the room. Tears glistened in eyes the color of faded brown cloth. She swiped the edge of her hand beneath her nose. "And Oy'm terrible sorry about breakin' the missus'—"

"Enough, Alice." Folding the newspaper, he forced himself to draw in a calming breath. "What is the rule about the morning room?"

She sniffed, lowered her eyes.

"Well . . . ?"

"We ain't to come in 'ere if the door's closed, m'Lord," she replied in a small voice.

"And was the door closed?"

"Oy can't as recall, m'Lord. Me . . . mind was filled wiv uvver things."

"Indeed?" He tapped the dimple in his chin with the tip of a long finger. "Weighty matters, I should think. The harvest troubles in Ireland?"

"No, m'Lord."

"Hmm. Mr. Laveran's discovery of the malarial parasite, no doubt."

"Malar . . ." The girl's eyes faded even more. "It's me sister Bessie, m'Lord. She's took up wiv a married 'ackney driver and me mum's beside herself wiv—"

Sidney waved a hand. "Pity, but unfortunate things do happen. Do you know the reason you're not to come near the door if it's closed?"

A hesitation, and then, "Because you're readin' newspipers, m'Lord?"

He winced. "Not newspipers, Abigail. News*papers*." His long hand automatically touched the stack beside him. *Illustrated London News. The Sun. News of the World*. "And reading requires concentration. Unlike dusting, which—as you've demonstrated—can be accomplished even when the mind is preoccupied."

"Yes, m'Lord," she replied with eyes lowered again.

"I do hope you mean that. You're forgiven this time, as you're so new with us. But if it happens again . . ."

Her lace cap bobbed up and down, but then she reconsidered and shook her head. "It won't happen, m'Lord!"

"Very good." He nodded toward the open door. "Now, leave."

She looked down at the broken pieces still on the hearth. "Now?"

"I didn't stammer. Did I?"

"But the—"

"Just because you cannot speak English is no excuse for not under-standing it. And do close the door behind you."

With what bits of Venus she had already gathered in her open palms, the maid rose from her knees and hurried to the doorway, pausing long enough to catch the knob with a forearm and pull the door closed. Muffled sobs mingled with muffled footsteps, fading into silence. Or at least *relative* silence, for his thirteen-year-old half brother, on a one-day school vacation for Founders Day, must have gathered up into the garden every lad from Belgrave Square.

He had no more raised the *Times* to eye level when a knock sounded again. "Enter!" he barked, vowing to send packing the servant who stepped through the doorway, regardless of rank or years of service. Everyone in the household knew full well that the morning room was his sanctuary. The chintz-covered sofa, soft with overstuffed plush arms, was perfect for study-ing the newspapers with his feet propped upon the ottoman. And the win-dow overlooking the garden was raised enough to allow fresh chill air to mingle with the warmth the coal fire produced. Only today the air was accompanied by the hoots from the terrace.

The doorknob turned. His mother stuck half her body through the opening, as one tests the temperature of a pond with one's toes.

"Mother . . ." he sighed.

"Forgive me, Sidney. Have you a minute?"

"Whether I have or haven't, you've interrupted my concentration—you and that son of yours. Can't you send him and his friends out to the Square or the Park?"

That pained look crossed her face, but she moved on into the room. Harriet Godfrey was still a handsome woman at forty-seven, her cheeks soft though a fair amount of grey dulled the brown hair. "I'm sorry, Sidney, but they're still muddy from yesterday's rain." She took a step toward the win-dow. "Shall I close—?"

"Then it would be too stuffy . . . wouldn't it?" he said. But he restrained himself from pointing out that he was well within his rights to demand some consideration, having inherited the house at age nine when his father, a judge in the Court of Exchequer, died of chronic bronchitis and heart failure. But his mother had wept the last time he said so, causing him to feel guilty for the rest of the day.

Aside from occasional trespasses upon his privacy and noises from his half brother, he was content to allow her second family to share the house, situated a stone's throw from Buckingham Palace and Green Park. Henry Godfrey's wages as director of the Midland Railway Company took care of household expenses, so that Sidney's sizable inheritance was allowed to accrue interest in stocks, India bonds, and similar securities. Mother's expertise in running the household spared him from having to give a moment's thought to domestic affairs—Abigail notwithstanding. And fortunately, Edgar spent the better part of his days in school.

"Well, what is it?" he asked, feeling the coal in his chest reignite. "If it's about that clumsy little skivvy . . ."

"I beg your pardon?"

Sidney glanced at the hearth, where shards of glass caught sunlight from the open window. "Never mind." Why expend the energy explaining if it wasn't necessary?

"You've a telephone call," she said.

"Yes?" He got to his feet, dropping his folded newspaper onto the stack. "Well, why didn't you say so?"

She stood with hands clasped, posture strained. "I wish you would ask that . . . Lady Kelly to be more discreet, Sidney. What if your brother had answered?"

Half brother, Sidney corrected silently halfway across the room. "Really, Mother, you're supposed to allow Rumfellow to answer the telephone. You don't answer the doorbell, do you?"

"Well, no."

"The telephone is simply another entrance to the house," he shot over his shoulder from the corridor.

"Yes, but about Lady Kelly . . ."

He hastened on as if she had not spoken, down the staircase and to the parlor just off the entrance hall. The Gower Bell candlestick telephone occupied its own small table at one end of the sofa. With one hand he picked up the corded earpiece from where it rested on the marble top, with the other he lifted the body of the telephone.

"Leona?" he said, settling into the sofa cushions.

The silence that followed caused him to wonder if the connection was still there. And who could fault her for hanging up, with his mother taking her own sweet time toddling up to tell him?

"Sidney?" came through, tinny and weak so that he had to press the earpiece into his ear. "You're back?"

"Yes, obviously. Where are you?" Telephone lines had not reached Hampstead yet, so she couldn't be at home.

"At the dressmaker's. I must speak with you."

He thought again of his mother answering the telephone. "You should know better than to call—"

"Today, Sidney."

He could recognize distress, tinny or not. Pushing aside his annoyance, he replied. "I'll meet you at Lambert's."

Over, then under, Sidney thought in his chamber upstairs, tying his silk paisley cravat. It occurred to him every now and again that he should have a valet, as his father had had all of his adult life. But he invariably talked himself out of hiring one. The chambermaids maintained his wardrobe and polished his shoes and cuff links. Why should he pay someone to choose his clothes, tie his cravat, and button his shirts, when he could invest the forty pounds per annum? Most of London's peerage were so fettered by tradition that they had no concept of trimming the excess in their lifestyles in order to increase their fortunes. Indeed, the land-rich-but-penny-poor gentleman was almost a cliché.

"Half the eligible women in London would give their last bonnets to be courted by you," came a voice from his doorway.

"But then, why would I wish for a woman with no bonnet?" Sidney quipped. "You may as well come in, Mother."

She stepped inside the room and folded her arms. "You're twenty-seven years old. Don't you think it's time you settled into a decent life?"

"I consider my life very decent, thank you." Sidney frowned at the knot and started over. "I've robbed no banks nor murdered anyone."

"Adulterers inevitably pay a price, you know."

"Then it's a good thing we're so rich," he couldn't help but say, taking up hat and gloves. He heard a sniff and looked at her again. Her grey eyes were lustered over. He sighed and wondered if female tear ducts ever wore out.

"I'm sorry," he said. "I shouldn't have said that."

"I didn't comfort you enough after your father died," she said, her voice heavy with regret. "And I assumed the Church was teaching you proper morals."

It was true that he had felt abandoned by the person he needed most, but maturity allowed him to look back at those bleak months—the servants' hushed voices and soft steps, the breakfast trays ignored outside his mother's door, frequent visits by the doctor—with some understanding.

"You were a good mother," he said, meaning it. One could not give what one did not possess at the time. "I never questioned that you loved me."

As to the Church, he could actually look back with gratitude for the ritual and routine that had provided some stability during those terrible fatherless days. But he simply no longer believed in its fables.

She was weeping, he realized. He took an extra handkerchief from a drawer and walked over to her. "There, there now, Mother," he said, wiping her cheek while she blinked watery eyes at him. "You mustn't work yourself up like this. Lady Kelly is an amusing conversationalist. And I happen to think myself well-versed in current events. We simply enjoy meeting for a chat every now and again."

"And what do you chat about, Sidney?" she sniffed, pain etched in every line of her face. "Her husband? Their three children?"

It was clear that nothing he could say would comfort her, that she was as intent upon having her say as he was intent upon leaving. So he handed her the handkerchief and patted her shoulder. "It's not healthy to worry as much as you do, Mother. A nap would refresh your mood, don't you think?"

The crimson and gold interior of Lambert's outdistanced garish into vulgar, in direct contrast to its nondescript grey stone facade. But it was one of the most popular places for London gentlemen of means. The maître d' greeted Sidney in the usual obsequious manner and escorted him upstairs to his usual room, appointed with a low table, beaded lamp that gave subdued light, Turkish rug, a print of Watteau's *Embarkation for Cythera* in a gilt frame, two plush chairs of gold brocade, and a red velvet sofa.

"Shall I send up some *Château Ausone*, your Lordship?" the maître d' asked as he helped Sidney out of his topcoat. He had the professional tact not to ask if Lady Kelly would be joining him, even though she had done so dozens of times over the past two years.

"Yes." Sidney wished he had thought to ask Leona if she would care to have lunch. Why pay for two meals if one would be wasted? He sighed. "And

Lady Kelly will be joining me. What do you recommend?"

"The *Moules Marinieres* are excellent today, your Lordship."

You'd say that if they scraped them from the bottom of old boats, Sidney thought, pulling off his gloves. But he said, "Yes, fine."

Ever since a friend at Lincoln College told him about a disgruntled footman, who had vented his ire at the friend's family for years by contaminating their meals in a vile manner, Sidney harbored a horror of someone doing the same to his food. And so even though he could leave shop clerks and chambermaids trembling in his wake, he treated waiters and maître d'—and especially his own cook and kitchen maids—with a degree of respect.

Five minutes after the maître d' had left, Sidney was sitting with his head against the back of the sofa, pulling on a Three Castles cigarette and blowing streams of smoke toward the ceiling. *Should have brought a newspaper,* he told himself, clicking the pointed toes of his patent leather boots together. He sat up at the soft knock at the door.

"Yes?"

The wine steward opened the door, stepped back, and allowed Leona entrance. She looked marvelous, Sidney thought, getting to his feet. Her tailored street suit of striped camel's hair in golden brown shades only made her look all the more feminine by emphasizing her lavishly endowed figure and tiny waist.

But at the sight of the crimson splotches upon her pale cheeks and bluish shadows beneath her eyes, he regretted ordering both meals. He had a feeling neither would be touched. *Out of the frying pan, into the fire,* he sighed silently.

"Please put that out," she said, fanning a gloved hand in front of her face.

She had never complained of his smoking before, but he shrugged and leaned down to extinguish the cigarette in a crystal ashtray. He helped her out of her cloak and handed her a glass of wine once she had settled onto the sofa.

"What is it, Leona?" he asked, sitting next to her after the wine steward was gone.

She raised her glass, draining it as if it were water while her green eyes stared dully at him from above the rim. Uncharacteristically she wiped her mouth with the back of a hand, not even glancing at the reddish stain left on her doeskin glove. But she shook her head when he reached for the bottle.

"Martin informed me Saturday that he's taking the children to New York," came out in a rush. "Last year he bought half-interest in his brother's hotel, but I had no idea—"

"Wait—just wait," Sidney said, holding up a palm. He shook his head. "He's threatening—?"

"Not *threatening*. He's already booked five passages on the S.S. *Patagonia* nine days from now."

"He expects you just to up and leave England? In nine days?"

She shook her head. "The other passage is for Betty. She's agreed to relocate."

Though Sidney had never met the nursemaid, he was well aware that it was her dedication to the Kelly children that had allowed Leona ample opportunities to be with him over the past two years. "But what about you?"

"He gave me three days to decide if he should book another passage. That time ends tomorrow evening." Emotion thickening her voice, she said, "I was frantic for fear you wouldn't return—"

"There, there." He picked up her gloved hand, squeezed it. "I'm here now."

"Yes," she breathed, managing a grateful little smile.

He had to think. "What happens if you refuse to go?"

"Then I shall be allowed to stay in the house only until his solicitor sells it," she said through trembling lips. "After that, I'm on my own. He says I've dragged the family name through the mire, and that our . . . children will never be able to hold their heads high in England."

Sidney let out an oath. Meek, soft-spoken, stoop-shouldered Sir George Kelly, who peered through spectacles as thick as the bases of sherry glasses? The same Sir George who could never have procured a wife on Leona's scale were it not for his money? "But surely he's suspected something about us for ages. Why now?"

She took a deep breath. "I have suffered nausea every morning for several days. When the housekeeper heard me—twice—on Thursday, she informed George. He sent for Doctor Lloyd in spite of my assuring him it was a reaction to some bad oysters."

"And . . . ?"

"It wasn't."

Studying her splotched face, Sidney said, "You mean . . . ?"

She nodded. "And he knows it's yours."

Sidney could feel the pulse in his Adam's apple squeeze against the cravat he had tied with such precision. "That's impossible, to know . . ."

"I've not allowed George into my chamber for months, Sidney. You know that." She drew in another breath, studying his face. "But he says he's willing to raise the child as his own—"

"If you leave with him."

"Yes," she murmured, tears puddling in her eyes again. "And become a proper wife and mother."

A knock sounded at the door. "Take it away!" he called, vexed that the kitchen staff would no doubt feast upon the mussels, which would show up on his bill next month. The irritation passed, overwhelmed by a larger sense of loss. Tears stung his eyes as he held her wrist gently and pulled the glove from her hand.

"Life without you . . ." he said, curving her fingers to press them to his cheek. "I don't know how I shall bear it."

When she did not speak, he opened his eyes again. She was staring back.

"You would have me go?"

Sidney blinked. "What other choice have you?"

Another silence, then, "I should think you could suggest one, considering I'm carrying your child."

The smooth fingers curved over his hand suddenly felt like a trap. It had never troubled him that his and Leona's names were whispered behind open fans. But it was one thing to have a married mistress, and quite another to be in the midst of a divorce scandal—with an out-of-wedlock child to boot. Just last summer Lord Hauxton was blackballed from the Club when it was discovered that his son was a homosexual.

Sidney credited most of his investing success to knowing the right people, belonging to the right gentlemen's club. Newspapers were not always privy to trade secrets discussed in a setting of soft leather chairs and fine pipe tobacco. Why, during his week of fox hunts, he learned of plans for an electrical power station in London within the next two years, a promising investment opportunity he intended to research.

The cutting off of his social connections wasn't the only thing to consider. Leona would leave the marriage as she had entered it—virtually penniless. After ten years of grand living, she would not be content with a little flat in Soho and modest allowance.

Her hand slipped from his. "Sidney?"

He cleared his throat. "I should think you would wish to be with your children, Leona."

Pain washed across her face. "And I should think you'd wish to be with yours."

The cravat felt even tighter about his neck. They stared at each other. Her lip trembled. A solution came to him, and he grasped for it, knowing that he would despise himself afterward. Focusing his eyes just a shade below hers, he said, "I've only your word that the child is mine."

He moved his attention from her face to his fingernails, studying them. He could feel the weight of her stare and braced himself for the outburst to come. But several seconds later she merely said in a dead voice, "Very well, Sidney. Lie to yourself if it makes you feel better."

Then she rose. He stood as well, moving over to the coatrack. But she shook her head and took her cloak from him when he attempted to put it upon her shoulders. The air seemed to have been sucked out of the room, and he had the strong desire to say something to make it right, to smooth away the cold resignation upon her face. But the words stuck in his throat like Macbeth's *amen*. He opened the door and stared at the floor as she passed through. After the door closed again, he leaned against it.

He did not leave the room until he had composed himself. Two more glasses of wine and another cigarette helped, along with the press of a cool flannel against his face at the washstand.

Out on Cannon Street he stood by the coach and tapped his foot while his coachman sprinted up the pavement with a brown paper parcel in his hand.

"Sorry, m'Lord. I thought I had time to nip down the street for a —"

"To the Club, Jerry," Sidney said with a seething tone.

"Yes, m'Lord." But once Sidney was inside, Jerry stood there with the door still open and peered at him. "Are you unwell, m'Lord?"

"That's hardly your affair, is it?" Sidney snapped, setting his hat beside him. "And I didn't appreciate having to wait for you."

The man's face colored. "It's just that I've had no lunch, m'Lord."

"Get a move on or you'll have no job!" Sidney barked. The relief at having someone upon whom to vent his sour feelings was a tonic, and by the time the coach turned up Saint James Street he was quietly whistling the third movement to Bach's *Concerto Grosso*.

Conversations rising from the leather chairs of the Brookes' Club mostly revolved around fox-hunting exploits on various estates. The hours spent there were not wasted, for even though Sidney acquired no information that could behoove him financially, his account of attempting to slip unnoticed back to the house with ripped trousers after being tossed from a belligerent horse brought knee-slapping laughter. He agreed with Emerson's observation that a person who wished to rule the world must keep it amused. He had no desire to rule the world, just to acquire his fair share of it, and then a little more for good measure.

When Sidney walked out to Saint James Street, he nodded approval at Jerry, who had hopped down from the box to get the door. He walked through the quiet house on Belgrave Square at half-past ten. A pencil of light shone beneath the library door. It was not his mother's custom to wait up for him, but he had a feeling she was in there. She looked up at him as he eased open the door, a sheath of papers on the desk before her.

"Sidney," she said. There was none of her usual warmth to his name, and reproach lingered in the hollows of her face. "I didn't expect you back so early."

He walked over to the desk and looked down at the lined page. "What are you writing?"

"I haven't given it a title yet. But it takes place in Epping Forest."

"Then why don't you title it *The Parker Twins in Epping Forest*?"

"Perhaps."

Touching her shoulder, he said, "I'm sorry I caused you grief, Mother. And it's over."

"You mean . . . ?"

"Lady Kelly is no longer in my life."

Some hope penetrated the reproach. "Are you just saying that because I want to hear it, Sidney?"

He shook his head. "She'll be leaving London with her family for the States in a few days."

Her shoulders moved with a deep breath. "Permanently?"

"Permanently."

There was a hesitant silence, then, "I hope this means you're giving some thought to your future, Sidney."

"I think about the future constantly," he told her. Why did she think he spent so much time poring over investment information?

"I'm not speaking of money," she said as if reading his thoughts. "While you're accumulating pounds sterling, the minutes of your life are slipping through your fingers. And there's no more pathetic creature than an old man who has squandered his youth instead of building a solid life."

He hated it when she attempted to lead his thoughts in that direction. And horror of horrors, lately his thoughts had begun to venture down that path of their own accord. For someone of his social class and financial advantages, it stood to reason that he should be happy. Amusements he had had plenty of, but happiness had flitted just beyond his reach for so long that he had begun to take it for granted that no one was truly happy.

"Is that the moral of the Epping Forest book?" he quipped to silence the voices of warning in his head.

"Sidney . . ."

"Sorry, Mother. You're so right." He leaned to kiss her furrowed forehead. "And that's precisely what I said to Lady Kelly."

❧ *Eight* ❧

Catherine was only slightly more fond of verse than she was of classics, though in third standard she won the Poetry Medal for reciting all thirty-six lines of Wordsworth's "Poor Robin." She wasn't quite certain who discovered Milly's great mental storehouse of poetry, but it never failed to delight her when someone pressed upon her to show it off. After all, she was the one responsible for nudging Milly out of her standoffish ways, so she claimed a tiny bit of the glory for herself. Only privately though, for she wasn't sure anyone else would see it that way.

Milly's fame had spread even to the older students. It was a junior who stood up during breakfast on Tuesday and said, "Do favor us with a poem to start the day, Miss Turner."

"Yes, do," others chorused.

"No rest for the wicked," Peggy murmured, eliciting smiles from Catherine and the other freshers at the end of their table. Milly mugged a face at her and rose to her full regal height. She sent a nod across the hushed dining room to the student who had made the request.

"From Lord Byron's 'Dear Doctor, I Have Read Your Play,' " she said, clasping hands beneath her bosom and raising her chin slightly.

> *"Dear Doctor, I have read your play,*
> *Which is a good one . . . in its way,*
> *Purges the eyes, and moves the bowels,*
> *And drenches handker—"*

"Miss Turner."

Milly fell silent. All eyes went to Miss Bernard, standing at the faculty table. The mistress gave Milly a look of mild warning. "We are at breakfast,

Miss Turner, as you're aware. Select one with more appropriate language, if you please."

"Yes, Miss Bernard," Milly said amidst hushed titters and traded smiles. She leaned her head thoughtfully for a second, then nodded.

"From 'Dream Pedlary' by Thomas Beddoes," she said.

> *"If there were dreams to sell,*
> *Merry and sad to tell,*
> *And the crier rang the bell,*
> *What would you buy?"*

"It's just that I have what my father calls a photographic memory," Milly said to Catherine and Peggy on their way out of the dining room a half hour later. "Or rather, what he *called* it, back when he took any notice of me."

"I wish I had one," Catherine said. "I wouldn't have to study so hard."

"I would settle for your hair," Peggy told Milly as they entered the reading room.

"Don't say that," Milly scolded. "Your hair is marvelous."

And they were carrying the envy a little too far, Catherine thought, when Milly claimed she would give anything to have the loving mothers she and Peggy took for granted. She spotted her name on an envelope on the chimneypiece.

"Who would be writing me from Cambridge?"

"Well, open it and see," Peggy told her.

"Perhaps you have a secret admirer," Milly said. She and Peggy had no mail, so they trailed Catherine to a window, out of the way of others.

Catherine shook her head, drawing out a single page. "Secret admirers are supposed to send flowers, not letters. It's probably a bill for the linens, but I'm sure my father paid—"

Some slips of paper fluttered to the carpet. She watched Peggy dive for them. "What . . . ?"

"Tickets." Rising, Peggy looked from the slips in her hand to Catherine. *"The Man of Mode."*

Oh no, Catherine thought with sinking heart. With both friends watching, she had no choice but to scan the letter.

Dear Miss Rayborn,
    I was delighted to make the acquaintance again of Miss Somerset on Sunday, for I have thought of you often since my attention was most

grievously directed toward you during that journey from London. Yet I could not recall your surname, so did not know how to address a letter.

Do you enjoy theatre, Miss Rayborn? It would give me great pleasure if you and your friends would be my guests at St. John's on Friday evening. Tickets for third-row seats are enclosed. And I hope that you will find the character of Bellair more endearing than you did Gloucester!

With warmest regards,
Hugh Sedgwick

"Mr. Sedgwick is inviting us to the performance," Catherine said with a bland smile, as if Peggy were not holding tickets.

"Yes," Peggy mumbled. Her freckles stood out against her pale skin like tiny copper pennies.

Milly bit her lip, giving Catherine a helpless look.

"I'm sure he thought it would be too bold of him . . . writing to you after you had spoken Sunday," Catherine said, grasping at straws. "And it was me seated across from him on the train, so obviously he still feels he owes me an apology."

Peggy held out the tickets. The smile she wore did not travel up to her hazel eyes. "I don't think I care to go after all. It was never my favorite story. But do go, Catherine."

"*I* don't want them," Catherine said, stepping backwards.

"Then that settles it." Milly snatched the tickets from Peggy's hand, the letter from Catherine's, strode over to the fireplace, and tossed them in. She stood there for a moment, ignoring the curious looks about her, then returned wearing a satisfied expression.

"We could have given them to someone else," Peggy murmured, staring in the direction of the fireplace. It was obvious that her grief was not for the wasted tickets.

"Well, I'm glad you did it," Catherine told Milly. "It'll send him a clear message if those seats are empty."

"That's the spirit!" Milly moved between the two of them to link arms. "No *Bellair* is going to break up the Three Musketeers."

But he managed to cause some damage, however inadvertently. For though Peggy treated Catherine with no less cordiality over the following week, even congratulated her for making a passing mark on her Hellenistic Age paper, an invisible curtain hung between them. Worse still, the two pretended not to notice its existence, which only gave it more substance.

"She'll get over it with time," was Milly's advice. "After all, you didn't *ask* him to write. And you didn't accept the tickets."

"Yes," Catherine agreed, but she could not admit to Milly that not all of the unspoken reproach was on Peggy's part. Ever since receiving the letter, Catherine thought of Mr. Sedgwick now and again in spite of herself. She would have enjoyed seeing him, if only to have watched him upon the stage.

Another letter in the same hand arrived one week later. Fortunately there was also a parcel from her parents, and so while Peggy and Milly admired and passed around two shawls of gossamer-like saffron and cobalt blue yarn, Catherine was able to tuck the envelope up her sleeve.

"What is pashmina wool, Catherine?" Eileen asked, draping the blue one over her shoulders.

"It's from a Himalayan mountain goat," Catherine replied, glad for the distraction. "Woven entirely by hand, because it's too delicate for power looms."

"Why, Catherine, you secretive girl!" exclaimed Elizabeth Macleod from the Tennis Club.

"I beg your pardon?" Catherine's pulse pounded so hard she could feel it where her cheeks met her ears.

"You've never told me that your parents live in India. Why, I spent my childhood in Sanawar!"

Which was a far distance from Bombay, but provided Catherine with the opportunity to distance herself from Peggy and Milly. She ambled down the corridor comparing experiences with Elizabeth, who explained that her father was an Army captain in their Sanawar days.

When she was able to get away to her sitting room, Catherine sank into her corner chair and opened the envelope.

Dear Miss Rayborn,
I dared a glance at the third row during the performance, but the seats were empty. My fault entirely, for sending the tickets with so little notice, when you no doubt had other plans.
The Man of Mode was received very well, despite the actor cast as Dorimant forgetting a line and having to be prompted. I do wish you could have seen it.

Laughter and footsteps sounded from very near in the corridor. She prepared to tuck the page down into the cushions. But the sounds faded and she read on.

And now on another subject, may I take the liberty of asking if we may correspond? I understand that your studies consume most of your

days, as that first year is the most difficult, but if you spare time to do so
it would please me greatly. I wait anxiously for your reply.

With warmest regards,
Hugh Sedgwick

She read it three times, then looked about the room for a place to keep it. Not that Peggy would snoop, but it was too volatile a thing to keep where she could stumble upon it. She decided upon the chest of drawers in her bedroom. The thought occurred to her, as she tucked the letter beneath the paper lining of her stocking and handkerchief drawer, that she should toss the letter into the fireplace. Sentiment overtook that thought as quickly as fire had consumed the first letter. After all, he was the first young man ever to write to her. It made her feel quite grown up and even attractive. And she found she rather liked the feeling.

Drizzling rain pelted the windows and sent damp chills through the corridors all morning on Wednesday, the seventeenth of November. But by noon at least the rain had ceased, though grey clouds still lurked ominously overhead.

"I wish the day could have been prettier for you," Catherine said after greeting and embracing her cousin in the entrance hall.

Sarah looked charming as usual in a day dress of buff oatmeal cloth and short coat of plum-colored cashmere. But the dampness had gotten to the blond fringe hanging in limp tendrils over her eyebrows. "Oh, but it was raining buckets in London," she said.

Catherine turned to the two beside her. "These are my dearest friends, Peggy Somerset and Millicent Turner."

"We're very pleased to meet you," Milly said, taking the hand Sarah offered.

Peggy was just as welcoming. "Catherine has told us of Mr. Doyle's work. Do you happen to know what sort of microscope he's observing?"

"Why, yes," Sarah replied, smiling. "It's quite new. Made in Germany by a Mr. Zeiss."

"I thought as much! I would give anything to see it. The microscope in our laboratory is older than—"

She stopped when Milly nudged her. Miss Bernard was coming through the doorway from the first lecture room. Catherine introduced her cousin, the two made pleasantries over the weather, and Miss Bernard took out her pencil and asked Sarah to sign her notebook. "Please take no offense, Mrs. Doyle. We strive to keep account of our young women's whereabouts when they leave campus, and in whose company they are traveling. Times being what they are . . ."

"That's very admirable," Sarah told her. After Miss Bernard wished them a pleasant lunch and excused herself, Sarah turned to Peggy and said, "I wish Mr. Doyle were joining us. He would enjoy discussing chemistry with you."

Catherine's heart sank. Did Sarah assume that, because she had asked her friends to come for introductions, that she desired to bring them along? Not that she wouldn't enjoy their company under any other circumstance. But she had so hoped to pour out her heart to her cousin regarding the events of the past eight days.

She held her breath when Sarah asked Milly and Peggy, "You will join us, won't you?"

She eased it out again when Peggy thanked her anyway and said, "You'll have so much catching up to do."

Milly nodded agreement. "Let's plan on that the next time you visit Cambridge, Mrs. Doyle. And I shall insist you all be my guests."

Catherine remembered her manners enough to ask about family during the short ride to Cambridge in the hired coach. Once they were seated in the busy, quaint dining room of the Nave and Felly Inn and had given the serving girl identical orders, she related her problem to Sarah. While she was very fond of William, she was relieved that he was lunching at Pembroke College. She would not be comfortable discussing such a subject in the presence of a man—kin or not.

The seven years between Sarah and her had seemed a huge gap when Sarah was reunited with the family five years ago. But the gap narrowed with every occasion they spent together. Catherine had even served as bridesmaid at Sarah and William's wedding. She could tell her older cousin things that she could not discuss with her own mother.

"Has Miss Somerset asked you not to correspond with Mr. Sedgwick?" Sarah asked.

Catherine shook her head. "But the friendship would be over if I did— even though she realizes he has no interest in corresponding with her. It would never occur to me to act such a way if the situation were reversed."

"You're looking at the situation rationally, Catherine. Like a mathematical equation. Her emotions are involved, and you can count upon them to muddy things up."

Catherine had to smile. "Funny you should say that."

"Why?"

"Peggy puts things to equation too." And it was one of the many things Catherine found endearing about her.

Their meals arrived—baked perch with Dutch sauce, roasted new potatoes, and cucumber salads. Sarah thanked the serving girl, and when she was gone, gave Catherine a helpless look. "I do wish your Aunt Naomi were here to advise you. She's much more wise about this sort of thing."

"Then pretend you are her," Catherine said while unfolding her napkin. "What do you think she would advise?"

"Are you quite sure you want to hear it?"

"Of course."

"Very well. Naomi would first ask if you're in love with Mr. Sedgwick."

"In love? Sarah, I've only met him once."

"Then tell me what you know about him. Besides the fact that he's handsome."

"I didn't say he was," Catherine was quick to point out.

"I see. Then he's not handsome."

"Well . . . no." Catherine narrowed her eyes. "I believe I would rather hear your counsel than Aunt Naomi's after all."

"Too late," Sarah replied, and smiled. "I suspect they would be one and the same anyway."

With a sigh Catherine sat as far back in her chair as her bustle would allow. "Well, he's enrolled in Saint John's College . . . is involved in theatre productions . . . and . . ."

She had to think for a second. "He had the good manners to apologize for the stunt on the train, and was generous enough to send us tickets."

But once all was spoken, Catherine realized how meager was the collection. "I'm not pining away after him, if that's what you're thinking," she said defensively. "But how can I become better acquainted with him if Peggy's feelings constrain me from doing so?"

Sarah picked up her fork but merely held it above her salad. "Catherine, you believe otherwise, but you're still very young. Even in such a restricted environment as Girton's, you'll have occasions to make the acquaintances of many men."

"I didn't enroll in college to meet men," Catherine protested. "Else I would have gone to London University."

"But of course you didn't. What I'm trying to say is . . . women need friendships with other women. William and Father are the kindest, most compassionate men I know, but most times when I have a problem to sort out in my mind, I go to Naomi. She knows just how I feel. Women have that sort of empathy with each other."

"We do have a bond," Catherine confessed. "I'm more fond of her than of any school friend I've ever had. Even though we've known each other less than two months."

"What if you were to trade that friendship for the opportunity to correspond with Mr. Sedgwick," Sarah said, "then discovered that you have very little in common with him? Or that there was something deficient in his character?"

"I don't want to trade Peggy's friendship. But what if . . ."

"He's the one meant for you?"

"It's not entirely impossible," Catherine said with a self-conscious shrug.

"No, of course not."

"Then what should I do?"

"Are you asking me or Naomi?"

Catherine smiled. "Both."

Returning her smile, Sarah said, "If I were you, I would send him a letter stating that a correspondence would not be possible at this time, due to circumstances that you're not at liberty to explain. But if he would care to write again in the spring—"

"The *spring*!"

"Five months, perhaps six. Not a long time in the grand scheme of life, but surely long enough for Peggy to lose the infatuation or come to the realization that she cannot hold claim to him forever. After all, she's spent only a little more time in his company than you have."

"Yes," Catherine agreed, and after a hesitation said, "But what if he forgets all about me in the meantime?"

"Then you'll know he wasn't the one, won't you? Or it may be that you'll lose interest yourself."

Lose interest? Panic must have shown in Catherine's expression, for Sarah said, "A little time is a good thing, Catherine. I once had a beau courting me so intensely that I had no time to think. He was a curate who preached brilliant sermons and visited the sick, and everyone—including me—could not see his serious flaws. Had God not prompted me to wait until I was certain of my feelings, I may very well have been pressured into marrying the wrong man."

"Hmm." Catherine forked part of a potato and made a show of sprinkling it with black pepper. It seemed but a degree removed from fanatical to speak of God as if He were a participant even in courtships. But the advice seemed sound.

You came here to study, not fawn over the first man to show you a little attention, she reminded herself. And it was true, she knew next to nothing of him. If academics did not remain her top priority, she would be packing up her romantic notions—along with her other belongings—by Lent Term.

"I'll do that," she promised.

"I don't think you'll regret it," Sarah said.

They abandoned the subject of Hugh Sedgwick for things such as Bethia learning the alphabet and the search for a house in Hampstead. Sarah asked about Catherine's lectures and daily routine. They were just finishing their meals when Catherine glanced toward the rain-flecked window and spotted a pair of legs under an umbrella, bobbing from hansom to door. It was William, who gave his coat and umbrella to the innkeeper and approached the table.

"Cousin!" He kissed the hand she offered. "I feared I wouldn't make it in time to see you."

They addressed each other as cousin in jest, but it was true in a round-about way, for William's Aunt Naomi was married to Catherine's Uncle Daniel. "I'm glad you did," she replied, returning his smile.

He merely touched Sarah's shoulder while pulling out a chair, but the lightning-quick look that passed between his dark eyes and her green ones was more intimate than a kiss. "Is college all you expected it would be?" he asked Catherine.

"And more so. The days fly so quickly—I'm afraid four years will be over too soon."

William chuckled. "You may change your thinking on that later on. And are your lectures interesting?"

"Vastly! I'm learning so much."

"Even Classics?" Sarah asked, for most of the extended family knew of her anxiety over them.

"While they absorb most of my study time, they're not as overwhelming as I feared, thanks to a friend's tutelage." *A very, very good friend,* she thought.

"I'm glad to hear it," William said, but then was distracted by the cloud drifting over from the table to his right. Two women, appearing to be in their late twenties, had finished their meals and were enjoying cigarettes with their coffee.

Leaning forward a bit, he lowered his voice. "I hope you've not been pressured into doing the same, Catherine. I remember how it was, college students away from home experimenting with new things."

"William . . ." Sarah said.

"Well, we did promise your Uncle James we'd look out for her."

Catherine wrinkled her nose at him. "I only know of two girls who smoke." It was against Girton's rules, but the nose didn't lie. "And I tried it once but didn't care for it."

"Good for you. I realize this is monstrously unfair, but men talk amongst themselves about women who smoke, and their words are not usually flattering."

The concern in his expression was too much, so Catherine couldn't resist adding, "Besides, snuff is so much more convenient, what with not having to carry matches."

The two stared, until the corners of Catherine's mouth betrayed her.

"Why, you little . . ." William said with a chuckle.

Sarah and Catherine smiled at each other. Presently Sarah touched her husband's hand and said, "Don't keep us guessing, William. What did you think of the microscope?"

He blew out a long breath. "It was superior to any I've ever seen, Sarah. I intend to write to Mr. Zeiss and order three as soon as we're home."

"Very good." But Sarah seemed distracted, pressing a fingertip against her chin thoughtfully.

"What is it?" William asked.

She looked at him. "Do you think you could order four instead?"

"Four? Not without applying for extra funds. But I don't see the need for another."

"Not for the Commission. To donate to Girton College. What they have now is . . . how old, Catherine?"

"I'm not sure," Catherine told her. "I can recall something like *Pillischer* and the number 535 engraved on the base. Does that help?"

"535?" William shook his head. "It was efficient enough in its day—over twenty years ago."

"Doesn't seem fair that the men have all the best equipment, does it?" Sarah asked.

"No, it's not." His smoke-colored eyes crinkled at the corners. "An excellent idea, Sarah. We'll do that."

"Thank you!" Catherine exclaimed. "I can hardly wait to tell Peggy."

"Peggy?" William asked.

"I'll tell you all about her," Sarah promised, picking up her reticule from the empty chair. "But if we're to make our train, we have to leave now."

Back at Girton, Catherine stood outside the gate and watched until their coach was out of sight. Then she hurried into the building and down the main corridor, stopping at number four. Peggy, clad in a Bloomer suit, answered her knock.

"Catherine," she said with a weary smile. "Do come in."

Moving into the sitting room, Catherine said, "If this is an inconvenient time . . ."

"Of course not." Peggy closed the door. "I'm just winded. Playing Milly at 'fives' is like playing a tornado. Did you enjoy your lunch?"

"Yes, thank you."

"Would you care to have a seat?"

"Oh, I'm staying but a minute. I just wanted to deliver some news."

"News?" Peggy said with raised brow.

Catherine told her of the microscope soon to be donated, and all because Peggy had so impressed Sarah with her desire that the college laboratory have a better one.

"It'll be your legacy to Girton College," Catherine told her.

"Remarkable!" Peggy shook her head in wonder. "It'll be the Doyles's legacy rather than mine, but still . . ."

"You have a share in it too." Impulsively Catherine stepped forward to wrap arms about her. "I'm so glad we're friends."

Peggy submitted, arms stiffly at her side. Then she loosened and embraced Catherine. She was silent for a moment, then said in a soft voice, "Can you ever forgive me? I was so jealous."

"He's nothing to me," Catherine replied thickly. And she meant it. The curtain that had hung between them evaporated, and ten minutes later they were seated and laughing over Peggy's account of how Milly leaped like a ballerina to return an out-of-bounds return to win the game.

That evening Catherine took Hugh Sedgwick's letter out of the drawer and read it. Twice. She intended to throw it away and forget about it. But then she told herself that, even though he meant nothing to her, he had done nothing deserving of having both his letters ignored without the favor of a reply. So she sat, drew out her pen, and after chewing on the wooden tip for five minutes, dipped it into the ink.

Dear Mr. Sedgwick,

Thank you for the theatre tickets. I apologize that we were not able to take advantage of them, but as you suggested, studies do consume a vast amount of time here. Thus, I cannot engage in any correspondence with anyone other than family.

The lines before her faded as her mind pictured Hugh Sedgwick holding the same letter. His wheat-colored hair fell untidily over his forehead, his lips were frowning.

"Cold as a carp," he muttered. *He crumpled the page and tossed it into an ash bin. "I'll waste no more time on her."*

And she realized she minded. Very much. She thought again of Sarah's counsel, which she had intended to follow before being swept by the emotion of reconciling with Peggy. *Who knows how any of us will feel in six months?* she asked herself. Dipping her pen again, she added,

But if you still desire to correspond in the spring, I should like that very much.

Nine

Rapid population growth and modern improvements were wreaking havoc upon many of London's picturesque areas. The baleful stream crept out in all directions like a lava flow, swallowing up green fields with flowers and hedgerows, quaint houses with red tiles and gabled roofs, and leaving in its wake railways, factories, and blocks of flats.

But the flow of modernization had treated Hampstead more kindly. Sarah loved the area more than any she had ever visited. Four hundred feet above sea level, it was London's most elevated village. Its main street, Highgate, was just four miles from the teeming heart of the metropolis, yet the area still retained its old-world charm, with winding, hilly streets, quaint nooks, and byways.

The house happened upon William and her on the twenty-ninth of November, over seven weeks after deciding to relocate. They were only hours away from purchasing a redbrick Georgian home found for them by a house locating agency. While it was only a little larger than the Berkeley Square house, it was conveniently located on Church Row in Hampstead and an easy stroll from Saint John's, the parish church.

But Mr. Mitchell had recently learned of a situation where a gentleman of title had emigrated with his family to New York and wished to liquidate all properties in England. "You should give the house a look," the solicitor advised around the briar pipe clenched in his teeth. "The fellow's eager to sever all ties here, so he's asking far less than it's worth."

The following afternoon William left the Commission early. Sarah and William, Father and Naomi bundled into coats and cloaks, leaving Bethia and Danny in the care of Avis and Marie. In their traces in front of the coach, Comet and Daisy snorted vapory plumes and stomped their impatience to get going.

"They ain't afraid of them hills," Stanley said, blue eyes brighter now that little Lottie was sleeping longer stretches. Almost a half hour later the coach turned eastward from Christ Church Road onto Cannonhall Road, named for the old cannons that served as kerbposts. Presently they were confronted by a three-storey stone conglomeration of pointed arches, buttresses, and mullioned windows. Numerous chimneys rose from a slate roof stained by time and lichen to a richly variegated greyish red.

"Thornfield," Sarah breathed, her gloved hand wiping away more of the glass condensation.

"Yes, Thornfield," Naomi echoed. "I can just picture Jane Eyre sitting beneath a tree with her sketching tablet."

"And a madwoman locked away in the attic," Father said.

Sarah gave him a wry smile. "Father . . ."

He winked at her. "But in an interesting, Gothic sort of way."

"A dozen chimneys," William said. "Must be a coal mine underneath."

Mr. Mitchell, standing on the gravel drive with another gentleman, stepped up to open the door. "Keep your seat, Mr. Russell," he instructed Stanley as he helped Sarah from the coach. "Mr. Prout's coachman is in the kitchen laying a fire. Riley's his name. Why don't you drive around to the stables, blanket the horses, and go warm yourself?"

"Aye, Sir," Stanley said. When all eight human feet were on the ground, the empty coach rumbled away.

Sarah kissed the solicitor's cold bearded cheek. "You could have waited inside," she said with a little shiver.

"It's just as cold inside. It's been empty for three weeks." He put his hand on the shoulder of his companion, a man with liberal grey in his side-whiskers and crow's feet behind his spectacles. "May I introduce Mr. Prout? He represents Sir George Kelly, the owner."

"Shall we go inside?" Mr. Prout asked when introductions were concluded. But in the empty entrance hall he excused himself to join the servants downstairs in the kitchen. "I'm too old to be gadding about from room to room, and the house speaks for itself. You'll know where to find me."

The men carried lamps to light the nooks, crannies, and corridors without access to windows. Some pieces of furniture remained, a pianoforte in the sitting room, a rug and painting in the morning room, a chess table in the library. "Sir George shipped most of it, gave some to servants, and a fellow will be collecting what's here to sell on consignment," Mr. Mitchell explained. He ran a finger along the dusty top of a chess table. "But Mr.

Prout says if any particular pieces strike your fancy, you're welcome to buy them."

By the time they stepped into the upstairs parlor, all images of the red-brick Georgian on Church Row dissolved in Sarah's mind. She could see herself rocking a baby at the oriole window from which one could look beyond the grey stone house across the road and see Hampstead Heath, 240 rolling acres dedicated for public use.

"It's straight out of a novel," she said, her voice ringing against oak paneling and marble flooring.

"The lady of the manor," William teased, but in such a tone that assured Sarah he was just as awestruck. "We would need more servants."

"Mr. Prout could supply you with information on the ones who haven't yet found other situations," Mr. Mitchell said, his lamp resting upon a half-table while he lit his pipe.

Naomi ran fingers along a section of carved wainscoting. In a voice filled with maternal concern she asked, "Can you afford this?"

"You mustn't overburden your finances," Father cautioned.

"We can afford it," William assured them, stooping to test the chimney flue as he had in other rooms.

Thankful for the *we*, Sarah nodded. It had taken William months and months to accept that her inheritance—as well as the shipping income—was as much his as hers. "Please don't worry, Father."

"Very well." But concern lingered in his green eyes. "Still, shouldn't you pray over it before making any decision?"

"We've prayed God would lead us to the right house for almost two months now," Sarah told him. "Don't you think it's remarkable, that this one should practically fall into our laps within hours of buying the other one?"

Father smiled. "Yes, remarkable."

"I think Avis will be pleased with the fireplaces," William said. Wiping the soot from his hands with a handkerchief, he walked over to Sarah's side. "You're that certain this is the one, Sarah?"

She drew in a lungful of chill, tobacco-tinged air. How could she explain, even to those she loved most, how much at home she felt? No matter that the cornerstone was laid at the turn of the century, it was as if this house was built with her in mind. And as she had assured her father, she had prayed so fervently over the past two months. Surely God had led them there. "I'm certain, William."

The look upon his face said he would find a way to give her London

Bridge should she desire it. "Well, let's finish our tour. We do want to make sure that madwoman isn't lurking about."

They all started moving toward the door. Naomi reached out for Mr. Mitchell's lamp when he tried to manage it, the doorknob, and his lit pipe at the same time.

"Why, thank you, Mrs. Doyle," he said with a little inclination of the head.

"You're welcome," Naomi replied. "Tell me, Mr. Mitchell, do you know why Sir George left England in such haste?"

The solicitor took his pipe from his lips, holding it aloft as he opened the door. "It's quite a tragic story, actually. As Mr. Prout tells it, he could no longer abide his young wife's infidelities. She was carrying on with some baron she'd met at a soiree, a scoundrel of the lowest order."

"How sad," Sarah said. But that such a marvelous house would have its history tainted did not dampen her enthusiasm for it. After all, Jeremy Blake had brought dishonor to the Berkeley Square house long ago, and still she had spent many happy years there.

"Indeed, sad," Mr. Mitchell agreed. "And the irony of it is, the scoundrel's mother authors children's books with moral lessons. Pity she didn't teach them to her son."

Sarah and William's eyes met. *Lots of people write children's books* was the silent message she sent him.

And his to her was, *We both know of whom he's speaking.*

"Do you happen to know the mother's name?" Sarah had to ask. *Not that it has anything to do with us* was the next silent message she sent her husband.

"Why, I'm not certain. But my granddaughter reads the stories. They have to do with a set of twins—"

"The Parker Twins?" Naomi asked.

"Yes, that's it," the solicitor said, then glanced up at the high ceiling. "The bedchambers are above. Shall we?"

They went up the grand curving staircase and moved from room to room, each as grand and welcoming as the last. Yet whenever Sarah pointed out some structural adornment—such as the balcony leading from the master bedchamber window, William merely nodded or gave her a pained smile. After inspecting every room, they ended up back downstairs in a kitchen three times the size of Berkeley Square's. Mr. Prout, Stanley, and a man with brown hair and ruddy cheeks rose from a worktable six feet from a cavernous fireplace. Beneath, a long sinewy tom uncurled himself to rub his side against the table leg and give them a mildly interested stare. He was a mixture of grey, amber, and black, and three of his legs were white, looking as if he wore white boots.

"Hector comes with the house," Mr. Prout said. "The Kellys feared he'd not make the journey. He's an excellent mouser. Well, what do you think?"

"It's a wonderful house," Sarah replied with strained voice.

"Very nice," Naomi said.

Sarah felt a touch on her coat sleeve and turned. William was giving her an odd look. To the others he said, "Will you excuse us?"

Mr. Prout waved them on and pulled out a chair for Naomi. "But of course. Take your time."

They walked down a corridor, turning into a room that appeared to be the parlor of the cook's apartment. *Trudy would love that,* Sarah thought.

William set the lamp upon a dusty chest of drawers and turned to face her.

"What's wrong, William?" she asked.

"You've fallen in love with this house."

"Well, yes."

He winced. "I can't live here, Sarah. I'm so sorry."

She stared at him. "Just because of Lord Holt?"

Dark eyes pained, he nodded. "But you liked the Church Row house, remember? The stained glass windows . . . being able to stroll down the street to Saint John's . . ."

"Yes, I did. And you liked *this* house until Mr. Mitchell brought up his name. I could understand if Lord Holt had ever lived here, but—"

"The fact that he is connected in any capacity ruins it for me, Sarah. You heard of the damage he did to the family who lived here. Look at how he treated you at the bookshop. And you haven't any idea how he thrived upon tormenting me at Oxford. That man taints everything in his path, and the less I'm reminded of him, the happier I am."

Sarah allowed her protests to die in her throat. He was already making a sacrifice by having to drive to work a longer distance each day. And buying a house wasn't like buying a new bonnet, but a huge investment of not only money but emotion. She could not ask him to live in a place where he would never feel at home.

"Very well," she said.

"But do you understand?"

"Not completely," she admitted. Raising a hand to touch his collar, she mustered a smile and said, "But I know how difficult it is for you to deny me anything. I don't have to have this place to be happy."

"Thank you." He gathered her into his arms. "I'll make it up to you, Sarah."

"You don't have to," she murmured into his shoulder. "You're more important than any house."

When they returned to the kitchen, William said to Mr. Prout, "Thank you for meeting us here. But it's not for us."

"Ah, but one can't expect everyone who looks to buy," he said with a good-natured shrug. "And it'll sell quickly, once our advertisements are published next week."

The one on Church Row was lovely, Sarah reminded herself.

"Why don't we take the back door out to the coaches?" Mr. Mitchell suggested.

The garden's winter dreariness consoled Sarah a bit. Her eyes drank in the dead vines clinging to the low stone wall, icicles hanging from bare shrubbery limbs, and brown grass crackling beneath their shoes. Anything to lessen her adoration of the house. And then she raised her head. "Oh my . . ."

William looked beyond the low wall. To the far southeast Saint Paul's regal dome rose above the whole hazy spread of the eastern metropolis. The country to the east and west was picturesque in the highest degree—fine old homes against a backdrop of richly undulating land diversified by pleasant pasture slopes and wooded hills.

Beautiful, was his grudging thought.

"Why, that can't be . . . Windsor Castle?" Daniel said, pointing off to the east.

"It is at that," Mr. Prout said, and William thought he detected a subtle note of victory in his voice.

Sarah moved beside him and took his arm. "It's all right, William." When he looked at her, she smiled. "Truly it is."

There was no guile in her expression, and William's heart gave a little lurch. Womanhood and proper nourishment had softened the planes of her face, yet there was still the trace of the fragile waif lurking in the wide green eyes, almost translucent skin, and delicate features. She had spent over half her life in want, and he was driven by the need to protect her.

And to make her happy. Though he had never told her so, he was starting to doubt that he had the power to give her what she desired most, a child. But he *could* see to it that she lived in the surroundings of the heroines of her novels.

It's not as if he ever lived here, he forced himself to reason. *And a grown man shouldn't live in the past.* Why should he give Lord Holt the power to affect his family's well-being?

He tucked a cornsilk tendril resting upon Sarah's pinkened cheeks back into her black felt hat. "You know," he told her. "On second thought, the one on Church Row wasn't as large a house as we had hoped for."

"You . . . don't want that one either?"

"I'm afraid not. I want this one. But I also believe your father's right. We shouldn't make such a large commitment without praying over it until we've a clear answer."

She gave him a grateful smile, even as she shook her head. "You're saying that just for me. But I don't think God would lead us to buy a place where it is impossible for you to be happy, William."

"I'll be happy."

"How can you be sure?"

"I'll be happy because I will choose to be happy. Trust me, Sarah."

"Oh, William!" She seized him into an embrace, and he grinned at Daniel and Aunt Naomi over her shoulder.

Mr. Mitchell smiled at Mr. Prout. "I have the distinct impression you'll be hearing from us again."

———

Because of the season, moving into the Cannonhall Road house had to wait. Catherine came down for Christmas vacation, spending most of her time at study, but also endearing herself even further with the children because of her untiring agreeableness to read any book placed into her lap. Even Danny would cock his head and listen, reaching stubby fingers to help turn pages when he felt one had been dwelt upon long enough.

January lay heavy upon England. Colds and sniffles were passed about like a potato in the child's game, and on the eighteenth the worst snowstorms in a century blew in, with easterly gales at over seventy miles per hour at Great Yarmouth and snowdrifts twelve feet deep in the Isle of Wight.

By April the snows had melted but rainstorms were frequent. Benjamin Disraeli died on the nineteenth, the eleventh anniversary of Sarah's having come to Berkeley Square from the orphanage. William's twenty-seventh birthday was celebrated the following Sunday.

May waltzed in on sunny breezes rife with aromas of clematis and lilac, and the servants began packing and sending nonvital household items to Hampstead. Much of Sarah's time was spent with the Mitchells, arranging modifications in shipping schedules so that a cargo ship could be refurbished to accommodate passengers. Russian Jews, suffering brutal pogroms since the March third assassination of Czar Alexander III, were pouring into London. Many hoped to secure passage to the States, but possessed little more than the clothes upon their backs. Once she and William learned the gravity of their situations from the Rothschilds next door, they had prayed for a way to help beyond just donating money.

By the eighteenth of May, Sarah's twenty-fifth birthday, the S.S. *Dorothea* had made its maiden voyage across the Atlantic with cargo more precious than Wedgwood china and Yorkshire wool, the house agency had found a buyer for the Berkeley Square house, and the last stick of furniture from the same was acclimating itself to its new Hampstead setting.

They were welcomed to their new home with such offerings as baked goods, jars of preserved figs, and baskets of gooseberries and strawberries from every neighbor on Cannonhall Road, including pensioned Admiral Kirkpatrick from next door on the west, and from the other side, the Morlands, proprietors of the Corinthian Hotel on Heath Street. All offered advice on the best places to dine and shop, the best spots on the Heath for horseback riding or picnics, and the best location for Mr. Duffy's vegetable patch. And while some were aware of Sarah's connection with Blake Shipping, none expressed any curiosity over Rayborn and Doyle pedigrees.

Sarah and William also had purchased some of the Kelly furniture, such as the mahogany writing table they placed at one of their bedchamber windows overlooking the Heath. But only temporarily, Sarah told William, for she had faith that it would be moved aside one day for a rocking chair.

---

Ten

*O*n the sixth of June, Catherine knelt over an apple crate in which tins were packed among crinkled newspaper. They bore the labels of Droste's Cocoa, Mackintosh's Toffee de Luxe, Yardley Solidified Brilliantine Lavender Soaps and such, but when opened revealed biscuits of all species cradled in tissue papers—arrowroot and chocolate the size of guineas, ratafia and cinnamon like large buttons, shortbread in neat planks, and macaroons heaped like haystacks.

Just a little something to tide you over during examinations was penned in Aunt Naomi's neat hand.

Three quick raps sounded at her door, and Milly and Peggy swept in before she could bid them enter.

"Milly said you got a—" Peggy started, then cut herself off. "Goodness!"

Catherine handed the Yardley tin up to her. While Peggy's mother was an excellent cook, she was also a busy woman who often did alterations in the tailoring shop. She stocked up on shop-purchased treats such as Peak Frean biscuits and Cadbury chocolates to give to Peggy whenever she visited home. Milly received money for purchasing her own, so they both appreciated Aunt Naomi's homemade thoughtfulness as much as Catherine did.

"I wish I had an Aunt Naomi," Milly sighed, pulling apart a macaroon. She popped half into her mouth, and with a lump in her cheek said, "You have enough here for a party."

That gave Catherine pause. While she had been invited to several informal suite parties during the year, she had never hosted one herself. She was certain Aunt Naomi wouldn't mind her sharing the wealth. She glanced about the room. "That's an excellent idea. Do you think there's room for all the freshers?"

"All eighteen?" Chewing, Peggy looked about too. "Hmm . . . if we opened your bedroom door."

"We could push the table against the wall and put all the chairs in my room," Milly suggested. She sighed, reached into the tin again. "And I suppose there will be nothing left of these."

"Well . . ." Catherine was having second thoughts over that one. As fun as it would be to share and soak up praise for such fine refreshments, it would also be nice to have some set aside later for intense study sessions. "I'll set out half and buy more." Byrde's Fine Pastries in Cambridge supplied treats for special occasions such as Girton's annual Old Students' Dinner that were almost as tasty as Aunt Naomi's.

After breakfast the following morning Catherine stopped by Miss Welsh's office to ask permission to go into Cambridge.

"Mr. Willingham is off visiting family," the vice-mistress replied after Catherine explained the nature of her mission. Whenever any student had shopping to do that involved bringing back cumbersome parcels, the grounds keeper could be pressed into delivering her in the wagon, which had benches fitted along the sides for passengers.

"I don't mind hiring a carriage," Catherine told her. But that still left her without a chaperone.

"Miss Sinclair mentioned needing to purchase some shoes after lunch," the vice-mistress replied as if reading her mind. She pulled out a desk drawer and handed over a shilling. "Do bring me a couple of those little apricot cakes, will you?"

Miss Sinclair, a plump young woman with a hearty laugh, was the most popular resident lecturer. According to those students reading Mathematics, she treated Calculus as if it were the most exciting subject in the world. *That's the sort of schoolmistress I'd like to be,* Catherine thought. Surely difficulty in keeping her mind focused was not unique to her own experience. Even her father once admitted that he would never have passed King's College in London were it not for Uncle Daniel's tutelage. How many children today were being unjustly accused of laziness?

"We'll wait to take a carriage back with our packages," Miss Sinclair said as they set out on foot for the exercise, and so that the honeysuckle-laden breezes would not be wasted. Accompanying them was Miss Berryman, a third-year student who wished to purchase a pair of gloves. She was also in the Tennis Club, and while she was pleasant enough, she was one of the very few older students who had never invited any freshers to address her by her given name—something freshers were not allowed to do without permission. She shocked Catherine by yawning with mouth uncovered during Miss Sinclair's relating of her student days in the early seventies, when the College was moved from a rented house at Hitchin to its present location.

"As all our errands are so close together, I shall trust you both to complete yours and meet me at Fordham's," Miss Sinclair said when they came upon the shops of Market Street. Scents of yeast rising, cinnamon, and almond icing met Catherine inside Byrde's. While a woman at the counter made her purchases, Catherine scanned the trays of biscuits and cakes behind the glass. The bell over the shop tinkled, and she automatically turned to look. Hugh Sedgwick entered, clad in brown tweed jacket and navy blue trousers. He blinked as if adjusting to the indoor light, then gave her a crooked smile.

"Why, good afternoon, Miss Rayborn," he said, removing his boater hat.

"Good afternoon," she replied with a delicate balance of casualness and breeziness. Casual, because she did not wish him to suspect for a moment how she had hoped for the sight of him at the Cambridge and London stations between terms, and breezy so he would not suspect her disappointment every time she checked the chimneypiece in the reading room once winter was behind them.

". . . and half of that apple cheesecake," said the woman at the counter, while Catherine and Mr. Sedgwick stood in awkward silence.

He cleared his throat. "Congratulations on the Newnham match."

How did you . . . ? she started to ask, then told herself it was not necessary for him to know of her membership in the Tennis Club. His statement was simply generic, based upon the fact that she was a Girton student.

"Thank you." Because she had no idea what else to say, she added, "I wasn't good enough to participate this time. But my friend Millicent Turner did."

"I see. Well, there is always next year, isn't there?"

"Yes, perhaps," she replied, and a nervous little laugh escaped her.

His expression became glazed, like the icing on the eclairs. He looked down at the shiny leather toe caps of his ankle boots, then up at her again. "The goods are excellent here, aren't they?"

"Oh, quite," Catherine replied. "I'm having a little party for all the freshers before examinations."

"Very nice. I haven't the excuse of entertaining. I simply have a craving for scones that aren't as dense as bricks."

She caught herself in the middle of another nervous titter. *Stop that!* she ordered herself.

"What's your pleasure, Miss?"

Catherine turned to the vacant counter, while the bell tinkled the departure of the first patron. The baker's wife was looking expectantly at her, grey hairs dusting her brown topknot like the flour dusting her gingham apron.

"I beg your pardon," Catherine told her, but on a whim turned to the young man behind her. "I have so much to buy, Mr. Sedgwick. Why don't you go ahead?"

"Oh, but I couldn't . . ."

"Please do. I'll need another moment to decide."

"Well, thank you," he said, and smiled at her as he stepped up to the counter.

Catherine watched him ask the baker's wife for a half dozen scones. When he turned with paper sack in hand, she was quick to divert her attention to the baked goods behind the glass.

"How will you get all your purchases back to Girton?" he asked.

She looked up at him, as if she had not stared at the back of his head for the past minute. How easy it was to forgive him, she thought with some annoyance. "One of our resident lecturers is just two doors down at the cobbler's. We'll be taking a carriage from there." She managed to stifle the nervous laugh that time.

"What's your pleasure, Miss?" came again from behind the counter as the bell over the door tinkled and two chatting women entered.

"I'm in the way—forgive me," he said quickly, taking a step backwards.

"I hope you have a pleasant summer," Catherine told him just as quickly.

"And you as well."

She devoted her attention to the baker's wife, pointing to trays without taking time to think. "And two dozen lemon squares." After all, they wouldn't be for sale if they weren't good. As she walked toward the door with pasteboard box in her arms, she could not help but hope that Mr. Sedgwick would be out there waiting. But she wasn't surprised when he was not. If he didn't care enough to write, why should he care enough to wait?

Did I write too soon? Hugh pictured himself asking her as he turned up Sidney Street. *You did say spring, didn't you?* But of course she had, for he still had her letter in the stationery chest with his correspondence from home. *You could have at least sent a note that you'd changed your mind. How difficult would that have been?*

It wasn't shyness that had held him mute in the bakery, for he could not very well act on stage if such were his problem. But the setting was all wrong—the impatient baker's wife, new customers. He had waited outside the door only for a minute before reason told him that it just wasn't meant to be. She was probably besieged by suitors who had not squandered their first impressions by making fools of themselves on trains.

Anyway, she giggles too much, he told himself as consolation.

On Green Street he turned into Underwood's Grocery, dimly lit because of all the placards in the windows. "A half dozen packages of Black Jack, please," he said at the long counter, then amended his order.

"Rather, make that a dozen." He seldom chewed gum, for it stuck to the porcelain filling of his upper right back tooth if he wasn't careful. But on the near horizon loomed the Tripos examination, which would decide whether or not he graduated. His fingernails were bitten to the quick, so it was either gum or he just might gnaw his fingers to the bone.

"Very good, Sir," said the grocer, a thin man of about thirty with blond hair parted in a straight center line and slick with macassar oil. He opened a wide-mouthed gallon jar and began counting packages into a small paper bag. Over his left shoulder were stacked several tins of Sedgwick Tea. The lotus blossoms on a royal blue background had not changed since Grandmother Sedgwick painted the first template forty-seven years ago. It was fortunate that she was skilled with brush and palette, for Grandfather Sedgwick could not have afforded to hire an artist during the early days of trying to carve a niche for himself in the tea market.

The brand was now ubiquitous across England, and the family business so commonplace to Hugh's childhood memories that the sight of a Sedgwick Tea magazine advertisement or placard on the side of an omnibus or in a grocer's window stirred little more sentiment than did the sight of trees or mailboxes—also commonplace to his childhood memories.

"Good afternoon, Mr. Sedgwick."

The voice that came from behind him rumbled, as if the speaker's vocal cords were lined with gravel. Hugh knew who was there before turning, for that same voice had filled lecture halls with teachings of axioms and theorems and such over the past four years. Abel Billingford, Ph.D., Fellow of the Royal Society and Head of St. John's Mathematics Department, was as thick as a tree trunk, though stooped with the weight of seventy years. Thick white curls framed his hatless head so that he resembled later portraits of Beethoven. One spotted hand curved around the ivory handle of a cane, the other clutched a small silk purse.

"Dr. Billingford," Hugh said, snatching off his hat, although etiquette did not demand that he do so for one of the same gender in a public building. "Good afternoon, Sir."

"And to you, Mr. Sedgwick." The man's faded green eyes took in the bag in the grocer's hands. "That's a lot of chewing gum."

The tone was not accusatory, but just the fact that Dr. Billingford would notice and comment caused Hugh to feel as guilty as if he'd been caught purchasing opium. "Yes, Sir. A vulgar habit, I realize." He cleared his throat, set the bakery bag on the counter, and dipped into his coat pocket for his purse. "I assure you I don't normally buy it, but—"

"Do you know the difference between a man chewing gum and a cow chewing her cud?" Dr. Billingford asked.

"Why, no, Sir."

The faded green eyes glinted humor. "The intelligent look on the face of the cow."

"Heh-heh, that's a good one, Sir," Hugh told him over the grocer's guffaws. He paid for his gum, pocketed his purse, and stood aside while Dr. Billingford purchased two tins of sardines. Everything within him wanted to bid the old man *Good day* and escape. But he stood rooted to the ground and watched the crooked fingers rake two shillings from his purse. And when the grocer handed the bag over the counter, Hugh had no choice but to step up again.

"Please allow me, Sir. And I'll hail you a carriage."

"Thank you. But my physician says walking is good for me. If you will be so kind to carry my bag, we'll toddle along and have a chat."

A chat?

A brow cocked over the aged eyes. "Unless you were not yet planning to return?"

A way out was being offered upon a platter, but Hugh could not bring himself to seize it. Besides, if he were to be given another lecture over his marks, it would be best to get it over with now, while he could at least ingratiate himself with Dr. Billingford by carrying his bag. "I'm finished shopping, Sir."

Foot traffic on the pavement was light, and they ambled along at half of Hugh's usual speed. Yet Dr. Billingford seemed in no hurry to converse. After traveling thusly for some forty feet, Hugh could bear it no longer. He shifted the parcels to his left arm and turned to the man on his right.

"Sir, I would like you to know that I'm studying diligently these days. I intend to pass the Tripos and graduate."

"I've no doubt you will," Dr. Billingford replied.

Hugh gaped at him. This, from the man who had called him into his office every midterm to scold him for not applying himself?

"Why, thank you, Sir," he said. "That means a lot, coming from you."

The old man did not reply, his attention devoted upon finding the appropriate spots to strike his cane. But after ten steps or so, he said, "You will pass the Tripos because you have made it your goal to do so, Mr. Sedgwick."

Hugh opened his mouth to thank him again, when it struck him that, while the words were complimentary, something sounding very much like resignation colored the gravely voice. But why? Respectfully, he said, "Is there something wrong with that, Sir? That's every student's goal, after all."

"Not every student's, Mr. Sedgwick. I can assure you it was not mine, fifty years ago."

A trap was being baited, Hugh began to suspect, and he had stumbled into it all because of a hankering for gum. There was nothing to do now but wade his way through it.

"What was your goal, Sir?" he asked, only because it was expected of him. Like any actor worth his salt, he could recognize a prompt line.

"My goal was to become educated. It was my passion, young man." Faded green eyes studied Hugh's face. "And what is your passion, Mr. Sedgwick?"

No one had ever asked Hugh that in his twenty-one years, thus he had never thought to ask himself. His passion? "I enjoy acting and rowing," he replied, then hastened to add, "But only as hobbies. Having my degree is far more important to me."

"Why, may I ask? Your place in this world is secure, degree or not."

Hugh did not have to ask him to explain. Since early childhood, it was naturally taken for granted that he would help his father run Sedgwick Tea one day. But why single him out? There were others in his position, such as Neville, who stood to inherit his father's horse-breeding business, and whose marks were so poor that he was sent down for the term and would have to return in the fall.

"With all due respect, Sir," he said, shifting the packages again. "I'm not the only person here from a successful family trade."

"Indeed you are not," the old man agreed, then sighed heavily. "And it is not a crime to inherit another man's dream."

"Another man's . . ."

"But when that dream insulates a promising young man from discovering his own dream, it saddens me. I have watched you for almost four years now, drifting with the current, content to settle for mediocrity. Why did you even enroll here, Mr. Sedgwick? Is it because your father demanded it?"

"No, Sir," Hugh replied defensively. "I wanted to come. My father wanted me to start working right after Harrow." His father would have no difficulty convincing Lane and Brian, students there now, for they were champing at the bit to get started in the business. That Hugh's younger brothers had inherited the Sedgwick entrepreneurism was in evidence by the time they were ages four and five and collected their old toys into a cart to sell, until a housekeeper five doors down informed Mother of what they were doing.

"Then, could it be that you resented having your future mapped out before you were even born?"

"No, Sir. Not at all." But resentment was creeping in all right. For the man beside him. His range of influence in Hugh's life was supposed to be limited to academic matters. What business had he meddling in his life beyond Saint John's? Other than accepting the occasional foolish wager—which he had vowed never again to do since the handkerchief prank—he had striven to live a moral life.

Fortunately, the old man seemed to have said all that was on his mind, and appeared to be concentrating solely upon staying upright. Between defending himself further and having the conversation end, Hugh chose the latter.

A quarter of an hour later, they stood across the street from the college's arched main gate, with its blend of early Tudor brickwork and painted heraldry. "I feel humbled every time I pass through the same gate through which the likes of Wordsworth and Wilberforce passed," the old man murmured just barely over the street traffic.

If the remark was intended as a barb, it found its mark in Hugh's chest. "Sir," he said. "I can't be another Wordsworth or Wilberforce."

The faded eyes blinked at him. "Do you think I would wish that of you, Mr. Sedgwick?"

"You obviously don't think highly of the tea business."

"Then I have failed to communicate my concern to you. I happen to respect any man with imagination enough to build a profitable trade—provided that trade is ethically sound." A smile softened the heavy features. "And . . . being particularly fond of tea, I am grateful that there are those who would spare me the task of attempting to dry the leaves myself."

"It's called *withering*, Sir," Hugh told him.

"I beg your pardon?"

"What's done with the leaves after they're picked."

"Withering, eh? You see, one is never too old to learn something." Dr.

Billingford rested a spotted hand on Hugh's shoulder as the somber expression resumed itself. "What I am suggesting, Mr. Sedgwick, is that you search your heart. Prayerfully so. Discover whether your feet are treading the path they are on because you are heeding your life's calling, or because habit and security—and the expectations of others—have blinded you to any other paths."

That he should have such concern, whether it was warranted or not, lightened some of Hugh's resentment. He was even able to honestly say, "I appreciate that, Sir. And I'll think over what you said."

"Indeed you will." The old man's voice became almost tender. "I only pray it is while you are still young enough to act upon it."

Eleven

On the evening of the twenty-fourth of June, the doors to the reading, first lecture, and dining rooms were propped open for a party to celebrate the completion of the Easter Term and to herald in the long vacation. Even Miss Emily Davies came up from London. She reminded Catherine more of a nanny than intrepid pioneer, with her small, neat figure, pointed features softened by fifty-one years, and laurel of greying brown braid. She and co-founder Barbara Bodichon had encountered much hostility in their quest to establish a women's college. Some of that hostility remained in a more subtle degree, for the University refused to confer degrees upon even those female students with exceptional scores on the Tripos examinations.

"You must taste this," Peggy told Catherine, handing her a cup of cherry punch. "Pineapple bits."

"Very good," Catherine said after a sip. "Just don't spill it on your dress."

"Oh . . . good idea." Peggy held her cup farther out in front of her. She looked like a titian-haired princess in her ivory armure gown. Circling her lace collar was the strand of seed pearls her Aunt Mabel had given her.

Catherine's eyes strayed in the direction of the piano and settled briefly upon two matronly heads together in conversation. She looked away again when she realized the target of the two sets of eyes. "Is it just my imagination, or are they talking about us?" Catherine said in low tone.

"Who?" Peggy said, looking about.

"Don't do that!" Catherine whispered. "Miss Bernard and Miss Davies. Over by the piano."

Peggy slanted a discreet look in that direction, then said through stiff lips, "Not us. *You.*"

"But why?"

Her friend took a sip from her cup. "Miss Davies probably asked her to point out the greatest woolgatherer in Girton's history."

Catherine laughed. "I doubt that."

"We'll see. They're on their way over."

Sure enough, a sweeping glance leftward took in the two women advancing upon them. Miss Davies smiled and said, "Miss Rayborn! Miss Bernard tells me we have you to thank for influencing Mr. and Mrs. Doyle to donate the microscope."

"I'm afraid I had nothing to do with that," Catherine told her. "I was simply present when they decided to do so. It was Miss Somerset here who influenced them."

"Indeed?"

Both women smiled at Peggy, who smiled back but shook her head. "Miss Rayborn gives me too much credit. She's the one related to the Doyles."

"But I had *nothing* to do with our being related," Catherine argued and looked at the women again. "If Miss Somerset had not been so enthusiastic over the microscope at Pembroke, the idea never would have occurred to them."

Miss Davies laid a hand upon Peggy's sleeve. "Modesty *and* school loyalty. You're a credit to Girton, Miss Somerset."

"What was that all about?" Milly asked, sidling up to Catherine after the two women moved on to a group of assistant lecturers and older students.

"The microscope." And to forestall another friendly argument with Peggy over who should take credit, Catherine looked at the remnant of pavinni cake in Milly's dish. "How is it?"

"The carbonate of soda wasn't mixed well. You taste salty patches now and again. I'll probably not go back for thirds. But shall I get some for you?"

"No, thank you," Catherine told her, and Peggy demurred as well.

"Miss Turner, will you recite for us?" Miss Welsh came over to ask.

Milly agreed, but before leaving to stand in the center of the room with the assistant headmistress, she bared her teeth discreetly at Catherine. "Anything there?"

"No, you're fine," Catherine said, taking her dish.

Miss Welsh asked for silence. Milly delivered an excellent rendition of Felica Hemans' "Casabianca":

> *"The boy stood on the burning deck*
> *Whence all but he had fled;*
> *The flame that lit the battle's wreck*
> *Shone round him o'er the dead . . ."*

After the applause, a senior sat at the piano and struck the C chord. "Gather 'round, ladies," Miss Welsh said, the ruffles at the ends of her sleeves fluttering with her beckonings. A couple of low groans mingled with the dull thuds of punch cups and dishes being set upon tablecloths, but minutes later a gentle brook of layered voices flowed through the room carrying strains of "The Girton Pioneers," "Gaudeamus Igitur," and "Forty Years On."

> *"Forty years on when afar and asunder*
> *Parted are those who are singing today*
> *When you look back and forgetfully wonder*
> *What you were like in your work and your play,*
> *Then it may be there will often come o'er you*
> *Glimpses of notes like the catch of a song,*
> *Visions of girlhood shall float them before you,*
> *Echoes of dreamland shall bear them along."*

"What's the matter with Peggy?" Ann Purdy whispered under the strains of "Girton, My Friend."

Catherine automatically glanced beside her to the left, at the vacant spot that had contained Peggy just a moment ago. She whispered the same question to Milly, who looked about the room from her superior height and shrugged.

"I'll see about her," Catherine said, and eased her way back to the nearest door.

Peggy, already in her nightgown, answered her knock. "I'm fine," she said with a weary smile. "I should have told you I was leaving. But I've not caught up with sleep since exams, and my mind's in a fog."

"Then sleep well." Catherine stepped up to kiss a freckled cheek. "I'll wake you in time to dress." They would be riding back to London together, as usual. Milly, however, would be catching the Midland Railway for Saint Ives from the Histon Station, northeast of Girton.

"Thank you," Peggy said, then gave her an odd little look as if she would say more.

When she did not, Catherine studied her friend's face and said, "Are you sure you're all right?"

"Yes." Peggy nodded. "Go join the others."

Back at the gathering Catherine explained Peggy's fatigue to those who inquired. All about the room embraces and promises to write were exchanged, though almost half of the students, including Peggy, would return after short visits with family. Study went on at Girton even during the weeks the lecterns were vacant.

"I don't think we can consider ourselves second-year students until next term," Milly said in Catherine's apartment an hour later, while Catherine was folding a blouse for her trunk. Milly sat on the bedroom rug in nightgown and wrapper, slippers pushed aside from her long bare feet so that she could trim her toenails with a pair of grooming scissors.

"But we're no longer freshmen," Catherine argued, then gave her a worried look. "I hope you're not getting any—"

"Got them." Milly grinned at her and held up a closed hand. Resuming trimming, she said, "I'd wager Evelyn will have to take a sleeping powder tonight. She'll be as eager to see me as I am her."

"At least she didn't talk your father into making you spend the summer at school," Catherine said, resuming her packing.

"Actually, I wouldn't mind staying, were the situation different. It would certainly be easier to study. But I have to protect my sisters and brother."

"Surely she wouldn't harm them."

"Hmph! Did I tell you she was a witch?"

At least a dozen times, Catherine thought wryly.

"She's probably reading her book of spells as we speak. If I don't return, you'll know she's turned us all into toads."

Catherine smiled and rolled up a pair of stockings. She was leaving her coats, some dresses, and winter woolens in the wardrobe and dresser, with smooth bits of cedarwood tucked in sleeves or pockets to repel moths. She would be away for a little over two months. The voyage to and from Bombay requiring thirteen days each way, she would spend a month with her family, then a week with the Hampstead kin. That would give her the month of September back at Girton to study ahead before Michaelmas Term would begin on the fourth of October. And for those two months away, she was bringing along Pope's 1200-page translation of Homer's *The Iliad.*

You'll be a walking authority on Homer by summer's end, she promised herself.

". . . sends a servant to meet my train," Milly was saying. "How welcome do you think that makes me feel?"

Realizing her thoughts had drowned out the first part of Milly's sentence,

Catherine turned from her trunk. "I wish you and your sisters and brother could come to Bombay with me."

Milly smiled up at her. "Wouldn't that be—"

Three low urgent knocks sounded. The door opened when Catherine was four steps away. Peggy entered, cheeks splotched and eyes red and puffy.

"I saw your light . . ."

"I'm glad you could join us." Catherine was about to ask what was the matter but changed her mind. *Better give her a minute.*

"Peggy, what's the matter?" Milly asked.

Peggy blinked, and the eyes reddened even more. "It was so typical of you, Catherine. The way you praised me to Miss Davies, when I don't deserve it."

"But you *do* deserve it," Catherine protested, relieved that was all that was the matter. "But if it's going to upset you, then we'll share the credit. Now, why don't you help me latch my trunk and we'll all have a nice chat?"

But Peggy just batted her watery eyes.

"Peggy?"

"I don't deserve your friendship," she sniffed.

Catherine sent a curious glance Milly's way, but Milly was studying her toenails as if trying to be as inconspicuous as possible. She turned to Peggy again. "Why would you say that?"

Her friend swallowed, then whispered, "I did a terrible thing."

"Well, I believe I'll turn in now," Milly said, getting to her feet.

"No. Please stay." Peggy leaned against the bedpost as if in need of support and looked at Catherine again. "You received another letter from Hugh Sedgwick. About two months ago."

"I did?" Catherine looked at Peggy's empty hands. "Where is it?"

"I burned it."

"Burned—?"

"Oh, Peggy . . ." Milly said.

A tear slid down Peggy's freckled cheek and clung to her jawline. "You had come back here for a pencil when I checked the reading room. I regretted it the minute I did it, but . . ."

"Why did you do it?" Catherine asked.

She closed her eyes, sending a tear down the other cheek. "I had thought I'd gotten over the jealousy," she said when her eyes opened again. "And you'd said he didn't mean anything to you, so I told myself the letter wouldn't matter to you anyway."

All Catherine could do was stare at her. *What must he think of me?*

"That was a hateful thing to do," Milly said.

Peggy burst into sobs, buried her face in her hands. "I know, I know!"

Catherine exchanged somber looks with Milly, while her mind pictured a letter blackening and crumbling in the fireplace. *How could you?* she wanted to scream.

At length Peggy wiped her face with her sleeve and peered miserably at her. "I'll go to Saint John's in the morning, Catherine. Perhaps he'll still be there. I'll tell him what I did."

"You can't go there alone, Peggy," Milly reminded her. "And I can't imagine anyone agreeing to chaperone you for such an errand."

"Then I'll write to the college, ask his London address." Her eyebrows rose hopefully. "Or I could send him a letter, in care of Sedgwick Tea!"

He'll want nothing more to do with me, Catherine thought, recalling how quickly he had disappeared after they came across each other at Byrde's. The fact that he hadn't asked why she didn't write back was proof that he had decided she was too much bother. She shook her head. "Just forget about it."

"But—"

"No!"

Peggy flinched as if she'd been slapped, then stared at the carpet with lips trembling. A tiny bit of pity penetrated Catherine's outrage, but she pushed it away. She could feel the weight of Milly's stare and resented that the two were hoping she would swallow her hurt and act magnanimously.

Indeed, Milly said in a tentative voice, "At least she owned up to it, Catherine. She could have kept silent, and you would have never known."

That was so. But had Peggy somehow injured her *physically*, she would not be expected to up and forgive while the wound was still throbbing. "I'm very tired," she murmured. "I'd like to go to bed now."

No one moved for several seconds. Laughter drifted from somewhere down the corridor. Peggy nodded resignedly. "I love you, Catherine," she whispered just before turning for the door.

Catherine did not reply. When the door closed behind Peggy, she said to Milly, standing behind her. "I'm just not ready."

"No . . . um . . . of course not."

At the sound of a sigh, Catherine turned. Milly's face was a mixture of somberness and uncertainty. She made an awkward little gesture. "But perhaps I should . . ."

"Go ahead and look in on her," Catherine said.

"Are you sure you—"

"Yes, I think you should."

And she meant it, though it disgusted her that a tiny part of her wanted to make certain Peggy would not go and do something rash. She paced the floor after Milly left, wishing she could go outside and run, anything to burn up the emotion surging through her.

The following morning she did not go to breakfast, but gathered up her last-minute things to leave early for Cambridge Station. She could not imagine sharing a carriage with Peggy. What would they talk about?

She had just pinned on her hat when Milly knocked to wish her farewell.

"I know I'll have to forgive her eventually," Catherine said as they embraced. "But I can't imagine the friendship ever being the same."

"I just thought with her helping you study . . ." Milly said uncomfortably.

Et tu Brute? Catherine thought, but it was nothing that she had not said to herself several times during the long night. "I just don't know."

She waited at the farthest end of the station platform, seated next to a tall, dark-haired woman of about thirty who said she was traveling alone and would be happy to share the bench. Catherine preoccupied herself with scanning the gathering crowd in the hopes of not seeing Peggy, and the woman, seemingly occupied with her own thoughts, did not attempt any idle chit-chat. *The perfect seating companion,* Catherine thought, and determined she would try to share the same carriage with her too.

But when a trio of male Indian students passed by, the woman snorted and said, "Do you imagine they ever bathe?"

Catherine turned to her. "I beg your pardon?"

The woman wrinkled a pert little nose and nodded in the trio's direction. "They always look so smarmy, those—"

"What an ignorant twit you are!" Catherine seethed, rising and ignoring the gasp of outrage from the bench. It felt good to have a target for her anger, and for two shillings she would have lingered to deliver a lecture on prejudice. The remaining benches were occupied, so she stood off to herself. She caught no sight of Peggy, who must have decided upon a later train. She also caught no sight of a shock of wheat-colored hair.

During her three days in Hampstead, she managed to push aside thoughts of Girton and her disappointment with Peggy. She explored the nooks and crannies of the magnificent house, shopped with Sarah and Naomi at T.J. Paxton's and Harrods for gifts for her family and their servants, read storybooks to Bethia and Danny in the garden, and pedaled Sarah's bike north across the Heath.

After breakfast on Tuesday the twenty-eighth, Uncle Daniel and Bethia accompanied Catherine on the thirty-mile journey to Tilbury to meet the steamer and her chaperone. It was through Uncle Daniel's association with William Blackwood and Sons that they had corresponded with an editor's aunt, a Mrs. Jennings from Norwich, who desired to visit her daughter and the daughter's army colonel husband in Bombay.

"You really didn't have to escort me," Catherine told her uncle in the London and Tilbury railway carriage. "I know you've a book to write."

Uncle Daniel smiled at her. "Bethia and I were ready for an adventure. Besides, I'll rest easier when I'm certain Mrs. Jennings is there."

"And what will you do if she isn't?" Catherine teased. "Send Bethia in her place?"

She kicked herself mentally when her young cousin's countenance brightened. "Oh, may I, Father?"

"I'm afraid not," Uncle Daniel said with a hand upon her shoulder. "However would we manage without you for two whole months?"

The girl's blue eyes took on a faraway glaze as if her four-year-old mind was considering how the family would manage. Presently she gave Catherine a look that said *I'm sorry, but my parents need me.* "She'll be there, Catherine," Bethia assured her. "Why would she write you if she wasn't going to come?"

Catherine tugged gently at the braid resting upon the girl's narrow shoulder. "Why indeed, Bethia?"

Mrs. Jennings was waiting in the Bursar's office of the Peninsular and Oriental Steam Navigation Company. She was a hardy-looking woman of sixty years or so, with weathered skin, light brown hair drawn into a no-nonsense knot, and a taupe gown devoid of bustle and frills.

"I took the liberty of reserving a portside cabin so we may avoid the worst of the sun," Mrs. Jennings said after introductions were made. "Starboard upon return. That's where the term *posh* originated, you know—Port Out, Starboard Home. And I've a gallon of ginger biscuits for the both of us. Good for seasickness. Not that I expect to need any, for my constitution is exceptionally sturdy."

"I can see you're in capable hands," Uncle Daniel said with a smile.

Twelve

*I*t so happened that Mrs. Jennings was the one in capable hands, as this was her first trip abroad, and her information was gleaned from letters from her daughter and newspaper travelogues. Once the S.S. *Heron* met the treacherous waters of the Bay of Bascal, she alternated between berth and deck railing, her complexion greenish like verdigris upon copper.

"I wish I could *die!*" she would moan.

"Try swaying gently against the roll so your head stays vertical," Catherine advised, between wiping the woman's face with a damp cloth, fetching the ship's doctor, and coaxing ginger biscuits upon her. She suffered only warning twinges of sickness herself, such as when she attempted to read Homer. But the waters became calmer once the ship entered the Suez Canal, in spite of almost daily showers from the monsoons swelling in from the southwest. It was calm enough to allow Catherine and Mrs. Jennings to join two dowagers, Mmes. Horton and Mead, in the ladies' public room for games of Whist. And thirteen days after leaving Tilbury, Catherine stood with Mrs. Jennings on the upper deck under the shelter of the bridge, watching the rain-muted panorama of Bombay grow more and more vivid as the steamer rounded Colaba Point into Bombay Harbor on the eastern side of the peninsula.

"I'm glad I didn't know how rough the trip would be beforehand," Mrs. Jennings said, fanning herself against the steamy heat. "Or I should never have had the courage to come."

Catherine smiled at her. "I think you would have, still."

The woman gave her an appreciative look and took her hand. "My daughter will want to meet the young woman who kept her mother from pitching herself into the sea. We'll be sending you and your family an invitation to lunch—you'll join us, won't you?"

"I'm sure we would enjoy that," Catherine told her.

Once the ship tied up at pier in the P & O Dockyard, passengers under umbrellas began moving toward the gangplank. Native porters in rain-soaked white uniforms swarmed against the flow, calling out "Luggage! Baggage! Luggage! Baggage!"

Catherine's father and Mrs. Jennings' son-in-law, Colonel Timbs, were waiting on the pier, having made each other's acquaintance minutes earlier. The officer was a compact man, with dark eyebrows almost as thick as his mustache. After introductions and a repeat of Mrs. Jennings' promise to invite them for lunch, they bade each other good-day and parted company. The clouds veiling the sun cresting Malabar Hill were streaked dark crimson, and Bombay's congested streets were difficult enough to navigate in the daytime.

"How was your journey?" Father asked, drawing Catherine into the shelter of his umbrella as he escorted her to a hired horse-drawn *gharri*. Two porters followed with the trunk.

She smiled. "It had its ups and downs."

He chuckled at the old family joke. Girton and Hampstead seemed like other worlds entirely—albeit drier, more sedate ones. Even in the rain the pier was thick with people of countless nationalities moving amid a clamor of languages and dialects. The mile-and-a-half ride to the Byculla area took three-quarters of an hour. Her family lived in a red sandstone cottage within the walled school grounds, next to the administration and hospital buildings. Little diamonds of light seeped out between the slats of the chick screens, fashioned to keep out bees, wasps, grasshoppers, squirrels, snakes, and monkeys while allowing in the scents of jasmine and tuberose, hibiscus and lotus. Father's hand was inches from the knob when the door opened, and a girl pitched herself into Catherine's arms.

"Catherine!"

Smiling, Catherine squeezed the girl tight. Her sister's arrival in the Rayborn household over nine years ago was nothing short of a miracle, for Mother had given up hope of having another child. Cosseted by family and servants alike, she was remarkably unspoiled.

"How I've missed my Jewel!" she said, kissing the top of the ash brown head. "And I've paper dolls for you in my trunk."

"Oh, thank you! My others are starting to—"

"Ladies?" Father said in a long-suffering voice from behind. "If you please?"

Mother came into the hall and embraced her, while manservant Dasya slipped out to assist the driver with the trunk. The women servants, Jarita and Neerja, waited with shy smiles to greet her, and Naeem, the Muslim cook, had prepared a special meal of *patrani machi,* hilsa fish topped with chutney and baked in banana leaves, and a dessert of *gulab jamun,* fried cakelike balls in rose-scented syrup. Afterward Catherine and her family chatted in the parlor. It warmed her heart that her parents and sister remembered the names and situations of the friends and classmates from her photographs and letters. She did not tell them of her hard feelings against Peggy.

"My heart aches for poor Milly," Mother said. Plump, dark-haired, and grey-eyed, she possessed a sort of energy and efficiency that made her seem younger than her forty years. "And her little motherless siblings. It will only get worse if her stepmother has a baby, you know."

Father wanted to know more details of her lectures. Jewel, allowed a rare extension of bedtime, asked, "Whatever happened to those men who tricked you on the train?"

"I saw one of them at a bakery once," Catherine replied casually.

"You ignored him, of course," Mother said with an indignant narrowing of the eyes, and Father nodded, though he looked away when the briefest of smiles touched his lips.

Not wishing to lie, Catherine covered a convenient, though authentic, yawn. She was just too travel fatigued to submit to a lecture, no matter how lovingly delivered.

But the lecture came from within, as she lay in her bed an hour later listening to the persistent whine of a mosquito foiled by the netting draped from the canopy. *You have to stop thinking of him,* she told herself. For all she knew, Hugh Sedgwick could have written that he was engaged to be married or going off to join the foreign service after graduation, and Peggy had spared her some pain.

She immediately withdrew that thought. Not knowing was far worse.

But you have only four weeks to be with family, she reminded herself. And would she rather store memories that would tide her over the coming year, or waste time dwelling on what might have been? She chose the former. She rose long enough to light her lamp and bring *The Iliad* into her fortress of mosquito netting. A chapter would surely put her to sleep. But Homer proved powerful enough to transport her to the Land of Nod after three pages.

The following morning, after Father had left for the school office, Catherine sat on the parlor carpet cutting out paper dolls with Jewel while

Mother sat behind the marble and teak tea table, unscrewing the back from a clock ruined by humidity. Through the windows came the tree frogs' nasal *quank-quank-quank.*

"I do wish you could stay here forever," Jewel said, her sparsely lashed green eyes following her scissors around the image of Princess Vicky.

"You have Allyson," Catherine reminded her, carefully trimming around a pink dress. Allyson was the daughter of one of the schoolmasters. They shared lessons with Miss Purtley, the governess who had taught Catherine and who was home in Devonshire for the summer.

"Yes, but she's not the same as a sister."

"I know. I've missed you too. But what would I do here?"

The girl thought for a minute. "You could help Miss Purtley tutor us."

"Your sister wishes to finish college, Jewel," Mother said, going over a rusted coil with fine sandpaper. She looked at Catherine. "But speaking of governesses, your Aunt Phyllis's letter says she's looking for one for Muriel and the twins."

"Oh, my. Better to tend lions at the zoo."

Jewel ducked her head, hiding a smile. Mother smiled too, even though her tone admonished. "Catherine . . ."

"Forgive me, Mother. But why a governess?"

"She's been told that Sheffield's schools are lacking, and can't bear the thought of sending the children to boarding school. When I wrote back I suggested that a male tutor would be more appropriate—after all, Bernard and Douglas are nearing twelve."

"Sheffield?"

"Uncle Norman's imminent transfer. Which you would have learned of if you had visited your aunt before you left."

Catherine grimaced. "I know, Mother. But I only had three days . . ."

"And so you couldn't spare an hour?" Her mother set the coil and paper on the table. "Now, Catherine, I've told you how Aunt Phyllis came to stay with us a whole month after you were born. I was very weak, you know, and could not have managed the household without her. She may dote excessively upon the children, but she does love her nieces."

"I'll visit before I go back to school." When her mother looked skeptical, Catherine added, "I'll even spend a couple of days with them."

In the time it took the latter thought to travel from her lips to her own ears, Catherine regretted it and added quickly, "If they invite me, of course. But if they're planning to move, I certainly wouldn't want to be a hindrance."

"Catherine . . ."

"You've always said that we shouldn't take anyone for granted. Even family."

"Very well." Mother was pacified enough to resume sanding, and Catherine resumed manipulating the scissors around the paper dress. Yet the issue was evidently still in Mother's mind, for presently she said, "After all, once they move away you'll see them only at Christmas. If that often."

The thought was not too distressing. Catherine winked at Jewel, who grinned and winked back. Truly, she loved her aunt and cousins. Some relations were just easier to love from a distance.

The majority of the school's one hundred and nineteen male students had joined their families for the summer. Still, Father had much to do in planning the next term. But he made time to accompany Catherine, Mother, and Jewel on Saturday shopping forays at the Crawford Market and Chor Bazaar, and on strolls through the Hanging Gardens. On Sundays they walked to Saint Thomas Church, a steepled stone structure that could have been transplanted from any London neighborhood, though the congregation was more colorful with the scatterings of military uniforms and some natives in English dress.

Father took the whole day off on the twenty-sixth of July, Catherine's nineteenth birthday. Her parents presented her with a strand of jade beads with gold clasp and matching earrings, and the family took the ferry to the island of Elephanta to picnic and tour the caves. When they returned there was a note from Mrs. Jennings, written in a sprawling hand.

> *My dear Miss Rayborn,*
>   *Please forgive me for not extending this invitation sooner, but Colonel Timbs, my son-in-law, was called away on official business to Bangalore shortly after my arrival, and has returned only yesterday. Will you and your lovely family pay us the honor of joining us for lunch next Tuesday?*

During the monsoon season, invitations between acquaintances living some distance apart tended to be more for lunch than supper, for there was always that uncertainty of rain—an inconvenience during the day, but a hindrance to safety on the roads after dark. On the second of August, Catherine's family took a hired *gharri* four steamy miles down the Colaba Causeway to the point of the peninsula, to the garrison of the Durham Light Infantry, 2nd Battalion. Officers and their families resided in a row of tan brick *bungalows,* from the Hindustani word *bangala,* one-storey cottages with low roof lines extended to create verandahs. A manservant in white *kurta* pajamas ran out to meet them and led them to Colonel Timbs's bungalow and into a parlor strewn with colorful dhurrie rugs. Two men in scarlet coats trimmed in gold rose from chairs, along with two women from the sofa.

"And here is my very own Florence Nightingale," Mrs. Jennings caroled, hastening forth to embrace Catherine.

"Welcome to our home," Colonel Timbs said with a courtly bow. His introductions included his wife, a younger, fairer-cheeked version of her mother, and his adjutant, Lieutenant Elham, a tall, striking figure with long side-whiskers neatly trimmed and wavy, almond-brown hair.

They took seats and chatted, at least the older adults did, while Catherine and Jewel listened. Once the weather, the school, and army matters had been discussed lightly, a female servant paused at the door to send Mrs. Timbs a discreet nod. In the dining room, Mrs. Timbs directed Lieutenant Elham to take the chair across from Catherine's. Two female servants efficiently placed bowls of soup upon the white cloth. Each time Catherine's eyes met Lieutenant Elham's, she shifted her gaze to the Constable landscape over his right ear. She was so absorbed with pretending not to notice him that she could barely taste the yam soup or follow the discussion flowing about her.

"Can you imagine suffering a bullet in the back for a whole month?" Colonel Timbs was saying from the head of the table. Even though mail delivery from England took thirteen days, the telegraph ensured that the *Times of India* was up to date.

"Has anyone discovered why he did it?" Mother asked.

Lieutenant Elham forked a curried shrimp into his mouth and turned to his left. "I believe he expected a consular position that was denied him, Mrs. Rayborn. Bitterness apparently drove him insane."

It wasn't that Catherine had no sympathy for the States's President Garfield. But the lieutenant's elegant, eligible presence caused her to feel extremely self-conscious. Especially with her father seated at her right elbow.

"What is your impression of Cambridge, Miss Rayborn?" the lieutenant said presently, when the subject of the attempted assassination was exhausted.

"It's a fascinating town," she replied, relieved that she could stop pretending not to notice him. "Have you been there?"

"Actually, I graduated from King's College. Did you enjoy your year at Girton?"

"Very much so."

"She's in the Tennis Club," Jewel told him.

"Is that so?" The lieutenant smiled at Jewel. "I should ask your sister for some lessons. My sister trounces me unmercifully every time I visit home. My *younger* sister."

Jewel covered a smile, and Catherine was about to ask where *home* was, but Father cleared his throat and said pleasantly, though pointedly, "Indeed Girton is a fine college. Catherine will be eager to return there as soon as possible after she leaves us on Friday. We're delighted she's willing to delay such frivolous pastimes as courtships in favor of education."

Such frivolous pastimes as courtships? Catherine stared down at her plate, her cheeks on fire. *Could you be any more blunt?*

"This is excellent shrimp," Mother said to Mrs. Timbs with strained voice. "Do convey our compliments to your cook."

"Yes, excellent," Father echoed. There was only self-satisfaction in his tone. And Lieutenant Elham did not address Catherine directly again for the remainder of the meal.

Thirteen

After the dessert of *kheer,* rice cooked in sweetened milk with raisins and almonds, everyone retired to the parlor. Through the chick screens rolled volleys of not-too-distant thunder.

"I was hoping the rain would miss us this afternoon," Father said.

"Those are target drills," Colonel Timbs corrected, crossing one polished boot over the other. "The men are acquainting themselves with our new carbine Martini-Henry rifles."

"Indeed? Are they vastly different from what you had before?"

Father had no interest in guns and was only being polite, Catherine knew. She told herself that if Lieutenant Elham had voiced an identical statement about the rifles, Father would have replied something in the order of *How good that you keep your men occupied so that they aren't gadding about trying to romance colonists' daughters* or something equally humiliating. She just knew it.

"Five ounces lighter, a good six inches shorter," Colonel Timbs replied. "But you see, even the most minuscule change requires some adjustment. A weapon must be as a third arm to a soldier, and the heat of battle isn't the time to make that adjustment."

He turned to Mother. "Pray, don't be alarmed by that, Mrs. Rayborn. There are no foreseeable battles here in India. Still, it is a soldier's duty to be prepared."

"I see." Mother's smile only minimally softened the taut lines of her face. Catherine could feel identical lines in her own.

"Perhaps Mr. Rayborn would care to see your gun collection, Frank," Mrs. Jennings said to her son-in-law.

"Really, I shouldn't wish to trouble—" Father began, but Colonel Timbs had uncrossed his boots and was on his feet.

"Nothing would give me greater pleasure. Lieutenant, do stay and keep the ladies company. Will you excuse us?"

"But of course, Colonel Timbs." Mother's smile was guileless as she watched Father rise from his chair. "James is immensely fascinated with guns. Isn't that so, James?"

"Immensely," Father replied, but the grey-green eyes above his smile made Catherine think of King John being presented with the Magna Carta.

"Fine fellow!" Colonel Timbs clapped him on the back on the way through the doorway. "We'll begin with the pistols . . . wait, muskets. My favorite was captured from an Iroquois warrior during the French and Indian War . . ."

The atmosphere of the parlor was lightened by the older women's conspiratorial smiles. Conversation eddied from one subject to another: Mrs. Jennings' tour of the Taj Mahal, Mother's discovery of a stall in the market selling fine silks cheaply, and Mrs. Timbs's enthusiasm over the telephone exchange to be built in Bombay by the beginning of next year.

"But here we are, boring the young ones," she said abruptly, and turned to the lieutenant. "Lieutenant Elham, why don't you escort the two Misses Rayborn to the roof to watch the drills?"

"It would be a pleasure, Mrs. Timbs," he replied. He rose and offered a white-gloved hand to Jewel first, with her being seated the closest to him, then Catherine. "May I?"

He accompanied them down a corridor. Just before a narrow set of stairs, Catherine heard the Colonel's voice from one of the rooms.

". . . as you can see, the internal coiled spring striker was a welcome improvement over the external hammer and firing pin . . ."

"One moment, if you please," Lieutenant Elham said pleasantly. He climbed the steps, his boots striking against the wood, unlatched and pushed open a door in the ceiling. His body disappeared through it, then his face and shoulders reappeared. Holding out a hand, he said, "It's quite safe."

"May I go first?" Jewel asked.

Catherine smiled at her. "Go on."

The girl scurried up the steps and disappeared. Catherine took his hand next, and was helped out onto a railed area above the slate-tiled verandah. On the parade ground a half dozen targets were set up before huge bales of hay. A half dozen soldiers loaded rifles and fired off volleys at an officer's command, then hastened to the back of the queue while others took their places.

"We've some talented marksmen in the regiment," the lieutenant said. "Five were awarded VCs during the Battle of Kambula." He nodded at Jewel's puzzled expression. "That was in South Africa, against the Zulus."

"VCs?" Catherine asked, resting both palms against the wooden railing and trying not to think of how it felt to have him take her by the arm and elbow just minutes ago.

"Forgive me. It's so seldom that I speak with civilians that I forget how. The Victoria Cross—the highest decoration for gallantry."

"Is that what you're wearing?" Jewel asked.

Catherine turned to look. Chin dipping to his chest, Lieutenant Elham touched the medal attached to a red and blue ribbon. "No," he said modestly. "For distinguished conduct in that same battle."

"Your parents were proud?" Catherine said.

"Yes." His white teeth flashed with his grin. "But then, they were proud the first time I washed my ears unassisted."

Jewel's girlish laugh rang out over the railing, and Catherine smiled, put to ease by the shared humor.

"Does the noise hurt theirs?" Jewel asked when sober again. "Ears, that is."

Lieutenant Elham looked out toward the parade ground. "Only those foolish enough not to put cotton in them as advised."

"But then how can they hear the commands?"

"It only muffles the loudest noises. Give it a try sometime and you'll see."

"How long have you been quartered here, Lieutenant Elham?" Catherine felt comfortable enough to ask.

"One year," he replied. "We spent five in South Africa."

"You've not been home in six years?" Jewel asked, green eyes filled with sympathy.

"I've been twice, actually," he said. "Spennymoor, in Durham. Have you heard of it?"

Catherine and Jewel shook their heads.

"I can understand that. The roads into Spennymoor weren't even surfaced until I was—"

"Ah well, there you are," came a familiar paternal voice. Catherine turned. Father's head stuck out of the opening. "How good of you to show my girls the drill, Lieutenant."

"Would you care to join us?" the lieutenant asked, taking a step in his direction.

"I've seen quite enough, thank you," Father replied with an innocuous smile. "And now we must beg your leave, for we must be getting on before the rains come again."

On the way home in the *gharri,* Mother stared straight ahead with hands clasped. By the time they passed the railway works, Father was sending puzzled glances her way. She excused herself to her chamber once inside, saying she intended to take a nap.

"Your mother never naps," Father said, peering up the empty staircase as her footfalls faded in the landing.

"Do you think she's ill, Father?" asked Jewel, too young to notice the undercurrents swirling below the surface of the adults' behavior.

"The humidity," Catherine suggested for Jewel's benefit. While Father's remarks at the table grated in her mind like fingernails against a chalkboard, she tried to swallow her anger. It was frustrating not to give it vent, but she would soon be enmeshed in the routine of University again, and Lieutenant Elham's smile would fade from her memory. What if she poured harsh words upon her father, and then he contracted malaria or some other fatal tropical disease while they were two weeks apart?

The headstone in Saint Thomas's churchyard looked as if it had just left the stone carver's table. Not like those surrounding it, weathered by monsoons and the overbearing sun. Catherine reached out, touched the cold granite, and murmured, "If only I could take back what I said!"

Her very-much-alive father's voice penetrated the daydream. "I should see to her," he was saying, and when Jewel moved to follow, he shook his head. "Stay with your sister."

"But—"

"She'll be all right," Catherine reassured her, and motioned toward the parlor. "Why don't we play draughts? I'll be the red this time."

They started the game, but Jewel looked up at Catherine as if trying to decide whether to speak.

"Well, what is it?" Catherine asked after the fourth such look.

The girl hesitated, moved her draughts piece, and said, "Lieutenant Elham will be sad when you leave too. I think he was in love with you."

Catherine gave her a loving smirk. "Oh, you do?"

"I could just tell by the way he looked at you." The narrow shoulders shrugged. "And he smiled at you a lot."

"He smiled at you more."

Jewel sighed, rolling her green eyes. "Catherine, people aren't as shy about smiling at children."

"Jewel?"

Both heads turned toward the doorway, where Father stood. "Fetch your mother a glass of water, please."

"Yes, Father," Jewel said.

He patted the top of her head as she passed, then walked over to take the chair she had vacated. "Your mother says I behaved boorishly today."

His expression begged contradiction, but the resentment Catherine had pushed aside came welling to the surface again. "He was only being courteous, Father."

He winced. "I know."

"Would you have preferred it if he had acted rudely and ignored me?"

"Truthfully?"

"Father . . ."

"You're too innocent to understand how these soldiers long for the company of eligible English women, Catherine. Lieutenant Elham seemed a decent sort, but there are countless opportunists wearing scarlet coats these days."

"And so being in the Army automatically makes one an opportunist?"

"Of course not." He blew out a breath, ran a hand through his greying brown hair, and tempered his voice. "Can you fault me for wanting a man to court you for your character and goodness, and not because his options are limited by society?"

"I can't imagine your wanting *any* man to court me."

"Is that what you think?" he asked, giving her a wounded look. "I look forward to the day my daughters are happily wed, Catherine. Nothing will make me happier than when the right men come along."

Such earnestness tempered some of Catherine's resentment. And there was the matter of her having only three days remaining. Not enough time for the most whirlwind of courtships, even if Jewel's assessment of the man was correct.

"Can you ever forgive me?" he asked.

She reached over the board, touched the back of the hand absently rolling a black draughts piece upon its edge. "You're a good father."

His grey-green eyes were pensive. "I realize I'm overbearing at times."

"Not *all* times. You don't scold me over my marks."

He chuckled. "Yours are higher than mine were. If my students only knew how your Uncle Daniel had to tutor me all the way through college."

They smiled across at each other, and then he turned serious again.

"Had I the opportunity to do it all over again, I would treat the young man differently."

And so with the memory of his words, Catherine felt no guilt over accepting the envelope Mrs. Jennings handed her on the promenade deck of the S.S. *Heron* on the fifth of August, when Bombay had faded to a speck on the watery horizon.

"It's from Lieutenant Elham," Mrs. Jennings said, though Catherine already knew. "He brought it by yesterday evening."

"Would you mind if I . . . ?" Catherine began.

"Of course not," Mrs. Jennings said, smiling.

Their cabin was less roomy because of the two crates of mangoes they were bringing back—each fruit wrapped in a sheet of newspaper. But there was ample room to pull a chair over to the porthole light and read.

> *Dear Miss Rayborn,*
> *It was an honor to make your acquaintance on Tuesday past. I only wish we could have spoken longer.*

Diplomatically he did not mention her father's statement at the lunch table. He wrote on to tell her of himself, describing his duties in the infantry and his family background—his father was a blacksmith in Spennymoor, and his mother kept house. He had an older brother, married, and two younger sisters, one the organist at Saint Edmund's in nearby Sedgefield.

"You were right, Father," Catherine murmured dryly. "He certainly sounds like an opportunist."

He also professed to enjoy poetry, particularly Keats . . . *but ever since I was commissioned into the Army, I cannot read 'Ode to a Nightingale' without a lump in my throat.*

I wish Milly could meet you, she thought, but then discarded the idea. Milly was just too beautiful. Just because she was a loyal friend did not prevent a young man's eyes from making comparisons. That evening when Catherine discovered that a lecturer on British Literature at Owens College was one of the eight people sharing the dinner table with her and Mrs. Jennings, she asked if he was familiar with the poem.

The old man smiled, set down his fork, and began to recite.

> *"My heart aches, and a drowsy numbness pains*
> *My sense, as though of hemlock I had drunk . . ."*

By the time he was halfway though the seventh stanza, the lump of which Lieutenant Elham wrote had found a place in Catherine's throat.

". . . Perhaps the self-same song that found a path
Through the sad heart of Ruth, when, sick for home,
She stood in tears amid the alien corn . . ."

Catherine blinked tears from her own eyes. *He's homesick,* she thought. *How sad.*

And how touching. She reread the letter by lamplight just before bedtime.

"Do you plan to write him back?" Mrs. Jennings asked from her berth, where she sat propped on pillows with Henry James's *The Portrait of a Lady.*

"Yes," Catherine replied. She could post her letter from Aden, the first port of call. It was her duty, with him serving Queen and Country far from home.

And he did have that nice smile, she reminded herself.

Fourteen

"Why, yes," Sir Ronald Hill replied to Sidney's inquiry at the Club on Monday the eighth. They sat adjacent to each other and near an open window, for the August heat was as severe upon the upper-crust Londoners as the lower. "I'm doing quite well with Montreal Rolling Steel. Are you thinking of purchasing some shares?"

"I'm leaning in that direction," Sidney said, elbows propped upon the arms of a leather chair.

"Why don't you follow me home? I'll show you the percentages in my ledger."

It was the old *quid pro quo* practiced in the Club. Last year Sidney had shared with Sir Ronald the knowledge he had gained of G Costa & Company food exporters, and they were both starting to reap decent profits from those investments.

His coach trailed Sir Ronald's barouche into the mews behind Charles Street in Mayfair. In the garden, hollyhocks, roses, and delphiniums wilted under the unrelenting sun. Two young girls and a boy ceased tossing a ball with a nursemaid in black-and-white to squint at them with hands shielding eyes.

"Papa!" one of the girls cried, breaking from the game and advancing with dark curls flying. The other children were at her heels. The nursemaid folded her arms and smiled indulgently. Beset by all three, Sir Ronald lifted each child up one at a time and submitted to kisses upon his smiling bearded face.

"What do you think of children?" Sidney asked Roseline Dell late that evening at Palermo's. She ate heartily after a performance at the Strand

Theatre, her knife sawing through one slice of steak as her painted mouth chewed another.

"Children?" she said, her little pearl teeth barely pausing from their work on the steak. "I like Eric, the stage manager's brat. He runs errands for me, and sees that I've always a filled tumbler offstage. But should I ever have children, I would want girls. Boys are too plain. You can dress girls up in velvet and fine lace, curl their hair, and teach them to dance."

Sidney slanted a bemused look at her. "Everything's for show, isn't it?"

Her blond ringlets bounced with her shrug. "And you're one to speak of showing off?"

It was so, he reckoned, so he picked up his fork and resumed his *Cannelloni della Casa*. While Roseline filled the void Leona had left, he would never have been interested in her if she did not turn the heads of other men while hanging on to his arm.

And it mattered little what she thought of children, for as much as she amused him, she was not suitable wife material. He would not sully his father's name by giving it to a burlesque actress. Besides, he would never be sure if she were faithful to him, therefore he would never be certain if the children were really his. And she was too self-absorbed to devote herself to children, the way mothers were supposed to do.

Beauty without grace is a hook without bait, someone had written. Emerson, he thought. It certainly applied to Roseline. But as he didn't think himself ready yet to be caught, he didn't mind so much the absence of bait.

And yet on the heels of that thought came the memory of Sir Ronald's pleased expression. What must it be like, to return home every day like a prince to one's own cozy little kingdom? To know that one's own bloodline would be carried forth in the veins of another generation? *Legitimately carried forth*, he reminded himself with a thought for the infant Leona must have delivered by now.

Roseline's throaty voice broke into his reverie.

"Are you listening at all, Sidney?"

"I beg your pardon?"

With an aggrieved sigh, she said, "I asked what's got your mind so busy."

He smiled across at her. "I was just telling myself how beautiful you are."

"Liar," she growled, but grinning so that some of the little pearl teeth were exposed. "Do order me another steak, will you, love?"

On the following morning, workers from the London Telephone

Exchange made the final line connections on Cannonhall Road. The first call Sarah Doyle placed was to Blake Shipping.

"I can hear you very clearly, Mr. Mitchell," Sarah said into the telephone mouthpiece. "Can you hear me?"

"As if you were just up the street," came the voice through the receiver. "Welcome back to the nineteenth century, Mrs. Doyle."

Sarah nodded at Naomi, seated at the other end of the parlor sofa. On the floor near Mrs. Blake's piano, Danny stacked blocks to form a haphazard tower. At three, he had figured out that the marble floor made a more secure surface than carpets for his building projects. Hector the cat, stretched out across the keyboard lid, watched lazily through narrow slits, not a muscle flinching when the blocks crashed to the floor.

"It's good to be back, Mr. Mitchell," Sarah said. "And do please tell young Mr. Mitchell I look forward to hearing his report tomorrow."

"I assume the *Servia* didn't sink," Naomi said, looking up from the winter cap she was knitting for Bethia.

"*And* reached speeds of over seventeen knots," Sarah said. "Can you imagine?"

Avis, collecting teacups and saucers from the tea table, shook her head. "Beggin' your pardon, Missus, but I don't see how a steel ship stays afloat."

"It's the principle of displacement, Avis. The ship is lighter than the amount of water it takes the place of."

"Um-hmm," Avis said with a blank look in her owlish eyes. Sarah smiled and scanned the room for something with which to illustrate. The dull clinks of wood against marble got her attention.

"I'm going to build a big castle," Danny said aloud to himself.

Sarah walked over to her half brother and got down to her knees, propping herself against the heels of her slippers. "May I borrow two, Danny?"

He looked uncertain, but placed two in the palm of her right hand. She turned to face Avis. "Let's imagine one of these is made of water, and the other of steel. Which would be the heaviest?"

"Why, the steel one, Missus," Avis replied warily. "Yes?"

"Very good. And so it would naturally sink in water. But . . . if you were to hammer this steel block into a thin sheet, and then turn up the sides to form a boat, the whole thing would take up a whole lot more room. Agreed?"

Avis looked at Naomi, who nodded back.

"Of course, Missus," the maid said.

"And if you could somehow construct a boat of water the same size, the water boat would weigh far more. Can you imagine why?"

The long-case clock ticked twelve silent seconds, thirteen, while Avis stood with tray in hands and lips pursed. Even Danny ceased stacking blocks, as if anxious to hear her reply.

At the fourteenth tick the maid smiled. "Because the insides of the steel boat would just be air. But as you can't go hammerin' water into a sheet, the water boat would have to be *all* water."

"And air is less dense than water," Sarah said, smiling. "You have it!"

"Who has what?" came from just inside the doorway as Sarah's father entered the room. Under his arm were his Tourograph Field Camera and stand, his fiftieth birthday present from Sarah and William two years ago.

"Avis understands the principle of displacement," Sarah told him.

"Good for you, Avis," Father said.

"Thank you, Sir," she said with a pleased flush and carried the tray from the room.

"Time to go to the zoo?" Danny asked.

"Yes, dear, we're going to the zoo," Naomi replied, tucking her knitting back into its basket. To Sarah's father she said, "Bethia asked if Guy could come along, so I gave her permission to invite him. Do you mind?"

"Of course not." Father turned to Sarah. "Are you sure you won't join us?"

"Thank you," she told him. "But I'm going to be lazy today."

And there were too many mothers with children at the zoo. Sarah did not begrudge any woman her maternal joys, but there were days when the longing to join their ranks was too much.

While her father carried the camera equipment, Sarah took Danny's other small hand and helped Naomi guide him toward the landing. He was at the age where he balked at being carried, but did not mind assistance on the staircase. Just outside the stables and carriage house, Bethia and Guy stood with a picnic basket on the gravel between them, watching Stanley check the traces connecting Comet and Daisy to the six-seater open phaeton. Shocks of brown hair were beginning to loose themselves from the wetting-down Guy's mother had given them.

Presently the five were seated, with camera equipment and picnic basket at their feet. Sarah returned their waves until the carriage turned from the drive onto Cannonhall Road. Hoofbeats and wheel rumblings were fading as she started again for the house.

The garden was like an impressionist's painting of light and shadow and texture—a half-acre profusion of flower beds and trellises, shrubberies, vegetable patch, and shade trees. A cobblestone path bordered with jonquils, bluebells, and forget-me-nots meandered out to a set of benches under an ancient apple tree, then out to a sunken stone pool—where a stone angel stared pensively down at a half dozen goldfish huddled on the shady side. Framing this natural work of art was a stone wall draped in the vines of a clematis.

Paradise, she thought, and immediately felt a pang of guilt.

Why isn't it enough? Thousands in the world would trade places with her. Through the labor and dreams of someone she had never met, Mr. Blake, she had inherited beautiful surroundings, financial security, a worthy occupation. She was loved by her husband and the people in her life. Saint Paul wrote of contentment from a prison cell. Why couldn't she be more like Saint Paul and less like Eve, who, when given everything, still wanted more?

Penny Russell, pegging out the wash on the line by the west wall, waved. "Good of them to take Guy along!"

Sarah called back, "He's good company!"

Baby Lottie's wide eyes peeked above the rim of the basket near her mother's feet. By paying a call to Saint Matthew's Foundling Home, she and William could have a child just as adorable within a fortnight. *If that's what is in your plan for our lives, Father, please take away this longing to bear a child in my own womb.*

"Mr. Doyle on the telephone for you, Missus," parlormaid Claire said from the back door, just as Catherine stepped onto the terrace. The hazel eyes studied her face as she held open the door. "Are you unwell?"

"I'm fine," Sarah said, smiling to prove it, for any sympathy at all would send her spiraling back into self-pity.

She had once asked Claire how she could reconcile herself to having borne no children. *Helping rear fourteen sisters and brothers took the longing for them out of me,* was her frank reply. *I was ready for some peace. And Mr. Duffy, well, he's always had his garden.*

"So, we're back in the nineteenth century," William said over the receiver.

"Mr. Mitchell said the same thing when I called him earlier," Sarah told him and added silently, *How did you know how much I needed to hear your voice right now?*

"Did everyone get off to the zoo?"

"Just minutes ago."

"Well, I've a call to make at noon on Highgate—a chemist has suspicions over a case of liver tonic he bought. If you can bear a late lunch, I'll come for you at about one and we'll nip over to Spaniard's."

Sarah smiled. "I was going to ask Trudy just to send me up a sandwich. The Spaniard's and your company sound much better."

She replaced the receiver in a much better frame of mind. She read the *Times* in the chair near the window, then went upstairs to ask Marie to arrange the blond hair hanging limp past her shoulders. The lady's maid crafted a long braid, then twisted it into a coil anchored with pins.

"You should wear your sea-green silk," Marie suggested, walking over to the wardrobe. "How often do you meet your husband for lunch?"

A soft knock sounded. "Come in," Sarah said.

Mrs. Bacon entered, calling-card tray in hand. "I'm afraid Mrs. Pearce is in the sitting room."

"Mrs. Pearce, you said?" Sarah asked, clinging to a thread of hope that she had misheard.

Thick spectacle lenses magnified the regret in Mrs. Bacon's eyes. "And the children are with her."

"Oh dear." Mentally Sarah raced from room to room. "The nursery—"

Mrs. Bacon jangled the chain of keys clasped to her apron. "Locked."

Sarah blew out a breath. At least Bethia's and Danny's toys were safe.

"And we must lock the parlor," Marie advised.

The housekeeper blinked. "The parlor?"

"The telephone. A boy in the house where Nicolette works was caught ringing people and barking like a dog."

"The chess board is set up in there too," Sarah remembered aloud. "William and Father didn't finish their game Saturday."

"I'll see to the parlor," Mrs. Bacon said.

"What about Hector? Should we put him away somewhere?"

"The cat will protect itself," Marie said. "It would be more simple to lock the children up, I think. You have only to send word that you are not able to receive guests."

The thought was tempting. And Sarah would certainly have no qualms over doing so if the guests waiting in the parlor were not Aunt Virginia's sister, and Catherine and Jewel's cousins. One had to be mindful of family feelings, even when not related by blood. And if she entertained them now, it would probably be months before they called again. Receiving them now would spare Naomi, who was so nervous in the Pearce children's company that she kept Bethia and Danny close at hand. "I can't do that. But surely they won't stay long, with Father and Naomi away."

Marie blew out a breath. "Then you must at least put on a bonnet in the hopes she will take the hint."

"Good idea," Sarah said, waiting for Marie to pin on the straw hat with a simple maroon velvet ribbon about the crown. Were it not August, she would have worn a cloak to convey a stronger hint. Outside the sitting room she paused to pray under her breath, *Father, help me to be gracious.*

"Mrs. Rayborn!" Mrs. Pearce exclaimed, rising from the settee. "I'm simply green with envy! This house is more beautiful than I imagined!"

"Thank you, Mrs. Pearce," Sarah said, moving across the carpet to offer her hand. "How do you do?"

Eleven-year-old twins Bernard and Douglas, clad in identical blue sailor suits, did not turn from the window overlooking the heath to acknowledge her entrance. Eight-year-old Muriel stood facing the locked case holding Grandmother's collection of Oriental dolls.

"The better for seeing you," Mrs. Pearce replied. The ethereal looking brown eyes moved up to her hat. "Oh dear, were you leaving?"

"Not until one o'clock. Mr. Doyle is taking me to lunch."

Sarah repented mentally when she realized her mistake by giving the exact time. *Lunch* to most people meant *noon,* two hours from now instead of three. But there was nothing she could do about that now. "Do please have a seat."

"And do forgive my popping in unannounced this way," Mrs. Pearce said, smoothing her skirts as she settled again upon the settee. "But with your not having a telephone . . ."

"We have one now. Just this morning. But I'm afraid Father and Naomi are not here."

"Yes, your housekeeper informed me they took the children to the zoo."

Sarah slipped into a chair and looked at Avis, standing to the side of the doorway. "Avis, please bring tea. Or would you children prefer lemonade?"

"Lemonade," a twin barked from the window. The other grunted something that sounded like agreement.

"Nothing for me, if you please," Muriel said, turning to give Sarah a dimpled smile. Lace pantaloons peeked from beneath the hem of her ruffled pink dress. "May I hold a doll?"

"No, dear," Mrs. Pearce said.

The child looked so disappointed that Sarah smiled at her and said, "They belonged to my grandmother, so they're very special to me."

"I would be very careful."

"Of course you would. But some are very old, so they're best kept where they are. My sister's not even allowed to play with them."

"That's because Bethia's only four."

"Muriel . . ."

The violet eyes sent Mrs. Pearce a hard look, but the girl didn't press.

"They eat with sticks, the Chinese," she murmured to the porcelain faces behind the glass.

The boys migrated to the table, upon which sat a model clipper ship that had once belonged to the Blakes. "It's very fragile," Sarah said, easing to the edge of her chair. The ship had already been repaired once at Berkeley Square, after Danny knocked it and its glass case over during his climbing days. A shard had cut his little hand, which was probably why no one had gotten around to purchasing a new case.

"Look, boys, but mustn't touch," Mrs. Pearce said, twisting in her seat to speak to them. She turned again to Sarah. "You really should put it under glass, you know, if only for the dust."

The twins traded grins behind their mother's back. Giving Sarah a smirk, one slowly brought his index finger to within an inch of the muslin mainsail. Not to be outdone, the other made a great show of touching the foremast. Heat rose to Sarah's cheeks. She had known only one other set of twins personally in her life, David and Reuben Rothschild, now at Oxford. They were fine fellows, and so their company was a pleasantry multiplied by two. With the Pearce twins, the opposite was the case.

"Really, boys . . ." she said benignly but firmly. "That ship is an heirloom."

Mrs. Pearce turned, waving a hand at them. "Get away from it!"

"There's nothing to *do* here," one whined.

"Then go out to the garden." Mrs. Pearce turned to Sarah again. "Do you mind?"

"Of course not," Sarah replied as her nerves unwound a bit. "We'll send their refreshments out to them. The badminton net is set up too—you'll see the rackets and shuttlecocks in a basket on the terrace."

"Muriel?" said one twin from the door.

Muriel turned from the doll case. "May I stay?"

"If you wish," Mrs. Pearce replied, extending an arm. As her brothers clamored through the door, the girl walked over to the settee, dropped into the cushions, and leaned against her mother.

"Has Virginia written to you that we're leaving London?" Mrs. Pearce asked.

"Leaving?" Sarah sat a little straighter. "For how long?"

"Sun Insurance Company is founding a branch in Sheffield, and Mr. Pearce has been asked—"

"I want to go outside now," Muriel cut in, sitting up.

Mrs. Pearce smiled at her daughter and fondled a golden curl. "Very well, dear. Mind you stay with your brothers. And don't overexert yourself."

When the girl was gone, Mrs. Pearce said, "She played in the sun too long yesterday and has a tiny bit of fever. But as I was saying . . . it's quite a move up the career ladder for Mr. Pearce. Not that we're desperate for increased wages, what with the inheritance from my parents. But you know how men are about their jobs."

"I do at that," Sarah said. "Please congratulate him for us."

"I will, thank you." Mrs. Pearce hesitated, then added, "The children are eager for the change. They aren't fond of their schools and think it will be a grand adventure to be tutored. But as for me, even though we moved to Belgrave Square little more than a year ago, I've made such good friends. I fear I'll be terribly lonely."

Sarah could not help but feel sympathy. Sympathy and admiration, that Mrs. Pearce would make such a sacrifice for her husband's sake. "You'll make new friends, Mrs. Pearce. Perhaps you should think of this as a grand adventure too."

When the woman gave her an uncertain look, Catherine went on. "A new world to discover. Twenty years from now you may even look back and tell yourself it was the wisest thing you ever did."

Mrs. Pearce pursed her lips in thought. "I confess that notion never crossed my mind, but I'll certainly try to look at it that way." She brightened and smiled. "And our new house will seem more a home once we're there with all our belongings. I'm so glad we stopped by. I really do feel better."

"I'm glad," Sarah said, returning her smile.

Avis wheeled in the tea trolley, and Sarah asked her to bring the children's lemonades outside. After the maid left, Mrs. Pearce said, "As for my unannounced visit, we're having a garden party on Sunday the twenty-first. A farewell to all our friends. You'll receive an invitation via post next week, but I do want to impress upon you how much I hope you and your family will attend."

There was nothing Sarah could do but accept the invitation so graciously extended, especially considering the occasion. And she imagined the Pearce children would be far less taxing upon the nerves in their own arena, with any misbehaviors directed toward their own property.

"Very good!" Mrs. Pearce clasped her slender hands together. "I'm overjoyed! *And* I must warn you that I plan to steal Catherine away from you for a little while. Virginia's most recent letter says she's eager to stay a couple of days with us."

"But of course." Sarah poured the two cups, sipped her tea, and made the appropriate sympathetic sounds as her guest described the turmoil that packing had put the household into. When the clock struck eleven and the children still played outside, Sarah was feeling quite magnanimous. "Would you care for a tour of the house?"

Mrs. Pearce brightened, setting her cup and saucer on the silver tray on the tea table. "I wanted to ask, but feared with your leaving for lunch—"

Sarah rose. "We have time."

It was on their way down the corridor that she remembered the parlor and nursery rooms were locked. In front of those doors, she simply tried the knobs, gave her guest a bemused smile, and moved on. She caught no sight of Hector, and reckoned the same survival instincts that made him an excellent mouser served him well in other areas too.

Fifteen

"We'll give you another day," Roger Duffy mumbled as his big soil-stained fingers gently released the Sim's Mammoth Tomato. But its brother, sharing the same vine, was the perfect deep red, so he picked it and placed it in his basket, atop those he had gathered from the first row of the vegetable patch.

He stepped outside every day in awe that he, of all men, should be so privileged to be allowed to coax living things out of the soil. On mornings such as this one he felt especially blessed. Breezes flitted about from all directions, carrying to his appreciative nose the slightly musty aroma of figs one minute, sweet roses the next, and every now and again, freshly turned dirt—from where Trudy's sixteen-year-old nephew, Jack Woodley, planted a bed of autumn-flowering Guernsey lilies near the dovecote.

The sounds were pleasant too. The *chip-chip-chip, tell-tell-tell, cherry-erry-erry, tissy-chee-wee-oo* from a chaffinch perched upon a wire cucumber trainer just five rows down, the dull scrapes of the shovel, the clicking of the mower from the Morlands' garden, the faint whistled notes of "Alice Grey" from the Pearces' coachman in the carriage drive, and the laughter of children from the terrace. They weren't from the Rayborn children or little Guy Russell, who could be easily coaxed into sitting on an upturned pail and playing the harmonica, but the happiness in their voices was pleasant to his old ears.

He moved down the row, and had just started a third when a childish voice said, "Are those apples?"

There was a fluttering of wings as the chaffinch took flight. Roger turned slowly because of the catch in his back. A girl stood staring at him. Though they had only visited twice at Berkeley Square that he could recall, he was aware of who the Pearces were; relatives of Mr. James Rayborn's wife. The children had not addressed him during those two visits, but then, he couldn't fault them for that, with his fierce black brows and wild grey beard. And so he arranged his heavy features into as pleasant an expression as possible. "No, child, they're tomatoes. Apples grow in trees."

"I lost a tooth in an apple once."

Roger chuckled. "Well, no tomato never snatched anybody's teeth. Is there no vegetable patch in your garden?"

"No. Cook buys them at market. Father has them with his eggs sometimes. I don't like them."

"Well, now, there's different sorts of tomatoes."

When she gave him a blank look, Roger nodded toward the row of Sutton's Dessert Tomatoes, shining like greenish-orange jewels in the sunlight. "Ever have a plum tomato?"

She stepped over to the row he was motioning toward and gingerly stretched out a finger to touch the skin. "I don't think so. May I taste one?"

"They ain't quite ripe, but if you've patience, you'll have yourself a fine treat." Roger set the basket down in the valley between rows and walked over to the potting shed. She was still waiting when he returned with a small lard pail, and she watched him twist a dozen tomatoes from their stems.

"Mind, you'll just have to get someone to set them in a window for three or four days."

"Thank you," she said and started to leave, but then paused in mid-turn to give him a worried look. "What if I eat one before it's completely ripe?"

"Why, you'll know when it's ripe." He picked up one from his basket. "It'll be red. Like this one."

"I brought up my eggs this morning." She put a hand up to her neck and grimaced. "I don't want to do that again. It hurts."

"Poor mite. Green tomatoes ain't tasty, but they won't make you ill like that—unless you fill your stomach with 'em. Or unless you're a horse."

"A horse?"

"Aye. They'll give a horse colic, could even kill 'em." He narrowed his eyes in mock suspicion. "But you ain't a horse, are you?"

She smiled at his joke, shaking her head.

"Well, that's good." He returned her smile, touched the brim of his felt hat, and turned his attention back to his tomatoes. When his basket was filled, he set it under the shade of a leafy turnip plant and stepped over to the three bare rows where he had sown a winter crop of spinach. "There's a good little fellow," he said, when the bit of green he knelt to inspect was indeed a sprout of spinach and not a weed.

The sounds of splashes and not-so-pleasant laughter met his ears. He turned on one knee. The two look-alike boys stood at the goldfish pond with badminton rackets, striking the water with ax-like motions.

His knees creaked as he pushed himself to his feet to hurry over. Jack, in the distance, watched with dirt-heaped shovel in midair. "You mustn't do that!" Roger yelled, and again. After the third time one of the boys heard him, stopped, and said something to his brother. By the time Roger reached them they were panting and grinning, soaked to the gills in their blue sailor suits.

"We didn't hurt the fish," one boy said. "They're too fast."

"Aye, but you're scaring 'em, and that ain't nice." Helplessly Roger looked westward. No sign of the coachman, which likely meant he had ducked into the kitchen for a cup—a usual hospitality. But movement in a pink dress caught his eyes. The girl was walking toward the horses with pail crooked over one arm and a hand extended.

"My father was so fond of his library," Mrs. Pearce said, fingertips brushing the top of a leather chair as she looked about her. "But mother was never a reader. Just *Family Herald*."

"You must miss them terribly," Sarah replied. She had met Uncle James's in-laws only once, at a Christmas party he and Aunt Virginia had given four years ago.

Mrs. Pearce's alabaster face clouded. "It took the longest time for me to accept that I couldn't just pop over to—" But she stopped and leaned her head. In the silence Sarah's ears picked up sounds of commotion, growing in volume so rapidly that by the time she turned toward the door, it was opening. In the doorway Sarah caught Mrs. Bacon's anxious expression, just before one of the twins pushed past her, dragging a sobbing Muriel by the arm. The other twin and Claire followed close behind.

"He pushed Muriel down!" The first twin released his sister's arm so she could run for her mother.

"Pushed her?" Mrs. Pearce clutched Muriel to herself and glared at the second twin. Over the girl's wails, she said, "What have I told you about mistreating your sister, Bernard?"

"Not me! That old man outside!"

"The gardener!" Douglas piped.

For a couple of seconds Mrs. Pearce stood there as if trying to absorb his meaning. Then she turned a somber face to Sarah. "Mrs. Doyle?"

"That's impossible," Sarah said.

"My husband has never struck anyone," Claire said with hands clasped in front of her so hard that the knuckles were white.

Sarah nodded. "There has to be some mistake."

"We saw it all, Mother!" one twin exclaimed.

That settled it for Mrs. Pearce. "If you will direct me to your telephone, Mrs. Doyle, I will ring my husband. And the police."

"Please," Mrs. Bacon said. "At least allow Mr. Duffy to explain."

"What more is there to explain?" Mrs. Pearce said tightly. "When a grown man assaults a child . . ."

"Please, Mrs. Pearce," Sarah coaxed, taking a step closer. "We should see what he has to say."

They walked the staircase in tense silence, save Muriel's whimpering and her mother's soothings. Outside, Mr. Duffy, Mrs. Pearce's coachman, and Jack were gathered around the Pearces' horses. Mr. Duffy looked over his shoulder and limped toward them.

"What's wrong with his leg?" Sarah said to everyone in the vicinity as she hurried across the terrace.

"He's the one, Mother!" came a boyish voice from behind. "And I kicked him in the shin for it!"

The Pearces' coachman sprinted toward them, passing Mr. Duffy. He was a compact man with sandy hair and cheeks that were flushed. "The horses are all right, Missus," he said, panting.

Mrs. Pearce squinted past him. "What have the horses to do with this?"

"Your girl here tried to give 'em these," Mr. Duffy said when he caught up with the group. He held out a lard pail filled with greenish-orange tomatoes. "That blue roan almost had one in its teeth. Alst I did was take her by the arm—I didn't intend to make her fall."

"I didn't know they would hurt them!" Muriel sobbed, burying her face in her mother's arms.

Mr. Duffy turned a stunned face to Sarah. "I told her they would when I gave 'em to her, Missus."

"Muriel?" Mrs. Pearce said with a shade of uncertainty in her tone.

"Mr. Duffy is an honest man, Mrs. Pearce," Sarah pressed.

The girl look up at her mother, tears trembling from her long lashes. "He's lying, Mother. He said nothing of the sort. He's just a hateful old troll!"

"And he shouted at us at the fish pond," one twin said while the other bobbed his head.

Hurt and helplessness settled upon Mr. Duffy's craggy features. "I wouldn't harm no child."

Sarah moved over to touch the back of his big work-hewn hand, recalling the comforting feel of her small hand in his so many years ago when they learned the Rothschilds' baby had died.

"Tell me, Mrs. Pearce," she said. "Do hateful old trolls give gifts to children?"

But Mrs. Pearce was pressing a hand against the child's forehead. "She's still warm. Small wonder she forgot." Her eyes moved from face to face, like a lioness searching for the most defenseless gazelle in the herd. They found their target.

"And where were *you* all this time, Jim?"

Her coachman colored deeper and motioned toward the carriage house with a shoulder. "In the . . . privy, Missus."

She looked disappointed and raised her chin. "Well, then . . . get the door."

"Yes, Missus." He spun on his heel, sending Mr. Duffy a regretful look before jogging off toward the coach.

"Thank you for showing me your home, Mrs. Doyle." Mrs. Pearce's tone was reservedly civil. She ignored Mr. Duffy. "Come, children."

The parade of Pearces left the terrace with Mrs. Pearce holding Muriel's hand and the twins at the rear, attempting to elbow each other off the cobbled path. Sarah watched with heart pounding against her ribs, then happened to look again at Mr. Duffy. He was staring at the ground in front of him, lips slack and soil-colored eyes faded with resignation.

You have to say something, she told herself.

"Mrs. Pearce?" she called.

The group halted at the coach's open door, turning to watch her advance.

"Your children owe Mr. Duffy an apology."

Mrs. Pearce blinked. "I beg your pardon?"

Stopping six feet away, Sarah said, "He was only showing Muriel a kindness. And he probably saved your horses. He doesn't deserve such abuse."

The wary expressions on the children's faces turned into triumph as their mother replied, "I sorely regret that the misunderstanding happened, Mrs. Doyle. But as there was wrong on both sides, I see no need for apology."

"Wrong on both sides? And how is that?"

"Granted, Muriel should have remembered what she was told, and

Bernard should not have resorted to violence—even though he was defending his sister. But your gardener should have used some restraint. Muriel could have been seriously injured, being pushed in such a way."

Frustration quickened Sarah's pulse. "But he didn't—"

"My children say otherwise."

"Your children did not tell the truth."

"A mother can tell when her children are telling the truth, Mrs. Doyle. If you had any of your own, you would understand."

The pity in Mrs. Pearce's tone, the superiority in her expression, were too much. Sarah's temples throbbed. Taking another step forward, she said, "When I have some of my own, I will pray to God that I'm not so foolish over them as you are yours!"

The woman gasped, her porcelain cheeks stained crimson. "How dare you!" Mrs. Pearce sputtered, the "ethereal" of her eyes burned up by rage. She herded her children into the coach as if she feared Sarah would lunge, calling over her shoulder, "You may consider the invitation to our party withdrawn!"

The coachman closed the door behind them and scampered up into the box. Sarah fought an impulse to sprint over to the window and inform Mrs. Pearce that she wouldn't attend their party for all the money in the bank. She was restrained by the sight of Penny Russell's face between the curtains above the stables. Other curious eyes probably watched from the house windows. As the coach rumbled up the drive with wheels snapping gravel, she returned to the group near the terrace. Claire stood at her husband's side, a hand resting upon his broad shoulder.

"Mr. Duffy, I'll telephone Doctor Lloyd to look at your leg," Sarah told him.

He raised his left leg and swung it from the knee. "Just a bruise, Missus. It's better already."

"I'm glad." Her pulse began slowing, and she realized how drained of energy she felt. "And I'm sorry for what my guests put you through."

"Ah, it's naught to worry yourself over, Missus."

"It isn't Christian of me to say this," Claire said, "but it did my heart good . . . hearing what you said to Mrs. Pearce."

"It felt good to say it," Sarah confessed. She shook her head. "But I should have used more tact to make my point."

"Beggin' your pardon, Missus," young Jack told her. "What you said was nothin', compared to what them boys said to Mr. Duffy. Why, it would make a fishmonger blush!"

"Really, Mr. Duffy?" Mrs. Bacon's brows raised above her spectacles. "Just what did they say to you?"

He wagged a finger at her. "Now, Mrs. Bacon . . ."

"I'm not asking you to repeat it word for word, just . . . oh, never mind. I'll ask Claire later."

"But Mrs. Duffy weren't out here," Jack reminded her.

Sarah smiled at the knowing look that passed between housekeeper and parlormaid, even as Mrs. Bacon replied, "That's so, Jack. I quite forgot."

Cloth-covered tables were laid out in the garden of The Spaniard's Inn, in the shadow of the white weatherboard building that had provided hospitality to the likes of Dickens, Reynolds, Keats, and Shelley. Locals insisted that highwayman Dick Turpin was born there almost two centuries ago, and it was a fact that his father had owned the inn for a time. Over plates of sausage and mash, Sarah related the morning's incident to her husband.

"Incredible," William said, shaking his head.

"Where do boys so young learn to swear?" Sarah asked.

"Perhaps their sister taught them."

"She's only eight, William."

Affection shone from his smoky eyes, even as he teased, "Old enough to murder horses, but too young to swear?"

Sarah mugged a face at him. "As horrible as she was, I can't allow myself to believe that was her design. You know how curious children are. Surely it was just that—wanting to see what would happen."

"Hmm. Perhaps." He looked at the untouched sausage on her plate and the small crater her fork had made in the potatoes. "Aren't you hungry?"

"Oh." She picked up her knife and sawed off a bit of sausage. But after raising it level with her chin, she returned it to her plate.

"What's the matter?"

"It smells funny," she replied. "Don't you think?"

"Mine didn't." He reached for the fork and brought the bit of sausage up to his nose. It disappeared into his mouth. "Nothing wrong with it," he said after chewing and swallowing.

"Please, take it all," she said and pushed the plate toward him. The unpleasantness with Mrs. Pearce and her children was too fresh in her memory and had robbed her of her appetite.

"Are you sure?"

"Yes." She watched him sprinkle salt onto the potatoes. "I just hate the thought of Catherine being caught in the middle of this."

"That won't happen." He shook his head. "They're her relatives, not ours. And you'll never have to see them again, so just put them from your mind."

She was able to do just that the following day, as she and the Mitchells discussed the information Harold had gleaned regarding steel-bottomed ships. But the Pearces popped into her mind again on Thursday as she hastened down the corridor for the bathroom after lunch.

"Sarah?" came Bethia's soft voice and knock.

"I may be in here a bit longer, Bethia," Sarah called, rising from her knees with cautious slowness. "Can you use the one downstairs?"

"Yes. But are you all right?"

"Of course, dear. Now run along, will you?"

A hesitation, then, "Are you quite sure you're all right?"

"Bethia, I'm fine." She washed and dried her face, and thought she could detect a pink tinge to her cheeks in the basin mirror. *Fever,* she told herself, chills prickling her arms as she took her toothbrush from the cupboard. She would have to confine herself to her chamber, away from Bethia and Danny in particular. She only hoped none of the servants who were unfortunate enough to be in Muriel Pearce's vicinity were suffering the same.

Nausea welled again, and she dropped her toothbrush into the basin.

"Madame?" Marie's voice this time.

"I don't want anyone near me, Marie," she said when she was able to speak. "Do please go away."

———————

Belle picked up speed as the runabout passed Christ Church. William Doyle switched the reins to return Admiral Kirkpatrick's salute from the other side of the low stone wall. Their neighbor seemed to spend every waking hour pottering in his garden, the topiary so geometrically precise that branches appeared to have been trimmed with a shaving razor.

And that was just fine with William. Hampstead's water was touted to be the best in London, the area having even been a popular spa a century past. He thought there must be something in that water that caused the residents to mind their own affairs. Friendly they were, but not so concerned with whether the apples on a newcomer's family tree were golden or rotten. He reckoned his and Sarah's trees had a little of both.

"*Will*-iam!"

"Mis-ter Doyle!"

Speaking of trees . . . he thought, returning the waves of Bethia and Guy, perched upon a low limb of the elm between the carriage drive and house. He called, "Mind you, hang on there!"

Stanley came out to take Belle by the bridle.

"How are you keeping, Stanley?" William asked, taking his umbrella and satchel from the seat before stepping down to the gravel drive.

"Fine, Sir." Stanley sent a worried nod toward the house. "But Mrs. Doyle's taken ill."

"Is it serious?"

"Can't say. The doctor just left."

Sarah's father came out of the parlor and met him on the landing. "Daniel," William asked, "why didn't anyone ring me?"

"She wouldn't allow it," Daniel replied.

"You should have anyway."

The older man nodded understanding. "Trust me, we would have if it were more serious. But Doctor Lloyd says a mild ague is going around, and most people stricken with it are fine after a day or so."

Still, William hurried up the stairs, propping satchel and umbrella against the wall just inside their bedchamber. The curtains were drawn against the evening sun, a lamp burned on the bedside chest. Marie and Naomi sat in chairs, Marie sewed onto a hooped canvas while Naomi knitted.

"How is she?" he asked.

"Better, we think," Naomi said. "She was able to hold down some broth an hour ago."

"But she is exhausted," Marie added. "It took all of her strength for us to walk her to the bathroom."

William walked over to the high bed. Sarah looked more the child than a businesswoman, pale lashes resting against too-white cheeks, right hand beneath the covers and left tucked beneath the thin pillow she favored. Her green eyes opened, blinked, and then rested upon him.

"Hello there," he said softly.

She gave him a weak smile, barely whispered, "William. You're here."

"Yes, I'm here, sweetheart. Now go back to sleep."

She made a slight nod and closed her eyes.

Heal her please, Father, he prayed, heart swelling within his chest. Mild ague might be nothing to worry over, as everyone seemed to think. But as scarlet fever had taken the lives of his parents and infant brother, he did not take any rise in temperature lightly. Especially when it concerned his wife.

"Thank you for all you've done," he said to the two women. "I'd like to sit with her now. Please have my supper sent up."

William shook his head at their offers to stay longer. When the door clicked softly behind them, he took the current issue of *The Analyst* from his satchel and sat in the chair Naomi had occupied.

"Are they gone?"

He put the magazine aside and fairly bolted from the chair.

"I thought you were asleep," he said, feeling her forehead with the back of his hand. Warm, but not hot, which gave him a rush of relief. "Shall I get them?"

"No." She turned on her pillow, drew her right hand from beneath the covers, and touched his cheek. "It was cruel of me to cause everyone worry, but I so desperately wanted you to be the first to know."

That made no sense. With sickened heart he wondered if the fever, mild as it was, was affecting her brain. "But sweetheart . . ." he said cautiously, taking the hand. "Doctor Lloyd told them before I even got here."

She shook her head. "He agreed to tell them there is a mild ague going about. Which is the truth. He never said *I* had it." Her smile faltered a fraction. "I pray God will forgive us that. While it wasn't technically lying, the intent to deceive was there."

Humor her, William thought. Why had he sent Aunt Naomi and Marie away? He didn't even think to ask them if Doctor Lloyd had given her any medicine that could account for her peculiar remarks.

"You know, I'd like Aunt Naomi to see how much better you're looking," he said, placing her hand gently back down upon the coverlet. "I'll just ring for—"

She gave a little laugh and pulled herself up a bit on her pillow. "Oh dear," she gasped, swaying a bit. He took her by the shoulders. She stared down at the coverlet, while he stood there, helplessly out of reach of the bell cord.

"Sarah?"

Presently she raised her chin and pulled in an even breath. "Better, now."

"Good." William reached across her for his pillow and propped it against her right side. "Can you manage to sit there long enough for me to ring for help?"

"We don't need help, William." Her emerald eyes caught the lamplight. "Hold me close, and I'll whisper something wonderful to you."

For a bit longer William's face held on to the perplexed, worried expression it had worn since he entered the room. And then a slow grin brought dimples to his clean-shaven cheeks. "Is it what I hope it is?"

"It is," she said, smiling back at him.

She was gathered into his arms—gently so. Resting her cheek upon her husband's shoulder and listening to his endearments, Sarah wondered if she had ever had a happier moment in her life. The wonder of it all caused her to lie awake hours later, after the household and William were wrapped in slumber. Sometime during the course of her thankfulness she reflected upon those Rachels and Hannahs still waiting with empty arms. *Pour down grace upon them, Father,* she asked. *Help me never to forget how it felt to be among their ranks.*

---

Sixteen

*U*ncle Daniel was waiting in Tilbury when Catherine disembarked at noon on Thursday, the eighteenth of August. "What has been going on?" she asked in the railway carriage moving toward Waterloo Station, their first opportunity for a chat.

"Oh, a little of this, a little of that," he replied. "Naomi and I are planning to take Bethia—which means Guy too—to the opening of the Natural History Museum on Saturday morning. We would enjoy having you with us."

"I'd like that, thank you," she told him. Londoners had been anticipating the Museum's completion for months, and news of the upcoming Grand Opening had even reached the *Times of India*. Odd, though, that he did not mention Sarah and William, when they took so many outings together. So she asked. "Will Sarah and William be along too?"

"If they wish. Now tell me all about your summer. How is the family?"

The change of subject distracted Catherine from puzzling over his enigmatic smile, but she discovered the reason for it that evening. She was unfolding the nightgown Susan had placed upon the foot of her bed, when Sarah stopped by her room.

"Everything unpacked?" her cousin asked.

"Yes, very nicely," Catherine said. She tossed the nightgown onto the bed and hurried over to move her reticule from the seat of the chair near the idle fireplace. While Sarah had never had high color, she appeared pale. Also, at supper she had passed up the seasoned roast chicken and did not finish the meager servings of buttered boiled potatoes and asparagus on her plate.

Catherine had asked Susan about it earlier, when the chambermaid came into the room with a fresh water carafe. "The Missus' appetite's been off for a few days," was the evasive reply. Susan had seemed so uncomfortable even surrendering that bit of information that Catherine hadn't pressed.

Sarah did not demur when invited to sit. "Thank you for the *saree*," she said. "William says it makes my eyes look like fresh-shelled peas."

"Peas?"

"It was a compliment. He's very fond of them."

Catherine laughed, relieved that her cousin wasn't too unwell for mirth. "You're very welcome," she said, and then became serious. "I couldn't help but notice your supper plate. Is anything the matter?"

Her cousin nodded but her smile did not fade. "That's why I'm here. I wanted you to hear it from me, because the whole household already knows. Except for the children, of course. They're too young to understand."

"Understand what?" Catherine asked when Sarah paused for breath.

But she was frustrated by her cousin's determination to deliver the whole preamble. "We would have preferred to keep it to ourselves," Sarah said. "At least until my condition became too obvious to hide. But after Doctor Lloyd came by . . ."

All Catherine could think of was some fatal illness. *How brave she is,* she thought with throat thickening. Her mind conjured a picture of Sarah's pale face staring up at her from her pillow.

"But you must return to school," Sarah was saying with strained voice.

Catherine shook her head and took up her cousin's frail fingers. "I've already written Girton that I'm sitting out the term. It's the least I can do."

"Oh dear." Sarah's voice dissolved the scene. Apology and mirth filled her eyes. "It's not what you think. We're expecting a baby."

Relief washed over Catherine, though she had not the foggiest what a baby had to do with uneaten supper. She was ten when Jewel was born, and could not recall Mother complaining of any loss of appetite or other malady. But then, she had not been told that a sister or brother was on the way until days before the birth. "A baby!" she breathed, clasping her hands. "And so you're not ill?"

"Not ill. Unless you count the constant nausea, which Naomi says will pass eventually."

"I'm so very pleased! May I write and tell Mother and Father?"

"Yes, please do that. And give them my love."

They embraced at the door, and Catherine discovered that her travel fatigue was replaced with a new vitality. She went to the writing table and composed a letter to her parents.

I have the most wonderful news! was her first sentence.

And as long as she had out pen and ink and paper, she decided to write Lieutenant Elham. Only, not much had transpired since the ten-page letter she had posted from Aden, which he should have received by now. She didn't feel right about mentioning Sarah's condition to a young man so recent to her acquaintance. But she started out with a paragraph that she hoped was witty, telling him how every discussion she had overheard from Tilbury to London had to do with the heat wave. *Everyone who complains of the heat should spend a summer in India, don't you think?*

Her mind went blank as she held her pen poised for the second paragraph. When no idea entered the void for several minutes, she blotted her pen and decided to finish tomorrow. A decent night's sleep would sharpen her mind. And sure enough, as soon as her feet slid into her slippers the next morning, she was struck with a marvelous idea.

"Didn't John Keats live in Hampstead?" she asked at the breakfast table.

"Less than a mile and a half away," Uncle Daniel replied, his fork cutting into a slice of mango. "What a treat these are, Catherine."

In the kitchen were some for the servants' breakfast, and two baskets were put aside in the pantry, which Catherine would deliver to Aunt Phyllis's family and the Somersets after breakfast. Catherine had included the latter because they were so gracious to her the three times she had visited Peggy on Saville Row. Now she was glad she had done so, for her anger at Peggy had begun dissolving soon after she read Lieutenant Elham's letter.

"I wish I could have brought you some bananas, but they would have spoiled," she told her uncle. "A mile and a half, you say?"

"East Heath Road leads directly to it," Sarah said, pulling the crusts from a piece of dry toast. "It's a private residence, but there's no harm in asking Stanley to stop by for a look at the outside.

Catherine smiled at her. "I'd like that, thank you."

"I gather you're fond of Keats?" Aunt Naomi asked. On her right, Danny used fingers and spoon to transport poached eggs from dish to mouth, in the special high chair Mr. Duffy had constructed of oak. Bethia, previous owner of the chair, sat between Sarah and Catherine, absorbing the conversation.

"I never realized it until just lately," Catherine told her. Fortunately, the lecturer aboard the S.S. *Heron* had offered to lend her a book of Keats's poetry, and during the journey Catherine drank in every metaphor. At the expense of Homer, but she still had time to catch up.

She went back up to the guest chamber to pin on a straw hat, trimmed with pink silk orchids, and a gown of burgundy and white gingham. A half hour later she stood among the lime trees bordering Albion Lane, facing the two-storey cottage where the poet, suffering from the consumption that would take his young life, penned "Ode to a Nightingale" in the spring of 1819. Her eyes drank in every window and chimney of the white building so that she could list it all in that second paragraph of a certain unfinished letter.

"She stood in tears amid the alien corn," she murmured.

She could feel Stanley's eyes upon her, and turned her face to him. "It's from a poem."

"Ah," he said, nodding. "Never cared much for corn myself."

Mrs. Somerset was a petite woman with light brown hair coiled into a topknot. She thanked Catherine effusively for the mangoes, which no one in her family had ever tasted, and insisted she stay long enough for a slice of bakery coconut cake. "Peggy'll be here tomorrow," she said, her small hands arranging teacup and cake upon a tray. "She's been studying so hard, we've rarely seen her this summer."

If she was aware of the scene that had occurred at Girton on the eve of vacation, her expression did not reveal it. "Why don't you come for lunch?"

"Thank you, but I'm afraid my uncle and aunt already have made plans for me," Catherine said, relieved to have an excuse. The minute she set foot in the apartment over the tailor's shop, she had found herself missing Peggy more than she could ever have imagined she would at the start of summer. But she wasn't certain how Peggy would feel about seeing *her*.

"Then I'll have her ring you, and you two can make your own plans," Mrs. Somerset said. "Aren't the lines through to Hampstead now?"

"They are." Catherine swallowed her bit of cake past a sudden lump in her throat. "And please do tell her I would like to speak with her very much."

She left with Mrs. Somerset's promise to do just that. The Pearces' house on 42 Belgrave Square stood amidst a row of pale stone Georgian town houses with Doric pillars flanking front doors and wrought-iron railings separating service entrances leading down to kitchens. A maid had just welcomed Catherine inside the hall when Aunt Phyllis entered with the twins and Muriel. The boys tarried at the door long enough to mumble thanks for the mangoes—under their mother's prompting—then set out for a cricket match at nearby Green Park.

Eight-year-old Muriel, on the other hand, showed uncharacteristic welcome, lunging at Catherine and wrapping her arms about her waist. "Catherine! I'm so happy to see you!"

"And I'm happy to see you too," Catherine told her.

"Mind you don't injure yourselves!" Aunt Phyllis called out the door to her sons, then backed away so the maid who had answered Catherine's ring could close it. "That's very sweet, dear, but you may turn loose of Catherine now."

The small arms tightened around Catherine's waist. "We missed you so-o-o much!"

Catherine patted her golden curls, smiling at Aunt Phyllis. "And I missed you."

"You're quite her heroine," Aunt Phyllis said, beaming. "Why, just last week over supper she said she would like to attend Girton when she's grown. Didn't you, Muriel?"

The girl nodded, cheek pressed against Catherine's ribs.

"That's quite enough, Muriel," Aunt Phyllis told her. "I'm serious."

Muriel simply craned her neck to grin up at Catherine, as the maid in the background stared at the floor. However sweet Muriel's smile, the violet eyes danced with mischievous joy of capturing the attention of all the adults in the hall.

"Muriel," Aunt Phyllis cooed. "We've tea waiting in the parlor. But we can't very well have it until you—"

"Does Jewel miss me?" the girl interrupted.

"Yes." Catherine had to fight the urge to reach down and force away the little leech's arms.

"And Uncle James and Aunt Virginia?"

"Really, Muriel . . ." Aunt Phyllis's voice was developing an edge. "Don't force me to ring your father."

If this threat intimidated Muriel, she concealed her feelings well. Aunt Phyllis tightened her lips, but an instant later sent Catherine a conspiratorial smile. *This will work,* she mouthed, stepping closer. "My, my! Who do I see sliding down a sunbeam?"

Muriel giggled and buried her face in Catherine's side again.

"I do believe the tickle fairy has come to call!"

The girl shrieked and twisted as her mother's fingers attacked her unprotected sides. Finally the grip loosened. Catherine followed mother and giggling daughter up the corridor that ran the length of the town house. She held her own arms rigid at her sides, so she could not easily be seized again. *An hour,* she told herself. *Sixty minutes.*

The parlor was a cheerful room, its walls hung with very pale violet damask and covered with sketches and paintings. Queen Anne furniture with graceful cabriole legs sat upon Brussels carpeting. Bric-a-brac and framed photographs were artfully arranged upon crocheted table scarves, and flowers spilled from a stand at the window. Catherine and Aunt Phyllis took seats upon the sofa with Muriel between them.

"I'm going to miss this room," Aunt Phyllis sighed, leaning toward the tea table to pour cups. "I've already ordered the same wallcovering for our new parlor, and I intend to make it as much like this one as possible. I believe I'll make the adjustment more easily with familiar settings here and there."

"Mother always tried to keep Jewel's and my bedrooms looking the same with each move," Catherine told her.

"Your mother and I have always thought alike. You remind me so much of her. I do hope you'll plan to spend a couple of nights with us."

"It's so kind of you to invite me," Catherine said, the only response she could give. To declare that she was looking forward to the stay would not be truthful. "But I'm afraid I've already made plans for tomorrow." Not only was there the museum visit, but she had to stay in Hampstead afterward in the hopes that Peggy would ring.

"That's just as well." Her aunt handed her a saucer and filled cup, Spode's *Blue Italian* design. "It would probably be better if you waited until after the party anyway. I'm afraid I'll not be fit company until it's over. But as we're moving into a hotel Tuesday so the rest of the furniture can be packed, you must promise us Sunday and Monday nights."

"Yes, of course." The full extent of what Catherine had just heard registered in her mind. "Party, Aunt Phyllis?"

"Why, yes. Our farewell party on Sunday afternoon. Didn't you receive the invitation? I posted it in mid—"

"Mother, you can barely see the scrape," Muriel interrupted, having endured not being the center of attention for long enough. She twisted her elbow around to show her mother, then grinned at Catherine. "Bernard dared me to climb the mimosa tree in the square. I'm not allowed to cross the street without Nanny, so Father sent him to bed without supper."

"I'm glad your arm has healed, dear," Aunt Phyllis told her. "But the adults are speaking." She looked again at Catherine.

"It must have been misdirected at one of the stops," Catherine told her.

"Well, there is no harm done, is there? I'm just glad you'll come."

From upstairs came a dull hammering. Aunt Phyllis sighed. "I'm afraid you'll have to get used to that while you're here. The servants are already crating the nonnecessities from upstairs. But we have to keep everything intact down here, just in case it rains Sunday. If this dry spell will hang on just a bit longer . . ."

"The pictures from my walls are all gone," Muriel said. "But Mamma says I may keep out some of the dolls to play with."

"It took her half a day to decide upon six," Aunt Phyllis said with a fond look at the child.

"Not half a day," the girl corrected with rolled eyes. "That's exaggerating."

"Well, a long time."

"A long time and half a day aren't the same."

"Yes, dear." Aunt Phyllis looked at Catherine. "I'll send Jim for you after lunch Sunday."

I'm sure I could ride with Sarah and the others, Catherine started to say but caught herself. Surely if her aunt had invited them, she would have made that suggestion herself. She was a little surprised at the exclusion, being that the occasion was a farewell party, but then, they did not socialize often and were not blood relations to Aunt Phyllis. "That's very kind of—"

"Our new nanny's name is *Metcalf,*" Muriel interrupted. "Lora Metcalf. It's as if you're saying 'Lora met-a-calf.' That's funny, don't you think?"

"I've told you that it's unkind to make sport of people's names, dear," Aunt Phyllis scolded gently.

"But she agrees it's funny." The girl turned again to Catherine. "I'm glad she's moving with us, because she's nicer than our other nannies were."

Or more desperate, Catherine guessed.

A glance at the Wellington clock on the chimneypiece told Catherine that the obligatory hour had passed, with five additional grace minutes. She did not know how she would bear two nights, but staying any longer today would not make them any more bearable. She set her cup and saucer on the table and started to rise. "Now I should—"

"Has Mrs. Doyle mentioned . . . anything?" Aunt Phyllis asked.

Catherine eased back into her seat. Was she referring to Sarah's pregnancy? Not certain if she had the right to carry the news outside the household to anyone not directly related, she assumed a blank expression. "Anything?"

Her aunt chewed on her lip for a second and then sighed. "I trust you'll keep this to yourself, Catherine, although I did write your mother of the . . ."

She stopped herself and cut her eyes to the child between them. Muriel, having obviously sensed that her mother's cryptic remarks signaled that the conversation was only appropriate for adult ears, sat silent as held breath.

"Muriel dear, speaking of Nanny . . . run up and see if she's finished packing your toys."

"Please let me stay, Mamma."

"Just go up there and see. You may come back down afterward."

Muriel shook her head. When her mother attempted to take her arm, she dropped chin to chest, folded her arms, and tucked her hands into the opposite armpits with such smooth motion that Catherine suspected it was not the first time the girl had employed this maneuver. After several attempts to insert a word into the midst of the arguments and pleadings and cajoling and weeping that followed, Catherine got to her feet. Aunt and cousin paused, looking up at her.

"Don't mind me, I'll show myself out." she said, leaning down to plant a quick kiss upon her aunt's flushed forehead and, as an afterthought, pat the top of Muriel's head. She kept one arm rigid again at her side, just in case the child should lunge and cling again.

"My nerves felt like ants were inside my skin," she confided to Sarah after lunch, as they sat in wicker chairs on the terrace. Doctor Lloyd had paid a visit while Catherine was at Aunt Phyllis's and insisted that Sarah spend time outside every day, heat wave or none. Uncle Daniel was inside writing, Aunt Naomi putting Bethia and Danny down for naps.

Catherine felt no qualm over criticizing her Pearce cousins, but loyalty to both sides of the family prevented her from betraying Aunt Phyllis's vague confidence. Loyalty did *not* prevent her, however, from hoping Sarah would volunteer the information. But if her cousin knew anything, her face did not betray her.

"Well, a warm bath tonight will settle your nerves," Sarah said.

"That sounds lovely." Catherine sighed. "An hour was sheer torture, Sarah. I don't know how I'll bear it over there. If Aunt Phyllis rings you searching for me, you'll know I've run off and joined a convent. Or a circus."

It was another hint, but Sarah either did not recognize it or was allowing it to fly past. "Just remind yourself that it's only temporary."

"They say the same thing to prisoners in dungeons as they tighten the rack."

Sarah smiled. "Now, you know it won't be *that* bad."

"I do?" Catherine feigned a little shudder before returning her smile. "Sorry. And I'll drop the subject, as my ranting and raving isn't going to do any good."

"If it made you feel better, it did some good," Sarah said, then changed the subject herself. "Did you and Mr. Sedgwick correspond last spring?"

Catherine shook her head. How many days had it been since he had visited her thoughts? It seemed of little use to go into detail about Peggy burning the letter. "It just wasn't meant to be. And as you pointed out once before, I hardly knew him. *But* . . . another young man did ask me to correspond."

"Yes?"

"An army lieutenant I met in Bombay," Catherine said, and smiled at how wide her cousin's eyes grew.

"A soldier? And Uncle James allowed this?"

"He and Mother were there. Jewel too. Father's behavior was beastly, now that you ask, but he apologized later. He isn't aware that we're corresponding, but then, *I* didn't even realize it when we said our farewells. But Father can hardly object, with Lieutenant Elham being thousands of miles away."

"Tell me about him."

Gladly Catherine complied. And having read Lieutenant Elham's five-page letter until the creases were felting, she had quite a lot of information to impart. "Well, his father is a blacksmith . . ."

---

Seventeen

*O*n the following morning, Catherine, Uncle Daniel and Aunt Naomi, Bethia, and Guy joined hundreds of other Londoners at the cathedral-like Museum of Natural History, peering at fossils, insect and herb collections from around the globe, and skeletons of such animals as the whale and giraffe. Afterward they had a late lunch at a café near Holland Park. While she had a lovely time, Catherine found her thoughts drifting more and more toward Peggy. What if Peggy did not wish to resume the friendship?

Her fears were put to rest at half-past four, while she was lying across her bed willing herself to concentrate on *The Iliad* instead of sending glances toward the door. She sprang to her feet at the knock.

"Miss Rayborn, you've a telephone call," Avis said after being bade to enter.

"Bless you, Avis!" Catherine said, pausing in the doorway to squeeze the surprised maid's hands. Downstairs, she crossed the empty parlor and scooped up the earpiece from where it lay on the table scarf.

"Good afternoon?" she said into the telephone.

"Catherine? Is that you?"

Hearing her friend's voice brought tears to Catherine's eyes. She gushed, "I'm so sorry I was angry!"

"Oh, Catherine . . . you had every right to be," Peggy said. "I couldn't believe it when Mother gave me your message. After what I did . . ."

"It's forgiven and forgotten, Peggy."

Silence, then, "It's haunted me all summer. I thought of writing so many times."

"Well, please don't trouble yourself over it any longer. Let's put it all behind us, shall we?"

"Thank you, Catherine."

"And thank *you* for being my friend. I can't wait to see you!"

"And I, you. It was so thoughtful of you to bring mangoes—we're enjoying them immensely. Perhaps we can ride back to Girton together. Do you plan to return soon?"

"Wednesday," Catherine told her. "And you?"

"Monday," Peggy replied, sounding disappointed. "I'm in charge of our study group, so I can't stay away for too long." Her tone lightened. "But we don't have to wait until Girton, do we? Say you'll come for tea tomorrow."

Now it was Catherine's turn for disappointment. She explained about her aunt's party.

"Then we'll simply save our catching up for later," Peggy said.

A better idea popped into Catherine's head. "I have to make another call for a minute. But please stay by the telephone."

Sure enough, Aunt Phyllis graciously said, "But of course you may invite your friend. Just direct Jim to her house when he comes for you."

". . . and his mother's African violets almost always win the blue ribbon at the village flower show," she was telling Peggy in Aunt Phyllis's coach the following afternoon, after attending Christ Church with her Hampstead kin— except for Sarah, who still feared venturing too far from the house. "He became fascinated with the military as a boy, when a regiment quartered in Spennymore, and so his mother's brother purchased his commission."

"Thank heaven for wealthy uncles and aunts." Peggy touched the pearls above the modestly scooped neck of her gown, a pale brown silk run through with sage green threads. "Or your lieutenant would be forging horseshoes, and I would be married to Oliver Piggot."

"Really! So you feel some affection for him after all?"

"Absolutely none. At least not the sort of affection that leads to marriage. But you seem to feel some of that for your lieutenant."

"Marriage? I still hardly know him, and won't see him again until next summer." Which was not to say that the idea had not entered Catherine's mind once or twice. Perhaps thrice. She was about to tell her of Lieutenant Elham's fondness for Keats, when it occurred to her that she was monopolizing the conversation. Worse, it was more monologue than conversation.

"Do forgive my selfishness, Peggy. I've not even asked about your summer."

Peggy smiled. "If you were selfish, we wouldn't have had those lovely mangoes for breakfast. But there is little to tell. We study on our own, and those of us taking the same courses have formed discussion groups. It works quite well, for we assign text readings so that no one lags behind."

Catherine could picture it all in her mind, and she felt a twinge of envy. "You're returning tomorrow?"

"Yes. I wish you were going up there with me. Are you quite sure you can't leave early?"

Catherine sighed. "I've promised to spend two nights with Aunt Phyllis, and I daren't even try to get out of it. And I planned to spend Tuesday back in Hampstead, to pack." She thought for a second. "*But* . . . there is very little to pack, actually. Sarah's servants went ahead and laundered the clothes from my trunk Friday." She raised a brow hopefully. "Do you think you might—"

"Wait until Tuesday? Of course."

"Thank you!" Catherine leaned forward and took her hands. "We'll have a wonderful year, won't we?"

"We will."

"I just wish I had read more Homer," Catherine confessed.

"You will when we get to Girton," her friend said. "I'll keep your nose to the grindstone."

"Ouch!" Catherine said, wrinkling her nose in jest. Another subject popped into her mind, or rather, three smaller ones. Should she warn Peggy what to expect?

Surely they'll be ordered to be on their best behavior, she thought. Aunt Phyllis's commands carried very little weight, but on special occasions she effectively managed to bribe them with offers of rewards. Why borrow trouble that might not even happen?

Riles the butler answered the door and directed Jim to take Catherine's portmanteau up to the guest bedroom. He escorted them to the parlor, where Uncle Norman put newspaper aside and rose from an armchair. Catherine had just started making introductions when Aunt Phyllis hurried through the doorway in a gown of pale bluish-green silk. She was not without virtues, and her chief one was an ability to make a person feel that he or she was the most important person in the room. She clasped Peggy's hand and said, "How good to make your acquaintance, Miss Somerset! Shame on Catherine for not telling us what beautiful hair you have! And those pearls, they're exquisite!"

"Thank you," Peggy replied, blushing to the roots of her red hair. "And for inviting me here."

"It's our pleasure. And I want you to know that my husband and sons buy exclusively from Somerset's. Isn't that so, Norman?"

"They do quality work," he confirmed, stepping forward to shake Peggy's hand and to smile at the kiss Catherine planted upon his cheek. He was a broad-shouldered man, almost completely bald, with a mustache as thick as a hairbrush. He wore an air of quiet competence befitting his management position at the Sun Insurance Company. But in matters pertaining to his children, he reminded Catherine of a rider who, having given up hope of grasping the reins, hangs on to the edge of the saddle for dear life.

"Bernard and Douglas are dressing," Aunt Phyllis said, as Uncle Norman returned to his newspaper. "And Muriel is napping. She's so beside herself over having guests that her nanny couldn't coax her to settle down. I had to read three chapters of a Parker book to her before she fell asleep."

"Parker book?" Peggy asked.

"The Parker Twins adventure books," Catherine explained. She had read several to Jewel before her sister could read them herself.

Aunt Phyllis narrowed a playfully shrewd eye. "You've no young siblings, Miss Somerset . . . correct?"

Peggy smiled back. "Correct, Mrs. Pearce."

"Well, the books are quite popular with the younger set. Mrs. Godfrey, the authoress, will be here today with her husband, in fact."

"You know her?" Catherine said with eyes wide.

"Why, yes. Hasn't your mother told you? She lives just on the other side of the square. We serve together on the flower committee at Saint Peter's." She looked at Catherine and sighed. "Unfortunately, her older son, Lord Holt, sent his regrets. I was hoping to introduce you. Every unmarried woman in Belgrave has her cap set for him."

"And some of the married as well, I hear," Uncle Norman said from behind raised newspaper.

"Norman . . ."

He lowered the newspaper and shrugged. "I'm just telling you what I hear."

"You can't fault a man for drawing the attention of some silly women, Norman," she said as if explaining to a small boy why he mustn't climb on the banister. "They're an upstanding family and deserve our respect."

"May we help you, Aunt Phyllis?" Catherine asked, jumping into the awkward moment.

Aunt Phyllis turned again to her and smiled. "Thank you, but now it's just a matter of making certain the servants lay the tables properly."

"We'll keep you company as soon as I've changed," Catherine said, for she had worn the blue silk to church.

"There's a good girl. Just give your dress to Rose."

Catherine led Peggy up the staircase to a guest chamber and took from her portmanteau a gown of Belgian linen in a damask-like pattern of light mauve upon cream. Susan had ironed it yesterday, so it only required a light pressing. "Won't take but a minute," Rose the chambermaid said. "The iron's already hot. And I'll take tomorrow's gown too, if you've a mind."

"Thank you," Catherine told her.

"Do I look appropriate?" Peggy asked after the maid had left with a dress over each arm.

"You look very nice," Catherine said, though she had the thought that the pearls, lovely as they were, were not quite right for the gown. She withdrew her jewelry pouch from her portmanteau. "But would you mind trying these on?"

"Aren't you going to wear them?"

"Not with mauve. I brought my coral necklace."

Peggy allowed Catherine to unfasten the pearls and clasp on the jade beads and earrings her parents had given her for her birthday. The effect was dramatic. The jade not only enhanced the green tint to the gown's fabric, but deepened the rich hues of Peggy's red hair.

"My word!" Peggy breathed, staring at herself in the long mirror.

"Beautiful," Catherine told her.

Her friend turned to her and smiled. "Thank you. But you do exaggerate."

"Catherine doesn't exaggerate," said a small voice. "She's very honest."

Muriel stood in the doorway, resembling an angel in nightgown of ivory satin and lace. "Why, thank you, Muriel," Catherine said.

The girl covered a yawn with her hand. "Excuse me," she said with a sheepish smile. "Nanny's polishing my shoes. May I come in?"

"Of course." After introducing her cousin to Peggy, she motioned to a chair. "Why don't you sit here?"

"Thank you." Muriel obliged, then folded her hands in her lap. "I have some pearls too, Miss Somerset."

"Yes?" Peggy said.

"They were my Grandmother Pearce's. Only, they're put away. Mamma says I mayn't wear them until I'm sixteen."

"Sixteen will come before you know it," Peggy assured her. "Trust me."

The violet eyes were doubtful. "I'm only eight."

"Eight? But that means you've reached the halfway peak. The rest of the way will be downhill."

"Downhill." The girl thought it over and smiled. "And going downhill is easier, isn't it?"

"Much easier," Peggy agreed.

Until you reach fourteen or so, Catherine thought, becoming a little annoyed that Peggy was devoting her attention to Muriel. There was still so much catching up to do.

"May I hold the pearls, Miss Somerset?"

Catherine answered that one before Peggy could open her mouth. "I'm afraid not, Muriel. They were a gift from her aunt."

But Peggy contradicted her. "Yes, certainly." As she took them from Catherine's hand, she gave her a look that plainly said, *Aren't you being a little harsh?* "Eight is certainly old enough to take care of things."

"I'll take care of them," the girl promised, holding them aloft and swirling them gently so that they formed a heap in her open palm.

"Careful, Muriel," Catherine said.

Muriel nodded and held them so that they draped over both small hands. "Mother says we shouldn't be unkind to people who aren't pretty, for if an ugly oyster can make a pearl, then even homely people can have something beautiful inside them."

"Why, that's a lovely thought," Peggy told her, her expression positively maudlin.

"Yes, lovely," Catherine said, and stepped over to the girl with her jewelry pouch. "Now, let's put them away."

Muriel surrendered the strand and climbed down from the chair. "Miss Somerset, would you like to see my Queen Victoria doll? She has a real ruby brooch."

"Why, yes," Peggy replied.

"Most of my dolls are packed. But I was allowed to keep out six."

"Why don't you show them all to me?"

"You don't have to," Catherine told Peggy.

Peggy gave her another reproving look as she offered the girl her hand. "I'll be back shortly."

She returned when Catherine was sitting at the dressing table while Rose pinned on her pale wine-colored straw hat with satin trim. "What a delightful child!"

"Um-hmm." Catherine did not remind Peggy that her first sight of that delightful child was during a conniption fit over lemonade. In the mirror she could see Rose's lips pressed as if suppressing a laugh. After the maid was gone, Catherine said, "I should telephone Sarah that I'm leaving Tuesday, so they don't make any plans for me."

Not only was her cousin understanding, but, after asking Catherine to wait for a minute, came back on the line to ask if Peggy would care to visit the Hassall Commission laboratory with William tomorrow.

"Yes, absolutely yes!" Peggy exclaimed, embracing Catherine.

But will they catch on? Sidney, Lord Holt thought, holding up the smoked-glass spectacles to the parlor window. He had noticed a pair in a spectacle shop window on the Strand yesterday, on his way to The Crown Hotel to meet Roseline. At least something promising had developed from the evening, for he was becoming increasingly bored with Roseline's self-absorption. Not to mention how she took for granted that he was now responsible for all of her living expenses, including the small fortune her dressmaker charged for trussing her up like a peacock.

The spectacles came from a small factory in Birmingham, the shop owner had told him. And he had wired a triple order just yesterday, for the dozen pairs he had had in stock last week were gone, with the exception of the pair that Sidney had then decided to purchase.

Sidney did not normally invest, especially in small endeavors, unless he had a strong inkling. That inkling had served him well in the past. He likened himself to a ship navigating between the mythical monsters Scylla and Charybdis. Scylla coaxed him to take risks, and Charybdis, to be too conservative. The trick was not to veer too close to either side.

A knock sounded at the door. "Enter," he said, holding the spectacles up to the window again.

Rumfellow entered, silver calling-card tray balanced upon splayed fingers. "You've a visitor, Your Lordship."

"Yes?"

Sidney reached for the card, but drew his hand back when the butler said, "A Lord Faircliffe, Your Lordship."

"Here?" Sidney said. "In our house?"

A brow made scant movement over the butler's impassive face. "In the hall, Your Lordship."

"Well, tell him I'm out. And if he calls again, do the same. Do you understand?"

"I understand, Your Lordship."

"Very good." The butler had taken only three steps when Sidney said, "And Rumfellow?"

Rumfellow turned.

"The hall. Have it scrubbed." He had learned of Malcom Faircliffe's condition only three months ago, from a mutual friend and Oxford alumnus at the Club. The affliction was commonly assumed to be contagious only through intimate association, but who could tell what scientists would discover ten years from now? Better to err on the side of caution. "Also the door . . . anything he may have touched."

"Yes, Your Lordship."

Turning again to the window, Sidney stepped to the side, then pushed aside just a sliver of curtain. A bowler-hatted figure took halting steps toward the waiting coach, where a footman waited.

Ah, Malcom, you poor chap. Remorse spread through Sidney's frame. It seemed only yesterday that they were staircase chums at Lincoln College. In those days Malcom was more the brother than Edgar could ever be. Whenever the doldrums threatened, Malcom could be counted upon to find some new amusement. *What a sorry end to such a decent fellow.*

He focused his attention upon the coach again, and realized with a start that Malcom had turned to stare up in his direction. Even from a floor above, Sidney could detect the pallor of the skin. He let go of the curtain and moved farther to the side, resting his head back against the wall. Not until the hoof-beats faded did he allow himself a deep breath.

It could happen to you, too, he told himself. He would have shrugged off that notion in his younger days. Slum creepers were the only ones afflicted, not gentlemen in custom-tailored suits. But Malcom was the second upper-crust man of his acquaintance to be afflicted thusly. Given his own past, Sidney sometimes felt he was living on borrowed time, and even wondered whenever gripped with a cold or sore throat if something more sinister lurked beneath.

"Sidney?"

He blinked. His mother stood by the lamp table, only six feet away.

"Who was here?"

"Just an acquaintance from Oxford," he told her, and when she gave him a puzzled look, he shrugged. "I'm not in the mood for guests."

Concern replaced the puzzlement in her grey eyes. "Is something the matter?"

You're not a doctor, Sidney reminded himself. *What could you have done for him? Better to put it out of your mind.*

"No, nothing," he replied.

She came closer. "What have you there?"

"Guess," he said, hooking the spectacles over his ears and peering at her through their dark lenses.

"Hmm. Surely not for reading."

"Hardly. Here, try them on."

He helped her hook them over her ears, and smiled as she raised her chin to look about the room.

"Not very efficient, are they?" she said hesitantly.

He chuckled. "They're for shielding one's eyes against sunlight. I'm going to nip over to the Park to try them out." The garden was too shady, as was Belgrave Square.

"Must you do that now?" she asked, removing the spectacles.

"Why? What's wrong?"

"Henry's just left for Euston Station. There was a train derailment somewhere near Liverpool."

"You don't say! Any injuries?"

"I'm afraid so. At least one death."

"Pity," Sidney said, meaning it. But he could also feel some relief that his investments in the Grand Junction Railway line were minimal, and so hopefully the damage to his finances would be as well.

"Yes, a tragedy," she agreed. "I expect he'll be gone for days."

Sidney raised an eyebrow, not sure what his stepfather's departure had to do with him, for as bad as the news was, it was not something that couldn't be saved for the supper table.

"Would you mind going with me for a stroll?" she asked.

"Stroll?"

"Across the Square to the Pearces'. The farewell par—?"

But he was shaking his head before she could finish. "Sorry, Mother, but I can think of a hundred things I would rather do—including having my corns shaved. Just go alone."

Anxiety washed across her face. "Alone?"

He sighed. She really needed to get out more, instead of closeting herself away with manuscripts most of the time. "These are the eighties, Mother. It's quite proper for a married woman to attend a party without an escort."

"We wouldn't have to stay long," she said as if he had not spoken. "A half hour?"

He shook his head. "That Pearce fellow tried to sell me insurance at your tea. And he's dull as dishwater."

People with inheritances usually were. Almost always they were content to live on whatever a solicitor doled out to them every annum, and did not go out and actively seek new opportunities to compound that wealth. More than likely the Pearces' friends would be of the same ilk. *Or perhaps they're all insurance salesmen,* he thought with a little shudder.

She was standing there, disappointed, so he suggested, "Why don't you ask Edgar?" At fourteen, surely his half brother knew how to conduct himself in social situations. Or at least to sit quietly somewhere out of the way.

"He has a cold."

"Then you have an excuse to stay home, haven't you? What do you care if they're offended, if they're leaving London soon?"

"Sidney," she said with a little sigh.

Her persistence was most vexing. But because he did not care to see reproach in her eyes over the next few days, he stifled a groan and replied, "Very well. But only a half hour . . . understood?"

"Thank you, Sidney," she said with a relieved smile. "You'll be dressed soon?"

He waved a hand. "Yes, soon."

Eighteen

*I*n the Pearces' garden, Riles and parlormaids Mildred and Valerie bustled through the doorway with silver trays laden with sandwiches and plovers' eggs, olives and pineapple slices, assorted cakes, and little dishes of sugared raspberries. The gardener arranged chairs facing the gazebo. Up on the platform three men in fitted breeches, silk stockings, blue satin coats, and powdered wigs, and a woman in embroidered silk with square neckline, tuned a viola, cello, and two violins.

Aunt Phyllis stood at the center table under a huge open canvas canopy, turning a vase of white Madonna lilies this way and that, and stepping back from it.

"It's all so lovely, Mrs. Pearce," Peggy said.

"I hope so." Aunt Phyllis rotated the vase again. "Should they face this way?"

Brushing a petal from her aunt's sleeve, Catherine replied, "Yes, that looks nice."

A half hour later, strains of chamber music provided backdrop to a dozen conversations rising from a dozen knots of people dressed in Sunday finery. Aunt Phyllis and Uncle Norman moved from group to group, soaking in compliments and best wishes for their futures.

"I can't imagine living this way," Peggy told Catherine when they were finally able to withdraw and listen to the string quartet play what Peggy informed her was the second movement to Haydn's *Emperor*. "So serene and elegant."

"They don't live like this *every* day," Catherine assured her. She could see Muriel's nanny, a plump young woman who looked no older than seventeen, admonishing Bernard and Douglas against chasing each other around a plum tree and pelting each other with olive pits. *And most days are not so serene.*

As if to confirm Catherine's thoughts, Muriel broke loose from the nanny and dashed about the garden as if she had been locked away for a year. Twice Catherine witnessed near-collisions between the lace-and-frills cyclone and a guest whose attention was divided between walking and keeping steady a dish and cup.

"We're terribly late," Sidney's mother fretted over the rustle of her skirts.

"*Fashionably* late," he corrected, hands in pockets. Because his legs were long and unencumbered with a skirt, his shoes made one strike against the grass of the Square for every two of hers. "Besides, it's just a garden party, not a formal dinner."

She nodded, but after a hesitation said, "Still, I asked—"

"Yes, yes," he seethed. "You asked!"

But however humiliating it was to be chastened like a small boy, he had to admit to himself that he had lingered too long in the morning room reading the *Times.* She was looking straight ahead, but he could see the crimson spot upon her cheek.

"I do beg your pardon, Mother," he said with calmer voice. "I should have dressed earlier."

Now that his pique at her was tempered, his resentment of the Pearces swelled for having nothing more productive to do than gather neighbors for sandwiches and shallow conversation. *A half hour, no longer,* he promised himself. If his mother protested, she knew the way home.

"Please don't tell your aunt, but the costumes and music don't actually match," Peggy leaned close to murmur as the quartet played the first movement to Mozart's Symphony no. 40 in G Minor. "The costumes are baroque, but the music is classical."

Catherine stared at her. "You're the only person in London who would know that."

"Not so," Peggy said, but with a pleased smile. "Any devotee of music would know. But one can't fault the musicians. Powdered wigs lend a more theatrical atmosphere than top hats."

"Then, why don't they play baroque music?"

"I'm sure because it's too dramatic and emo—"

"*Cath*-erine!" a female voice trilled. "How long has it *been!*"

Catherine and Peggy rose from their chairs, and Catherine introduced her friend to Christina and Georgina Lorimer, second cousins twice removed on Mother's side. Christina was three months younger than she; Georgina, eighteen months. With her family moving about so much, Catherine had rarely seen them over the years, the last time being a Christmas supper at her grandparents' four years ago. Now each had a husband attached to her arm. Christina introduced hers as Thomas Smith, dentist, and Georgina's as August Crane, bank clerk.

"It's a wonder no man has led you down the aisle, Catherine," Georgina purred, wedded bliss lustering her blue-green eyes and pinkening her flawless cheeks.

Christina cut her younger sister a sharp look. Turning to Catherine again, she consoled, "Oh, but there is still time."

Until what? Catherine thought. Would she turn into a pumpkin if not married by twenty? "I've wanted to go to college since I was a girl," she said, as if that would explain, and then despised herself for feeling she had to justify the lack of a spouse upon her arm. Especially with Peggy as a witness.

"And we so *admire* you for—" Georgina began but turned silent when the music faltered. Heads were turning in the direction of the canopy, and the hum of conversation tapered, even as the music quickly resumed.

"We should see if Aunt Phyllis needs us," Catherine said, not even trying to hide her relief. "Come, Peggy."

Under the canopy, Aunt Phyllis held up the cloth at one end of the punch table and leaned to peer underneath. "Sweetheart . . ." she coaxed. "If the string breaks, we'll never find them."

Catherine held her breath. *What string?*

"I'm being careful, Mamma!" came from beneath. "And she said I could wear them!"

"Aunt Phyllis?" Catherine said after exchanging glances with Peggy. "She hasn't Peggy's pearls . . . has she?"

Aunt Phyllis blew out her cheeks and gave Peggy an apologetic look. "I do apologize, Miss Somerset. But she'll give them over at once. Won't you, Muriel?"

"I just want to wear them for a little while!"

Uncle Norman stepped beneath the canopy. "What's going on?"

"She has Miss Somerset's pearls," Aunt Phyllis replied, and wheeled upon the nanny hovering at her elbow. "Why weren't you watching her!"

"I was, Missus! But she's been giving me the slip all afternoon!"

"Well, how hard can it be to keep up with an eight—"

"Phyllis." Uncle Norman sent a slight nod toward the nearest knot of people, seven or so who either stared at the ground or pretended not to have noticed.

While her husband walked around to the back of the table, Aunt Phyllis gave the group a helpless smile. "We've been so preoccupied with packing—haven't paid enough attention to her."

"Muriel, you will remove yourself from there this instant," Uncle Norman said calmly, lifting the cloth.

Two small black velvet slippers appeared on Catherine's side. Crystal cups clinked, and punch swayed against the sides of the Bristol cut glass bowl as Muriel thrust out her body. The strand of pearls swung from around her lace collar.

"Here Muriel, let's put them away now," Catherine said, reaching out. But she wasn't quick enough. Muriel made a ninety-degree turn, arched out of her mother's reach, and hitched up her skirts to sprint toward the house.

Catherine started to follow.

"Catherine . . . wait!"

She turned. Aunt Phyllis was sending her a pleading look. "If we'll just ignore her, she'll bring back whatever she's taken."

But a glance at the freckles standing out on Peggy's stark white face was enough to galvanize Catherine into action again. "What if she breaks them?" she said, and did not wait for an answer.

Up ahead the girl sprinted across the terrace and through the door propped open for servants bearing trays. Catherine walked as briskly as modesty would allow, slowing only when she reached the terrace and heard footfalls behind her.

"I'm so sorry, so sorry," Catherine said, pausing for the fraction of a second so that Peggy could catch up with her. "I should have hidden the pearls . . . warned you."

"Not your fault," Peggy said.

In the corridor they had to step around a red-faced maid scooping sandwiches from the floor onto a tray. "Out the front," she muttered before being asked.

Sure enough, the door stood open. They were halfway to it when a child's shriek and the whinny of a horse rent the air.

"No!" Catherine exclaimed, breaking into a run with Peggy beside her. They stopped short on the top step. On the pavement Muriel twisted and pulled as a tall man held her arm.

"MUM-MEEE!"

"Hush, Muriel." Catherine continued down the steps, her pulse still sounding in her ears. The man looked up.

"Does she belong to you?" he said tightly.

"No," Catherine said. "Well, yes." Just across the street she could see a mimosa tree with inviting branches. Clearly that was to be her hiding place.

"She dashed out in front of a horse," he said, as an older woman joined him.

Catherine's pulse jumped again. She took hold of Muriel's other arm as the man released her. "Time to give it over, Muriel."

Peggy stepped down onto the pavement. Teary eyed and sniffing, Muriel looked at Peggy, eyed the stern-faced man, then took off the necklace. "I wasn't going to keep it." The instant Peggy's hand closed over it, the girl jerked her arm away, darted around Peggy, and ran up the steps. Her sobs carried through the house.

"Thank you ever so much, Sir!" Peggy said, clasping the necklace to her chest.

"Yes, thank you," Catherine echoed.

"Just a matter of being in the right place at the right time," he said, his voice as refined and resonant as an actor's. He was strikingly handsome, with auburn waves beneath the brim of his bowler hat, thin mustache over full lips, and dimple centered in a square chin. While his smile was more politeness than warmth, his voice was affable as he said, "May I introduce my mother, Mrs. Godfrey?"

"Mrs. Godfrey?" Catherine forgot all about Muriel. "My sister will be so pleased to learn that I made your acquaintance. She has your stories practically committed to memory."

The woman smiled. "Will she be here today?"

"I'm afraid not. She's in Bombay with our parents."

"Well, do send her my regards."

Mrs. Godfrey introduced her and Peggy to her son, Lord Holt. The difference in names had not struck Catherine when Aunt Phyllis mentioned them earlier. Mrs. Godfrey was probably widowed at one time and remarried, she thought. She wondered why the son had decided to come in place of the husband, before reminding herself that it was none of her business.

"I'm Catherine Rayborn, and this is my friend Peggy Somerset."

Lord Holt's sharp blue eyes slanted a look toward the door. "And who was the little hoyden?"

Mrs. Godfrey put a hand upon his sleeve. "Sidney."

But Catherine was not in the frame of mind to defend her. "My cousin, Muriel Pearce."

"Catherine?"

All turned to Uncle Norman, standing on the porch.

"She was almost hit, Uncle Norman," Catherine told him. "Lord Holt stopped her."

He blew out a breath, the thick mustache curving down with his frown. "Thank you, Lord Holt. She's not allowed to cross the street. She'll be disciplined, of course. And the necklace?"

"I have it now, Mr. Pearce," Peggy told him, holding out her hand.

"Well, very good." He descended the steps and made a little bow. "How good of you to come, Mrs. Godfrey, Lord Holt. I do apologize for my daughter's misbehavior."

"Children will be children," Mrs. Godfrey said in a tone not quite sincere.

As Catherine and Peggy trailed behind the three down the corridor of the house, Catherine overheard that Mrs. Godfrey's younger son, Edgar, had attended the same academy as the twins. Knight-in-shining armor that he was, Lord Holt contributed nothing to the conversation.

A few covert glances were sent in their direction in the garden from guests who had resumed socializing. There was no sign of Muriel nor the nanny. Aunt Phyllis came hurrying from the house just as Uncle Norman was telling Mrs. Godfrey and Lord Holt of the Sun Insurance Company's recent boom in business. She shook her most recent guests' hands, and gasped when Mrs. Godfrey explained that her husband had been called away to a train derailment near Liverpool.

"Was anyone hurt?" she asked, hand up to the base of her neck.

"We can only speculate as to how many," Mrs. Godfrey replied somewhat evasively.

Uncle Norman shook his head. "If statistics follow their usual course, only one-fourth of the passengers on that train will have any sort of insurance."

Aunt Phyllis clucked her tongue. She seemed to be purposely avoiding Catherine's eyes. Did that mean the invitation to spend two nights was withdrawn? The prospect was not too grievous, however much Catherine loathed to sow any seeds of family disharmony.

"You're welcome to stay with us," Peggy leaned close to whisper. The pearls were wrapped, bracelet style, around the hem of her glove. Catherine knew better than to offer to put them back into her pouch.

"May we offer you some refreshments?" Aunt Phyllis said.

Uncle Norman offered an arm to Mrs. Godfrey. "Yes, may we?"

"None for me, thank you," Lord Holt replied, making no move to budge from the terrace. "Do have some, Mother."

Mrs. Godfrey was more gracious. She ambled with Aunt Phyllis and Uncle Norman toward the canopy, pausing to meet other guests. That left Catherine and Peggy sharing company with Lord Holt. Or at least sharing the terrace, for he stood staring out at the mingling guests with an unreadable expression.

You have to be sociable, Catherine told herself, and cleared her throat. "Have you lived in Belgravia all your life, Lord Holt?"

"Mostly." The polite smile returned. "And you?"

"I've lived all over. I'm a sophomore now at Girton College. Miss Somerset here as well. Are you acquainted with Somerset Tailors on Saville?"

Resuming his stare at the assemblage of guests, he said, "I have not had that pleasure."

Catherine shot Peggy a puzzled look and received one in return. Should they just walk away and leave him to the comfort of his own company? But what if he was simply timid in social situations? That did not seem likely, given his commanding presence, but who could tell what was inside another's head?

That he was so handsome made Catherine more willing to give him the benefit of the doubt.

Obviously Peggy felt the same, for she said, "You must be very proud of your mother, Lord Holt."

"Yes, I am," he replied with the same wearied tolerance one reserves for small children who ask too many questions. The message was clear.

Are you this rude to everyone? Catherine thought.

She looked at Peggy again. Her friend nodded, hazel eyes stormy. "If you will excuse us . . ." Catherine began, then realized she had no reason to give for walking away.

The relief that came to Lord Holt's expression told her that none was necessary.

"What a bundle of conceit!" she said to Peggy as they sat again in chairs facing the baroque-classical musicians.

"He would drown in a rainstorm," Peggy replied with a glance over her shoulder. "Did he think we were flirting with him?"

The thought had not occurred to Catherine. But if women threw themselves at Lord Holt all the time, as Aunt Phyllis implied, it would only be natural for him to assume they were doing the same. "Oh dear. I hope not."

Peggy shrugged. "Perhaps he resented having to rub elbows with us commoners."

Suddenly the musician playing the viola twitched, raised his bow to brush his cheek, and glared out toward some shrubbery at the edge of the gazebo. Catherine saw two brown heads duck. Douglas and Bernard had finally found something with which to amuse themselves.

"Did you see that?" Peggy asked as a bit of green landed in the woman's high white wig.

"My cousins." Fortunately, before Catherine could expend too much angst wondering if she dare involve herself, Uncle Norman strode around the gazebo and quietly ordered the twins into the house. They obeyed, grinning and unrepentant.

The next time Catherine sent a casual glance toward the terrace, there was no sign of Lord Holt, nor Mrs. Godfrey.

"Gone?" Peggy said.

"Apparently."

"At least he saved my necklace."

Catherine nodded. "And he didn't throw pits at anyone."

But she decided that when she wrote home of meeting Mrs. Godfrey, she would leave out the part about her snobbish son, so as not to spoil any of Jewel's fondness for the books.

It occurred to her that Lieutenant Elham might be familiar with Mrs. Godfrey's stories, having such a large family. She could picture him patiently reading to a younger niece or nephew. He was just the sort of man to whom children would be drawn. And even though a medal was pinned to his chest, it would never occur to him to behave snobbishly toward anyone.

A little ache pricked her heart. How was it possible to miss someone with whom she had spent so little time? *You hardly know him* entered her mind, but it was as if the voice of Sarah were saying it. Deep within herself, Catherine was certain that she knew him, better than she knew most people. The brief meeting, combined with his letter, had given her a glimpse into his soul, and it was a good one.

If only she had met him earlier in the summer! But then, she told herself, perhaps she would have stayed in Bombay and forgotten about Girton. She realized that the idea of doing so did not distress her as much as it should.

Aunt Phyllis did not hold a grudge after all. When the last guests were gone and Peggy delivered back to Saville Row—with a bandbox of leftover sandwiches and cakes—she linked arms with Catherine, surveyed the litter of food bits remaining on the tables, and pronounced the party a roaring success.

Catherine managed to conceal her surprise. Perhaps with family rows being so commonplace at 42 Belgrave Square, her aunt did not realize how unsettling they were to the outsiders who witnessed them.

"I have to say I was disappointed that you spent so little time with Lord Holt," Aunt Phyllis said.

"Oh, he obviously thought it was more than enough time."

"Indeed?" She gave Catherine a puzzled look. "I can't imagine that, but then, they did leave early. Perhaps they were more upset over the train derailment than they let on."

Somehow, Catherine didn't think that was the case. They strolled toward the house, trailing behind a chambermaid carrying a chair, while other foot-weary servants hastened back and forth from house to garden.

"If we *weren't* moving," Aunt Phyllis said, "I would certainly never think of hiring those same musicians again. They expressed no gratitude whatsoever when I paid them. You know, talent is one thing, but if one is to market one's talents, one must learn common etiquette."

"Mm-hmm," Catherine murmured.

A nightgown-clad Muriel bounded down the staircase with curling rags bobbing in her hair, and handed Catherine a fairly good picture she had penciled of a robin perched upon the edge of a birdbath.

"Will you give this to Miss Somerset, and tell her I'm sorry I was naughty?"

"Now, there's a dear," Aunt Phyllis purred.

"Ah . . . certainly," Catherine told her, moved in spite of herself. Still, as the child's hapless nanny escorted her upstairs to finish the preparing for bed-time ordeal, Catherine went into the guest room to check the contents of her jewelry pouch before locking it inside her portmanteau.

Nineteen

*L*aborers employed by Sun Insurance arrived the fol- lowing morning, assisting the servants with disassem- bling the household. Now that the garden party was in the past, they would be able to crate all but the most essential items such as beds, linens, dining table, and the kitchen pots and dishes required for one more day.

Tomorrow, Aunt Phyllis informed Catherine at the breakfast table, everything else would be packed, requiring the Pearces to move to Queen Elizabeth Hotel on Piccadilly Street for the duration of the week.

Muriel was cross, having won most of last night's bedtime skirmishes— which eventually involved Aunt Phyllis as well as the nanny. The twins were no better. As little control of the children as Uncle Norman possessed, he gave at least an aura of fatherly discipline that held them somewhat in check. Aunt Phyllis placated and pleaded, mediated every petty argument, and even offered bribes, to the point where it seemed that every bite Muriel consented to fork past her rosebud lips, every civil word the twins said, earned them some future treat, plaything, or privilege.

But instead of making the children happy and obedient, these indul- gences only worsened their moods and escalated their misbehaviors.

"Mother . . . make Bernard stop repeating every thing I say," Douglas complained.

"Mother . . . make Bernard stop repeating every thing I say," Bernard echoed.

"Now, Bernard . . ."

"Cook put those green things in the eggs," Muriel whined. "I don't like those green things."

"They're onions, not green things," Douglas said. "Don't you know anything?"

"They're onions, not green things. Don't you know anything?"

"Mo-therrrr!"

"Mo-therrrr!"

"Bernard, I'm not going to tell you again to stop that," Aunt Phyllis said for the second time, then looked up at Catherine. "You've hardly touched your food, dear."

"I'm a girl-l-l," Douglas singsonged, daring his brother with his eyes.

"I'm a girl-l-l," Bernard echoed, nonplused.

"Boys!"

"I'm feeling a little unwell," Catherine replied in the first space of silence. Three-quarters of what was an excellent omelet was growing cold upon her plate. Her tea had turned lukewarm. The buttered mushrooms had developed an oily sheen. *Unwell* was no exaggeration, for it described perfectly the condition of her nerves.

"Tell Cook I want one without the green things," Muriel whined.

"Wait, dear," Aunt Phyllis told her. "I'm speaking with Cath—"

"Ouch! You didn't have to hit me!"

"Ouch! You didn't have to—"

Catherine pushed out her chair with such abruptness that it rocked on its back legs before settling against the carpet. "Some fresh air will help."

"Of course," Aunt Phyllis told her. "Why don't you sit in the garden, and we'll join you once we've finished?"

"And sunlight," Catherine added with an apologetic smile. "Lots of sunlight would make me feel better . . . just coming from India . . . you know."

She left her aunt puzzling over her meaning, and fortunately, Muriel provided a distraction by bursting into tears over the wretched green things.

On her way to the upstairs landing, after cleaning her teeth and grabbing a hat and gloves, Catherine happened to glance through the open doorway to the nursery. Even with most things packed, it was a wonderland of color, from the ceiling mural of fairies and forest creatures to the William Morris "Daisy" wallpaper and canopy-covered bed with a half dozen frilly pillows and bolsters piled up against the pink coverlet. Muriel's nanny stood at the foot with a small nightgown draped over her arm. The side of her head rested against the bedpost, her eyes were closed. Already she looked fatigued.

Hurry, or you'll be sorry, Catherine warned herself, starting again for the staircase. But just as her hand touched the banister, she turned and went back to her room. Her reticule was locked in the portmanteau with her jewelry pouch—a precaution she had thought of later last night. She took a couple of pound notes from it, then on second thought added two more. This time when she paused in the nursery doorway she cleared her throat, gently.

The nanny snapped to attention, her round face flooded with alarm. "I'm sorry, Miss!"

Catherine stepped into the room, took the girl's hand, and placed the folded notes in it. "Buy yourself a nice frock or two," she whispered. She left the girl gaping and stammering thanks. Outside, she strolled briskly up Halkin Street, crossed Grosvenor Place, and passed the Wellington Arch. Used in the seventeenth century for hunting and duels, the fifty-three-acre Green Park still retained much of its old-world charm. Dew-covered grass glistened in the morning sun, and the air carried a hint of the coming autumn. Catherine's nerves slowly unraveled as she strolled the meandering paths through stands of trees and open ground.

One more night. A person could bear almost anything for twenty-four hours. And who was she to complain, when others had suffered much worse? Lieutenant Elham, for example. On the scale of human suffering, war surely occupied a place at the top. Being confined to a house with whining, argumentative children did not rate even being on the same page.

Blinded by black spots, Sidney squeezed his eyelids tight and removed and folded the spectacles. They would not slip into his left coat pocket—he remembered the pear he had snatched from a bowl in the hall—so he switched them to the right, thinking, *Not very effective for staring at the sun.*

But then, how many imbeciles went about staring directly at the sun?

Just one that I can think of, he thought wryly, rubbing his eyes. The caws of a colony of rooks, which had been taking short soaring flights from the branches of a nearby oak, sounded like laughter.

"Lord Holt?"

Sidney opened his eyes, blinked. One of the young women from the garden party stood amidst the black spots.

"Forgive me for intruding upon your privacy," she said. "I was just . . . it looked as if you'd taken ill."

"I'm very well, thank you," he replied, squinting up at her. Guileless grey-green eyes studied him from an oval face. Soft curls of dark brown lay about her brow; the sides of her hair were drawn up into a straw hat, with several long strands curling over her shoulders. The faintest tinge of rose shaded her cheeks.

Yesterday during their walk home, his mother had remarked on how lovely the girl was, in that hinting sort of way Mother used whenever she happened to cross paths with any woman one degree removed from a nun. Ire at his mother and the Pearces had apparently dulled his perception then, just as the sun affected his vision today, for he found her fresh-scrubbed beauty refreshing. Quite a difference from Roseline's perpetually bored expression, an affectation she assumed to be the height of sophistication.

Her name, he asked himself as courtesy propelled him to his feet. She had remembered his. Why hadn't he paid closer attention yesterday? He dipped into his pocket again. "I was testing these."

She looked at the spectacles and nodded. "I noticed some soldiers wearing them in Bombay," she said. "The Indian sun can be relentless."

"Indeed?"

"Oh, yes. Even during the monsoon."

Realizing she had misinterpreted his question, he rephrased it. "Pardon me . . . what I meant was, were many soldiers wearing them? I'm thinking of investing in a company that makes them."

"Why, I can't recall. Ten or so, I should think. But surely they're rare, because this is the first time I've seen a pair up close."

"Would you care to try them?"

For a fraction of a second it seemed she would reply in the affirmative, but then the warmth faded from her eyes. "No, thank you," she said, and gave him a civil nod. "Do have a pleasant day, Lord Holt."

My behavior yesterday, he thought, wincing. He watched her walk away, admiring the determined set of her shoulders and the dark curls falling below her hat. Should he go after her? He took the watch from his waistcoat, allowing the hour to be the deciding factor.

Half-past nine. Which meant he really did not have the time to dally about in the Park, even though the noon appointment at Broughton Stables in Hammersmith, West London was not set in stone. After weeks of enduring Roseline's begging and nagging, he had promised her a horse and sidesaddle, along with a place near Hyde Park to stable the animal so she could parade herself about on the occasions she managed to rise before afternoon. His coachman, Jerry, knew good horseflesh, being half horse himself. The other half was Scottish, which meant he could sniff out a bargain.

She's just a child, really, he told himself with one more admiring glance. It was then that she wheeled around and faced him. Her pretty face worked up as if she were trying to decide whether to say something.

"Yes?" he said, lifting a brow.

"My friend and I were just being sociable yesterday," she said with a bravado that obviously was costing every bit of her inner strength. "And for your information, I'm corresponding with an army lieutenant in Bombay."

"An army lieutenant in Bombay?" he echoed, trying not to smile.

"Yes. A war hero too."

"Hmm." Sidney rubbed his dimpled chin thoughtfully. "That could be tricky. Does the war hero know about the lieutenant?"

"Know about . . . ?" she echoed, gaping at him. Knowledge flooded her expression, and she turned sharply on her heel and resumed walking.

Sidney jogged forth to catch up with her. "Wait, please."

She continued looking straight ahead, even as he fell into step beside her.

"Forgive me for making sport. But you were so serious that I couldn't stop myself."

Still she did not turn her face toward him.

"And I must ask you to forgive my rudeness yesterday," Sidney continued. "To you and to your friend."

"Very well," she replied in a tight voice.

"It never entered my mind that you were being anything but sociable."

It was not true, for he assumed any eligible woman—and sometimes ineligible—who initiated conversation at a social gathering was interested in him as a potential suitor. He did not think himself vain for assuming so, for he was fully aware that his money and title were the main draws. A handsome face was an asset, but London was filled with handsome wheelwrights and shop clerks and fishermen. And daughters of polite society did not pursue them for husbands.

One lie told, he was compelled to follow it with another. "I was suffering a fierce headache yesterday, which was compounded by the tragic news from Liverpool. I desired nothing more than to crawl into a corner somewhere. But as I had promised to escort Mother to the party . . ."

She ceased walking. Sympathy filled the grey-green eyes, as crimson flooded her cheeks. "Oh dear."

"Please don't look so stricken. You had every right to say what you did."

"I had no right," she argued, shaking her head.

"I'm grateful that you did. If you had not, I wouldn't have had the opportunity to explain."

Her posture eased slightly. "That's very gracious of you, Lord Holt. Has it left you?"

"Left me?"

"The headache."

"Yes, thank you. Though it's tempting fate to be out here staring at the sun, isn't it?"

That made her smile. She had a nice curve to her lips, the corners disappearing into tiny semicircles.

"Would your lieutenant-war hero be terribly offended if I asked to accompany you on your stroll?" Sidney asked impulsively.

She seemed to think that over, then shook her head. "He's in India. But still, he wouldn't mind."

"Very mature of him. Jealous men are such boors, aren't they?"

"Yes."

"Pray tell me," he said as they resumed walking, "was it recently that you noticed the soldiers with the spectacles?"

"Why, barely over a fortnight ago. I was in Bombay visiting my family."

"Your father's in the military?" They had reached the northernmost part of the park. Sidney could hear the traffic noises on Picadilly Street.

"He's headmaster of the Victoria School," she replied. "I'm only able to visit them during long vacation."

Long vacation. That meant she was a student somewhere. Secondary school or college? Had she mentioned that yesterday? If he was clever enough, he could figure out her name without being forced to admit he had forgotten it. "You live with Mr. and Mrs. Pearce between terms?" Surely he would have recalled seeing her, but then, he did not normally take strolls in Green Park.

She shook her head. "With relations in Hampstead."

"I see." And he was feeling increasingly awkward, not mentioning her name. He made one more attempt. "I'm quite familiar with Hampstead. But I can't recall meeting anyone there by the name of Pearce."

"The Pearces are on my mother's and Aunt Phyllis's side of the family. My Hampstead relations are Rayborns. And Doyles."

He recalled her name now. *Rayborn.* And it rang another mental bell, especially when linked with Doyle. But the Doyles lived in Berkeley Square. "Have they resided in Hampstead long?" he asked casually.

"Only three or four months. They moved from Berkeley Square to a house on Cannonhall Road."

Something in his blue eyes was unsettling. Catherine wondered if the headache had returned. "Lord Holt?"

He blinked, smiled. "Do forgive me. I was just wondering how long it has been since I've enjoyed such pleasant company."

"Thank you." Heat rose in her cheeks again. Flattered as she was, she realized that she had stretched the rules of propriety for long enough. It was not seemly to spend so much time, unchaperoned, with a man to whom she was not betrothed.

And she could not abandon her aunt all morning, no matter how severely her nerves had been taxed. No matter how much she was enjoying the company of this handsome lord. She offered her gloved hand. "I should go now. Do have a pleasant—"

"Please," he said, closing his hand over hers. "Must you?"

"I left my aunt halfway through breakfast."

"Then you must be hungry." With his other hand he motioned across Picadilly. "There is a decent café . . ."

"No, thank you." Propriety would scream at that one, and her father have an apoplexy if he ever found out.

He nodded toward a nearby bench under an elm. "Then at least sit and share my breakfast with me, and I'll escort you back to your aunt's."

Before she could decline, he released her hand and withdrew a pear from his pocket. Another smile deepened the dimple in his chin. "How long can half a pear take?"

"Very well," she said, and not reluctantly.

He sat a respectable distance from her, long legs crossed at the ankles, and drew a small folding knife from his fob pocket. Just as his voice seemed meant for the stage, his hands seemed meant for peeling fruit, so white and well-shaped with long fingers and clean nails. A splendid ring, a single diamond set in a massive gold claw, flashed blue and purple as the sun struck it at every turn of his hand. And the finger it was on—the little one—held itself aloft slightly as if to show off the diamond the better.

Catching herself staring, she raised her eyes again to his face.

Lord Holt smiled. "You should remove your gloves."

"Thank you." She removed them and folded them in her lap, and then accepted the slice of fruit he handed over.

"Please tell me about your family," he asked. "How long have they lived in Bombay?"

"Three years." She told him of her recent visit home. "And yours?"

"There isn't much to tell." The modesty in his tone suggested otherwise. "My father was an Exchequer judge, but he passed on when I was nine."

"I'm sorry."

He nodded. "Thank you. It was a very difficult time, but Mother and I slogged through it. And fortunately, she and Mr. Godfrey struck up a friendship that led to marriage a couple of years later."

"You didn't mind?"

He chuckled. "After being head of household for two years? Can you guess?"

Catherine covered a smile with her hand. "But you grew used to him?"

"Oh, absolutely. And I'm grateful that he makes my mother happy. He's the one who encouraged her to write. They even have a son together, my brother, Edgar, who just recently turned fourteen."

"He looks up to you?"

"I wish that were the case. I was thirteen when he was born and more interested in playing cricket than visiting the nursery. Then I was off to Eton, and then Oxford. Now that I'm home, well, he's the one who'd rather be out swinging a cricket bat with his friends, and I'm too stuffy ancient for him. How is it with you and your sister?"

"I was only nine when she was born," Catherine said, surprised at the easy flow of conversation, so different from yesterday's attempt. "And so I played with her instead of dolls. We shared the same governess too. Even though our academic interests are different, we do have those bonds."

"Then I gather she's not like your little cousin?"

"Not in the least. In fact, she's an absolute dear."

He handed her another slice of pear. "But then she would have to be, wouldn't she?"

"What do you mean?"

"What do you think I mean?"

She chewed on the bit of pear to distract attention from her cheeks, which were surely betraying her again.

"Why does it embarrass you to be complimented, Miss Rayborn?" he asked.

"I'm not embarrassed," she murmured, and the fact that he could tell otherwise made her cheeks even warmer.

He did not contradict her, just tossed the pear core into a shrubbery and offered her the damp handkerchief he had used to wipe the bench. "It's a bit soiled. But better than pulling gloves back over sticky hands. And we should be delivering you back to your aunt's before she sends the cousin after you."

Did I say something wrong? Catherine asked herself as she cleaned her hands. True, it was past time to be moving on toward Belgrave Square. But she should be the one to bring that up, not him.

"Thank you for breakfast, Lord Holt," she said, rising when her gloves were on.

He wiped his hands quickly and got to his feet. "The pleasure was mine."

He stuffed the handkerchief into a pocket, crooked an elbow, and smiled. "Shall we?"

"You aren't obliged to escort me," she told him.

"Nothing would give me more pleasure, Miss Rayborn."

When he did not move, she slipped a hand into the crook of his arm. It was her first time to walk such a way with a man, other than her father or Uncle Daniel. Her self-consciousness eased a bit when she realized how little notice they attracted. Another couple strolled in the distance, two elderly men played chess at a table set up under a dogwood tree, and nursemaids aired children or gossiped in little groups. Douglas—or Bernard—sent her a wave from a group of boys taking turns trying out a pair of stilts.

"They'll all be wanting to run away and join the circus," Lord Holt told her. "At least until suppertime."

"Father took me to see some acrobats when we lived in Malta. One turned three backwards flips on stilts strapped to his feet."

"You've lived in Malta? You're quite the cosmopolitan woman, Miss Rayborn."

That made her smile. She explained how her father had tutored the son of the Naval Hospital's Inspector General. When he asked about her studies, she told him how pleased she was to be at Girton. "Have you ever been there?"

"Not there, but close. My father has some relations in Chesterton—to the east a bit, just across the Cam from Cambridge—but my mother fell out of favor with them by remarrying, so I've not been up there since the college was built."

"I'm sorry. About your family."

"They were bores anyway." His blue eyes glinted as they waited for a lull in Grosvenor Place traffic. "Cambridge and Oxford, walking arm in arm. There is hope for world peace after all."

"Well, the women's colleges aren't officially part of the University," she said.

"Indeed?"

"We're allowed to take the Tripos exam, but the scores don't count toward a Cambridge degree."

"How positively medieval! The old dons probably worry that the women will prove themselves brighter than the men."

"How nice of you to say."

"I mean it. And what about the students from the male colleges? I imagine they're delighted to have you there. Do they make pests of themselves, flirting and all that?"

Suddenly college students seemed so young. Catherine shook her head. "They're not allowed past the gates unless they're family. And we're not allowed to go into Cambridge without chaperones."

"Very wise," he said. "There are a lot of wolves out there in sheep's clothing."

"Now you sound like my father," she told him.

He chuckled. "I'll accept that as a compliment."

Twenty

As they neared 42 Belgrave Square, Sidney noticed two men in shirtsleeves and corded trousers carrying a piano down the steps toward a waiting wagon. His mother had mentioned that the Pearces were moving soon, but as their comings and goings had no effect upon his life beyond the inconvenience of sacrificing a half hour at their dull party, he had not thought to wonder when that might occur.

Now, he found himself a little more interested. He asked Miss Rayborn, "Your aunt and her family are moving soon?"

She nodded. "Tonight is their last night in the house. They'll spend the rest of the week at the Queen Elizabeth Hotel."

"And where after that?" Not that he gave a tinker's curse, but once one initiated a subject of conversation, good manners compelled one to see it through.

"Sheffield. My uncle will manage a branch office."

They had reached the front of the house and stood a little to the side of the steps, in front of the cast-iron railing. "Where will you go tomorrow?"

"Hampstead," she replied. "But only long enough to say farewell and collect my things before catching the train for Girton."

The Hampstead relations, Sidney thought, as it occurred to him that it was probably Leona's house that the Doyles had moved into. Grand old estates like that were passed down through the generations and seldom came on the market. *I just hope Doyle has enough couth to wipe the manure from his boots when he goes inside,* he thought. He only wished he could be a fly on the wall, watching William Doyle's face as he learned that this innocent creature had spent the morning in the company of the man he and his wife considered the biggest rakeshame in London.

She was giving him a curious look, and he realized he was smiling.

"I wish you a pleasant journey tomorrow," he said.

"Thank you." The corners of her mouth tucked into their charming little semicircles. "I'm glad to have had my first impression of you corrected."

"Hear, hear," Sidney said. The Hammersmith appointment nagged again at his mind. And there was no point in lurking here, when the Pearces were too occupied for guests. Not that he would wish to set foot inside anyway, just in case he should happen upon Mr. Pearce with his insurance policies or that girl with her shrill mouth.

As if reading his thoughts, Miss Rayborn moved her hand from its nest in his arm. "I'm afraid I can't invite you in."

"Please don't trouble yourself." Sidney took up her hand and brushed a quick kiss against the back of her glove. "It's time for me to nip on home for hat and carriage. I've an important meeting at the Stock Exchange."

Will I ever see you again? Catherine thought. But she could only say a much safer, "I hope you're on time."

"Thank you." He touched his forehead as if the brim of a hat rested there. "Good morning, Miss Rayborn."

Catherine smiled. "Good morning."

She watched him hasten across the Square at almost a jog, but only until telling herself that she would be mortified if he were to happen to look back. Two laborers paused from stacking crates in the corridor to nod politely at her. Aunt Phyllis was in the library, holding up a sheet of foolscap for Riles, a parlormaid, and another laborer. "Paintings and any wall ornaments should be crated together according to their respective walls," she was saying. "I've drawn up a plan here—everything from the fireplace wall shall be labeled *A . . .*" Eventually she looked toward the doorway and smiled.

"Did you have a pleasant outing, Catherine?"

"Most pleasant," Catherine replied with a bittersweet little pang. "May I lend a hand?"

"Heavens, no. We'll do them a greater service by moving out of the way. Isn't that so, Riles?"

With a subtle lift of the brows, the butler replied, "It is a wise servant who does not contradict his mistress."

Aunt Phyllis laughed, and Catherine marveled at how much fun her aunt could be away from the company of her children, and when matters did not pertain directly to them. After giving the butler the sketch, Aunt Phyllis propelled Catherine toward the parlor. "And now it's time we had a nice visit without any distractions. Who knows when that will happen again?"

"Where is Muriel?"

"Her nanny took her to Harrods for nightgowns and stockings. There is no telling what sort of merchandise we'll find in Sheffield. And I sent the boys out to play."

"I saw them at Green Park," Catherine told her as they passed the crate stackers. "They were having a jolly time with a pair of stilts."

"Stilts is fun," murmured one workman to the other. "I built some for me son."

But Aunt Phyllis had stopped walking. "How high were they?"

With a sinking feeling that she shouldn't have volunteered that bit of information, Catherine held up a hand, shoulder height. "Not terribly high."

"My boy's was as high as a horse's ears," the crate assembler said.

Aunt Phyllis was not mollified. She turned toward the library door.

"Riles?"

"Madam?"

"Send someone over to the Park to tell the twins they're *not* to play on stilts."

The candlestick telephone rang as they stepped into the parlor. A maid hurried through the doorway to answer it.

"For you, Missus," she said to Aunt Phyllis. "A Lord Holt."

Lord Holt? Aunt Phyllis mouthed to Catherine as she took earpiece and telephone and seated herself upon the sofa.

Catherine perched herself on a chair, barely allowing herself to breathe.

"Good morning, Lord Holt!" her aunt said. "To what do we owe this unexpected pleasure?"

She assumed a listening pose, forehead denting.

"Very kind of you to say so," she said eventually. "Mr. Pearce and I were honored that you and your dear mother could attend. But I'm distressed to learn of your headache. Has it eased any at all?"

After another silence, "I'm relieved to hear it. A good night's sleep is usually the best tonic—although you may wish to try Biliousine, should one persist to the next day. Our holiday to Portsmouth would have been ruined, had I not had some in my luggage for Mr. Pearce. Be sure to take it with a little food, or your stomach will give you grief."

Halfway through the silence that followed, Aunt Phyllis angled her head to send Catherine a smile. "No, she hasn't told me, but we're just now having the opportunity to talk."

Another brief silence, then, "Yes, Catherine is indeed a charming young woman. From a good family, I might add. My sister is a saint. And with a three hundred pound per annum legacy from her grandfather—"

No! Catherine mouthed, shaking her head.

"—she'll be no liability to any man wise enough to ask her hand."

I want to die! Catherine's face burned, and nausea gripped her.

"Yes . . . yes . . . I see . . ." Aunt Phyllis went on, oblivious to Catherine's misery. "And you were given only two tickets? But you mustn't apologize, Lord Holt. We're quite occupied here. And Mr. Pearce and I would have no objections, given my friendship with your mother, and the good name of your family. You would bring her back here immediately afterward, yes?"

Still another silence, then, "Very good, Lord Holt. Would you care to speak with her?"

Aunt Phyllis ignored Catherine's frantic shakes of the head and waved her over insistently, until she had no choice but to comply. Handing over the telephone, her aunt whispered, "He wants to ask you to the opera."

Catherine stared at the earpiece until a nudge in her side prompted her to put it to her ear. "Miss Rayborn speaking."

"Good morning again, Miss Rayborn!"

"Good morning," she replied. The normality of his voice made her feel better. Perhaps every family had an Aunt Phyllis, whose words sometimes had to be taken with a grain of salt. But she wished her aunt were not staring so intently. The raised eyebrows gave her the air of a spaniel with its ears cocked.

"Won't you be late for your meeting?" she asked.

His sigh came over the telephone line. "I'm afraid that's inevitable. But yes, I must make haste, and so do pray you'll forgive my lapse in etiquette by ringing instead of stopping by."

"Of course," she said, and tried to recall her aunt's words. *Did she say opera?*

"And I realize this is terribly last-minute and highly irregular, but I am suddenly in the possession of two tickets to Verdi's *Rigoletto* at the Lyceum. Mrs. Pearce has granted me permission to ask you to accompany me. Would you pay me that honor?"

She could barely keep her thoughts in order. "This evening, do you mean?"

"Forgive me . . . yes, this evening. The curtain opens at eight, and we could have a light supper at Gatti's if I come for you at half-past five."

I'll lend you a dress, her aunt mouthed.

Catherine needed little more encouragement than that. In fact, less would have sufficed. "Very well, thank you."

Roseline will be furious, Sidney thought, closing the front door after himself for the second time. She was terribly fond of attending the opera, if only because it meant seeing and being seen by the right people. But she had little call to complain. Not considering the money he would be spending on her horse and all its trappings.

Jerry started to climb down from the driver's seat of the landau.

"I'm fine," Sidney said, and stepped inside unassisted. "Let's get a move on."

A sudden whim had prompted him to leave Jerry at the reins just minutes ago and return to the house for the telephone. Miss Rayborn would be here in Belgravia for only another twenty-four hours or so. He had spoken truth when he told her that he couldn't recall a more pleasant morning, and had an unshakable feeling that he would enjoy the evening more in her company than in Roseline's.

There was only one fly in the ointment. He happened to know, as would any stockholder worth his portfolio, that telephone lines were now extended to most of Hampstead. If Miss Rayborn happened to ring her relations today, the opera would be off. True, he would still have the satisfaction of having angered William Doyle again, but the victory now seemed a little hollow.

Catherine. He had not known her Christian name until Mrs. Pearce spoke it over the telephone. It seemed to fit her looks and personality, and even somehow added to her attraction.

You're turning into a sentimental sop, he told himself, but smiling.

"Are you quite sure I should?" Catherine asked Aunt Phyllis. Not that she could do anything to alter the situation now, after accepting Lord Holt's invitation. "That's less time I'll be spending with you."

Her aunt took her by both hands, the brown eyes filled with excitement. "My dear, this is vastly more important! You would be foolish not to seize this opportunity. And you'll simply have to visit us in Sheffield to make up the time, won't you?"

A nagging little thought lurked in the back of Catherine's mind as she accompanied her aunt upstairs and listened to how dozens of young women would gladly trade places with her. *What would Mother and Father think?* But she tried to silence that voice by reasoning that Aunt Phyllis and Uncle Norman represented her parents as long as she was their guest. Why, her parents would expect nothing less than for her to obey them! And Aunt Phyllis had all but ordered her to accept the invitation.

"Let's go ahead and lay out your clothes," Aunt Phyllis said, flinging open her mahogany wardrobe. "I do believe my pearl grey satin would be a perfect contrast to your dark hair. Thank goodness we've not gotten around to packing the extra clothing. I've slippers covered in the same fabric. I only hope they fit you. I think my feet are more narrow than yours."

"I'll make them fit," Catherine said, and felt a little like Cinderella when they did. Cinderella with cramped toes, albeit.

Peggy rang at ten-past five, just after Aunt Phyllis had dabbed some *Jardin de Coeur* on Catherine's wrists and behind her ears, and the maid Rose had put the curling iron away. "I can't talk long," Peggy said over the telephone line. "Father's expecting a call from a customer. But I've discovered what I want to do after college!"

"I gather you had an interesting day," Catherine said, touching the ringlets cascading from the pins at the crown of her head. They swayed gently with her every movement, as did the sapphire and gold ear wires Aunt Phyllis had lent her.

"Vastly! We analyzed samples of stock from a chemist shop in St. Giles. But I'll tell you all about it tomorrow. Mr. Doyle said he was impressed with my analytical skills, and that there's no reason a woman shouldn't work for the Commission. Of course he was being kind, but—"

"William wouldn't have said that if he didn't mean every word."

"You're quite sure?"

Catherine smiled as if her friend could see her. "I am. William's wise enough to see what an asset you would be to them."

"Thank you, Catherine," Peggy gushed. "Well, Father's making motions to me. But I just couldn't wait to tell you."

"I'm glad you didn't wait, or I should have missed your call," Catherine said, and tried to imagine the shock on her friend's face as she added, "Lord Holt will be by very soon. We're going to the opera."

The pause that followed was as gratifying to Catherine's ears as the exclamation at the end of it. "*Lord Holt?*"

"Yes. You remember, the man who—"

"I remember! But how . . . ?"

Catherine smiled again. "I'll tell you all about it tomorrow."

There was another pause, then a hesitant, "But what about Lieutenant Elham?"

He had not visited Catherine's thoughts since she and Lord Holt shared the pear. "Well, we're not engaged. And it's just one evening at the opera."

"Yes, of course," her friend said with a little less conviction than Catherine would have wished.

Muriel and Aunt Phyllis came through the parlor doorway as Catherine replaced the earpiece.

"You're so pretty!" Muriel cried.

"Why, thank you Muriel." Catherine folded the girl into her arms, aware that she was risking another clinging episode, but too giddy with anticipation to be cautious. And fortunately, Muriel detached herself when the embrace concluded.

———

In 1834 when Parliament rescinded the charter given to the East India Company, breaking up a monopoly of two and a half centuries, the late Cyril Sedgwick was one of the small independent merchants who seized this new opportunity. Offering his greengrocery on Baker Street as security, he borrowed money from the Bank of England to build a two-storey brick building on Aldgate. There, family members and a growing number of hired workers packaged tea, purchased through the auctions in Mincing Lane, into the distinctive Royal blue tins for crating and shipping to shopkeepers in a widening circle of patronage.

Whereas Cyril had the initial dream, eldest son Fuller made Sedgwick Tea a household name by blending different varieties of teas from differing Indian regions to achieve a consistent taste. He offered free tins to families on holiday in such resorts as Brighton and Portsmouth, so that the fame would spread as those travelers returned home, and took advantage of the freight services offered by railways in the 1850's to reach markets as far north as Yorkshire and later, Scotland.

And so it was expected that Fuller's three sons would make their marks one day, especially Hugh, the eldest. Since leaving Cambridge, Hugh had been making those marks in accounting ledgers. None of his sons would be figureheads, Fuller determined, but would be competent in every aspect of marketing tea. It was the only way a family business should operate, if they expected to hand it down through generations of Sedgwicks to follow.

It made sense to Hugh, and so he did not mind in the least that he would have to prove himself before being given his own office, on the top floor of the four-storey building across Aldgate from the one Grandfather Sedgwick had purchased almost fifty years ago. The desk placed near the desk of Mr. Culiard, head accountant, afforded him contact with the other accounting staff—to include, besides Mr. Culiard, three bookkeepers and two secretaries—and any workers or visitors with business on the fourth floor. A solitary office would have limited the human contact, and when one spent hours with one's nose following a pencil, that contact was vastly important.

He was not alarmed over his lack of passion for his work. He had only been employed for two months, so surely that would come later. Besides, London would be a very giddy city indeed, if every person felt a passion for work. Competence and commitment to duty were more important than passion. His father seemed pleased with both in Hugh's regard, and just this morning had assigned him his first actual project. Under Mr. Culiard's mentoring, he was to determine the profitability of extending Sedgwick Tea's range of marketing to the States. Several factors had to be considered, including overseas—as well as railway—shipping, storage, advertising, and maintaining a branch office to control such operations.

"Fortunately, we would not have to add tariffs to our expenses, as the U.S. Congress exempted coffee and tea nine years ago," Mr. Culiard explained that afternoon, his chair drawn up beside Hugh's desk. He was forty or so, long-nosed and lean and usually in want of a haircut. He could have been a caricature of Dickens' Bob Cratchet but for an awareness of his own competence that gave him the courage to speak his mind.

"How long do you think that will last?" Hugh asked.

The accountant nodded approval. "Excellent question. They could vote to withdraw that exemption at any time. And so we would have to set prices with that in mind, else we could find ourselves having to raise them sharply and lose customers if the tariff is applied."

Hugh scanned the rough figures he had collected from other departments earlier this afternoon. "Is there a way to trim shipping costs?"

"I don't see how. The price per tonnage has already been negotiated."

Mindful of overstepping the bounds of his own limited experience, Hugh said respectfully, "But just because Morgan Shipping has always handled the transport from India, how do we know that they're offering the best price to the States?"

Mr. Culiard opened his mouth to reply, but then closed it again and looked at the figures on Hugh's page. "You know . . . it certainly can't hurt to get figures from other companies, can it?"

"You're not just humoring me, are you?" Hugh asked with lowered voice.

The man laughed, causing other workers to look up from their desks. "It was an excellent idea, Mr. Sedgwick. I only wish it had been mine."

A secretary, a young man fresh out of typing school, approached ten minutes before the office was to close at six. "Telephone for you, Mr. Sedgwick."

The fourth floor boasted two telephones, one in Hugh's father's office and the other attached to a wall over a desk and stool in the accounting department. It was to the latter that Hugh went.

"Mr. Sedgwick speaking."

"And why isn't Mr. Sedgwick *here*, is what I would like to know."

Hugh smiled at the sound of Neville's voice. "Ah, but I happen to know that Mr. Sedgwick is indeed here."

"Not here . . . *here*."

Returning the waves of two bookkeepers heading for the staircase with hats and coats, Hugh said, "Neville, if you recall, I said I didn't think I could—"

"Ah, but that wasn't a definite *no*. And Margery is desperate for you to meet Lillian."

That was the part that had made Hugh leery last week when Neville approached him about the outing. "I'm not sure I want to meet someone who's *desperate*."

"Lillian's not desperate, good man, and you'll see why when you set eyes upon her. *Margery's* the desperate one. She doesn't like the man who's been courting Lillian, though he's twice as rich as you. We've just gotten a table at Dyer's. I'll order you a steak, so just hurry on over and—"

"Impossible. I would have to go home and change."

His friend's groan came clearly over the line. "Very well. It'll give us an opportunity to talk about you anyway. We'll leave your ticket at the *on call* desk at the Lyceum."

"Neville, I really don't think . . ."

"Look, Hugh," Neville said with peevish tone. "I promised Margery you'd come, and she'll be sullen for a week if you don't show. Also, you know what they say about all work and no play."

"Very well," Hugh sighed. Rubbing his forehead as if that would somehow wipe out his stormy thoughts, he went down the corridor to his father's office.

"Mr. Sedgwick has not returned from the auction," his father's secretary, Mr. Westbrook, informed him.

"Please tell him I've gone ahead." He took up hat and umbrella and satchel and left the building for the half-block walk to Aldgate Station. The London Underground, the network of trains running beneath the streets, had been steadily expanding over the eighteen years since the initial four-mile track was laid. Even with having to switch trains at Paddington, the trips to and from work were cut by at least half the time his father's coach would have taken in London street traffic. South Kensington Station, where he stepped above ground again, was but a pleasant shady three-hundred-yard stroll from their three-storey Georgian home on Queensgate.

The kitchen was his first stop. He asked Mrs. Kiddy, the cook who had been with his family since before his birth, if he could have a sandwich packed in ten minutes.

"Can't you see how busy we are?" she grumbled from the work table, where she rolled a pastry while kitchen maid and scullery maid scurried about.

"Sorry," he said in a contrite tone. He winked at the scullery maid, who covered a smile. "I'm not *too* terribly hungry."

She shook her grey head and pointed the rolling pin at him. "Ten minutes, Master Hugh. But next time give us warning. You've a telephone in that office, yes?"

"Next time!" he promised. Leaving the kitchen, he considered and discarded the idea of having Amos, their coachman, bring the carriage around. Mrs. Kiddy was right about giving warning, and the poor fellow would miss his supper.

He stopped in the parlor just long enough to greet his mother and sisters, Claire and Noelle, ages thirteen and eleven. "Father will be along later," he said. "And I'll not be here for supper."

"But where are you going?" Mother asked, as she looked up from her needlework.

"The opera with Neville and Margery."

"*Just* Neville and Margery?" Claire asked with a mocking little smile.

He smirked at her. "There *may* be a young lady involved, if you must know. And I'm in a dreadful hurry, so I must beg your pardon."

Upstairs he washed his face and changed into a formal black tailcoat, with white cravat and gloves and top hat. He stopped in the parlor long enough to plant a kiss upon the cheeks of his mother and sisters, and another upon Mrs. Kiddy's lined cheek, for she had wrapped *two* roast beef sandwiches.

Kensington had settled itself into an evening tranquillity, the sun bisected by Saint Clement's steeple. He ate as the hansom bore him down Gloucester. Halfway through his first sandwich, he wished he had specified ham, for Mrs. Kiddy stuffed her roast beef liberally with garlic cloves. But the damage was done, and he was famished, so he consumed the other.

Gas lamps lit up *Rigoletto* on the marquee above the white columns of the Lyceum Theatre. Carriages and coaches were still pausing on Wellington to discharge people, a good sign that the opera had not yet begun. But having left his watch in his other waistcoat, Hugh could not be certain how much time until opening curtain. He paid the driver, brushed crumbs from the front of his coat, and hastened toward the entrance with top hat under his arm. About six steps from the entrance, he happened to glance toward Wellington, where a tall gentleman was helping a young woman from a coach. The first thing he noticed was that she was beautiful. And then he recognized her.

No wonder she didn't write back, he thought, and quickened his pace toward the Lyceum's entrance before she could look his way. Provided she were to take her eyes off the tall man, and that did not appear likely to happen anytime soon.

Twenty-One

L a donna e mobile
qual piu-ma al vento,
muta d'accento e di pensiero . . ."

The song resonated from the tenor's throat in tones as rich as the colors of the sixteenth-century Italian court setting. Lord Holt leaned close to translate. "Women are fickle, like a feather in the breeze."

Catherine nodded, her heart pounding to the tempo of the timpani. Her aching toes throbbed to the same rhythm, but she was glad she wore the shoes, for when he came for her at Aunt Phyllis's, he said she looked as stunning as a Nattier portrait. She had never heard of the artist, but the appreciation in her escort's blue eyes told her it was a compliment.

"E sempre misero
qui a lei s'affida,
chi le confida,
mal cauto il core!"

". . . and that a man will be miserable if he trusts her without guarding his heart," Lord Holt went on.

When she looked at him he smiled. "Verdi's sentiments. Not mine."

Never had she known anyone like him; elegant, sophisticated, witty, knowledgeable, and confident. Thoughtful, too, beginning the evening with roses for Aunt Phyllis, cigars to Uncle Norman, and box of Cadbury's chocolates for the children. At Gatti's, where he had thought ahead to reserve a table, he had guided Catherine past a queue of at least two dozen theatergoers to a secluded corner. The *Lobster a la Mode Francaise* he ordered for her was so excellent that she was glad she had not mentioned beforehand that she was not fond of lobster. And once they were seated in the box at the Lyceum, he presented her with a pair of opera glasses on a silver chain.

Mother would have made her return a gift from a man to whom she was not betrothed, but it was purely a practical gift. Not that she needed them, for their seats in box four were among the best in the house.

"What did you think?" he asked over the applause during the final bows.

"Wonderful performance," she replied, clapping gloved hands. But then, she could have accompanied him to a recitation of the London Telephone Directory, she told herself, and would not have enjoyed the evening any less.

In his coach again, Catherine ignored her aching feet, half-fearing and half-hoping that he would take her hand. And hoping *completely* that he would not attempt to kiss her. From what she had learned from Mother and friends at Girton, she would be required to slap him lest he assume she was of questionable virtue and despise her afterward.

"Are you sure you absolutely must leave tomorrow?" he asked, the side lamp bathing half his face amber.

He wants to see you again! Catherine told herself with wonder. Surely such a man could keep company with any woman he wished. So easily could she have agreed to stay. And she *wanted* very much to agree. After all, formal lectures would not begin until October fourth, six weeks from now. What would a few more days matter?

But Peggy had put off the trip a day for her. She did not wish to put a strain upon their resumed friendship.

And another reason rose from the murky depths of will and sentiment. She should not appear too eager, as if she had never been courted before. Which she hadn't. Not officially.

Lieutenant Elham's face appeared in her mind and evaporated. *He spoke with food in his mouth,* she remembered. How could she have purposely overlooked such a thing? *You were a silly girl,* she told herself. *Just as you were with Mr. Sedgwick. A man pays attention to you, and you lose your head.*

But it was different with Lord Holt. Because he was so much more mature, he enhanced what maturity she possessed. Just as she didn't wish to appear too eager, she didn't want to discourage him. How did one tread such a fine line?

"I didn't spend as much time with my Hampstead relations as I had intended," she said carefully, as if that were the chief consideration. "I should really return next week for a few days."

She could study just as well in Hampstead as Girton, if she would but make herself. *It's just a matter of conquering the will.*

"Now, that's the sweetest music my ears have heard all evening," he said. But an odd melancholy touched his smile, and he turned his face from her to stare through the window at the gaslit houses of Victoria Street.

Catherine's cheeks heated. *You've done it now!* she chided herself. He was probably thinking that she was no different from those dozens of other women Aunt Phyllis had mentioned. If only she had given it more thought before agreeing to return so hastily!

There's no mystery to you at all, is there? she told herself.

He faced her abruptly. "Miss Rayborn, there is something I must say."

"Yes?" She braced herself for whatever was to follow:

Investing occupies too much of my time.

I'm not interested in courting.

Or perhaps even, *Hampstead is too far away.*

"As much as I would like to see you again," he continued, "that will not be possible in Hampstead."

I knew it! Catherine thought, but joylessly. Still, she possessed enough pride to reply with forced flippancy in her voice, "Think nothing of it, Lord Holt. I shall be too busy anyway, what with needing to study, and—"

"Will you please listen?" he interrupted, blue eyes mildly annoyed. "If I didn't *want* to see you again, I wouldn't have asked you to stay."

The ache in Catherine's heart lightened. "Hampstead isn't so far."

Inexplicably, he chuckled in a flat sort of way. "I'm aware of that. It's your family there who would prevent it."

"My . . . family?"

"Would William Doyle happen to be one of those Hampstead relations?"

"Why, yes. He's married to my cousin Sarah. How do you know him?"

A silence of several seconds passed. "From Oxford. I really didn't intend to enjoy your company so much, Miss Rayborn. You've put me in a quandary."

"Why would he try to stop me from seeing you?" In fact, the reverse would be the case, for the family would be more favorable to her seeing someone who wasn't a total stranger.

She was about to point this out, when he frowned and said, "I'm afraid I treated him most shamefully while he was a servitor at Lincoln College."

She couldn't imagine Lord Holt treating anyone shamefully. Hadn't he shown patience with the waiter at Gatti's, even when the man mistakenly addressed her twice as "Miss Dell"? But the fresh memory of his behavior at the garden party came back to her. *He had a headache,* she reminded herself.

"William is a forgiving person," Catherine assured him, relieved that the obstacle between them was so easily vanquished. "But if you think it would help to clear the air, all you have to do is apologize."

He shook his head and groaned. "How I wish it were that simple."

"Then I'll speak with him."

"It won't do any good. Trust me."

"But why?" she asked.

"Truth is, there is more." Another silence passed, and then, "During the years Mr. Doyle was acquainted with me, I was young and foolish and full of myself. I had lost my father as a boy, and my stepfather and mother were too absorbed in their own child to provide any moral guidance."

Two emotions tugged at Catherine. Pity for the man beside her, for the regret in his tone could only have come from deep inner pain. And frustration, that while his confession was obviously heartfelt, it was so vague. What was she to think?

And the confession obviously was to remain vague, for he said in an apologetic, yet adamant voice, "I know I've confused you, Miss Rayborn. But that's all I can say. I just want you to understand that it's not lack of wanting to see you again that forbids me from calling on you in Hampstead. And as you're not allowed callers at Girton . . ."

"I don't have to tell them," Catherine said, barely able to keep the words from gushing forth. She had to see him again! They had known each other only for a day, yet oddly, she felt as if she had always known him. As if on the calendar of her life, this certain day had been circled many years ago.

"I can't ask you to deceive your family," he told her.

She appreciated that. "It would only be until we figure out a way for you to make things right with William." And she just knew that was possible. She had never seen William act toward anyone with anything less than kindness. Or at least toward anyone not guilty of adulterating food or medicine.

"I'm afraid his opinion of me will not be so easily changed."

"You don't know him as well as I do."

"Indeed." He was thoughtfully silent for a minute. "On High Street there is a grocer, J. Porsters. It's less than a half-mile walk from Cannonhall Road. Do you know it?"

She shook her head.

"If you'll keep a watch out, you can't miss it. Between it and the iron-monger's, Skoyle's, there is an arched entrance over a narrow little lane, Perrins Court, where there is a nice café called Banton's."

"I believe I could find it."

Finally he smiled. "But of course you can. If you still wish to see me again, just wire me from Girton telling me the day and time to be there."

Catherine wished they were speaking of tomorrow.

He scooped up her hand and held it for the remainder of the ride, squeezing so hard that the press of his ring against the inside of her fingers was painful even through the gloves. But she didn't wish to spoil the moment, so she endured it. Besides, it took her mind off her toes.

Under Aunt Phyllis's portico he brushed a kiss against the back of her hand. "But for a pair of smoked spectacles, our paths may never have crossed again, Miss Rayborn. Life is strange, isn't it?"

"Yes," she replied. *Strange and wonderful!*

Chambermaid Rose answered Lord Holt's soft knock right away, obviously having waited up for just that purpose. Once the door was closed behind her, Catherine leaned upon Rose's shoulder for support and took off Aunt Phyllis's shoes. The maid helped her limp upstairs on her throbbing stockinged feet.

"Have you ever been in love, Rose?" Catherine whispered in the guest room as the yawning girl unfastened the buttons along her back.

"Aye, Miss. I've a young man that works in the docks. He takes me to supper with his sister on my half day. I expect we'll marry."

Catherine was glad. She wanted to ask how she came to *know* she was in love, but she took pity on the girl and gave her a half crown for staying up.

"Thank you, Miss!" the girl exclaimed softly. "May you sleep well."

But sleep was a long time in coming. Beginning from when she descended the staircase and met Lord Holt's smile, Catherine relived every moment, every look and conversation as if her mind were a stage, herself and Lord Holt the actors. *And he didn't even try to kiss you,* she reminded herself. At least not on the face. Wasn't that proof that, no matter what occurred in his past, he was now a decent man?

Let's see . . . seventy pounds wouldn't bankrupt you by a long shot, Sidney told himself in the study just off his bedchamber. He looked over the figures again, glanced at the folded pair of spectacles upon his desk. *But you'll be kicking yourself if they catch on and you didn't take a greater risk.*

He was used to staying up late, and in fact, would still be out if he had used the tickets on Roseline. *And nursing a bloated head in the morning,* he thought, flicking the ash from his cigarette into the crystal tray. *With your purse considerably lighter,* for Roseline would have mentioned some need or want, even after he had spent all afternoon purchasing and arranging board for the horse. In his mind's ledger, her liabilities were beginning to outweigh her assets.

He sat back in his chair and took another pull from the cigarette. *Your*

Oxford chums would have a good chuckle, he told himself, letting out a stream of smoke. He would have laughed himself, had someone told him a month ago that he could find himself interested in someone so fresh and unworldly. Catherine Rayborn brought something out of him he didn't even know he possessed.

William Doyle and his dull wife were another matter. They could go to blazes for all he cared. But in the course of a few hours, his thoughts had evolved from wishing to upset their comfortable little world, to hoping they would not upset his.

Catherine shot up from her pillow and blinked at the unfamiliar surroundings. As her mind regained its focus, an auburn head appeared in the doorway.

"Are you awake, dear?"

"Yes, come in," Catherine said, while every molecule of her body strained to sink back into the mattress.

Aunt Phyllis hurried inside in a glow of expectancy and rustle of plisse dressing gown. "I thought of nothing but you all evening!" she gushed, as Catherine swung her feet out of the covers.

Catherine smiled and fished for her slippers. "I had a lovely time, thank you."

Her aunt lifted her dressing gown from the back of a chair and helped her into it. "If you think that's enough to satisfy me, dear niece, you're quite mistaken. Cook is sending a pot of tea out onto the terrace, and I expect you to join me there and provide some details before the children are up."

Hastily Catherine performed her morning toilette. The splash of cool water upon her face helped clear the cobwebs from her mind. She sat out on a wicker chair beside a stack of crating slats and a pail of nails, describing their meal at Gatti's, and then the opera.

"Oscar Wilde and his wife occupied the box opposite ours," she recollected, because she knew Aunt Phyllis would get a thrill from it. Funny, she had barely thought to be impressed when Lord Holt pointed them out, for even the Prince Regent's presence wouldn't have outshone her companion's.

Her aunt poured second cups of tea, the smile never leaving her face. "I hope you realize how fortunate you are. Your mother will be so pleased."

"Do you really think so?"

"When I tell her how high his family is esteemed? Your father will be a bear about it, but he's too far away to do anything but growl." As she handed Catherine the cup, a frown finally found its place. "The timing, however, couldn't be more disastrous."

"Yes." Catherine agreed.

"Must you return to Girton today?"

"I really must."

Aunt Phyllis took a sip of tea and inclined her head in thought. "That may be best, on second thought. He'll consider it a refreshing change from the women who throw themselves at him." Her face became anxious. "But he did ask to see you again, didn't he?"

"Yes," Catherine assured her.

"But of course," Aunt Phyllis said as the lines of her face eased. She sighed. "But that means he'll be courting you in Hampstead, and your father's relations will get to witness all the excitement instead of me. You must promise to write to me faithfully, and tell me everything that goes on."

Her aunt had not referred to that side of the family since Catherine's parlor visit on Friday. However disturbing was the breech, Catherine realized it was a convenient thing. It would not do to have Aunt Phyllis in communication with the Hampstead kin just now. Not until they could be made to understand the decent side of Lord Holt, as she did.

The movers were swarming about after breakfast. Catherine embraced her aunt and uncle and wished them happiness in Sheffield. Muriel clung to her with theatrical sobs until her brothers peeled her away by the arms. That led to the girl biting Bernard's finger and his cuffing her in return, and Aunt Phyllis and Uncle Norman becoming caught up in the fracas. Meanwhile the helpless nanny stood by, looking for all the world like a soldier about to be beckoned into the heat of battle.

Uncle Norman's coachman delivered her to Hampstead, carried her portmanteau to the door, and bade her farewell with a tip of his hat. Up in the guest room, Avis helped her pack her last-minute things. Before lunch she sat out by the goldfish pond with Sarah, Uncle Daniel, Aunt Naomi, and the children. Sarah still looked peaked, but handled the nausea better, she said, by nibbling on some ginger biscuits Trudy had concocted.

"I'm afraid it's going to rain on you this afternoon," Uncle Daniel said, cocking a speculative eye toward the grey clouds building in the northeast.

Catherine smiled at him. "After the monsoon, a little English rain is nothing."

They chatted of other things. Harmonica notes drifted pleasantly from the vegetable garden, where Guy, the coachman's son, sat on an overturned pail and played for Mr. Duffy. As much as Catherine cherished her father's side of the family, her thoughts were preoccupied with Lord Holt. She was tempted to mention his name casually in connection with other guests at Aunt Phyllis's party. Just a simple little test of the waters, to prove to herself that the years had tempered their low opinion of him, if indeed they had ever held one. But the fact that Aunt Phyllis had not invited them would make mentioning the party tactless.

"May I come back next week?" she asked Sarah as they left the dining room after lunch.

"But of course," her cousin told her. "Your room is always ready here."

"I just don't want to take you for granted."

"As if it would ever occur to you to do so."

Catherine gave her a little sideways embrace, greatly relieved that no explanation was asked of her. But just in case Sarah or anyone else was wondering, she paused before the staircase and added, "I didn't get to spend as much time with all of you as I would have liked."

It was true, she told herself to soothe the stab of guilt. Just because they were not her primary reason for returning did not make the secondary reason any less genuine.

"Are you limping, Catherine?" Aunt Naomi said, joining them.

Catherine turned to her and made a little grimace. "I stubbed my toe on the bedpost."

Two hours later at King's Cross Station, she whispered to Peggy, out of Uncle Daniel's and Bethia's hearing, "I'll explain later, but please don't say anything about Lord Holt."

Twenty-Two

*T*hough Girton's summer pace was refreshingly relaxed, it was still a routine to which Catherine had to readjust herself after two months away. But she thought she was applying herself fairly well until the twenty-seventh of August, four days after her return to school, when Peggy took it upon herself to inform her otherwise.

They sat at Catherine's sitting room table with a tin of chocolate Preak Freen biscuits between them. Catherine was penciling notes from *The Iliad*, and Peggy was reading the May issue of *Philosophical Magazine*, in which, she explained, chemist G. Stoney proposed that electricity was composed of discreet negative particles he referred to as "electrons."

"But if they can't be seen under a microscope, how can he be so sure they even exist?" Catherine asked.

"By the way they're influenced by other materials. He used a cathode ray tube—" She stopped and squinted curiously at Catherine's notebook.

"What is it?" Catherine asked, shielding her writing with her hand.

Peggy lay down her magazine and shook her head. "We've less than six weeks before term starts. At this rate, you're not going to finish *The Iliad*. Remember how adamant you were about studying ahead so you wouldn't have to struggle so?"

"But what do you think I'm doing now?"

Peggy reached over, brushed Catherine's hand aside so that the half dozen penciled *Lady Catherine Holt*s were visible. Mortified, Catherine covered the writing again and opened her mouth to snap something about Peggy minding her own business. But the concern in her friend's expression gave her pause.

"You're right," she admitted, shame heating her cheeks. "I'm just not quite used to being back. But I'll try harder to concentrate."

Peggy pressed her lips together, the hazel eyes skeptical.

"I really will," Catherine said. "Don't you believe me?"

"I believe you *think* you will."

"What does that mean?"

"I don't want to make you angry."

"I won't be angry," Catherine promised, trying to mean it. "Please, say what's on your mind."

Hesitantly, Peggy said, "You know how we've complained of Milly's obsession with her stepmother?"

"Are you implying that I'm obsessed with Lord Holt?"

"How long did you spend with him? A day? And now you speak of leaving Tuesday to see him again, when we've only been back four days?"

The past five sleepless nights chose that particular instant to extract their toll from Catherine. Suddenly she could not fill her lungs with enough air. "I can't help it, Peggy," she whispered. "You'll understand when you're in love."

Peggy stared, and at length said softly, "As you were with Lieutenant Elham?"

"I never said I was in love with him," Catherine protested, chagrined at the memory of how she'd prattled on about the man. On her dresser sat another long letter from Bombay. She dreaded the duty of having to inform him that she would be too busy to correspond. "That was a schoolgirl infatuation."

"And so it's different this time?"

"Yes." Catherine nodded to emphasize her answer. "I can't explain it, but it's very different."

"I'm just worried about you. Girls who give their hearts so easily can end up in all sorts of trouble. And the fact that you can't mention his name to your family is an ominous sign."

"But I *plan* to tell them about him."

"When?"

"Soon. And I sheltered my heart for nineteen years, so you needn't worry over me."

"You mean your *father* sheltered your heart." Peggy blew out a breath, muttering, "It's a curse to be pretty. I could save a man from a burning building, and he would thank me and perhaps toss me a shilling. All you have to do is ask why one is rubbing his eyes, and you're taken to the opera."

Catherine laughed. "You overdramatize everything, you know? You should be writing plays instead of analyzing compounds. Or analyzing me, for that matter."

Rolling her eyes, Peggy said, "I just don't want you to be hurt. Please promise you'll be careful, and not allow him to take advantage of you. I have a feeling he's used to an entirely different sort of woman."

"I'll make that promise, if it will make you feel better. But it's not necessary."

A knock sounded. Beatrice Lindsay stuck her head through the doorway.

"We're making taffy in the kitchen. Join us!"

Catherine turned to Peggy again. "Go ahead. I won't slack off while you're gone."

But Peggy smiled and reached over to take her pencil. "No one says you shouldn't have some fun."

In the train carriage bearing down upon London three days later, Catherine took little heed of fellow passengers or passing scenery, her attention fastened upon the text she held open before her.

> *Then after he had wrought this shield, which was huge and heavy, he wrought for him a corselet brighter than fire in its shining, and wrought for him a helmet, massive and fitting close to his temples, lovely and intricate work, and laid a gold top-ridge along it, and out of pliable tin wrought him leg-armour. Thereafter when the renowned smith of the strong arms had finished the armour he lifted it and laid it before the mother of Achilleus . . .*

You'll regret not protecting the heels too, Catherine thought. She was proud of herself for concentrating more diligently on Pope's translation since the heart-to-heart chat with Peggy three days ago. Even Peggy had noticed, expressing amazement over the eight notebook pages of notes—without a single *Lady Catherine Holt* penciled in the margin.

———

Because Perrins Court was not open to carriage traffic, Banton's drew very little patronage from those merely passing through Hampstead. Sidney only knew of it himself because he and Leona had met there occasionally during their early days together. Locals filled about half of the dozen tables, yet the absence of gasoliers in favor of candles gave an atmosphere of privacy.

Sidney was pleased to discover, as he entered the café at two in the afternoon on the last day of August, that no painful memories of Leona swooped down upon him. In fact, he found himself hoping that her relationship with Sir Kelly had improved. It was good for the children, when their parents loved each other. When the waiter, a man of thirty or so in white shirt, waistcoat, and apron, brought coffee, Sidney decided to go ahead and order their meals. There was little risk to doing so, he told himself, for she *would* be here.

His own appearance had not been decided definitely until yesterday evening. *You probably wouldn't even be here if not for the glove.* Not that he wasn't smitten with the girl. But that was exactly the problem. He had always prided himself on maintaining control of his feelings. The thought that some little part of his heart would be attached to someone, of its own doing, was frightening.

Finding the calfskin glove at Roseline's flat was the factor that pushed him over the edge. For an actress, she could have at least constructed a decent lie. But she had merely insisted that *he* had left it there, even after he tried it on and showed her the slack in the too-large fingers. He was relieved it was over, only regretting having spent so much money on her. Especially the horse. *She can buy her own oats.*

He was certain she wouldn't be without male attention for long, for some other twit was sure to come along, if he wasn't there already. Perhaps the glove's owner. *And more power to him!* Sidney thought. *I'll buy him a drink if I ever find out who he is.*

Catherine Rayborn appeared in the doorway, cheeks flushed and hair drawn back into a chignon under a narrow-brim straw hat. When their eyes met she looked surprised and relieved.

"Miss Rayborn," he said, getting to his feet as she approached the table. "I was relieved to receive your wire." Not that he doubted for a minute that he would hear from her, but because women liked to believe there was some element of mystery to them.

"Thank you," she said as she slipped into the chair he held for her.

"I'm happy to see you again."

"It's good to see you too." she said shyly.

"I took the liberty of ordering."

"Oh. Very good."

Seating himself again, he took her hand across the small table and said softly, "Tell me . . . how is it possible to grow even more beautiful in only one week?"

She gave him a little smile, averting her eyes. "The light is dim in here."

"Not from where I'm sitting. In fact, there's a little aura about you, like a painting of a saint."

"Thank you," she murmured.

Sidney smiled and thought that her chief charm was that she did not realize her own beauty. In the gilded world to which he was accustomed, of arched eyebrows and affected coy smiles behind fans, she stood out like a pearl on a strand of paste jewels.

He only wished she had worn her hair as she did in Green Park, the back long and loose, with tendrils curling over her shoulder. He could never fathom why women chose to braid and coil and tuck away one of their most unique and attractive features, but of course he would not tell her so and spoil the moment. She was no doubt trying to look mature for him, and he appreciated that.

"How did you get away?" he asked.

She looked uncomfortable. "I said I was going for a walk."

"Which is true," he reminded her. "You did walk, didn't you?"

"Yes."

A waiter brought two dishes of grouse pie and grilled mushrooms. Ordinarily Catherine was fond of both, but nervousness had driven her to consume seconds on boiled beef and suet dumplings from Trudy's kitchen. She had assumed she and Lord Holt were meeting for tea at such an hour in the afternoon. The suet dumplings were swelling in the pit of her stomach like sponges in bathwater.

But, because he was considerate enough to order for her, she speared a mushroom with her fork. Perhaps fungi did not require much room.

"Are you glad to be back at Girton?" Lord Holt asked after swallowing a bite of grouse pie.

Not as glad as I am to be here with you, Catherine thought, and lowered her eyes so that her expression would not betray her. "It was good to see some of my friends again."

"My fondest memories of University are of the times I spent with friends."

She raised her eyes to his again and smiled, pleased that he felt the same way.

He smiled back. "Tell me . . . what led you to enroll in college?"

"I hope to teach one day," she replied.

A faint look of distaste crossed his face. Catherine wondered if it had to do with the grouse pie or the notion of her teaching. "Is there something wrong?" she asked.

"Not at all." Dabbing lips with napkin, he said, "I just hate to see beauty wasted on brats too young to appreciate it."

An uneasy sense of disillusionment robbed her of any pleasure the compliment would have brought. This, from the man she loved? "I happen to be very fond of children, Lord Holt."

His blue eyes widened, as if he was just now realizing what he had said. "Do forgive me, Miss Rayborn. I'm actually fond of them myself."

"Than why would you—?"

"It was merely a term of endearment."

"Endearment?"

"Yes."

She wanted to believe that. But the word still hovered out there between them, refusing to be put aside.

He put his fork on the cloth. "Miss Rayborn, have you never lovingly labeled your sister a brat?"

"Only in jest."

"As I've done with my half brother, Edgar. And as I did just now." Lord Holt blew out a stream of breath. "I profoundly admire those with the patience to teach children. And had any of my schoolmistresses looked like you, I should have been the most excellent scholar in my class."

The pleading little smile he wore, the anxious lift of his brow, the charm of his words proved an irresistible mixture. Catherine's disappointment now turned upon herself, that she had taken offense so readily.

"Am I forgiven?" he asked.

"There is nothing to forgive," she replied. "The fault is mine for overreacting."

He winked at her. "I rather enjoy seeing you overreact. Such as when you sounded me out that day in Green Park."

Catherine winced at the memory and smiled. "May we change the subject?"

"Very well. What are you studying this summer?"

"I'm reading *The Iliad*," she replied while he took another forkful of grouse pie.

"*The Iliad*," he said after swallowing. "Are you aware that Troy may have been an actual place?"

"Why, no. I assumed it was mythical."

"As has everyone else, for centuries. But as we speak, a German named Schliemann or Schiulmann—or something equally difficult to pronounce—is excavating a site on the Aegean Sea believed to contain its ruins. I'm sure your lecturer will make mention of that when term begins."

Catherine was beginning to realize that he commanded a wide range of knowledge, like Uncle Daniel. After a tiny bite of grouse pie, she asked, "How do you know so much?"

As flattered as he was for her to notice, Sidney merely shrugged. "I go through newspapers like King Henry through drumsticks. And speaking of meals, you're not very hungry, are you?"

She gave him a look that could not be more wretchedly apologetic if she had confessed to stealing his purse. "I'm sorry. I—"

"It's unbecoming for a woman to have a large appetite anyway," he said, pushing his own empty plate aside. "We'll take a stroll."

Back on secluded Perrins Court, where they were not likely to bump into any of her kin, he offered his arm. "Now, tell me what's going on at Girton."

"Well, Peggy scolded me for not applying myself as diligently as I should," Miss Rayborn replied. "But I'm trying harder now."

"Peggy? You mean the friend from the party?" The party, where he behaved as a perfect boor, Sidney reminded himself. "Did she try to talk you out of coming?"

"She worries over me. That's all."

"And I didn't make a favorable impression on her, did I? There's a confectioner's around the corner. If I buy her a package of sweets as an apology, will you bring them back to her?"

Giving him a little smile, she said, "Peggy's very bright. She'll suspect you're trying to bribe her for my sake."

"And she would be right, wouldn't she?"

She pinkened modestly and changed the subject. "How is it that you're so familiar with Hampstead? Have you ever lived here?"

Sidney shook his head. "But a good friend once did."

"Where did he move?"

"To the States, actually. New York." The oddity of it struck him, that she would be staying at the house of his former lover. He would believe 5 Cannonhall Road held some charm for him, were it not now infested with Doyles.

"Do you miss him very much?" she asked.

"Not so much any more. It's not healthy to cling to the past." And because the subject needed changing, he smiled at her and said, "But if you'll promise not to blush too terribly, I'll tell you that suddenly the *future* appears brighter than it has in a long time."

"I can't make that promise, Lord Holt," she said, looking away while her cheeks flamed.

"Then, I shan't tell you," he teased.

The corners of her mouth tucked into the semicircles that he adored. For two shillings he would have kissed her, even though that would possibly frighten her away.

But the moment passed when she said, "I have to go back now, Lord Holt."

Sidney nodded, though disappointed. "Will I see you tomorrow?"

"Yes," she replied in such a way that he could tell she was hoping he would ask.

Back on Belgrave Square, he was just opening the *Times* when a knock sounded on the morning room door. "Yes?" he said, lowering the newspaper.

His mother entered, her face somber. "A woman rang for you a half dozen times while you were away."

"Mother," he sighed. "*Must* you continue to answer the telephone?"

She shook her head. "I only did so after the third time, when Rumfellow said she didn't sound sober."

That Roseline would be in such a state gave Sidney immense satisfaction . . . sweet revenge for the glove incident. Setting newspaper aside, he said, "Now, save that pained look for a real crisis. She's no one of importance. And I don't intend to see her again."

"Sidney." His mother's expression did not alter. "You said you were going to start considering your future."

"I am," he said, and partly to soothe the worry from her face, and partly because he relished the opportunity to say it, he told her, "I'm keeping company with a very decent young woman."

Hope mingled with doubt in her grey eyes. "Are you, Sidney?"

"I think I'm even her first beau." He had never considered the lieutenant-war hero a threat, and the fact that she never mentioned him again said volumes about how serious that relationship had been.

"Who is she?"

"Actually, you've met her."

When he informed her, she leaned down and kissed his forehead. "I can't tell you how pleased I am."

He smiled up at her. He could not recall the last time he had made his mother proud, and the feeling was quite nice. Especially considering the way he had achieved it. Keeping company with Catherine Rayborn was no great sacrifice.

Twenty-Three

*T*hat *should hold it,* Catherine told herself on the eighth of September, nine days after returning from Girton. She turned from the dressing table to look at Bethia, who sat pinned to the armchair, her lap filled by the dozing figure of Hector the cat.

"What do you think?" Catherine said.

Her young cousin eyed her bare forehead. "What did you do with the fringe?"

"Fringe is fine for schoolgirls." Catherine bowed her head so she could see the comb, which would soon be hidden by the brim of her hat. She eyed herself in the mirror again. "Do I look more sophisticated?"

"What's sophisticated?"

"Older," she said. She hoped the comb would stay without allowing too many stray hairs to dangle over her forehead. A second one, at the crown of her head, captured the sides of her hair so the rest could flow down her back. *Sophisticated, yet schoolgirlish.* Rather incongruous, she thought, but if it pleased Lord Holt, who had suggested the change, that was all that mattered.

"Avis wishes she were younger," Bethia said with an almost worldly sigh. "But she says she would want to know what she knows now because she was silly as a goose when she was a girl. She's teaching me to water-color."

Catherine smiled at her. "And what do *you* wish?"

The girl thought for a minute, then gave her an artful little smile. "That you would take me with you today? I'll be very quiet so you can study."

Catherine turned again to smile, ignoring the pang in her conscience. "I'm afraid not, Bethia. But I'll read to you again when I return, if you'd like. And tomorrow morning we'll take a stroll."

Atop her chest of drawers the tin of chocolates still waited to be brought to Peggy, who had written three days ago asking when she planned to return. *The Iliad* still waited on her bedside table to be read. Or at least given more than the scant attention she gave it. Which was not to say her eyes had not traveled many lines of print over the past nine days, but she might as well have read Mrs. Beeton's cookery book for all the information retained by her preoccupied mind.

"You do stay in the areas where there are other people, don't you?" Sarah asked during lunch that day, and not for the first time.

"Even Hampstead has its criminal element," Uncle Daniel warned.

Aunt Naomi nodded. "A young girl in a secluded spot . . ."

"Please don't worry," Catherine replied, "I'm never completely alone."

Her words were more true than they realized. Catherine's conscience, already starting to scar, felt another little stab. But an hour later, she could no more stop herself from peddling Sarah's bicycle northward than fly. And warnings notwithstanding, her relations respected her explanation that she could study more efficiently on the Heath than in the house or garden, where the temptation to visit with the others was so strong. So far only two occasions had altered that routine; a picnic after services on Sunday that she felt compelled to attend for the family's sake, and rain on Tuesday past.

At the end of the quarter-mile road bisecting the north Heath lay the Vale of Heath, once a malarial swamp and now a picturesque cluster of cottages around Hampstead Pond. The pounding of hammers rang out through the air, as laborers attached slate shingles to the roof of a bakery opening soon. Jerry, Lord Holt's coachman, was watering the horses in a trough outside the Suburban and Hampstead Hotel. "Good afternoon, Jerry," she said, propping the bicycle against the fence.

He looked around at her and touched the brim of his hat. "Good afternoon, Miss Rayborn. Did you have a pleasant ride?"

"Most pleasant, thank you." She was struck by how much more affable the man was to her, respectfully so, whenever Lord Holt was not present. Inside, the hotel proprietor led her from the hall into the dining room. Lord Holt rose from their usual table under a Constable painting of the Heath. Ever mindful of her comfort, he always arranged to be early so that she would not have to wait alone.

They were taking a risk, meeting in Hampstead, but as fond of Lord Holt as she was, she could not bring herself to accept his invitation to take the coach down to the City to a restaurant with private rooms. Some of her parents' protectiveness was ingrained in her, she had discovered, and besides, he would surely not respect her if she broke too many rules of convention.

After some strategic hinting, Catherine had discovered that the family preferred the Spaniard's Inn and Jack Straw's Castle to any other dining-out places in Hampstead. And with her leaving the house just after lunch, there was even less chance of being discovered. It was Sidney who suggested the Vale of Heath, away from the Hampstead shops.

Over tea for her and lunch for him, they discovered a little more about each other every day. Sometimes he would relate an incident from his boyhood or explain particulars of the Stock Exchange, and she would describe the goings-on at 5 Cannonhall Road. This particular afternoon she told him of the gifts she had bought on Highgate that morning to ship to Bombay so that they would arrive before Christmas, and the contents of her mother's latest letter—forwarded by Peggy from Girton, where Mother had assumed she would be by this time. As conversation flowed they found they had less need of it, and the spaces of companionable silence lengthened.

After Lord Holt finished his meal they strolled outside to their usual bench by the pond. He lit a cigarette and opened the recent issue of *Quarterly Review,* and she opened her text. If she read at least a page, she was justified in telling the family that she studied during these outings.

Justified, but becoming increasingly more miserable, at least where her relations were concerned. This weight chained to her newfound happiness was growing heavier daily.

"I hate this slipping about, Lord Holt," she said on that Thursday.

He did not move his eyes from the *Quarterly Review* but did pat her hand. "So do I, Catherine."

It was the first time he had addressed her by her Christian name, and it emboldened her enough to say, "If I knew everything William had against you, surely I could think of a way to put it all to right."

"Some things are irreparable."

"You don't know him as I do. He'll forgive you."

Now he lowered the magazine and gave her a weary smile. "You're too young to understand men, Miss Rayborn. While he may forgive me if I grovel enough, he'll still do all he can to prevent me from seeing you. That will not change, trust me."

But what could you have done that was so terrible? she wanted to ask. The question was one of the many things crowding out the absorption of *The Iliad* from her mind. But she did not persist, for she could tell he was becoming annoyed. She devoted herself to staring at the open book so that he could read his magazine. And just when she had convinced herself that he was regretting ever having gotten involved with her, he put aside the magazine and turned to her. "You know what I like about sharing your company?"

"What?" Catherine asked, holding her breath.

"I don't feel I have to bring along a dog and pony show to amuse you. We can just be quiet together. I've never had that with anyone else. That's rather nice, isn't it?"

She returned his smile. "Yes, very nice."

"You're a good influence on me, Catherine Rayborn." He offered her his arm and nodded ahead. "Shall we take a turn around the pond?"

Minutes later in the shade of a poplar tree, he drew her to him and kissed her for the first time. It was a gentle press of his lips against hers, but still potent enough to make her light-headed.

"You've captured my heart, Catherine," he said, his voice husky.

Her heart was filled to bursting, and she could scarcely believe her happiness. Leaning her head upon his broad shoulder, she said, "And you mine, Lord Holt."

"Sidney," he corrected gently, combing fingers through the hair behind her neck.

"Sidney."

He lifted her chin and kissed her again, this time not quite so gently. If she could freeze time, Catherine thought, she would wish to be there in his arms forever. But eventually and reluctantly she had to tell him that it was time to leave, lest a worried Uncle Daniel come searching for her.

Jerry, adjusting one of the horses' bridles, wiped his hands upon his trousers and hastened to open the door to the coach. He stood beside it, as formal as a palace guard. Sidney did not even look at him. Catherine's family had always relied on hired carriages and omnibuses, so the only other coachman in her acquaintance was Stanley Russell. While Stanley always maintained a respectful attitude, he was also treated as part of the Doyle-Rayborn family.

Perhaps that's supposed to be the exception, not the rule, Catherine thought as Sidney touched her cheek before entering the coach. Jerry closed the door behind his employer, nodded at her, and climbed up into his seat.

———

"Mrs. Doyle, may I have a word with you?" Mrs. Bacon asked the following afternoon.

"But of course." Sarah closed her ledger book and rose slowly from her writing table at a parlor window facing the Heath. The constant nausea was no better than when it started one month ago, but she was learning that she could at least hold her meals by avoiding certain foods and almost constantly nibbling on the ginger biscuits Trudy made for her. "Please, have a seat."

The housekeeper settled into a chair, and Sarah another. "It's none of my business, Mrs. Doyle, but I'm concerned over Miss Rayborn."

For a second Sarah thought she meant Bethia, but the gravity in the housekeeper's bespectacled eyes was in keeping with problems concerning someone older. "You mean my cousin?"

"Yes, Missus." Mrs. Bacon drew breath. "Susan gathers up the laundry at night. She told me the clothes Miss Rayborn wears for those walks on the Heath always come back smelling of smoke."

A ludicrous picture of Catherine gathering sticks to build a fire flashed through Sarah's thoughts.

"Tobacco smoke," the housekeeper clarified as if privy to the scene in Sarah's mind.

"I see." And that explained something—Catherine's professed need to find a spot on the Heath, when the house and garden abounded with private nooks and crannies. Perhaps the habit sprang from the pressure of studying so intensely, or perhaps it was the fashion among college women now. *Is she afraid we'll tell Uncle James?* Surely her cousin knew them all well enough to know they would not pack tales unless the matter was far more serious.

"Thank you for bringing this to my attention, Mrs. Bacon."

"There's something else, Missus."

"Yes?"

"Susan doesn't want Miss Rayborn to know that she's the one who told. The servants are all very fond of her, and . . ."

"I understand. Please tell Susan she has nothing to worry over."

"Thank you, Missus." Mrs. Bacon got to her feet. "Hate to see Miss Rayborn take up such a nasty habit, her so young and all."

"So do I." Sarah sighed. "And I suppose I should speak with her."

Because now that she had time to digest the information, she believed she would be failing her cousin if she did not at least express her concern.

Catherine and Sidney were in the middle of their third kiss when their solitude was infringed upon by voices with lilting Celtic accents. The four laborers from the bakery were seating themselves on the slope leading into the pond and digging into lunch pails.

"T'sn't fair that the wee one of us gets the biggest sandwich, now is it?" stated one in the tone that suggested he had made the same observation before.

"Can I help it if me wife loves me more than yer mum loves you?" was the merry reply.

"You had your chance, Kenny," said another. "That Flanagan woman would ha' married you at the drop of a hat."

"Better to have no sandwich than that woman," the first grumbled, to the chuckles of his mates.

Smiling at their banter, Catherine turned again to Sidney. He broke the severe look he was sending in the men's direction to shake his head at her and mutter, "No better than dogs, are they? Come, Catherine."

She walked with hand threaded through his arm, his remark echoing over and over in her mind.

"My mother would like to see you again," he said with a sidelong smile. "You two should get to know each other. One day soon, couldn't you say you're going shopping in the city? Or to study? The British Museum Library, perhaps?"

Her pulse jumped for two reasons. Delight, because it was common knowledge that when a man asked a woman to spend time with his family, he was fairly certain he wanted her for a wife. And panic, because while she could rationalize her outings over the Heath, this would be an outright lie.

Beneath it all surged a dull disappointment.

"Why did you say that?" she asked when certain that they were out of the workmen's range of hearing.

"Because we shan't have time any other way. By the time you—"

"No," she cut in. "Those men."

His blank look was followed by an arched eyebrow. "Frankly, they cheated me out of the opportunity to steal another kiss."

That brought back the still-fresh memory of the first three, and her knees went a little weak. Still, she could not understand the scorn that was in his voice under such benign circumstances.

Another young couple approached, holding hands. The four traded nods, and when there was some distance between them, Lord Holt turned his face to her again and frowned.

"You're not still fretting over that, are you?"

Catherine looked up at him. "They were just minding their own business. You sounded as if you hated them."

He sighed, patted the hand resting in the crook of his arm. "I admire how you see some good in everyone, Catherine. But you've spent much of your life outside of England, and you're still in a very sheltered environment. You haven't noticed what the Irish are doing to this country. Always with their hands out, too lazy or drunk to earn their bread like everyone else. Everyone I know despises them—except for my mother, who is just as sheltered as you are."

It was true that she was sheltered, even now with the relative independence of a college student. But one thing living abroad had taught her was that every culture had its good and bad elements. "How can you accuse them of being lazy when you've seen them working on that bakery every day?"

His second sigh was longer, tinged with impatience. "Very well . . . there are some exceptions to every rule, I suppose. But I reserve the right to associate with whom I please, and that will never include the Irish."

Catherine did not know how to respond to that, so she walked with him in silence and tried to push the disappointment from her mind. At length he stopped and turned to rest both hands upon her shoulders.

"But if this troubles you so much, dearest Catherine, I shall be only too glad to march over there and apologize. I can't bear to have you disappointed in me."

"Please don't," she said. That would be far worse, for she was certain they had not heard him.

"Then, will you forgive me if I promise to watch my tongue henceforth?"

He was giving her the look of a small boy caught sliding down the banister, and she melted under it. *He had a difficult childhood,* she reminded herself. Losing his father so young. A difficult childhood would naturally generate harsh opinions.

And he said you're a good influence on him. Wasn't his offer to apologize to the men evidence of that? Surely the more time they spent together, the more she could influence him to view people different from himself through less condemning eyes.

"I will," she said, smiling up at him.

"That's my girl," he said, and kissed her forehead. A childish laugh came from the lower bank of the pond. A small boy, holding the string to a toy boat, was pointing up at them.

"We don't stare at grown-ups, Master Charley," the boy's nursemaid admonished, sending Catherine and Lord Holt an apologetic look.

Sidney winked at Catherine. "We should get you back to Cannonhall Road before you—and young Master Charley—get into trouble."

––––––––

Upon her return, Catherine changed her clothes and sat out on the terrace with her young cousins. She read *The Butterfly's Ball and Grasshopper's Feast* twice to Danny, then to Bethia the final four chapters from *The Parker Twins and the Weeping Knight*.

"You'll wear Catherine out," Aunt Naomi said to the children when she fetched them to wash up for supper.

"I enjoy reading to them," Catherine told her, and reminded herself that she had done so countless times before meeting Sidney. The fact that holding a Parker Twins book made her feel closer to him was irrelevant.

"What is all that, Father?" Sarah asked that evening when Uncle Daniel entered the parlor with an armload of parcels wrapped in colored paper.

Uncle Daniel, who had excused himself after supper, replied, "I finished my first draft this morning—"

"Congratulations, Daniel!" William interjected.

"Thank you," Uncle Daniel said when all congratulations were given. He handed a parcel to Bethia, perched on the arm of William's chair. "And so I felt a little celebration was in order."

"*That's* where you went this afternoon," Aunt Naomi said.

Uncle Daniel gave his wife a wink and a parcel. "Did you think I had a secret *rendezvous?*"

"Daniel . . ." Aunt Naomi cut her eyes toward Bethia.

As if on cue, the girl looked up from picking at the ribbon about her parcel. "What's a ron-dee-view?"

"It's a meeting, Bethia." Uncle Daniel smiled at Catherine and handed her a parcel. "Father's just teasing Mother."

Catherine was glad to have something upon which to direct her attention, for the guilt that crept through her at the mention of the words "secret rendezvous" was surely apparent on her face. During the untying of ribbons and rustling of paper, Uncle Daniel placed two parcels on a lamp table, then sat again on the sofa to watch.

"Thank you, Father!" Bethia exclaimed, holding up a small Blue Willow china cup from a tea set. Sarah's gift was a calfskin case small enough to fit in a reticule and containing a hairbrush, comb, and mirror; William's, a pair of fine leather gloves. Aunt Naomi received a bottle of *Bouquet a la Marechal* perfume. Catherine received a cloth-covered papeterie with a hook-and-eye lid and fitted with cream-colored stationery and envelopes.

There was even a wind-up toy mouse for Hector, which Uncle Daniel allowed Bethia to open. Amidst the thanks going around, Sarah said to her father, "But you're the one celebrating. Didn't you get anything for yourself?"

"I did. The pleasure of watching you open them."

"Who are the other two for, Father?" Bethia asked.

"Danny," he replied. The boy was asleep in the nursery. "And Guy."

"How kind of you to think of Guy, Daniel," Aunt Naomi said.

He shrugged, but smiled at her. "I saw a flute in a shop window and decided he must have it."

They admired each other's gifts, and laughed over Hector's ignoring the wind-up mouse as if to say *You can't seriously expect me to chase that thing.* The lightness and camaraderie took Catherine's mind off her guilt for a little while, but when she retired to her bedchamber she was seized by panic.

Three weeks! She had read barely a third of *The Iliad.* It would be impossible to meet the study goals she had set at the beginning of the long vacation. *You should return to school,* she told herself. But the dread produced by the thought of leaving Sidney far overshadowed any panic over her studies.

Twenty-Four

*B*ut Catherine's plans were changed in the most abrupt fashion. A light knocking sounded at her door while she was sitting up on the pillows reading Homer. Or at least attempting, for the memory of Sidney's kisses kept interfering with the portion of her mind attempting to concentrate on the text.

"Come in?"

The door opened and Sarah entered, fair hair loose over the shoulders of her dressing gown of light blue *peau de soie*. She said, "Don't get up."

"Is something wrong?" Catherine asked, noticing the discomfort in her green eyes.

"There's just something I need to discuss with you, if I may."

"Of course." But Catherine could not lie there and allow her cousin, in her condition, to stand. She drew up her knees under the covers. "Do sit, will you?"

"Thank you."

She knows rushed into Catherine's head as her cousin hefted herself up slowly to sit on the bed's foot. *No, how could she? You're just imagining things.*

"What's the matter, Sarah?" she asked when her inability to bear the suspense outweighed the dread of knowing.

"Well . . ." Sarah tugged at the hem of her nightgown to cover her slippers, and leaned back against the bedpost. "You know how much I care for you, Catherine. You became as a sister to me when I was reunited with my family."

"You've always been special to me," Catherine told her.

Her cousin gave her an appreciative, if uneasy, smile. "I would never interfere with your life unless I was concerned you were involved in something that could harm you or your reputation."

For a fraction of a second, Catherine was back at Girton, hearing those same sentiments from Peggy. Her nerves prickled under her skin. "I appreciate that, Sarah," she said, trying to keep her voice composed.

"As unfair as it may be, society overlooks some things men do, but can be very harsh with their opinions when a young woman . . ."

She can't possibly know, Catherine told herself again. *And you're not acquainted with anyone in Hampstead who could have recognized you.*

". . . even at nineteen, you're still so very young . . ."

But what if it was someone with whom she was *not* acquainted, who had casually mentioned to Sarah of seeing her with a tall, auburn-haired man? She was introduced to at least a dozen people when she accompanied the family to Christ Church, people whose names had floated on through her Lord Holt-occupied mind.

". . . and once your reputation is damaged, it's almost impossible to repair."

Sweat chilled the back of Catherine's neck.

"I'm just going to have to come out and say this, Catherine." Sarah sighed. "I know why you go off over the Heath in the afternoons."

"To study," Catherine said in a small voice.

Her cousin shook her head. "That's not all, Catherine."

The nerves prickling Catherine's skin threatened to crawl through her pores. She and Sarah stared at each other for several long seconds, until Catherine could no longer hide the guilt in her eyes and lowered them to the coverlet pulled over her raised knees.

"How did you find out?" she asked.

"I'm not at liberty to say," Sarah answered. "But that's not important."

A weight pressed against Catherine's chest so that drawing in breath became a labor. She raised her eyes again. "I wanted so badly to tell you, but Sidney said you and William would never allow us to see each other if I did. He regrets mistreating William at Oxford, Sarah, and he really wants to have a decent life now, and I'm so *terribly* in love with him!"

It was almost a relief to get it all out. She held her breath and waited for whatever was to follow. But Sarah just stared at her with an unreadable expression.

"Sarah?" Catherine said when she could bear the silence no longer.

"Who is this Sidney, Catherine?"

Did you say too much? Catherine asked herself. But she had plunged in with both feet, and did not have the wits about her to make up a name.

Besides, she had already mentioned that William was acquainted with him. "Lord Holt."

Her cousin's face went as white as the bedsheets. "Lord . . . *Holt?*"

"He even confessed to me how insufferable he was at Oxford, and doesn't fault William one whit for his low opinion of him," Catherine said, unable to stem the gush of words. "And we were going to tell you eventually, as soon as we figured out—"

"How did you meet him?" Sarah said evenly.

There was nothing to do but tell her, while hoping that the description of Aunt Phyllis's garden party and the most-proper circumstances of their being introduced would soothe some of the discomfort in her cousin's expression.

"He saved Muriel's life. I met his mother, and Aunt Phyllis says she's a fine woman. Mrs. Godfrey. She writes those children's books that Bethia and Jewel adore, and serves diligently on the Saint Peter's Flower Committee."

But Sarah was holding her hand up to her throat as if she would choke. "Lord Holt, Catherine!" she said in a forceful whisper. "How could you?"

Did you not hear everything I just said? Catherine asked under her breath. "He's changed, Sarah. You don't know him as I do—"

"I don't want to hear that, Catherine," Sarah said with a shake of the head. "And isn't it just like him to go after someone as naive as you?"

"I'm nineteen years old!"

"As far as men are concerned, you're still a child." The green eyes widened as if Sarah were struck with a terrible thought. "Has he attempted to force himself upon you?"

"No! He's been nothing but a gentleman." Which was true, for the kisses were acceptable to both participants.

"Oh, Catherine, you don't even know whom you're up against!"

She was so wrong, and Catherine so helpless for words to try to convince her. She burst into tears instead, pressing her forehead against the knees raised under the covers. The mattress moved; she heard Sarah's feet lightly on the carpet and then felt a hand upon her shoulder.

"You don't understand him," Catherine rasped through a raw throat.

"I understand him all right," Sarah replied flatly.

"What has he done that would make you hate him so?"

"I don't hate him. Neither does Will, though yes, we share a low opinion of him. He conducted himself most shamefully during his Oxford years. I'm speaking of frequenting brothels, Catherine."

Catherine swallowed thickly. "Brothels?"

"Surely you know what they are."

While the news was distressing, Catherine discovered she was not over-whelmingly stunned. Her thoughts raced in the direction she had forbidden them to travel ever since he mentioned his dark past. Murder and robbery she had eliminated, for he would be in prison or the grave if he had committed either. That only left one immorality she could think of. And yes, she knew about brothels, for as inexperienced as she and her friends were, there had been the occasional whispered conversations at Girton about subjects not having to do with Classics or Mathematics.

She should hate him, she thought, but pity overshadowed the discomfort the news brought. *I was young and full of myself,* he had said. *With no moral guidance.* All that time he was a lost soul, searching for elusive happiness in one pair of strange arms after another and despising himself afterward, not even realizing that it was decency he longed for, that it was someone like her who could make him happy.

"And we have it on good authority that he had an affair with a woman who once lived here." Her cousin went on, unrelenting. "The woman had *children,* Catherine. Her husband had to move the family to the States to get her away from him."

That part was more disturbing than the news about the brothels. *That's how he's so familiar with Hampstead,* Catherine realized. The woman was the *friend* of whom he had spoken.

Just before he said that the future looks brighter than it has for a long time, she reminded herself. Proof that he regretted the affair, if indeed it did happen.

"Catherine, you do realize that adultery is a grave sin, yes?"

Catherine raised her stinging eyes from her knees. "Of course. But you've no idea how much he regrets his past, Sarah."

Her cousin groaned. "Have you not heard anything I've said?"

"Yes, of course." She grasped hopefully for something that Sarah, of all people, surely couldn't refute. "But aren't Christians supposed to forgive?"

"We are. But that doesn't give us permission to have romances with scoundrels."

He's no scoundrel. She knew Sidney's heart. And she desperately needed to speak with him. He would explain everything. Reassure her. *Tomorrow he'll make it all better.*

A horrid thought followed, more horrid than anything Sarah had told her. *What if they won't allow you to see him?* Cautiously, she asked, "Are you going to tell the others?"

Sarah appeared to wrestle with that. The chimneypiece clock ticked several times before she replied, "I'm not sure."

"Please don't, Sarah," Catherine begged. "Uncle Daniel will tell Father, and he'll make me go back to Bombay." While the worry was a valid one, she hoped it would distract Sarah from considering what should be done about *tomorrow.* She could not think beyond seeing Sidney.

But her hopes crumbled when Sarah said, "Then you're going to have to go back to Girton, Catherine. Tomorrow morning. We'll send whatever laundry you have."

"Tomorrow?" Catherine seized Sarah's right hand from her shoulder. "Please, *please* let me see him one more time. I'll ask him about everything you—"

"Impossible." Sarah shook her head. "You leave and forget you ever met him. You must give me your word, or I'll have to inform William and Father."

"You mean, you won't tell?"

"Not if you'll make that promise. I don't want my husband going fisticuffs with that man. But I'll do it if I must, and you can be sure Father will wire Uncle James."

"But what will everyone think if I up and leave so quickly?"

"You can say you're worried over your studies—which you *should* be, if your attention has been consumed with Lord Holt. Will you promise me, Catherine?"

Feeling as though the life had been drained from her, Catherine let go of Sarah's hand and wrapped her arms around her knees again. "I promise."

"I'm sorry it had to come to this, Catherine," Sarah said, stroking her hair. "And I know you don't believe this, but you'll thank me for this one day."

I'll never thank you for this, Catherine thought.

"You spoke with her?" William mumbled sleepily.

"Yes," Sarah replied, settling again into her pillow.

"That's good. Bad for the lungs."

"Um-hum." She stared up at the darkness as if she could see through the bed canopy into heaven. *William's not a brawler, Father,* she prayed, hoping God would understand. *And I wouldn't put it past Lord Holt to challenge him to a duel.*

She only wished she had not agreed to keep it from her father. Lord Holt could read railway timetables as well as the next scoundrel, and Cambridge was not that far.

But you gave her your word, Sarah reminded herself, as her husband's deep breathing melded into faint snores beside her. *And Catherine gave hers.* Her cousin had always been trustworthy before. Still, she added to her prayer, *Please protect her from that evil man.*

Candlelight flickered upon the smooth black surface of the telephone as Catherine picked up the earpiece. "Please connect me with Lord Holt's residence on Belgrave Square."

"One moment, please," came the operator's tinny voice.

Catherine turned away from the mouthpiece long enough to blow her nose into a handkerchief, fearing any minute the parlor door would open. Finally came the sound of ringing; once, twice . . . eight times before a sleep-filled, though dignified, male voice answered, "This is the residence of Lord Holt and Mr. and Mrs. Godfrey."

"Forgive me for the late hour," she said thickly. "But I must speak with Lord Holt."

The voice at the other end sharpened. "Madame, you have been warned repeatedly not to telephone here again."

"But I've never—"

After the click the line went dead.

She forced herself to go down to breakfast the following morning because her absence at the table, combined with leaving so abruptly, would arouse suspicions. She could not have anyone asking too many questions, lest Sarah allow something to slip. Besides, somewhere inside the stone in her chest, there was still love for her family. It would be indecent to just up and leave.

"All you all right, dear?" Aunt Naomi asked when Catherine entered the dining room.

"Yes, thank you. Just a little trouble sleeping." Catherine kissed her cheek and took a plate from the sideboard, where Uncle Daniel was dishing buttered eggs onto one of the children's plates. He gave her a concerned smile and forked some bacon onto her plate. She knew she looked a wreck; her eyes felt as if her lids were made of sandpaper.

"I'll be returning to Girton this morning," she said as she carried her plate to the table. "I really need to take advantage of the study groups before term begins."

"It's probably best," Aunt Naomi said, not looking as surprised as Cath-

erine had thought she would, "to become reacclimated to the school environment before lectures begin."

"But we were going to take a walk this morning," Bethia said. "And you
won't be able to say good-bye to William."

"Catherine needs to go back, Bethia." Sarah did not look up from spread-
ing marmalade on Danny's toast. "I'll tell William for her."

Though there was disappointment in her blue eyes, Bethia said, "I'll miss
you, Catherine."

"And I'll miss you, Bethia," Catherine said. She swallowed. "All of you."
Which was true. It was just that there was one person she would miss far more.

"Will you come see us again soon?"

"As soon as I can," Catherine replied and sent Sarah a hopeful glance.

This time Sarah looked back, and said with a firmness wrapped in a soothing tone that would escape the others' ears. "Yes, we'll all miss you, Catherine.
The months until Christmas vacation will seem forever."

It was her cousin's way of saying that she would be welcome back. But
not until later, when she hoped Sidney would no longer be an issue. Catherine
nodded and wondered how anyone who had felt love, as Sarah had, would
not feel pity for her plight.

"You really don't have to see me off," she told Uncle Daniel after farewells
were all said, and Stanley held open the door to the coach out in the carriage
drive.

"Oh, but Bethia and I enjoy the outings," Uncle Daniel replied with a
hand lightly upon his daughter's shoulder.

At King's Cross Station, they did not leave her side. Though still shaken
by last night's attempt, she longed to steal away to the stationmaster's office
and ask to use the telephone. Hopefully Sidney would answer this time, or at
least a sympathetic servant. But when she excused herself for the ladies' comfort room, Bethia asked to go too, and so she had no choice but to take her
along. She had given Sidney advance notice when the Sunday picnic interfered
with their plans, and on the afternoon it had rained, he had naturally figured
out that she would not be able to meet him. But this time would he worry
that they had been discovered? Or that she was angry over his remark about
the Irishmen?

You can wire him when you get there, she told herself as the train panted
out of the station. But that would not be until noon. If only there were telephones in Cambridge! She could only hope a wire would reach him before he
set out for Hampstead. She stared out the window, willing the train to go
faster, tormented by a mental picture of Sidney frowning at his watch at their

table at the Suburban and Hampstead Hotel.

"She's still peeved over that remark I made about the Irishmen," he was muttering to himself. *"If she can't be more forgiving than that, perhaps I shouldn't waste my time with her."*

With Michaelmas Term still three weeks away, only one other person shared her first-class carriage—a young blond-haired man, obviously a student. He held open a book, but many times Catherine sensed his eyes upon her. Eventually he cleared his throat and gave her a bashful smile. "Are you enrolled at one of the women's colleges, Miss?"

"Yes, Girton." She sent him a smile bland enough to convey the message that she was not interested, before turning again to the window. He did not disturb her again.

At Cambridge station she went into the telegraph office. "I'd like to send a wire to London, please."

"Very well, Miss." The man behind the desk held his pencil over a sheet of paper. "What would you like it to say?"

What she would have *liked* to have said was that Sarah had told her everything, and while the news was disturbing, she had confidence that Sidney had a good heart and would live his life differently if by some miracle he could go back in time, and that she hoped they would still see each other even though she would not be allowed to return to London until Christmas, and would he please write.

But one did not pour out one's heart to a telegraph operator waiting expectantly on the other side of the desk, especially when one was on the verge of tears. And so she shortened the message considerably.

"*Sent back to Girton,* Miss?" The operator asked.

"Yes. Please."

"No, Miss Rayborn, you've received no telegram since you asked an hour ago," Miss Bernard said to Catherine after lunch on Monday. "Rest assured, I will personally deliver it to you when it arrives."

"Thank you," Catherine told her sheepishly and walked down the corridor again. *He's received your wire by now,* Catherine thought. *Surely he understands it wasn't my doing.*

She only wished she had not chided him over his statement about the Irishmen. Yes, it was wrong of him to say what he did, but she could have put that to him in a milder way. Their last conversation had traveled through her mind over and over for the past two nights. She dissected every word she could recall, every look that had passed between them, to figure out if something else could be the reason why she hadn't received a reply.

She sent her plea upward, her first heartfelt prayer since she asked God to ease Grandfather Lorimer's suffering. *Make him answer my telegram, Father, please. I'll do anything you want, be anything you want, but please let me hear from Sidney.*

Twenty-Five

I'm afraid it's going to set in for a while," Mr. Babington, manager of the Bank of England, said over the cards fanned out in his long fingers.

As if on cue, the four men at the commerce table in the Brookes' Club glanced toward the nearest window. Mid-October rain ran down the glass in sheets and blurred the images of pedestrians dashing by with umbrellas.

"I'm glad I came by coach instead of carriage," Sidney said, pleased that the ten of hearts just dealt him gave him a three-card straight flush.

"Then you'll be a good fellow and give me a lift?" Sir Ronald asked. "I sent my coachman back for Lady Hill so that she could take the children to visit her mother. I planned to hire a cab, but . . ."

"But you'll do no such thing," Sidney told him.

"Neither of you has to worry over the rain." Mr. Preddy, author of two acclaimed texts on architectural design, frowned at the cards in his hand. "It'll be dry as the Sahara out there by the time we finish, if you continue to chatter on as if we're at Sunday tea."

"Is there any question of who's holding a bad hand?" Sidney quipped, bringing chuckles from the other two and a wry smile from Mr. Preddy.

"How were the pheasants in Northamptonshire, Lord Holt?" Mr. Babington asked after drawing three cards a half hour later.

"I bagged five," Sidney told him.

"You usually do better than that."

"I was tied up with other business. A farmer I evicted last spring managed to scrape up enough money for a solicitor." Sidney blamed the Agricultural Holdings Act of seven years ago, which protected tenant farmers from eviction without proper compensation. "If Parliament continues to chip away the landowners' rights, we'll be paying *them* rents."

"Hear, hear," said Sir Ronald.

Indeed the rain had let up by the time the game was finished—Mr. Preddy the unexpected winner. Still, Sidney steered Sir Ronald toward his coach outside the Club.

"Are you still seeing that actress?" Sir Ronald asked as they were carried toward Mayfair.

"No," Sidney replied, pretending not to notice the question in Sir Ronald's eyes. There were times he did not mind explaining himself, but Roseline was a sore subject. Not that his heart felt any pangs for her, but because he felt quite foolish for allowing her to plead her way back into his life after Catherine left. That arrangement had lasted less than a fortnight, simply because his first walking-out had left her so fearful of his doing it again that she clung to him like clematis to a wall.

Sir Ronald straightened in his seat. "Were you aware that Mrs. Marshall has returned from Hawaii?"

"Yes, I've heard."

"She asked Lady Hill about you. She's out of mourning now. You should consider paying her a call."

Sidney feigned a shudder. "That nasal voice. It's a wonder she has any nostrils at all."

A grin spread across Sir Ronald's bearded face. "She can afford to have others breathe for her. I'm told she reaped a tidy profit from the sale of Marshall's sugar plantation."

"No, thank you. My eardrums have served me well for twenty-eight years. I'll not abuse them now."

Husbands and wives were supposed to spend at least a little time together, Sidney thought. While the idea of adding to his wealth was always attractive, what good would it bring if he could not bear to be in the same room with his wife?

The thought of marriage brought to his mind's eye a face more fair than Mrs. Marshall's. Of late, he was beginning to wonder if he had made a huge mistake. His reason had seemed a valid one five weeks ago. The courtship was simply too inconvenient to maintain, what with her suddenly up at Girton and its barricade of rules against gentleman callers. And when she came home for vacations, he could expect again that she would not be able to absent herself too long from Cannonhall Road.

The brief reunion with Roseline, grouse hunts, cards at the Club, and spending more time at the Stock Exchange all helped keep his mind occupied. But as a moment ago, he found his thoughts more and more drifting toward her.

I wonder how her lectures are going, he thought, trying to imagine her taking notes, a little frown of concentration upon her pretty face. Did she finish *The Iliad* before Michaelmas Term?

"Lord Holt?"

He blinked at Sir Ronald, realized the coach had come to a halt in front of the Hill home on Charles Street. "Sorry," he said with a sheepish grin. "Woolgathering."

Sir Ronald smiled. "Would you care to come in for a drink?"

"No, thank you." He was not in the mood to witness Sir Ronald's domestic tranquillity today.

His newspapers were waiting for him in the morning room at home. He read through the *Times,* but ended up laying aside the half-finished *Chronicle* to stare at glowing coals in the fireplace. Loneliness gnawed at his insides.

You may possibly be the biggest imbecile in London, he told himself. He had enjoyed the affection of a decent young woman whose company was pleasing, and who gave not a whit about his money or title. He had held the potential for happiness in his grasp, and allowed it to slip through his fingers.

Was she terribly heartbroken? He had not even had the decency to reply to her wire. Perhaps she hated him now, and would want no more to do with him. Even as the thought passed through his mind, he knew that was not the case.

So will you do anything about it? he asked himself.

"I fear I'll regret not throwing *this* one in the fireplace," Peggy said at Catherine's sitting room door after morning lectures on Wednesday, the twenty-sixth of October.

Catherine held her breath and stared at the envelope in her friend's hand. She had stopped checking the chimneypiece in the Reading Room two weeks or so into her return. The day-after-day disappointment was just too overwhelming. Peggy, Milly, or sometimes one of the other sophomores had fallen into the habit of handing her mail to her in the corridor or dropping it by her room.

"Who . . . ?"

"It's from Belgrave Square," Peggy sighed. "That's all I know. And just when you were starting to act normal again."

Normal? Catherine thought, reaching for the envelope. Stuffing herself at the dining table—and between meals—so that her clothes were starting to wear tight? Racking her brains every night, trying to figure out what it was she did or said that had displeased him?

At least her studies had improved, for concentrating upon lectures and texts gave her respite from the other tormenting thoughts. She had even finished *The Iliad*.

"Thank you, Peggy."

Peggy nodded doubtfully and left. Catherine held the letter and paced the floor for a moment, willing it to be good news. When she felt strong enough, she sank into her upholstered chair and opened the envelope.

Dear Miss Rayborn,

I address you so because I do not know if I have the right to "Catherine" any longer. Your telegram caused me much distress, as I realized you could have only been sent away so abruptly for one reason, that our meetings were discovered.

I can only imagine what has been told you about me. And it grieves me to confess that much of what you have heard is probably true. While I wish I had been allowed the opportunity to hear those charges against me, how can I blame your family for wishing to protect you?

For weeks I have determined to absent myself from your life completely, in the hope that one day you would meet a man worthy of you. However noble that may seem, there was also an element of cowardliness. How could I ever face you again, knowing that you are aware of my shameful past?

With those stated, why do I write now? Selfishness, Miss Rayborn. I cannot pretend otherwise. I long to see you again. And I have begun to allow myself to hope that you have not completely blotted me from your heart. Else, why would you have sent me the telegram, when you could have just ignored me?

The letter went on to ask if she would possibly consider meeting him on the following Sunday afternoon at the home of a relation in Chesterton.

I have persuaded my aunt, a Mrs. Fry, to call for you under the guise of a family friend. If you do not wish to see me, please simply post her a letter at the address below and she will not call.

A half hour later, Catherine was standing just outside the open doorway to Miss Bernard's office. Eventually the headmistress looked up.

"Come in, Miss Rayborn," she said, blotting her pen.

Catherine advanced to the desk, arranged her face into a benign expression, and forced herself to meet the eyes staring up at her. "Pardon me for disturbing you, Miss Bernard. A Mrs. Fry, a friend of my family, has written inviting me to spend Sunday afternoon with her in Chesterton. After church, of course."

"Will she call for you here herself?"

"Yes."

"Very well."

"Oh, thank you!" she gushed before thinking.

Miss Bernard smiled. "She must be a particularly good friend. Why hasn't she called before?"

A fraction of a second passed. "She suffered ill health."

"Then I'm glad she has recovered," the headmistress said, clearly not noticing the hesitation. She dipped her pen in her inkwell. "Will that be all, Miss Rayborn?"

"Yes, thank you."

It's the only way, Catherine reminded herself on the way back down the corridor. But the thought was not as consoling as it should have been. When she was ten and told a schoolmistress at Saint Anne School for Girls in Malta that a composition she had forgotten to complete was carried off by the wind near a window, her punishment was to write a hundred times Sir Walter Scott's quotation—*Oh, what a tangled web we weave, when first we practice to deceive.*

They had been merely words those years ago. She understood them now.

Forgive me, Father, she asked, but her prayer had a hollowness to it. She knew, and God knew, that if she sincerely wished for forgiveness, she would be turning to head again for the schoolmistress's office.

"It's not right, his asking you to lie like that," Peggy said four days later. "Exhale now."

Catherine held on to the bedpost and emptied her lungs.

"Done," Peggy said.

"Can't you make it tighter?" Catherine rasped.

Milly, rifling through the top drawer of Catherine's chest for a ribbon to borrow, said, "Yes, Peggy, make it tighter. Blue is such an attractive color for the complexion."

Catherine ignored her and turned to Peggy. "Can't you?"

"It's tight enough." Peggy took a step back, then repeated, "He shouldn't encourage you to lie."

"You just don't understand," Catherine said tersely. Ordinarily she could stand up to their lectures, but her nerves had been on edge since Wednesday.

"That's right, *no one* understands," Milly said while tying a bow at the nape of her neck. Her hair flowed in waves from the purple ribbon, almost meeting the bustle of her light brown serge gown. "Your cousin . . . Peggy . . . me. Shouldn't that tell you something?"

"It's easy to judge someone you haven't met." Catherine looked into her open wardrobe. Yesterday she had finally decided upon the grey tailored suit. The lines were somewhat plain, yes, but when she tied the fringed ends of her cobalt blue shawl over the bodice, it drew attention away from the tightness of her blouse at the waist and looked quite feminine. But would the forest green velvet, definitely dressier, and with a sash that hid the tightness, be more attractive? *You've got to stop eating so much,* she told herself.

"You forget that I've met him," Peggy said.

"He wasn't on his best day," Catherine replied. "And you didn't think he was so terrible when he saved your necklace."

She turned to the two. They reminded her of severe schoolmistresses, both with arms folded, Peggy leaning sideways against the bedpost. "Please," Catherine begged. "Don't do this to me. I'm nervous enough as it is."

"Shouldn't that tell you something too?" Peggy asked.

"Peggy . . ."

Peggy gave Milly a helpless look. Milly sighed and took a step forward. "I'll just say one more thing, Catherine. Love can blind a person to faults, you know. My father still thinks Evelyn Singers is a saint."

"I don't think Sidney is a saint," Catherine told her. "He warned me that he had a past."

But the difference between Sidney and Milly's stepmother was that Sidney regretted that past and desired to live a decent life. As his letter said, it was shame that prevented him from contacting her for weeks. He had correctly deduced from her tersely worded telegram that she had been told everything.

"Just be careful, please," Peggy warned for the second time.

"I will. And you're both dear to worry over me, but do please stop." She gave her wardrobe another look and decided it was too late to change her plans. To Peggy she said, "Will you help me into this skirt?"

While the two helped her finish dressing—Milly even putting the curling rod to the ends of her hair—they did not offer to accompany her to church in the Village, but set out with the majority of the school in the opposite direction. Catherine was actually relieved. Sidney had not mentioned a time Mrs. Fry would call, hence Catherine's decision to attend where she could be back in the shortest amount of time. She hoped Milly and Peggy would still be in

Cambridge, not there to gawk and send each other messages with their eyes.

In the church of Saint Andrew, Catherine joined the five other Girton students, Miss Scott, and the rest of the congregation in responses to the Morning Prayers, the Anthems, the Apostles' Creed, and the Collect for the day. She did so absently, for her mind strained against its time constraint, willing the afternoon to come.

"We humbly beseech thee, O Father, mercifully to look upon our infirmities; and, for the glory of thy Name, turn from us all those evils that we most justly have deserved; and grant, that in all our troubles we may put our whole trust and confidence in Thy mercy, and evermore serve Thee in holiness and pureness of living, to Thy honour and glory; through our only Mediator and Advocate, Jesus Christ our Lord."

Her thoughts strayed even more once Reverend Murray began his sermon, for no verbal responses, no kneeling or standing, were expected from the congregation. Also, his soft voice and unremarkable appearance—receding hairline, spectacles, and slanting narrow shoulders—did not command attention. But her mind was captured halfway through his reading from the book of Saint Matthew, Christ's words from the Sermon on the Mount.

". . . Neither shalt thou swear by thy head, because thou canst not make one hair white or black. But let your communication be, Yea, yea; Nay, nay: for whatsoever is more than these cometh of evil."

As he expounded on the theme of *Truthfulness,* a passion burned behind the vicar's spectacles, which Catherine had been either too sleep deprived or prejudiced to notice during the one occasion she had attended here last year.

"You may live in the meanest hovel," he went on, "too poor to buy a decent coat, but dear brethren, you may still possess something that all the riches in the world cannot buy; that is, an integrity so pure and true that it is never necessary for you to embellish your words with 'I swear.' In fact, it would be redundant to do so. What peace of mind! What untroubled sleep! What a legacy to leave to your children!"

Catherine pressed her palms together as the vicar looked directly at her. *Peggy and Milly!*

". . . as written in the epistle to the Ephesians, *Wherefore putting away lying, speak every man truth with his neighbor.*"

But no, she reasoned with herself, arranging her face for the vicar's benefit into the same benign expression she had worn for Miss Bernard four days ago. Neither friend would do such a thing behind her back, and besides, she had not informed them that she would be attending Saint Andrew's until yesterday afternoon.

"We cannot fool God, dear brethren and sisters! Hear Christ's words as recorded in the eighth chapter of the Gospel of Luke: *For nothing is secret, that shall not be made manifest; neither any thing hid, that shall not be known and come abroad.*"

That brought a mental picture of the hurt and disappointment upon her mother's and father's faces as if they had learned somehow of her plans for the afternoon. Her heart pounded so violently in her chest that she glanced at Violet Newman, next to her, from the corner of her eye. Surely she had heard. But no, the fresher's attention was absorbed by the vicar and his sermon, her countenance so untroubled that Catherine felt a pang of envy.

And that was when she stopped listening. Not out of any spitefulness, but because she simply could not bear to have her conscience pricked any longer. As an accomplished daydreamer it was easy to do. She simply pictured Sidney, the relief that would be in his expression when she informed him that his past did not matter, that she believed he was a good person.

Still, she was glad when the sermon was concluded. There was a shuffling of feet and ruffling of pages as people rose from the pews to sing.

> *"Purer in heart, O God, Help me to be;*
> *Until thy holy face one day I see:*
> *Keep me from secret sin, Reign thou my soul within;*
> *Purer in heart, help me to be."*

Secret sin. She thought that the hymn would be the final stab at her conscience, at least at church. But another came when Reverend Murray clasped her hand at the door and said kindly, "Go with God, child."

She walked back toward the college, silent amidst the banter of the others, allowing the chill October air to bathe the heat from her face. If only it could bathe the guilt from her mind! She prayed again. *Forgive my lies and slipping about, Father.* But again, she could not bring herself to put a halt to them.

Indeed, she was able to feel great relief that it would be Miss Scott who would be in charge of the guest book, with Misses Bernard and Welsh in Cambridge with the larger group. While Miss Scott was amiable, she was a little shy and would be less likely to strike up a conversation with Mrs. Fry. After lunch the assistant lecturer settled in a chair in the entrance hall with a copy of Dr. Johnson's *Journey to the Western Islands of Scotland*, while Catherine sat in another chair and stared at the door, assuring herself over and over that Sidney would not have changed his mind, and would have wired her if circumstances prevented his coming to Cambridge.

The entrance door opened and a young woman stepped into the hall. Catherine met her eyes. *Too young to be Sidney's aunt,* Catherine thought as she and the visitor exchanged polite nods.

"Good day, Miss Ingle," Miss Scott said, getting to her feet to offer her hand. She turned to Catherine. "Would you please run upstairs and tell Maude Ingle her sister's here?"

Why can't Maude wait for her guests like everyone else? Catherine grumbled to herself on the staircase. On the way back, she suffered through Maude's chirpy detailing of the birthday tea she and her sister would be attending for one of their cousins in Barrington. She paused just inside the entrance hall, where an elderly woman stood with Miss Scott and Maude's sister.

"Ah, she's back," Miss Scott said, turning to smile at Catherine.

Twenty-Six

*H*ow good to see you again, Miss Rayborn." Mrs. Fry, clad in paramatta mourning clothes, extended a black-gloved hand. Colorless lashes blinked over eyes as hard as pebbles. "I've signed the guest book. Shall we?"

"Yes," Catherine said as they shook hands. She was relieved that she was not compelled to stage artificial small talk for Miss Scott's benefit, and then relieved again that when she turned just before the entrance door to send a farewell wave, the assistant lecturer was happily chatting with Maude and her sister as if no deception had occurred right under her nose. Past the gates, a coachman in livery dress and top hat waited at the door of a road coach. Mrs. Fry entered first, busied herself with arranging her skirts, and did not look up as Catherine settled into the rear-facing space.

She heard the snap of the reins overhead and braced herself as the pair of horses started moving. The college was a half mile behind them to the west when she could no longer bear the silence inside the coach.

"It's very kind of you to do this, Mrs. Fry."

Mrs. Fry gave her a thin, dry smile. "My nephew is a hard man to refuse, Miss Rayborn."

Catherine had no idea what that meant. But she was certain of one thing—the woman did not like her. *Why?* Catherine wished she had the courage to ask.

She racked her brain for something to say, something that would lighten the strained atmosphere. When nothing presented itself, she turned her face to stare out of the window.

Chesterton was a long, straggling village of mellow stone cottages and shaded lanes on the north bank of the River Cam. The coachman assisted them out in front of a quaint two-storey cottage of honey-colored stone. Drying ivy vines clung to the lower half, circling windows and porch posts, but left the upper storey bare and shadowed by a deep thatch overhang. There was no sign of Sidney, much to Catherine's disappointment.

"Good-day to you, Missus," said the coachman with a tip of his bowler hat. "I'll go water the horses and be back here waitin'." The coach was a hired one, Catherine realized. Did that mean Sidney had come from Cambridge in it, and was already inside?

"Miss Rayborn?"

Catherine blinked at Mrs. Fry, holding open the gate for her.

"Oh, I beg your pardon." She hurried through and waited to follow the woman up the short path to the house. "This is a lovely home," she said, making another effort.

"My husband was born here," Mrs. Fry replied, with no warmth but at least no hostility.

She opened the door and led Catherine into a hall furnished with hall tree and entrance table. To the left ascended a wooden staircase with worn carpeting. A young woman clad in a brown linen gown and white apron came through an arched doorway to take Mrs. Fry's black cloak. "No, thank you," Catherine said when the maid offered to take her shawl.

"Show Miss Rayborn to the parlor, Louisa," Mrs. Fry told her.

"Yes, Missus."

"And then bring me some tea upstairs."

"Thank you, Mrs. Fry," Catherine said, but the woman had already turned for the staircase. The discourtesy dampened her spirits for only a second, for the maid nodded toward the arched doorway and smiled.

"Come with me, Miss?"

"Yes, thank you." The maid led her through a dim corridor with wide oak-planked flooring, then opened the first door on the right. As Catherine went through the doorway, Sidney was rising from a sofa.

"Catherine!" he exclaimed, extinguishing a cigarette into an ashtray on a side table. The door clicked shut behind Catherine, and Sidney hastened toward her. He was as handsome as ever in a brown coat and tan trousers, and his auburn hair in waves from his high forehead. "I didn't even hear you arrive, or I should have come out there."

"Sidney . . ." was all she could say.

He smiled, taking her hands and holding them clasped against his chest. Footsteps faded in the corridor. "How happy you've made me by coming!"

She stared up at him, blinking away tears. "I feared I would never see you again."

"Never? My dear, what have I put you through? And yet, I am glad to hear it. It means you don't despise me after all."

"I could never despise you."

"Oh, Catherine," he murmured, moving a hand from hers to touch her cheek. "You've such a good heart."

For a fraction of a second she was back in the church pew. "No, not good."

That made him smile. "I beg to differ. Come, let's sit."

He led her to a faded medallion-back tufted sofa, centered over an equally faded carpet. Genteel shabbiness was the tone of the room, the furniture mostly mahogany and ebony from a half-century ago, with its heavy lines and scrolls. Faded green velvet curtains were drawn, and three kerosene lamps glowed from tables set about. Tea was spread before them on a rosewood table with legs curving into lion paws, but for a while they ignored the refreshment, sitting facing each other, Sidney holding both her hands between his own.

"I wonder how you can even bear to look at me?" he asked, blue eyes suddenly sad.

I would rather look at you than anyone in the world, she thought. "I know that you're not like that anymore. I tried to tell Sarah—"

"Mrs. Doyle? She's the one who told you about me?"

"Yes. I tried to explain how much you regretted your past, but it made no difference."

"I did warn you," he reminded her gently.

Catherine nodded. "She promised not to tell William or Uncle Daniel if I would return to school. I tried to ring you, but the man who answered wouldn't allow me to speak with you."

"Hmm. I'll have to speak with Rumfellow about that. Now, let's have some tea, shall we?"

"Yes." She poured steaming tea from a Wedgwood teapot with a hairline crack on the spout into Royal Worcester cups faintly stained inside. She liked performing the domestic little chore, for it reminded her of the countless times her mother had poured tea for her father when he returned from work. Her finger touched an odd spot in her saucer. A tiny chip had been ground away at one time, leaving a smooth shallow groove almost unnoticeable to the eye.

"My aunt Irene has seen better times," Sidney told her, sitting back with cup and saucer and crossing one knee over the other.

"What happened?"

"Her late husband ran up gambling debts for years, until he took mercy on everyone and put a bullet in his head last summer."

That saddened Catherine, no matter how cold the woman was to her in the coach. "Does anyone help her?" By *anyone* she meant Sidney and his family, though she did not wish to step too far over the limits of etiquette by asking directly.

"She receives a portion of the rents from the family estate in Northamptonshire. It was something my father set up when it was left to him. Even though he had two sisters, he was the only male, and the law of that time made him sole heir. The other sister is dead now, so there is only Irene to support."

"That was very decent of him. To share like that." Catherine wished that Sarah and William could be seated in the same room, listening. "And it's very kind of you to continue."

He nodded thanks and took a sip from his cup. "I promised my father. Mind you, it's just enough for necessities. And I don't consider modern furniture and unchipped china necessities, so don't pin a medal on me quite yet."

Catherine smiled and thought his modesty charming. They drank tea and chatted. He told her his mother and stepfather were in Bath, collecting research for a future manuscript. She told of Aunt Phyllis's recent letter saying she was adjusting to Sheffield better than she had expected, that one of her new neighbors was fast becoming a close friend. He said that his stock in East India Securities had jumped a half-pence per share, and laughed when she said, "Is that all?" She described her favorite and least favorite lecturers.

"Everyone whispers about Dr. Besant," she said. "He stares at my friend Milly. It makes her very uncomfortable."

"I can imagine," he said, followed by a thoughtful frown. "Actually, I cannot. We never had that problem at Lincoln."

She obliged his humor with a smile, but the subject of the lecturer's attention to Milly brought to memory something Sarah had told her. *Do you realize adultery is a sin?*

All in the past, she reminded herself, trying to keep down that pill she had swallowed whole back in September. *You've no right to ask for an explanation.*

The woman had children, Sarah had said.

Perhaps Sidney had not realized that fact, until he was so smitten that he could not help himself. Did he end the affair because he realized it was wrong? Or would it have continued had the husband not brought his wife

to the States? While he had vaguely explained his college debaucheries—
before she even knew what they were—as being the result of no moral guidance from a mother and stepfather preoccupied with their young son, he
had not explained this one.

She could not bring herself to ask, but she could hint, in the hopes that
he would volunteer. The subject at hand was a convenient one, and she
went on with it.

"If Dr. Besant were a bachelor, we would all be swooning over the
romance of it," she said casually.

"Swooning, eh?" He lifted a brow. "I've always wondered . . . how
exactly does one do that?"

"I'm not sure." She smiled and busied herself with refilling their cups.
The last drop dimpled the surface of hers, a half inch below the rim. Mrs.
Fry or her maid had apparently felt that two each were enough and so measured precisely. Handing him his, she looked up again. "But he has a wife
and children."

His blue eyes studied her over the rim as he took a sip. He lowered cup
to saucer again with a sharp *click*. "Indeed?"

"Yes. That's why it's so disturbing."

A tense silence stretched between them. She could no longer meet his
eyes, but felt their stare as she pretended to study the flaw in her saucer.

At length he said, "Just why are you telling me this, Catherine?"

"No reason," she lied, running her finger along the flaw. "I thought I
should ask your opinion of what Milly should do about it."

"Have your friend report him to the headmistress, if it gives her that
much discomfort."

"Yes, that's a good idea." She bit her lip, glanced up at him and down
again. "I think it's wrong—a married person behaving that way. Don't
you?"

"Obviously." Another pause, then, "Is there something else you wish
to ask me, Catherine?"

The sharpness of his tone frightened her. Not that she feared violence
from him, but that he would become annoyed at her prying and decide not
to see her again. She couldn't live with that. *He said he regrets his past.*
"Past" meant *everything* that happened before this day.

And he honors his promise to his father to support his aunt, she reminded
herself. Proof that he had a noble heart. She smoothed the anxiety from her
expression and looked up at him. "Yes. Would Mrs. Fry take offense if I
sent her a tin of tea? For her hospitality?"

He studied her for a second longer, then the tension began leaving his face. "No doubt she would appreciate it. But why don't you just bring it next week?"

Next week. Were there ever two such sweet words? Just to be certain, she said, "You'll be here?"

He smiled and took her hand. "But of course. Did you think I was suggesting you spend your Sundays with the old crosspatch upstairs?"

Catherine smiled, almost giddy with joy. And relief, that she had not said anything to damage their courtship! For this was indeed what it was, a courtship.

That fact was emphasized to her when he set his cup and saucer on the table, did the same with hers, and gathered her into his arms. "I never thought I would be holding you again, Catherine."

"Nor I," she murmured against his shoulder.

He put a finger beneath her chin and raised it, and then kissed her until she was drunk with lightheadedness.

She could have spent the rest of her life in his arms, but when a long-case clock against the wall struck four, he drew back and said with a reluctance gratifying to Catherine's ears, "We'll have to leave now. My train."

"We?"

He got to his feet and helped her to hers. "I didn't want to risk raising eyebrows this first time. But it'll not happen as long as Irene is along. That's why I hired a coach instead of hansom."

Voices drifted in from the other side of the door. But before opening it, Sidney smiled and drew her into his arms again. "One more?"

Gladly she obliged. When their lips drew apart, his arms were still around her waist. He raised an eyebrow. "They're feeding you well at Girton, aren't they?"

The spell was broken. Catherine had to fight a rush of threatening tears. *Your fault for not answering my wire!* She could not tell him this, though. Admitting her fear over never seeing him again was one thing, but it was quite another to admit that she had been so frantic that she filled her stomach as often as possible in an effort to dull the ache inside. He would think her a hysterical woman and be frightened off.

Lightly she replied, "Too well, I fear. I'm going to have to watch my portions."

There was another stab of pain when he simply smiled and opened the door.

———

"All these lovely treats, and you're simply giving them away?" Peggy asked in the reading room on the twenty-ninth of November. "They won't last the morning in here."

"Good." As Catherine placed the tray borrowed from the kitchen onto the wall table, she tried not to breathe in too deeply, for the combined aroma of chocolate biscuits and macaroons was enticing. "I can't very well send them back and hurt Aunt Naomi's feelings. And you're welcome to take more."

Her friend shook her head. "We've enough to last us until Christmas." By *we* Peggy included Milly, for the pair were allowed first claim on the package when the post delivered it yesterday. "But I'm worried over how you're—"

Voices came from the doorway as a group of students entered, sparing Catherine Peggy's usual lecture over "not eating enough to keep a gnat alive."

"What have we here?" Helene Coates asked with raised brows.

"Father Christmas came early?" said Susan Martin. "Yours, Catherine?"

"Yes. Please, help yourselves."

They did not wait for a second invitation. Catherine nudged Peggy on their way out of the room. "Oh, stop scowling. *It is more blessed to give than receive*, remember?"

Peggy made a face. "Let's study in my apartment. You've nothing to eat in yours."

But Sidney says I look lovely, Catherine thought. Her clothes were loose again, in fact even more so. That was better than any biscuit in the world, and surely worth the occasional hunger pang, or the embarrassment of her stomach sending off sounds like a rusty spring during Latin yesterday.

At least she was eating, not starving herself completely as she had during the first week of November, after Sidney's crushing comment. Fainting during tennis practice and spending the rest of the day in the infirmary had warned her she was carrying it too far. A week later and over Milly's protests, she resigned from the Tennis Club. She was having difficulty concentrating on her studies again and did not need the extra distraction. She could always rejoin next term, with a clean academic slate and not the heart-racing worries of lagging so far behind.

She sat at her study table to read a letter from her mother the following day.

> *Your father and I are sorely distressed! Aunt Phyllis writes that you attended an opera with a young lord of her acquaintance.*
> *Unchaperoned!*

You were not brought up that way, Catherine, no matter if he is the fine gentleman your aunt claims him to be, and no matter how many books his mother writes.

"Aunt Phyllis . . ." Catherine moaned, hammering the table with her fist.

Please explain what possessed you to do such a thing, and why you did not think it notable enough to mention in your last letter.
I am seriously considering catching the next steamer to London.

She reached for pen, ink, and stationery, in such a hurry to put down words that would appease her parents and ward off any action, that it did not matter that the letter would not reach them for at least two weeks.

Dearest Mother and Father,
This thoughtless daughter begs your forgiveness! Of truth, I did not think you would mind, as Aunt Phyllis granted permission and attested to Lord Holt's upstanding character.

She paused to consider what should follow. *It was a single occasion, he was a perfect gentleman, and I have not seen him since.*

But that would not work, she realized. Mother also wrote Uncle Daniel and Aunt Naomi. She could not be certain that Mother would not mention her distress over the single theatre outing. If word somehow got around to Sarah, Sarah would know she had lied to her parents, and feel compelled to involve herself in the situation again.

After some thought she ended up writing:

While he was a perfect gentleman, there is no reason for me to see him again, as my studies are of paramount importance.

It was still a careful fabrication, but one which Sarah could not refute if it came to that, for Sarah had no evidence that she was still seeing Sidney. She closed the subject by begging forgiveness a second time, then moved on to tell of school events, lest her letter give Sidney too much weight and thus arouse suspicion.

When finished, she stared at the sealed envelope on the tabletop. Her previous falsehoods were spoken ones. They faded into the air as all sounds did. But now she had put a lie to ink and signed her name to it. *God, forgive me,* she prayed, tears blurring the address on the envelope.

But again, repentance required action. *Her* action would be to send the envelope a quarter of the way across the globe, to the two people who had taught her to always tell the truth.

The fourth of December was her sixth Sunday to meet Sidney in Chesterton. He had her remove her hat and sit on a stool with hands folded in her lap, so that he could sit in a facing chair and sketch her portrait. He would not allow her to speak while he worked on the face, but did not mind chatting himself, and told her of the five pounds he had donated during a collection at the Club to benefit Saint Thomas' Hospital.

"I must confess that my only reason for extending charity to my aunt has been because of my promise to my father," he said as his pencil moved across the pad propped upon his knees. He had opened the curtains for more light, and so the ring upon his finger caught the reflection and flickered its range of colors. "This is the first time I've ever done so outside the family. I feel like the changed Ebenezer Scrooge, and I credit you for it."

"Me?"

"Don't speak, Catherine." He looked appraisingly at her chin and down at the pad again. "Yes. A happy man is a charitable one."

Catherine's smile, which had grown stiff from maintaining it for an hour, became effortless again. He could be so endearing, and make her so happy that she desired nothing else from life but to be in his company.

And yet sometimes he said things—little things—that made her feel inferior to him and filled her with fear that his affection might be waning.

Such as a half hour later. "I'm sketching your hair now," he said. "So you may speak if you'll hold your face still."

Now that she was allowed, she wasn't sure what to say. When she confessed as much, he glanced up at her while tilting his pencil to make little shading motions. "That will not do, Miss Rayborn. I've carried the burden of the conversation over the past hour—"

"Because you ordered me to keep silent."

He clucked his tongue. "Excuses, excuses. You'll simply have to come up with something amusing, or I shall be forced to explain the stock market to you again."

She wrinkled her nose at him. And after a little thought, she decided upon the account of the train ride to Girton, when the two St. John's students played the *King Lear* prank. Just as she was opening her mouth, Sidney stopped penciling and raised a hand.

"Sh-h-h."

"What is it?" she whispered, but he shook his head. She held her breath and listened. Sounds drifted from the corridor. Apparently Louisa the maid was entertaining herself while sweeping or some such chore.

"... *smile from the bar on the people below*
And one night he smiled on my love,
She wink'd back at him and she shouted 'Bravo!' "

Catherine and Sidney traded smiles. "What's she singing?" he said softly.

"It's 'The Man on the Flying Trapeze,' " Catherine replied.

He leaned his head to listen for a second, then nodded. "But how did you know that?"

"I've heard it at school. We sing in the evenings sometimes, just for a lark. Why?"

His face changed as if a veil had been drawn across it. With a tone of strained patience he replied, "That song is the sort of tripe the lower classes thrive upon, Catherine. People who would give you a blank look if you mentioned Schubert or Mozart. Not fitting for a young lady of refinement even to have heard of, much less admit to singing."

"Oh. I didn't realize ..."

"Doesn't the fact that a servant would know it give you a clue?"

His pencil started moving again, making sharp little motions. *He's going to make me look like Medusa,* she thought, appalled that she could have a humorous thought at such a time.

She had developed the habit of weighing her words before sending them to his ear, so that he would not think her unrefined and reconsider his affection for her. But she had stumbled headlong into this slip of the tongue simply because of her sheltered upbringing, and did not think the magnitude of her crime merited the chide she had just been given.

"Every servant in Britain knows 'God Save the Queen' too," she said quietly. "Should I not sing that as well?"

The pencil moved even faster. "That's a ridiculous analogy, Catherine."

This whole argument is ridiculous popped into her mind, shocking her. She pushed the thought away. The tension in the room was too much. She had to smooth the irritation from his face, the dent from between his brows. *And what do you know?* she asked herself. *You're nine years younger than he is.*

"Sidney, I'm sorry," she said.

She heard his sigh as he sat back and moved the pencil from the pad. "I can't fault you for hearing it at school, Catherine. You have people there from all sorts of backgrounds. But I have to say you've an appalling lack of interest in cultural things. You can't help having been raised middle-class, but one would think a woman pursuing an education would desire to rise above the limitations of her upbringing."

They stared across at each other.

Catherine's lip began trembling. "My upbringing was fine, thank you."

"Catherine . . ."

Hearing him speak her name broke down all restraint. She covered her face and broke into sobs. Presently she heard his footsteps, felt his arms about her.

"Now, now," he soothed into her hair.

She tried to shrug from his embrace. "Go away!"

"My precious Catherine . . ."

"Away!"

But his arms tightened about her. Finally she stopped struggling and allowed him to press her head against his shoulder. "Handkerchief," she rasped. His shoulder raised as he went for his pocket, and one was pressed into her hand.

Must you be so cruel? Sidney asked himself. Her sobs had quieted, but her shoulders still convulsed every few seconds. "I would cut off my right arm before knowingly hurting you."

Yet knowingly, deliberately, he had. But he took no pleasure from it, and in fact had to blink away tears from his own eyes. If only he could make her understand that his encouraging her to strive for perfection was for her sake. It did not matter that perfection was unattainable. He was a firm believer in a person's reach exceeding his grasp.

It wasn't yet time to say, *As the wife of a lord, you'll be under the scrutiny of every set of aristocratic eyes in London. They'll constantly be looking for any evidence of your family's inferior social status, any faux pas for which to amuse each other over tea the next day. Leave the common pleasures to the common folk.*

To counsel her thus before he had formally proposed would ruin his plans to surprise her at Christmas with the ring.

"It was unfair of me to criticize your family," he admitted. "They deserve an enormous amount of credit for raising such a lovely daughter."

"They're educated, and well-read," she sniffed.

"But of course they are," he said, rubbing her shoulder.

"And moral and generous."

"I shouldn't expect them to be any other way."

Once she was his wife and away from the Girton environment, he could tutor her in the finer elements of life. Take her to operas and concerts, school her in poetry and fine art, so that she could move among the *bon ton* without embarrassing herself. Or him.

They would have a short engagement, he had decided. He had never kept company with any woman this length of time without regarding his own physical needs, and it was beginning to take its toll upon him.

Twenty-Seven

What a joy to feel normal again! Sarah thought on Tuesday afternoon, the twentieth of December. She wiped condensation from a section of the coach window with her handkerchief. People scurried about with topcoat collars raised and scarves about their necks. Traffic was slower, the fog thick from thousands of coal fires, but the Christmas spirit was clearly present in London. And as if to underscore that thought, a fivesome of bundled Salvation Army workers stood at the corner of York Way and Euston Road, playing instruments and singing with vapory breath.

> *"Brightly shone the moon that night,*
> *Though the frost was cru-el*
> *When a poor man came in sight*
> *Gathering winter fu-el."*

She swiped her handkerchief across a larger area and turned to her father. "Can you see them?"

He sat on the edge of his seat and looked. "Very nice."

Seconds later Stanley was reining Comet and Daisy to a stop in front of King's Cross Station. Some of the old anxiety gripped Sarah. Though Catherine had kept up a correspondence with Father and Naomi, she and her cousin had not exchanged letters. Would she be bitter? She had sent up many a prayer that their friendship would be reestablished, and even more prayers that Catherine's infatuation with Lord Holt was a thing of the past.

"Wouldn't you rather wait?" Father said as she raised the hood of her cloak.

"I'm fine, Father." Inside the train shed she turned down his offer to find her a vacant bench. They spotted Mr. Somerset and joined him.

"How's the suit wearing, Mr. Rayborn?" the man asked after an exchange of pleasantries.

Father unfastened three buttons to his topcoat and opened it enough to reveal the black wool underneath. "Like skin on a sausage, Mr. Somerset."

The tailor chuckled. Presently the Iron Duke came squealing and belching cinders to a stop. From the window of a first-class coach, a hand waved enthusiastically beside Catherine's smiling face.

"Someone's glad to be back," Father leaned close to say above the noise.

"Yes." Sarah could only hope it was for the right reason. A guard began opening doors. Catherine stepped onto the platform, followed by Miss Somerset, and hastened over.

"How healthy you look!" her cousin exclaimed, squeezing Sarah tight. She drew back sharply. "Oh dear—I forgot! Should I have done that?"

Sarah laughed and embraced her again. "Yes, you should have!"

She could understand Catherine's lapse of memory. Five months into her pregnancy, she was still able to hide her condition under street clothes and winter coats. She had gained a stone weight; however, some of that was from what she had lost during the three sickly months.

Catherine looked thinner, Sarah noticed as her cousin kissed Father's bearded cheek. Her cheekbones were clearly more prominent. *You should have written her,* Sarah told herself. Perhaps she was ill, and needed looking after. But then, Aunt Naomi would have told her if that were so.

"Mr. Doyle has been saving back issues of *The Analyst* for you," Sarah told Miss Somerset as they shook hands. "I have them in the coach, if you and your father would care to walk out there with us." She wished they could offer them a ride home, but there was only room for four adults in their winter bulk.

Catherine's friend smiled. "How thoughtful of you both. Thank you."

"You're welcome." After the men had gone off to see about trunks, Sarah said to Miss Somerset, "We're having a Christmas party for the neighbors tomorrow evening. Why don't you come, and spend the night?"

"A Christmas party?" Catherine said. "What fun. Do say you'll come, Peggy."

But Miss Somerset regretfully shook her head. "Thank you, Mrs. Doyle, but one of my brothers' wives—Hannah—has invited us to her family party."

"Well, do come see us soon." Sarah became aware that Catherine was studying her with an odd expression. She asked her cousin, "What is it?"

Catherine glanced about, then leaned closer. "You don't even look . . . well, you know."

"Catherine!" Miss Somerset said.

Panic washed across Catherine's face. "Oh no! I don't mean that there would be anything wrong! I'm sure the baby's—"

"The baby's fine, silly goose," Sarah said, and lowered her voice as much as possible. "It's been turning somersaults all morning."

The two young women traded bewildered looks.

"Somersaults?" Catherine said.

"They do that?" Miss Somerset asked.

"That's how they feel," Sarah told them. "Didn't you know that they move?"

Both young women shook their heads.

"I assumed they slept the whole time," Catherine said.

Sarah laughed again. It was like old times, the barrier between them crumbling. Surely the matter of Lord Holt was over.

And to test the waters and reassure herself, she said in the coach on the way back to Hampstead, "Admiral Kirkpatrick has a grandson visiting from the University of Edinburgh. He's looking forward to meeting you at the party."

"I can vouch for him," Father said. "Very agreeable young man."

"He collects stamps as a hobby." Sarah looked at her father. "What is that called?"

"Philately," Father replied. "Your Aunt Naomi even gave him some from Bombay."

"Hmm. He sounds very interesting," Catherine said. "What time is the party?"

"Seven," Sarah replied.

"I'll be sure to be back in time to change. I plan to shop with Peggy tomorrow. It's just no use trying to buy gifts in Cambridge, what with exams and having to pack them up for here."

Sarah studied Catherine's face while trying not to appear to do so. Had she imagined a flicker of uneasiness in her eyes? Was she looking for things that weren't there?

But it was entirely reasonable that Catherine would need to shop, with Christmas just five days away. And Sarah did so want the tension between them never to reappear.

You don't have to be suspicious of every move she makes, Sarah told herself. *She's probably wondering if you trust her anymore. And she could be weary from the trip. And exams.* Still, Sarah knew that she would have much more peace of mind when she saw packages in her cousin's arms tomorrow.

———————

Six months into his employment at Sedgwick Tea, Hugh had an office right beside his father's. He had worked in some capacity in each department, had even unloaded and packaged tea. He knew most of the employees by name. Because the results of his investigation into the feasibility of shipping to the States was progressing well. On his desk sat a stack of American publications: *The North American Review, The Atlantic Monthly, The Living Age, Harper's New Monthly Magazine, The Century*. His immediate project was deciding in which ones Sedgwick Tea should purchase advertising, should the project prove itself profitable.

He was situated well in life, and possessed enough intelligence to appreciate it. Yet there were moments when a yearning for something more came over him. He didn't even know what the *more* was, so vague was its shape. His prayers that God would either take away those moments of discontent or reveal what it was he was lacking went unanswered. But he was usually able to quell those moments by reminding himself of the week he had spent on the loading docks, straining and sweating with men earning a tenth of his wages.

He was hopeful that the restlessness would visit him no more once he was married. His parents' marriage was a happy one, and Father had never seemed wanting for anything beyond the pleasant confines of home, office, and church. And Hugh did love Lillian and took pleasure in her company, a promising start to any union.

"You have the ring?" Neville asked when Hugh met him at Postgate's on Oxford Street for supper.

Hugh brought the velvet-covered hinged box from his pocket and handed it over his dish of *fillets of grouse* and *sauce piquante*. His friend's brown eyes widened appreciatively at the one-carat diamond, flanked by two pear-shaped sapphires.

"It should fit her," Hugh said. "I asked Margery to lift a ring from Lillian's jewelry box so the jeweler could measure it."

Neville did not ask how Lillian's sister was doing, but then, he had moved on to a banker's daughter—for now. "Very nice," he said, holding up the box to catch the gasolier light.

"You think she'll like it?"

"Do you jest? I'm tempted to marry you myself for it."

"No thanks." Hugh made a face. "I've seen you in the mornings. You're not a pretty sight."

"Just remember who introduced you." Neville handed over the box. "I expect the first child to be named after me."

"And if it's a girl?"

"Hmm." His friend stabbed a fried smelt with his fork and leaned his head thoughtfully. "*Nevillette* has a certain elegance."

"I'll certainly consider it," Hugh said with affected seriousness while pocketing the box.

"Can't blame a man for trying. When will you propose?"

"Tomorrow. I'm having supper with her family."

"She'll make you a good wife," Neville said, finally serious.

"Yes, I know." Hugh smiled at him. "A man can't ask for more than that, can he?"

The following morning, Catherine dressed in her favorite winter gown of rough-finished Pekin wool with stripes of alternating plain brown and rasp-berry. A black velvet hat with a cluster of black ostrich tips, tan suede gloves, black walking boots, and her cloak of soft grey velvet completed the ensemble. Sarah and Uncle Daniel would not hear of her taking a hired carriage into the City, so Catherine had to resign herself to allowing Stanley to deliver her to Saville Row, in front of Somerset's Fine Tailoring. Fortunately, the pavement was busy with Christmas shoppers, and no one from the shop came out as she waited for the coach to fade from sight. Then it was an easy matter of hiring a hansom. She did not feel comfortable being delivered to Sidney's house, so they had arranged to meet at Dalton's, the café on Picadilly he had once pointed out from Green Park. He was there, standing under the awning, and came forward to help her from the hansom.

"I'm sor-ry I'm late," she said, teeth chattering and cheeks stiff. "They m-made me take the coach, so I had to—"

"I understand." He looked up at the cabby. "How much?"

"One bob, Guv'nor," the man said, leaning down to extend his cupped gloved hand and then raising it again. He stared at his palm and gave Sidney a smirk, "Lovely, Guv'nor! Now I can buy the Queen that bonnet!"

Sidney took Catherine by the arm and led her toward the café. "I'll wager he's never even met the Queen. Your red nose is charming. But you must be freezing. We'll get some hot chocolate in you before we leave."

She sent an uneasy glance back toward the departing driver and spotted Jerry seated at Sidney's coach's reins. His eyes were visible between hat and woolen muffler. She sent him a wave, and he touched the brim of his hat with his whip.

"May I have tea instead?" she said once they were seated at a table. Hot chocolate was too filling, with its milk and sugar. She would have to eat more than her usual scant portion at Sidney's family table, lest they think she found some fault with the food.

He ordered tea for her and coffee for himself, then took her hands across the table. "I persuaded my stepfather to come home for lunch. I want you to know that rarely happens. He's a 'cold meat pie on the run' sort of person."

"Oh dear. Now I'm terrified."

"Terrified? But why?"

"I'm a nervous wreck," Catherine sighed. "I really want them to approve of me."

"Then you've no reason for worry. You've already impressed my mother. Henry will ask you all about Bombay, where he helped design some railroad. Edgar, at fourteen, has just decided that the female gender is not so annoying after all. See? You've not even stepped through the doorway, and you practically have them all in the palm of your hand."

A woman brought their coffee and tea. Catherine settled as far back into her chair as bustle would allow, and drew in a deep breath. "You always know just the right thing to say, Sidney."

He took a sip of coffee and nodded toward the window, where the trees of Green Park thrust skeletal limbs over the street traffic. "I thought you and I would bundle up and take a turn around the Park this afternoon. The place has deep sentimental meaning to me."

Her pulse jumped. His tone suggested this would not be just a simple stroll—especially considering the weather. But a distressful thought occurred to her. "I have to shop, remember? If I return with nothing—"

"That has been taken care of."

"What do you mean?"

"Last week I sent Rumfellow out to buy gifts. He has very good taste, for a servant. Two each, men, women, and children, yes?"

"Yes." She always gave money to the servants, assuming they would appreciate that more. "Sidney . . . I'm overwhelmed."

He winked at her. "It was money well invested, for it's buying me more time with you."

"Oh, but I'm going to repay you," she said, taking her reticule from her lap. "How much—"

"You're not to worry about that."

"But I brought money. Please."

"No." His voice was firm, and the shake of his head gave emphasis. "Jerry will put them in the coach while we're at lunch. And if any of the gifts don't quite match their intendeds, well, at least they provide proof that you spent the day in the shops."

The little stab to her conscience was not quite so painful as earlier ones, and was soothed quickly away by the affection in his blue eyes. "Thank you, Sidney," she said. "It was so thoughtful of you."

"Just proves what a good influence you are on me." He drained his cup and set it back upon its saucer. "Shall we?"

Outside, Jerry hopped down from his box as if his eyes had been glued to the café the whole time they were inside. "Merry Christmas, Jerry," Catherine said as he held open the door.

"Thank you, Miss," he said through his scarf.

"Are your children counting the days?"

The corners of his eyes creased. "They are indeed, Miss."

When the door was closed and the coach started moving, Sidney turned to her. "Catherine."

"What is it?"

He gave her a pained look. "I hesitate to bring this up in your anxious state, but I would appreciate it if you weren't so chummy with Jerry."

"But all I did was ask about his children."

"How did you even know he had them?"

"We chatted outside the hotel a couple of times last summer."

"He can chat up his own friends. I realize that your cousin is married to a former servant, but in the upper classes socializing with them simply is not done. Once you make a habit of it, the line between you becomes blurred. They lose respect for you, and their work becomes slipshod."

Catherine could not help but think of her parents' servants in Bombay, and the servants on Cannonhall Road, who maintained spotless houses and were certainly addressed with pleasantries. But the day had started off so promising, and she was on her way to meet his family. Was giving her opinion on the matter worth the argument that might result?

He has the right to dictate how his own servants are to be treated, she reasoned. Perhaps his servants were not as conscientious as Sarah and William's or those of her parents. Even so, she suddenly felt a little weary. Turning to the window, she allowed Belgravia's stately homes to parade by.

"You're not sulking, are you?"

She turned to Sidney again. "I'm just looking at the houses."

He patted her hand. "How can I fault you for having a tender heart?

You're just like my mother. If I weren't living in the same house, the maids would have *her* doing the work and serving *them*."

Relieved that she had had the sense to hold her tongue, Catherine returned his smile.

Twenty-Eight

"We laid twenty-one miles from Bombay to Thane in 1853," Henry Godfrey said from the head of the table. "It was the beginning of the Great India Peninsular Railroad. But after contracting malaria I determined if I ever got well I would never set foot outside of England again."

He was not a handsome man in the traditional sense, with crooked teeth and long nose listing a bit to the left. But the brown eyes shone with life experience and cordiality, and his head of greying brown hair was as full as any twenty-year-old's.

Fourteen-year-old Edgar had the beginnings of his father's nose and the auburn hair and height of Sidney's side of the family. He had spoken only when addressed when Catherine first arrived, but as the meal progressed, added more and more to the conversation.

"Why does your family have a Muslim cook when the other servants are Hindi, Miss Rayborn?" he asked.

Catherine smiled at him. "Because the Hindis refuse to cook meat."

His eyes widened with shock. "They eat it raw?"

He blushed when the men chuckled, so Catherine replied as if he had asked the most reasonable question, "They don't eat meat at all. Nor fish. It's against their religion."

"But what, then, do they eat?"

"Vegetables and fruit, I'm sure," Mrs. Godfrey told her son. She smiled at Catherine, with what seemed to be an encouraging mingling of approval and relief in her grey eyes. "Isn't that so, Miss Rayborn?"

"Yes. And lots of rice."

"You should send the Parker Twins down to India sometime, Mother," Sidney said, breaking off a portion of fluted roll.

"Yes, Harriet," Mr. Godfrey said. "Between Miss Rayborn and me, you would have a wealth of research available."

"Hmm." The woman nodded slowly. "What reason would they have for being there?"

Every male at the table mused over that one. "Why not give the old man a vacation this time?" Sidney said at length. It was the Twins' widowed father's occupation as newspaper reporter that sent them from adventure to adventure. "Make the viceroy his old chum from University, who has invited them to visit."

"And while they're guests in his mansion," Mr. Godfrey added, "the children are intrigued by a servant's tale of a Maharaja's legendary hidden treasure."

"Or you could have them lost in the Great Indian Desert with a caravan merchant," Sidney suggested.

"Or both," said Edgar.

Mrs. Godfrey nodded thoughtfully, and there was a visible relaxing of male shoulders. Catherine smiled. Clearly the books were a family enterprise.

The meal was more opulent than required of a simple weekday family seating. Three courses, beginning with mock turtle soup, on to ham and Brussels sprouts for the second, sweetbreads and lamb cutlets with *soubis* sauce for the entree, apple tart and cabinet pudding for the third. Catherine ate only as much as good manners dictated, relieved that no one scrutinized her plate, and was mindful to compliment the cook.

Sidney showed her the morning room afterward, his haven where he conducted research into financial matters. "Notice anything familiar?" he asked.

"I don't—" Catherine started, scanning the room, but then her eyes stopped at a writing table, where sat her likeness in a silver oval frame. *He really does love me!* she thought with wonder. They joined the family in the parlor for coffee and tea, but only for a half hour, for Sidney said, "You'll forgive us for dashing away, but we've an appointment."

"It's been a pleasure, Miss Rayborn," Mr. Godfrey said, and even Edgar nodded.

Mrs. Godfrey's grey eyes were warm upon her. "Do come visit again soon, will you?"

"She will," Sidney said.

A blast of frigid air assaulted them on the front steps. Jerry had brought the coach around again. "We'll ride to the Park," Sidney said. "No sense in freezing until absolutely necessary."

The inside of the coach was not much warmer, but cozier once the door shut out the wind. Six boxes rested on the seat across from them, tied together with twine.

"Won't you please allow me to repay you?" Catherine asked, making one more attempt.

Sidney gave her a mock stern look. "That subject is closed, Miss Rayborn."

She smiled and braced herself for the slight jolt of the horses setting out. "You have a lovely family."

"Yes." He glanced through the window at the house. "Mind you, those were our company manners, but we do get on much better now than before. I've asked Henry to start looking for another house. I expect they'll stay in Belgravia, with Mother so timid over new situations."

"They don't mind being asked to leave?"

"Of course not. They've always been aware that one day I would—" He checked himself abruptly, looking pained as if he had caught himself in a slip. Then he sighed and reached for her hands. "Blast it, Catherine, it has to be twenty-five degrees out there. I'm afraid comfort is beginning to look more appealing than sentiment."

"What is it, Sidney?" she said, barely daring to breathe because she so hoped her suspicion over what was coming next was correct.

He smiled. "I realized I'm required to get down on one knee, but I'll get motion sickness if I do. And I can't very well ask your father for your hand, with the situation as it is. But all that aside, will you pay me the honor of becoming my wife?"

As prepared as she thought she was, Catherine was still caught by a great rush of lightheadedness. "I will, Sidney."

"You've made me very happy, Catherine," he said, and leaned closer to gather her into his arms. The kiss was long and gentle and tasted of coffee—though not unpleasantly. "Oh, I'm forgetting something." Grinning, he sat back a bit and withdrew a black satin pouch from his coat pocket. He untied the strings and brought out a ring, an oval diamond set into a gold band, and circled by tiny amethysts. "It was my great-grandmother's on my father's side," he said. "My mother wore it too, and passed it on to me when she married Henry."

"Oh, Sidney," she breathed. "It's beautiful." She pulled the glove from her left hand and extended her fingers. The ring slid easily—too easily—over the third one.

"We'll have to have it tightened," Sidney said, holding her fingertips.

"Oh, but we can't cut into an heirloom."

"It won't even be noticeable. A jewelsmith on Cheapside does excellent work. I had them make my ring." He fished down between the buttons of his topcoat, brought out his watch, and clicked it open. "Only half-past three. Have we time?"

"We have," Catherine told him. They held hands and waited for the coach to halt on Grosvenor Place at the entrance to Green Park. Sidney opened the door before Jerry could hop down.

"On to Howe's in Cheapside, Jerry," he said affably, then turned to Catherine with a smile that said, *See? I don't abuse my servants.*

Catherine returned his smile. But as the first wave of romance settled into particulars, she realized that the ring was the least of their problems. "Oh dear," she said. "Sidney, I can't tell my family."

"I thought as much," he said with grim expression. "But I didn't want to be the one to say it."

The idea shook her world, coming on the heels of such bliss. Not have Mother and Father and Jewel sitting in the front pew of a church, smiling and giving their blessing?

She shook her head. "There *has* to be a way."

"I wish there were. But I've had longer to think this over than you."

Desperately she grasped for straws. "We could keep our engagement secret until summer, when you would come down to Bombay on the P & O and meet them. They wouldn't have time to write Sarah and William. We could have the ceremony at Saint Thomas's."

"And what reason would we give them for the secrecy? You've said that your father is overly protective. You think he would just hand you over to me like that?"

"I don't know!"

He gave her a sad smile, touched her cheek. "I'm sorry it has to be this way, Catherine. But once we're husband and wife, your family will have no choice but to allow me the chance to prove that I'll treat you with utmost decency."

Husband and wife, she thought. *Lady Catherine Holt.* The situation would be tense for a little while, but as he said, her parents would eventually give him the benefit of the doubt. After all, Mother and Father had married against the wishes of Grandfather and Grandmother Lorimer, and their marriage was certainly a success.

"When should we marry?" she asked at the risk of sounding forward. *He's your fiancé!* she had to remind herself.

He took her hands again. "You're not tempted to change your mind?"

"Never," she replied.

The affection in his blue eyes was so precious that Catherine wished she could marry him this instant. Still, it was a shock when he smiled and said, "The twenty-seventh of March."

"Three months?"

"Is that a problem?"

"No, of course not," she assured him.

It would be the day after she returned to London for Easter vacation. He explained that he would meet her train with arrangements for a place for her to spend the night, or she could ask to stay with Peggy if she so wished.

"Your relations won't be showing up at King's Cross, will they?"

She thought a second and shook her head. "I always write to let them know which morning I'll be leaving Girton. I'll simply tell them two days later. Then I'll wire them after the wedding, when I wire my parents."

Her family would be hurt, of course, but as much as she loved them, she could not trade her future happiness for their approval.

They would have a small ceremony just for family at his mother's church, Saint Peter's, Sidney told her. By then, his mother and stepfather would have moved into another house. "Or surely by the time we return from the honeymoon."

He had even thought that part out too. "We'll tour Egypt. I've always wanted to see the pyramids. And then we'll continue on to Bombay, where I promise you, I will do everything I can to endear myself to your family."

Sometime before they reached the jeweler's, Catherine realized that her Girton days would conclude after the upcoming Hillary Term. The thought was not distressing, for a person could only travel one path at a time, and how could any path be better than spending a lifetime with Sidney?

As for her desire to teach, she told herself that every little girl wanted to be a schoolmistress at some time in her life. Even Jewel pretended to teach her dolls at age four or five. But it was time to exchange that childhood dream for a happier reality.

Rows of shop-fronts on Cheapside displayed glittering watches, necklaces and rings, bracelets and brooches, and bales of silver spoons and forks. The jewelsmith at Howe's was a small man with soft voice and squinting eyes. He measured Catherine's finger and the ring. "Lovely heirloom," he said, holding it up so the gasolier reflected its facets. "We can have it ready by the twenty-seventh."

"That's after Christmas," Sidney told him, and nodded toward a placard on the wall behind the counter. "That says you can make repairs within
two days."

"Yes, Sir," the man said with an apologetic bob of the head. "Could
have it done that soon, if not for the season. But we're flooded—"

"And yet your sign is still up."

"Well, yes—"

"Then I'll take the two days, thank you."

The man blinked at him. "But you see, Sir—"

"Lord Holt," Sidney corrected quietly.

"Yes . . . ah . . . Lord Holt." The jewelsmith's eyes faded, as if he could
not quite find his place in the whole conversation. "You see, several patrons
have—"

"Your other patrons do not interest me," Sidney cut in. This time there
was an edge to his voice.

"Sidney." Catherine touched his coat sleeve. "I don't mind waiting." *I
won't be able to wear it in public anyway.*

He shrugged his arm away and placed both palms upon the counter,
leaning forward a fraction. "I don't think you quite understand. My father
was a barrister, and several of my friends are attorneys. So I know a bit
about the law. If you do not wish to be sued for false advertising, you will
have the ring ready on Friday afternoon."

The jewelsmith turned beseeching eyes to Catherine. She gave him a
helpless look.

"Do we understand each other, Sir?" Sidney said.

"Yes, Sir . . . I mean, yes, Lord Holt," the man replied, hands visibly
shaking.

"There you are, good fellow," Sidney said with gentle tone, and somehow that was worse than if he had yelled. He turned for the door. This time
Catherine could not bear to look at the jewelsmith. She could feel the poor
little man's eyes upon her back as she followed her fiancé out of the shop.

"Never contradict me in public, Catherine," Sidney said in the coach,
staring straight ahead.

Protests surged to her lips, and she swallowed them with difficulty. She
could tell by the set of his jaw that it would only annoy him. *He didn't
really mean that,* she consoled herself. The Sidney she knew and loved, the
Sidney who would soon be her husband, treated her like a queen almost
every second that they were together.

Even when they weren't together. Weren't the parcels resting upon the seat across from them proof of that?

"I'm sorry, Sidney," she said.

He nodded, blue eyes cold upon her. "Very well."

This time it was he who turned to the window. Uneasiness lay between them like a spiky hedge. Catherine fought back tears by promising herself that when a calmer time came, or perhaps after they were married and their love had grown even stronger, she would explain to him how sometimes his words hurt her.

"I had no idea," he said, taking her in his arms and pressing her head gently against his comforting shoulder. "Why didn't you tell me earlier?"

"I was afraid you wouldn't love me anymore," she confessed.

"Oh, my dearest Catherine. That will never happen as long as I draw breath."

". . . as Highgate."

She blinked at Sidney. "I beg your pardon?"

"I said, we'll deliver you as far as Highgate. Then you've only to take a cab for a half mile or so."

This has been an anxious day for him, she reminded herself, what with his planning to propose, and their having to keep the engagement a secret. Warily, she said, "Thank you, Sidney."

He actually smiled. "Purely selfish of me. I want to spend every minute with you that I can. Which reminds me . . . when will we see each other again?"

She had to think. It would not be wise to leave the house for any extended period of time before Boxing Day, five days away. But after that, surely returning today with packages would have purchased some freedom. She just needed an excuse as good as today's.

"Just give me a ring when you can find some privacy," he said at length. "This time, I'll be sure Rumfellow either takes the message or fetches me. I'll tell the same to Mother."

Catherine's pulse jumped. "Your mother?"

"She has this annoying habit of answering the telephone now and again. But you needn't feel awkward should it happen."

She nodded, knowing that every nerve in her body would feel awkward. But she could think of no other way. That brought something else to mind. "When will you tell your family?"

He smiled. "Soon."

And it will come as no surprise, Sidney thought. His mother's was the only approval that mattered, and that was assured. Hadn't she lectured him for years about settling down with a decent woman? But he could not make the announcement with Catherine present, because Mother and Henry would ask innocent enough questions pertaining to her family's part in the wedding plans. He needed to warn them ahead of time that this was not a comfortable topic of discussion for her.

His second reason was just as compelling. While Mother surely suspected he was no choirboy during his Oxford years, she had no concrete proof of his misbehaviors. And so for *her* sake, he had to base the cause for secrecy only on Catherine's relations believing the rumors about Leona and him. But that was not something he wished to discuss in Catherine's presence, even though he strongly suspected Mrs. Doyle had told her of the affair. He assumed the Doyles had learned of it during negotiations over the house, for they did not rub elbows with London's high society, in spite of their wealth.

Jerry reined the team to a stop directly behind an idle coach for hire on Highgate. "Fetch the packages," Sidney called while escorting Catherine to the other coach.

Once the packages were transferred and he had dropped some coins into the cabby's palm, he leaned into the doorway to say farewell. Catherine looked so becoming with the corners of her mouth tucked into little semicircles, the high color in her cheeks, and long hair tousled about the collar of her cloak. Only months ago he would never have considered marrying a woman who could not bring a dowry to their union. Having a good stable life mattered more now.

And who could tell? He knew by the way she spoke of them that her parents cared for their daughter a great deal. Perhaps once they warmed up to him, they would offer a belated dowry from the mother's inheritance. And at least there was the legacy from her grandparents to help maintain the household and her wardrobe and such, leaving him free to continue investing.

"I'll be counting the hours," he said.

"I'll miss you too." Her smile faltered. "You're giving me that lovely ring, and I have nothing for you."

"Not so," he corrected, and reached forward to tug a lock of her chestnut hair. "You've made a decent man of me."

Twenty-Nine

As Highgate's shops passed by her window, Sidney's parting words echoed through Catherine's mind. Incredible, that after his twenty-eight years of life experiences, he would credit her, a sheltered nineteen-year-old, with sparking his desire to turn over a new leaf. Already she missed him terribly!

But as 5 Cannonhall Road came into view, she was relieved that they had not tarried longer, for her watch showed ten-past five, almost an hour earlier than she was expected. That would surely earn her some grace points, should any suspicions linger in Sarah's mind.

That thought led abruptly to another. She had not informed Peggy that she was to be her alibi, simply because Peggy would become angry at being asked to be involved in any deception, and possibly even refuse. *She would have no reason to ring here today, not after our seeing each other yesterday.* Then she remembered the chemistry periodicals William and Sarah had given her. *What if she decided to thank them again?* If she did, she would write a note. *Wouldn't she?*

Mr. Duffy was hanging a garland of evergreen boughs around the front door. He walked out to the carriage drive to take the bundle of packages. When Catherine opened her reticule the cabby waved a hand. "Already bin paid, Miss."

Sidney . . . she thought, smiling.

"Yes, Miss." The cabby shook his head in mock wonder. "Paid me right down to the farthing, he did. Got to admire a man who's so precise."

Catherine's pulse jumped. She glanced at Mr. Duffy and received a blank look in return. "My friend's father," she explained. "Mr. Somerset. Must have used up all his change."

She fished out a half crown, far more than the short drive warranted, and handed it over.

"Thank you, Miss!" the cabby exclaimed. "And Merry Christmas to you!"

"You're welcome." As the cabby took the reins again, Catherine sent another look to Mr. Duffy, who grinned above the parcels in his great arms.

"Did y'leave anything in the shops, Miss Rayborn?"

She smiled, tension easing out of her. "I may have left a little, Mr. Duffy."

He chuckled as if she had told the wittiest of jokes, and relief made her so giddy that she joined in. At the door the gardener raised a knee to balance his burden and attempted to ease a hand toward the knob. Catherine waved him aside and turned the knob, holding the door open for him and closing it after he crossed the threshold. The seldom-used great hall had been transformed in her absence. Holly and mistletoe boughs wreathed the fireplace and draped the banister all the way to the landing. Red satin ribbons hung from every second railing. Red candles in lamp globes, decorated at the base with holly sprigs, waited to be lit on the chimneypiece and entrance table and piano, which had been moved from the parlor. Empty silver serving trays, tea service, and punch bowls gleamed under the reflection of the gasolier above the long table.

Mrs. Bacon, Claire, and Marie stood near that table with expressions decidedly less cheerful than their surroundings. "Good afternoon, Miss Rayborn," Mrs. Bacon said.

"Good afternoon," Catherine replied.

"What happened?" Mr. Duffy asked.

Marie scowled at the bundle in Mrs. Bacon's arms, which turned out to be Hector, studying Catherine through half-closed lids. "I walked in here just in time to see this animal prancing across the trays like a *ballerine*!"

"There are paw prints over everything," Mrs. Bacon said.

"Well, there's nothing to do but wash them," Claire sighed, picking up a tray. "At least we have time."

"Madame is not yet ready to dress," Marie said. "I will help you carry them to the kitchen. Just shut that beast up in a room somewhere."

The two other maids gaped at her. Even Catherine took pause, for as Sarah's lady's maid, Marie did not perform household chores beyond tidying Sarah and William's bedchamber.

"But you don't do that sort of—" Mr. Duffy said, but checked himself when his wife sent him a sharp look.

Catherine stepped forward and looped the ribbons of her reticule around her wrist. "Here . . . let me take Hector to my room."

Bethia met them upstairs in the corridor. She wore her dressing gown, her hair in little curling-ironed ringlets that had not yet been combed. "Catherine!" she said as if she had been waiting just for her. "We're to have sandwiches in the nursery for supper!"

"Yes?"

"Because we'll all be dressing and won't have—" her eyes widened. "What are those, Mr. Duffy?"

"Oh, it ain't for me to be tellin'," he said affectionately.

The girl looked disappointed, but hurried over to Catherine's door and swung it open. "Mrs. Bacon's angry at Hector," she said, following Mr. Duffy and Catherine into the room.

"And Hector's just crushed over it." Catherine looked down at the cat in her arms. "Aren't you?" She deposited him onto her window seat, holding a restraining hand lightly upon his back while Mr. Duffy placed the bundle upon the carpet beside her wardrobe.

"Thank you, Mr. Duffy," Catherine said, and when the door closed behind him, she looked at Bethia, who was leaning down to inspect the stack of boxes. "Now, you're not to handle them. They're Christmas gifts."

The girl said carefully, "For Uncle James and Aunt Virginia and Jewel?"

Smiling, Catherine moved her hand from the cat so that she could take off her hat and cloak—which would need a good brushing the next time she wore it. "No, I sent theirs weeks ago. It takes them a long time to reach Bombay."

She had not yet received their gifts to her. Perhaps they would arrive tomorrow.

A knock sounded as she was removing her gloves. She tossed them onto her dressing table on her way to the door. Sarah and William stood in the corridor wearing somber expressions.

Peggy rang, Catherine realized, a wave of queasiness rolling through her. "Please, come in."

"Thank you," Sarah said, and confirmed Catherine's worry by saying to Bethia, "Why don't you help Susan amuse Danny while your mother's changing?"

When the door closed behind a reluctant Bethia, Catherine looked at William and said, "You're home early." A stalling tactic to give her time to think, as well as a test to see if she could smoothe the gravity from their expressions by carrying on as normal.

"Just a bit," was his short reply.

You have to take the offensive, she ordered herself, taking long, steady breaths to calm her racing heartbeat. *Or you'll be packing for Bombay. Think fast, think fast!*

Sarah was opening her mouth to speak.

"Has something happened to my parents?" Catherine asked with anxious expression. "To Jewel?"

It would make her seem all the more innocent, she realized, if she hadn't the faintest idea why Sarah and William would come to her room like this. Didn't the Scriptures say that the guilty fled when no one pursued? If she had truly suspected some tragedy to her family, she would not have had to pretend to worry, but now she was dead certain that this had to do with Peggy and the telephone in the parlor.

Sarah's expression relaxed just a little. "Oh, no . . . not at all."

Catherine allowed herself a relieved sigh, but then sobered up again. "Then I'm glad you're both here. I've done something terrible, and it's weighing heavily upon me."

Husband and wife glanced at each other.

"I didn't ring you to let you know my plans had changed—and I should have. After Stanley dropped me off at Peggy's, I just couldn't bring myself to go in and invite her."

"But you had already invited her," Sarah said firmly. "That's what you said yesterday, that you and Peggy planned to shop."

"I said I planned to shop with Peggy," Catherine corrected. "But I hadn't mentioned it to her yet."

"Why wouldn't you mention it?" William asked. "You spent almost two hours on the train together."

"I didn't even *think* about shopping while we were on the train. It's difficult to get into the spirit of Christmas when you're recovering from exams." She looked at Sarah. "But when I was in the coach with you and Uncle Daniel, and saw all the other shoppers, I realized I needed to hurry and see to it."

"Why would you have taken it for granted that Miss Somerset would wish to accompany you?" Sarah said, green eyes still suspicious. "You could have given her a ring."

Catherine shrugged. "We spend every day together at school, so we practically read each other's minds. And she had already told me that she had no plans for the day."

Those parts were true. And it was a relief to insert *some* truth into her defense.

Folding his arms, William said, "Please explain this to me, Catherine.

Why would you suddenly decide *not* to invite Miss Somerset, when you were standing right there in front of their house?"

Catherine nodded and could only hope that sincere delivery would patch the gaping holes in her logic. "Because it wasn't until then that it struck me that Peggy would not be able to spend as much as I can. She isn't given a lot of spending money, and I'm always careful not to flaunt mine in front of her."

Again Sarah and William sought each other's eyes. This time some uncertainty had crept into their expressions. Sarah glanced at the bundle upon the floor. "And so you spent the day in the shops?"

"Yes. No, wait. I stopped for lunch at a tea room on Oxford Street. Other unescorted women were there, so I didn't feel it was improper."

"It must have been difficult, carrying all those around," William said, clearly still not shed of all his suspicions.

Catherine's thoughts raced. "Yes, quite. But the cabby I hired eventually helped me. He was the one who tied them up with twine." Her heart skipped a beat, for it was then that she recalled what she had said about Mr. Somerset for Mr. Duffy's benefit. *But what reason would Mr. Duffy have for repeating that to them?*

Her lie needed a bit more embellishing, she realized, and she allowed herself a faint sentimental smile. "I came across my grandparents' former housekeeper in the tea room," she said. "Mrs. Spear is her name. She said she's in a very good situation in Kensington, but that no employer has ever treated her as kindly as did my grandparents. It was a lovely thing to hear, coming at Christmas. My mother will be touched by it."

The two were starting to look a bit sheepish. While that was encouraging, it also sharpened the guilt gnawing at her insides. She had realized weeks ago that however mistaken they were about Sidney, it was love for her that had prompted Sarah to send her back to Girton. And it was the same reason they stood before her now. *But you can't afford to retreat now,* Catherine told herself.

"But forgive me," she said, forcing herself to look squarely into Sarah's green eyes while stretching her lips into an artless smile. "Here I am, rattling on and on when you have something to discuss with me."

For the third time William and Sarah looked at each other. William shrugged, and Sarah gave him an almost imperceptible nod.

"It's nothing," Sarah said. She glanced at the chimneypiece clock. "We've only an hour. I should change now."

"Yes, I suppose I should too," Catherine said, walking them the few steps to the door.

William paused halfway through it and turned. There was a spark of knowledge in the dark eyes that met Catherine's, but it faded again into uncertainty. "There are sandwiches in the nursery."

"Thank you." Catherine smiled at them. But once the door was closed, she went to her bed, threw herself across the coverlet and sank her face into a bolster pillow. *They still have doubts,* she told herself. *But they've decided to give you the benefit of them.*

For now.

She could not afford for anything like this to happen again. She had looked so forward to returning to London—*his* city, but she could not see Sidney for the remainder of the vacation. It would be terribly reckless to chance it. Which meant she would not have her engagement ring until he could bring it up to her at Chesterton.

Tears squeezed past her closed eyelids. *Love is supposed to make a woman happy,* she thought. But her only moments of happiness were when she was with Sidney. When she was not, her soul felt empty to the point of aching, and yet, paradoxically, filled with almost overwhelming guilt.

The only thought that consoled her was that they would be married in three months. Then she would never have to lie to anyone again. And one day, conceivably, when Sidney had proved himself to the whole family, they would sit about a fireplace with Sarah and William, and confess all the plots they had concocted in order to see each other, and everyone would laugh. Her mind's eye could see it so clearly, as if she were allowed a special glimpse into the future. William would cuff Sidney on the shoulder and say, "I was never so happy to have myself proved wrong about anyone, old chap!"

Her nerves quirked when a knock sounded. Had Sarah and William discussed the matter and decided they needed more proof of her whereabouts today? The name of the tea room, perhaps? *Is there even a tea room on Oxford Street?*

"Wait, please," she said, outpacing Hector to the door and scooping him into her arms. Susan stood holding the gown Catherine had chosen that morning, a Russian green cashmere with appliqué velvet leaves of the same color, and bouffant sleeves finished with a cuff of ecru embroidery. "All pressed, Miss," she said in her thick cockney accent. "Would yer like help dressin'?"

"Yes, please," Catherine replied.

The maid sent a glance at the tangles about her shoulders and added, hesitantly, "And combing yer hair?"

"That would be nice." Although appearance meant nothing to her this evening, Catherine had to put forth the effort or arouse more suspicion.

Susan worked quickly, careful to start with the snarled ends and work her way up with the comb, apologizing every time a snarl tugged. She formed several long braids and coiled them loosely at the crown of her head. With Catherine's permission she dashed downstairs and returned with a few small holly sprigs to pin among them. *May as well let her have her fun,* Catherine thought. A half hour later she stood at the mirror attached to her wardrobe door, the maid beaming from her elbow.

"Thank you, Susan." Catherine turned to smile at her. "You've made me look very nice."

"Pretty as a picture, Miss."

Eric Kirkpatrick apparently thought so too, for the admiral's grandson seldom left her side the entire evening. Were her heart not otherwise occupied, she would have been pleased, for he was an agreeable young man, and handsome, with a finely chiseled Roman nose and wavy brown hair as dark as hers.

"I'm fortunate in that my grandfather has kept up with his former navy mates," he told her after fetching her another cup of punch. "I've stamps from places as far away as Japan."

"Have you any from Malta?" she found herself asking. Just because she wasn't interested in him romantically didn't mean she couldn't assist him with his hobby.

"Several," he said, as if reluctant to confess it. "With the Navy Hospital being there. But it's kind of you to ask."

About four dozen people were present, almost evenly divided between adults and children, and all residents of Cannonhall Road. Aunt Naomi asked a neighbor's twelve-year-old daughter, Amy Jakes, to play the piano. The girl demonstrated remarkable maturity for her age in that she did not bang out carols, but played softly, her music a pleasant accompaniment to conversation. Bethia stood at her side to turn the pages of sheet music. Guy Russell, looking like a little man in his suit, his hair watered down with spikes sticking up here and there, stood at her other side and watched her fingers move along the keys.

"That boy should have piano lessons," said a voice from Catherine's left, during one of the rare times when Mr. Kirkpatrick was not at her side.

She turned to Uncle Daniel. "Has he learned to play the flute you gave him?"

"He took to it like a fox to chickens." He studied the boy with eyes narrowed thoughtfully. "But he should learn to read music. I believe I'll ask Amy the name of her tutor."

Beard aside, Uncle Daniel reminded Catherine of her father so strongly that sometimes she felt a little ache for her family in his presence. She knew him well enough to know that he would be paying for these piano lessons. She had no memory of her grandparents on the Rayborn side of the family, but appreciated how they had instilled generosity into both their sons. "That's so kind of you, Uncle Daniel."

He smiled at her. From the corner of her eye, Catherine caught sight of Mr. Kirkpatrick making his way over again.

"Pleasant fellow, isn't he?" her uncle said.

"Yes, very pleasant."

"I suppose he will appreciate it if I make myself absent."

"Really, you—" But her uncle winked and walked off to join Aunt Naomi and a circle of guests.

"You know, my grandfather has invited me to stay the summer with him," Mr. Kirkpatrick said with hopeful tone upon his return.

Carefully, so as not to hurt his pride, but with just enough formality to convey the correct message, Catherine said, "I'm sure Hampstead has lovely summers. I spend mine in Bombay with my family."

It did not matter, at least where the young man was concerned, that this coming summer would be quite different. A shadow of disappointment passed across his face, but he was game enough not to go off and sulk. And when his grandfather motioned him over to meet someone, Catherine took the opportunity to slip upstairs and ring Sidney's house.

He gave me permission, she reminded herself in the darkened parlor. His butler answered, asked her to wait, and a minute later Sidney's voice came through the earpiece.

"Catherine?"

"Sidney." A lump rose to her throat. "We can't see each other. Peggy rang while I was out, and Sarah and William are suspicious."

A muffled exclamation came faintly over the line. It almost sounded like a word she'd heard a cabby shout to his horses when she was a girl. Father had upbraided the man severely and removed the man from his hansom without paying. But she must have been mistaken, she told herself, for Sidney was not the sort of person to swear.

At length he said, "Yes, of course. We don't want anything interfering with the wedding. That's the most important thing."

"You're not angry?"

"At you? Of course not. Now, go try to enjoy your party, and I'll bring your ring to Chesterton."

His understanding caused her love for him to deepen even more so.

That love did not diminish even slightly three days later, Christmas Eve, when she finally got around to opening the parcels for rewrapping. But she could not help but feel dismay over the cheapness of the gifts.

For Uncle Daniel and William there was a muffler each, one of brown and the other of grey wool. The two women's gifts, hand-painted papier-mâché trinket boxes, were a little nicer, but she had seen similar ones in shops for a half-sovereign each. A pretty price for someone poor, but not nearly costly enough to justify her supposed reluctance to have Peggy witness how much she would spend.

Bethia's gift was a ceramic bisque doll with painted eyes, and Danny's, a kaleidoscope. *Could Rumfellow have spent less than he was given and pocketed the change?* Catherine asked herself. But the butler had not worn the look of an embezzler—however embezzlers were supposed to look. And besides, he would not risk losing his position should she mention the cheapness of the gifts to Sidney—which she could not do.

Perhaps it was Sidney's family's custom to exchange modest gifts, she thought. There was certainly nothing wrong with that. Still, if only he had informed her ahead of time of his plan, she could have insisted on giving his butler an appropriate amount of money, as well as a list of suggested gifts.

It's the thought that counts, Catherine told herself when some of the doll's rooted hair came off in her hand. She could not bear to imagine what William and Sarah would think. She got up and paced the floor, chiding herself for not opening the parcels sooner. But she had so wanted to allay Sarah and William's suspicions that she had spent almost every waking minute of the past two days involving herself with family. She read at least a dozen picture books to Danny, played paper dolls with Bethia, and helped Uncle Daniel organize his research files. The latter had consumed half of yesterday.

On Christmas morning the family followed the pleasant rituals being followed in thousands of households all over England, from the children squealing over the contents of their stockings, to the service at Christ Church, to the roast turkey and Christmas pudding, and then the presenting of gifts in the parlor. Small lit candles, fancy cakes and gilded gingerbread figures, little baskets and trays of candies and fruits festooned the branches of a seven-foot fir, and an angel with outstretched wings stared heavenward from its tip.

To Catherine's immense relief, the children drew so much attention—Bethia reverently touching a tiny shingle on the roof of her dollhouse, and Danny laughing until he hiccuped from the back of his hobby horse—that her gifts did not draw even one curious look.

"Thank you, Catherine," William said, winding the grey muffler about his neck and smiling. "Very nice."

Thank you, Catherine automatically prayed under her breath while her nerves untangled. A second later it occurred to her that she had just insulted God, who certainly was not party to her deception. Relief was replaced by guilt, and suddenly the three months until her wedding—three more months of lies—felt like a long time.

---

Thirty

*W*e'll see you at Easter," Sarah said, wrapping her
arms about Catherine's woolen-swathed figure in
the hall on the third of January, 1882.

Catherine patted her back, and said with a curious thickness to her
voice, "I appreciate how you've always made me feel welcome here."

"But it's been our joy," Sarah told her as they stepped apart. The little
Christmas shopping misunderstanding had been the only ripple in the
pond, but Catherine had certainly proved herself afterward by her cheerful
disposition and involvement with the family. "And we look forward to having you here many more times. Have you everything?"

"Yes, everything."

"We'll ship your other gifts as soon as they arrive," Naomi said as the
two embraced. That was the only damper on the season—slight that it
was—that no packages from India had arrived.

"Thank you, Aunt Naomi." Catherine knelt to embrace the children,
one in each arm. "And I wish I could take you both to school with me."

Sarah's father smiled. "We should leave now, Catherine."

When the door closed behind the two, Sarah and Naomi turned for the
staircase with the children. "I wonder if they're feeding those girls properly
at that school."

"I don't think it's the school," Sarah said. "She doesn't eat much here,
either."

"I eat much," Danny said, nodding righteously. "Huh, Mother?"

Naomi tousled his brown hair. "You do at that, Danny."

The temperature warmed slightly over the following two days, but not too
warm for snowflakes to form. By Saturday morning, rooftops and hedges were
dusted white, and there was enough accumulated for Father and William to

take the children—Guy Russell included—sledding on Parliament Hill on the Heath. A large box from Bombay arrived by parcel post that afternoon. Sarah and Naomi sorted through the contents in the parlor, under the watchful eyes of Bethia and Danny. Even Father and William looked up from their chess match now and again. The parcels labeled for Catherine were set aside, the others handed out. For Bethia there was a sari-clad Indian doll of coffee-colored china, with glossy black hair and thick dark lashes. Danny's gift was a mechanical tin elephant, which walked and raised its trunk when wound with a key. Sarah and Naomi received shawls of beautifully woven pashmina wool; William, a book of photographed scenes of India; and Father, a fine teakwood cane with carved ivory handle. There was even a gift for Sarah and William's yet-to-arrive baby, a soft cotton blanket embroidered about the hem with finely stitched honeysuckle vines and flowers.

"Pity Catherine's not here," Naomi said, trying on her shawl. She looked at Father. "You know, we could bring her gifts up to her tomorrow after church."

Father looked up from winding Danny's elephant and smiled. "Then let's go."

The children pleaded to be allowed along. Father was kind, but adamant that they should not. "Your mother and I haven't had an outing alone in years. We'll ask Avis to look after you. And when the weather warms, we'll take you on a special trip."

Both small faces fell, but with the distraction of new toys, disappointment was soon forgotten.

"Should we wire her?" Naomi said. "I believe she and her friends spend most of Sunday in Cambridge."

Sarah, wrapping her shawl around Bethia, said, "She told me she's been attending the parish church so she'd have more time to study."

"We'll just take our chances," Father said. "Even if we don't see her, we'll at least be able to drop off the gifts."

"She'll be surprised," Bethia said. "Won't she, Mother?"

Naomi smiled at her. "I expect she will be, Bethia."

"I like surprises," Danny said, cradling his elephant.

"*Everyone* likes surprises," Bethia told him.

"Did you put the ring away?" Sidney asked Catherine on the following day as the coach rolled out of Chesterton toward Girton.

"Yes." With an enigmatic smile she held up her gloved right hand. The ring made a little bulge in the base of her third finger. "Here."

"You're still wearing it?"

"There is less chance of losing it that way. I'll find a place for it in my room." She sighed. "But is it necessary? Who's to say it wasn't a Christmas gift, a family heirloom?"

"It *was* a family heirloom," Irene said from the rear-facing seat.

Sidney gave his aunt a warning look. The ring had been a bone of contention for years, after being passed down to his father instead of either of his father's sisters, and then not handed over to one of them later, when Mother remarried.

"It's best if you hide it away," he said to Catherine. "The purloined letter principle only works in stories."

"Purloined letter?" she asked.

"It's a story by Poe. Have you never read it?"

"No," she said, grey-green eyes sheepish.

He quelled his slight irritation by reminding himself that there would be plenty of time to broaden her horizons when they were married. Patiently he explained. "The protagonist hid a damaging letter in plain sight."

"I see." She gave him a grateful smile. "You don't mind if I show Peggy and Milly, do you? They won't tell."

"Very well," Sidney said, smiling at her eagerness to show off the ring, even though he was getting a little weary of hearing of the two friends. Again he had to remind himself of the limitations of her life experience, in spite of her family's travels. "And then find a safe place for it."

"Hmph!" Irene snorted, turning her face toward the window even though it was white with condensation.

Sidney pruned up his face, imitating her. Catherine covered a shocked smile. At least Irene was keeping her agreement not to intrude upon their privacy in the parlor. But he would have to speak with her about today's little barbs as soon as they were alone.

Another reason he would be glad when they were wed, besides not having to deal with Irene anymore, was that cab fare was costing him an arm and a leg. Fortunately his Express rides from London to Cambridge and back were free, owing to some favors traded between Henry and one of the line's owners. But cabbies were, as a rule, unpleasant creatures.

He forced all gloomy thoughts from his mind and took Catherine's hand. She squeezed his, and they rode on, not speaking because of Irene's presence, but so strongly aware of each other that words were not necessary anyway. And he dared to brush a quick kiss against her lips once they stopped outside

Girton's gates. Steamed windows were good for something. He could still hear the frame squeaking from the cabby climbing from his seat, when the door swung open.

"Catherine!"

The young woman who thrust herself halfway through the door was tall and fair, nose and cheeks pinkened by the chill, with ash blond hair spilling out of a mink hat. The eyes were of a startling shade of medium blue, one that Sidney could not put a name to in his mind.

"Oh!" she gasped self-consciously. "I didn't know—!"

"Milly, this is Lord Holt," Catherine said hurriedly. "And his aunt, Mrs. Fry. May I present Miss Turner?"

Irene mumbled some halfhearted acknowledgment, and Sidney said, "It's a pleasure to make your acquaintance at last, Miss Turner."

"Thank—"

"What's going on, Milly?" Catherine cut in. "Why aren't you in Cambridge?"

"We were too cold. And it's a good thing for you." She glanced back toward the school. "Peggy's been entertaining your aunt and uncle for the past quarter of an hour."

Catherine gaped at her. "Which aunt and uncle?"

"The ones from Hampstead."

"Oh dear! What should I—"

"Calm yourself, Catherine," Miss Turner said. "Miss Scott told them you're with a family friend. They assume it's a friend on your mother's side."

Indigo, Sidney thought.

The following Sunday in Irene's parlor, Sidney put his arm around Catherine's shoulders and said, "I would like to do something for your friends. They certainly saved us from disaster."

She turned her face up to him and smiled. "That's so typically thoughtful of you. But you don't have to do anything. I've already thanked them."

He caught something just a little odd in her tone, and realized what it was. "They were angry?"

"No, of course not." But after a hesitation, she added, "They just didn't appreciate being forced to become involved. They still don't like it that I slip around to see you."

"And do they think we have any choice?" Sidney pulled her closer and rested his chin against the top of her head as she leaned against his chest. "Anyway, I'd still like to try to change their opinion of me—as well as show my gratitude. Invite them to accompany you next week, and I'll order a nice meal from the inn upstreet."

"Very well," she replied. "But you won't be offended if they won't accept, will you?"

He shrugged, causing her head to move a little. "Then we'll have all the food to ourselves. You could use more nourishment anyway."

"What do you mean?"

With his free hand he picked up her left hand, pushed back the sleeve a bit to circle her wrist easily with his thumb and forefinger. "This is what I mean."

And she was looking almost gaunt, with little hollows deepening under her cheekbones. The change had been so gradual, their time together so limited, that he had barely noticed. But now her leanness was detracting from her beauty, and in addition, putting her at risk of falling prey to some lung disease like influenza or consumption. He didn't know what he would do if anything happened to her.

"I want you to start putting more on your plate. I want to marry a woman, not a skeleton."

"I will, Sidney," she said almost happily.

"That's my girl." He squeezed her shoulder, and reminded himself that moments like these would be the warp and woof of his life once they were married. How ridiculous, that he would allow Miss Turner's face to visit his mind several times over the past week, when he had only met her that one, brief moment. And especially considering that he was happily engaged to the most wonderful young woman he had ever met. He was almost tempted to tell Catherine he had changed his mind about the invitation.

———

One of the principles Hugh's grandfather established in the days of Sedgwick Tea's infancy was that a Sedgwick would always be the first to arrive at the office each morning. Doing so conveyed the correct impression in the employees' minds that the owners were not content to sit back and collect profits while managers ran the business. Fuller Sedgwick had carried on the tradition for almost thirty years and seemed happy to pass along the morning duty to his eldest son.

Hugh did not mind, though he had first shuddered at the notion of rising at four o'clock for six days a week. He was fortunate to have his position, he reminded himself often. And once he got on his way, he rather liked being one of the few awake and alert while the bulk of the city was still wrapped in gauzy slumber. Morning fog softened the lines of the businesses flanking Aldergate Street, transforming the atmosphere of blatant modernity into one of romantic centuries past, when the Saxon Gate stood here long before William and his Normans crossed the Channel.

After opening the lock on the front door to Sedgwick Tea, Hugh often stood a minute to allow his eyes one more pleasant sight before they would be attaching themselves to tonnage reports and advertising dossiers and the like. He was doing so on the nineteenth of January, head cocked to listen to a ship's bell lolling lazily in the distance, when he felt the light tug at his topcoat pocket, heard the padded scurry of feet on the snow-covered pavement. The shock was so great that for a second or two he could only gape in the direction of the figure fading into the darkness.

"Hey! You!" he shouted, dropping the keys into his pocket and giving chase—with care, for the thief clearly had had considerable practice at darting about on icy cobbled stones. Hugh had the advantage of a tenacity brought on by indignation. He caught up with the figure past Aldgate Station just before the Middlesex intersection, and flung his arms about him. He was a boy, Hugh realized. A squirming boy, who growled and then whimpered and pleaded to be let go.

"Not until you stop fighting!" Hugh growled back.

They struggled on, the boy even sinking his teeth into Hugh's sleeve, but the thick wool was a formidable barrier. Panting, the boy went limp. Hugh held his arms around the thin frame long enough to grab the lad by an ear.

"Ouch, Mister!"

"My purse," Hugh told him, tightening his grip.

The boy pushed back his coat sleeve and dipped a bare hand into his pocket. Even in the darkness, Hugh could see that the coat was too large for the lad, frayed at the sleeves and full of holes. "Here!"

Hugh shoved it into his own pocket and relaxed his grip on the ear just a bit. "If you needed money, why didn't you just ask?"

"Coos I ain't no beggar!" the boy replied. He had to be all of nine, his face filthy and pinched, his hair in clumps over his frayed collar.

"So stealing's better? What would your mother think?"

"Got none. You got yer money, Mister. Let go of my ear!"

Hugh let go, his anger replaced by pity. He reached into his pocket again. "Look, you don't have to go about picking pockets."

But the boy shot away from him, fast as a whippet, and was swallowed up by darkness.

"Wait!" Hugh called, taking a step in the same direction. "I'll give you—"

That was when he realized his purse was lighter. He opened it, to be sure, and jabbed a bare finger inside. He gave chase again, but by the time he reached the beginning of Whitechapel's slum, he had no clue as to which dark lane the boy had taken.

You were going to give him the money anyway, he told himself on the way back to the office. It was all of two pounds and some coins for the Underground—a pittance for Hugh but a tidy little bounty for a young street urchin.

A sickness of heart took hold of him and lingered on through the day, even after he reminded himself that the boy could buy several hot meals with the money. The wall surrounding his safe, insulated, well-fed, and well-polished little world had been scurried over by a visitor from a more desperate one. Even though the visitor was gone, a picture of his small footsteps in the snow refused to fade from Hugh's mind.

———

She's loyal to a fault, Catherine reminded herself in Mrs. Fry's parlor the following Sunday. Everything about Milly's manner said that she was unaware that she looked for all the world like a goddess standing atop Mount Olympus, while the lines of John Wilson's "By the Banks of the Clyde" flowed effortlessly from her lips.

> " . . *Here let me walk abroad when tempests fly,*
> *And careless hear them rage along the sky;*
> *Where forest trees with daring grandeur rise,*
> *Disdain the earth, and bold invade the skies.*"

And Sidney's fondness of poetry was the reason for the admiration in his eyes. After all of Catherine's babbling on about her two best friends' talents, it was only natural that he would ask Milly to recite. If Peggy had brought her violin, he would have asked her to play.

She should be grateful for his thoughtfulness, she chided herself with at glance at the remains of the feast on the table. Would she be this way when they married? A shrew of a wife who felt threatened by every face fairer than her own? If so, heaven forbid that she should ever allow herself to grow old!

But she could not help but wish she would have hinted to her friends that they should not accept the invitation. They would have followed her wishes. She felt Peggy's stare from the chair adjacent to the sofa and looked at her. Peggy smiled, and Catherine smiled back. But something in the meeting of their eyes told Catherine that Peggy knew what she was feeling.

Catherine stretched her smile wider. She didn't want any unwarranted pity.

Sidney loved her and her alone, and that was that.

"I'll wager you don't know any by George Peele," Sidney was saying.

"Hmm . . ." Milly murmured, arms folded and ash blond head leaning thoughtfully. "The name strikes a chord."

"You can't win that one, Sidney," Catherine said brightly. A little too brightly in her own ears, but she could not inhale her words again.

Milly winked at her and cleared her throat.

> *"Not Iris in her pride and bravery*
> *Adorns her arch with such variety;*
> *Nor doth the Milk-white Way, in frosty night,*
> *Appear so fair and beautiful in sight . . ."*

Because the coach would only accommodate four, and Catherine and her friends could not be caught with a single male, Sidney planned to hire another coach to take himself on to Cambridge Station.

"We should do this again next week," he said as Milly passed through the gate he held open.

Catherine halted in her tracks, but caught herself and managed to continue so that it appeared as if her boot was caught on the edge of a flagstone.

She could have saved herself the trouble, for Sidney did not even notice.

"You're very kind, Lord Holt," Peggy said, just ahead of Catherine. "But I'm afraid I have a composition due that Monday."

Milly nodded. "Yes, very kind. But it's my father's fiftieth birthday, and I want to surprise him."

Catherine let out the breath she was holding. Were Sidney and Mrs. Fry not present, she would have hugged her friends right there. Sidney did not seem disappointed. He even smiled and said, "How thoughtful. Where does your father live?"

"St. Ives. You know . . ."

"From the nursery rhyme," he finished.

After helping his aunt into the coach, he offered an assisting hand to first Peggy and then Milly, thanking each one for being such good friends to Catherine. And then he smiled down at Catherine and touched her cheek, his blue eyes as affectionate as ever.

Your imagination needs a leash, she told herself, returning his smile.

On the road to Girton, she fingered the ring beneath her glove, comforted by the feel of it. When she was not with Sidney she kept it in the jewelry box in her top drawer beneath her ribbons and stockings. She restrained a smile at Peggy's and Milly's attempts to make polite chatter with Sidney's aunt. They had been warned, and besides, they had achieved the same tepid results on the way to Chesterton.

"What was it like, attending a one-room school?" Milly asked.

"Yes, what was that like?" Peggy said, eyes wide as if the fate of the world depended upon the answer.

"I had nothing else with which to compare it," was the crisp reply.

Back at school Catherine followed Peggy into her sitting room, dragging Milly by the elbow.

"Well?" she said after closing the door.

Peggy started pulling pins from her hat. "Well what?"

Catherine gave an exaggerated sigh. "What did you think of him?"

"He's very handsome," Milly said.

"Yes, handsome," Peggy said.

Milly nodded. "And agreeable."

"Much improved over the last time we met," Peggy said, and held up a hand as Catherine was opening her mouth. "I know . . . he had that headache, and so that was understandable."

Still, their reservations hovered in the air and pressed against every corner of the room. Peggy set her hat upon the study table and drew a deep breath. "I can't speak for Milly, but I resented getting caught up in your assignations when your aunt and uncle were here. And I was uncomfortable today, allowing Miss Scott to think I was visiting a friend of your family. I'm sure Lord Holt meant well by including us, but please discourage him from inviting me again."

Milly nodded. "She does speak for me. I felt the same."

Catherine pulled out a chair from the study table and sank into it, torn between relief—at least over Milly's comment—and the desire for the two to see Sidney in the same light that she did. "You're simply never going to understand until you fall in love."

"I hope I'm never so much in love that I rationalize falsehoods." Peggy set her hat on the window ledge and shrugged out of her coat. "I can't reconcile myself with his encouraging you to lie, even arranging the situations for you."

"And on a *Sunday*," Milly said, unbuttoning her cloak. "With you fresh out of church!"

"But it's my only free afternoon," Catherine protested. Without Sidney's supporting presence, she felt besieged by the people who should be the most understanding.

Peggy pulled out the chair next to her and started pulling off her gloves.

"Catherine, Milly brings up a good point. His arriving here every Sunday afternoon means he does not attend church. What are his feelings about God?"

"God?" It had never occurred to Catherine to ask.

"Does he even believe in God?" Milly said.

"Obviously he's not hostile to religion," Catherine reasoned. "Or he would have ridiculed me for attending—"

"He *ridicules* you?" Peggy cut in.

"No, that's not what I meant."

How frustrating it was, to have the two jump to a conclusion before she could even finish a sentence. She could tell by the glance Peggy sent Milly that she was working up to another question.

"What I meant was," Catherine hastened to say, "Sidney is a Christian." She felt no guilt over the statement, for her heart was in tune enough with his that she would know this. And wasn't his desire to live a moral life proof that God was working in his heart?

"And he's told you this?" Milly asked. "With his own words?"

Not in so many words, rose to Catherine's lips, but both sets of eyes regarded her with such infuriating skepticism that she swallowed that reply and said, instead, "Yes. With his own words."

After all, what was one more lie?

Thirty-One

*W*ould you care to see my report?" Hugh asked his father late in the morning of the twenty-fourth of January.

Fuller Sedgwick stretched back in his chair, locking both hands behind his head with a cracking of knuckles. A stranger could have looked at the thick brown eyebrows and lashes and straight wheat-colored hair—Fuller's darkened a bit by time—and identified the two as father and son. Their eye colors differed, though, Hugh's brown and Fuller's green. And at that moment the latter's were crinkling at the corners over his smile.

"Finished already, eh? When your brothers get here, I may learn to play golf."

"Wouldn't that be nice?" Hugh said, smiling, even though they both knew the idea of his father staying away from the business for any length of time was inconceivable. As for the brothers, the place would practically be swarming with Sedgwicks once Brian graduated from Harrow this summer, and Lane the following year.

He pulled a chair around the desk and spent the next two hours showing his father the figures he had accumulated and the conclusions he had gleaned from them. "I believe the market would be extremely profitable. With the United States still so young as a nation, there is clearly a desire to maintain some of the old-country reminders."

Turning a page in his dossier, he went on. "As you can see, other food exporters to the States—Cadbury's Chocolates, Brand's A–1 Steak Sauce, Lea and Perrins' Worcestershire Sauce—have enjoyed a rise in profits every year over the past decade."

"And how did you acquire this information?"

"I visited them and asked." Hugh smiled at the surprise on his father's face. "A complimentary case of Sedgwick Tea and respectful attitude opens many doors, I have discovered."

He pulled out another sheet. "I even have some notes on what *not* to do, things they learned through trial and error. Lea and Perrins was most helpful in that regard."

"Amazing." His father scanned the page, absently rubbing his chin. "I wouldn't have imagined they would share that."

"Well, we don't present competition for them. But I knew better than to call on Twinings."

His father chuckled. Shuffling through the papers again, he said, "I want to read over all of this again, and have Mr. Culiard confirm your tonnage reports. This is a major undertaking, and we want to be certain we've dotted every *i* and crossed every *t*."

"I understand, Sir." In fact, Hugh felt a surprising relief. While success seemed probable, there were no guarantees, and bearing the sole responsibility for a failed venture was a little intimidating. He didn't mind that it diluted some of the credit due him. Sedgwick Tea was an important part of his life, but unlike his father and late grandfather, Hugh did not carry the business about on his shoulders once the doors closed behind him in the evenings.

"Why don't you take the rest of the day off?" his father said.

"You mean that?"

"You've worked hard. Go spend some time with Miss Henslow."

Hugh did not have to be convinced. But by the time he reached Aldgate Station, he had changed his mind. He continued on, leaning into a bracing wind.

He had never ventured past Sedgwick Tea to the east, had never had a reason for it. Saint Jude's was striking eleven as he entered Whitechapel High Street. Appropriately tagged "Butcher's Row" by Londoners, it was a long vista of windows boasting mutton and veal, legs, shoulders, loins, ribs, hearts, livers, and kidneys. "Buy, buy, buy!" came shrilly from butchers in stained aprons standing in doorways. The buyers were of all descriptions, from the middle to the very lowest classes, and mostly women, from housewives to servant girls. Beggars of all ages swarmed like locusts.

By the time Hugh turned down Plough Street, he had slipped his purse from coat pocket to waistcoat pocket. The makeup of the neighborhood changed dramatically the farther south he walked. Narrow lanes darted off in all directions, flanked by serried rows of shadowy courts.

He raised his muffler over his nose. An unwholesome vapor filled every inch of atmosphere, and refuse of all sorts was scattered about the cobbles, some of it suspiciously organic. A face peered at him from behind a filth and ice-encrusted windowpane, resembling a fish staring from the murky depths of a bowl. Few people were on the streets because of the cold, but every now and again some ragged person would call out from a doorway, "Got a bob to spare, Guv'nor?"

"Sorry," he replied to those queries, knowing better than to withdraw his purse. He had not really expected to see the boy, but managed to feel a keen disappointment when he did not. On Commercial Road he came upon dozens of people ambling toward him. Children outnumbered men and women, and all were bundled in patched and worn coats or simply wrapped into shawls. They spoke little to each other.

Hugh was struck with the expressions on the children's faces as they plodded past. Resignation mingled with weariness. A few sent dully curious looks his way. Two policemen watched from the corner, identically clad in blue double-breasted outer coats with two rows of brass buttons. "Lost, Mister?" one asked when Hugh drew closer.

Hugh shook his head and lowered the muffler from his nose. "Where is everyone going?"

"Umbrella factory just let for lunch."

"Children too?" Hugh said, even though he had heard his father say that it was the shame of England that thousands of children over the age of ten, when education was no longer compulsory, labored in factories and brickyards, textile mills and coal mines. They were limited by law to a "merciful" fifty-six hours per week and were paid a fraction of the wages of an adult male. "Is there no school?"

The second policeman pointed south with his nightstick. "Rupert Street."

"Why aren't they there?"

He eyed Hugh as if he were the most ignorant fellow whose path he had ever crossed. But the eye moved down to the cut of Hugh's finely tailored topcoat, and a bit of respect crept into his expression. "Law says the City only has to provide primary schoolin'."

"And there's nothing beyond that?"

"Nothing," affirmed the second policeman.

"They don't need it anyway," said the first, with a sage look at his companion. "Education just teaches them to steal the dearer thing."

The two chortled, and apparently expected Hugh to join in. When he did not, the first policeman sobered enough to shrug and say, "There's a

Wesleyan preacher on Gowers Walk who teaches reading on Sundays. Can't really call it a school."

Hugh looked about at the dismal surroundings. All his life he had taken education as simply his due, as he had his warm bed, fine clothing, and meals. He had not had to do one lick of labor until now, at age twenty-two. He thought of the resignation on the young faces, old before their time, and his heart felt a great sadness.

"Will you point me to Gowers Walk?" he said.

With a shrug the first policeman gave him directions, adding, "Watch your pockets, Mister."

The soot-stained brown brick building, with *Whitechapel Wesleyan Chapel* on a signboard over the door, had obviously been a shop in Whitechapel's more respectable days. Voices and bawdy laughter drifted from the gin shop next door. Obviously neither establishment had run the other out of business. There was a flat above, and smoke rose from the chimney. Hugh knocked as hard as his gloves would allow and waited, stamping his feet now and again. He was about to turn away when the door opened and a white-haired man with a face like old parchment looked out at him.

Hugh moved the muffler from his nose. "Good-day, Sir. My name—"

"Tell me where it's warm," the man said, beckoning him inside. Hugh followed him past a dozen rows of wooden pews, dimly lit by the sunlight seeping through the shop front window, and then up a flight of narrow stairs. They entered a tidy room with parlor furniture and a table and chairs. Hugh noticed the half-eaten bowl of soup and piece of bread on the cloth. "I've interrupted your lunch?"

"Easily enough mended." The man pulled out a chair. "Go stand by the fire. I would offer you some soup, but I just emptied the pot. Anyway, you don't look especially hungry."

"I'm not, thank you."

The old man picked up his spoon, and Hugh stuffed his gloves into his coat pockets and stood with back to the fire, warming his hands behind his waist. "Are you the minister here?" Just in case he wasn't talking to the minister's father. Or grandfather.

"For fifteen years." The man took a bite of soup. He had a surprisingly refined voice for his surroundings, as if he had been well educated. "Ronald Holland is my name. And you are . . . ?"

"Hugh Sedgwick, Sir. I'd like to find out more about your Sunday school." Why he wanted to know more, he wasn't yet sure. Perhaps to reassure himself that something was being done. To make a donation before retreating to his comfortable little world.

Between bites of soup and bread, Mr. Holland told him that from thirty to forty children, above the compulsory schooling age of ten, drifted into his pews after morning worship services. "We have a Bible lesson, and then I teach what I can for three hours or until my legs or eyes give way. Long division, geography, some spelling. They memorize a little Scripture and poetry—I'm partial to the Psalms and Lord Byron. Whatever they didn't get in primary school. Many come just for the soup, no doubt, but then, some soak it up."

Mr. Holland chuckled. "Soak up the lesson, that is, though you can say the same for the soup, can't you?"

Hugh smiled. "With all due respect, why do you only limit your lessons to Sundays?"

"Because I'm the pastor of a church as well, with a needy congregation. You caught me stopping here for a bite of lunch between rounds. Also, many of the children work at the factories, and Sunday is their only day off." He frowned down at the bit of soup that landed on his coat and dabbed it with his napkin. "And last but not least, I'm a tired old man, if you haven't noticed."

"Forgive me." Hugh took a step toward the table. "I didn't mean to imply that you don't do enough. Actually, I'm in awe of you, Sir."

"In awe of *me*?" Mr. Holland grinned at him. "Mrs. Holland will get a chuckle out of that one. She's sitting with a woman who has the ague."

"Then I'm in awe of her as well," Hugh said, reaching into his waist-coat pocket. "Please allow me to make a donation." He gave the man the fiver from his purse, saving the coins for the Underground.

"That's very generous of you, Sir," Mr. Holland said.

"It's the least I can do," Hugh told him.

"Remember, you have to try to be sociable with your stepmother," Peggy said, coiling Milly's hair into a loose knot the Sunday morning of the twenty-ninth. "For your father's sake."

"Don't you think I'm aware of that?" Milly said.

"We do wonder," Catherine told her as she brought a black cloak from the wardrobe to the dressing table. "This one?"

"Yes," Milly replied with scarcely a glance. Her lack of enthusiasm was clearly the reason she had slept late. If she missed the morning train, there was little sense in going at all. She could not even look forward to the company of her brother and sisters, as they did not have the liberty to take a Sunday train unescorted from their schools.

The clothes laid out, Catherine hurried down to the dining room, slapped together a bacon sandwich, and begged some brown paper of Mrs. Hearn to wrap it in. Then she stopped in the lobby to assure Mr. Willingham, who would be driving Milly to Histon Station in the wagon, that she was almost ready. Having a project kept Catherine's mind off the disappointment over not seeing Sidney today. He had some business having to do with the Northamptonshire estate, his letter of Thursday had said, and closed with: *I will count the hours until I see you again, my beloved Catherine.*

He was counting the hours, and she the minutes, or at least she was doing so last night when the ache of missing him forbade her sleep. Over ten thousand of them remained to be filled somehow before his presence would lighten her heart again.

————

"How did you sleep, Mister Holt?" asked the hosteller of the Hound and Bugle, just yards from St. Ives Station, as he set a plate upon the cloth.

"*Lord* Holt," Sidney corrected, unfolding his linen napkin. "My bed was lumpy, the mirror was spotted, and I could hear pipes groaning all night."

He would not be sending for seconds, this early in the morning, and so he had no fear of having his fried eggs, ham, and toast contaminated if the hosteller was so inclined toward pettiness.

"I'm sorry to hear it, Sir," the man said. Even with a beard, he had looked only to be about twenty-five. *Probably inherited the place,* Sidney thought.

The wife hastened over to refill Sidney's coffee. She stared at him with round worried eyes. "We just had the bathroom put in this summer, Sir. The pipes still ain't used to th' cold."

"We'll deduct a shilling from your bill," the man said. "And no charge for your breakfast. Next time we'll put you in a better room."

"Very well," Sidney said. No sense burning his bridges behind him—just in case.

But as far as *this* time, he still wasn't quite certain what had possessed him to come here. He loved Catherine with all his heart. Still, he was bewitched by a pair of indigo eyes, which clung to his imagination like shadow to pavement. "What time does the train from Histon arrive?" he asked as the two were turning to leave.

"Nine o'clock, Sir," the hosteller replied with the eagerness of one who wishes to repair a harsh opinion of himself.

At a quarter before the hour, Sidney put on his topcoat and bowler hat, took up his satchel, and stepped out into the cold. A light blanket of snow lay on the ground and dusted the grey slate roofs of cottages packed in the lee of a hill overlooking the river Great Ouse. Fifteen miles northeast of Cambridge, the town had roots in Saxon history, but was most famous for its international fairs in medieval times. Hence the nursery rhyme, which was painted in slanting letters over a window inside the railway station.

> *As I was going to St. Ives*
> *I met a man with seven wives.*
> *Each wife had seven sacks,*
> *Each sack had seven cats,*
> *Each cat had seven kits;*
> *Kits, cats, sacks and wives—*
> *How many were going to St. Ives?*

"Do ye know the answer?" came a voice from his left.

Sidney, seated upon a ladder-backed chair before the stove, gave the elderly ticket agent a weary look. "One."

The scant attention encouraged the man to launch into a story about a herd of cattle that broke through their hedgerow some years ago and gathered on the railroad track. Sidney ignored him and was relieved to hear a whistle at three-past nine. He rose and went out to the platform. The train squealed in seconds later, and a guard ran along opening doors. Some thirty-odd passengers exited various coaches. Miss Turner left a first-class coach, wearing a black cloak and the fur hat she had looked so fetching in when he first set eyes upon her. She did not look about, as would someone expecting to be met, but started toward Station Street.

You should be a detective, Sidney told himself, walking in the same direction. He had rightly supposed that a surprise visit home meant relying upon a hired carriage. He only wished he had taken some more time to think out what he would say to her. She was but five feet away, and he was beginning to lose his nerve.

Just as he was wondering if he should take that same train back to Cambridge and try to meet with Catherine this afternoon, Miss Turner glanced back over her shoulder.

"Lord Holt?" she said, turning.

In for a penny, in for a pound, Sidney told himself. He closed the distance between them and smiled. "Miss Turner."

"But what are you doing here?" She looked past him. "Is there anything wrong?"

"No. I thought you might need help hailing a carriage." He only wished she had worn her hair loose, rippling over her shoulders. He would give a guinea for permission to reach back and pull away the comb.

"Hailing . . ." The magnificent indigo eyes narrowed. "I don't understand."

"I think you do, Miss Turner."

She stared at him for several seconds. He stared back.

"I'm going to my father's," she said at length.

Sidney nodded. "As you made mention last Sunday."

"You're not invited."

"I wouldn't dream of imposing myself. But a beautiful woman such as yourself shouldn't be forced to find her own transportation."

"And so you came to help," she said flatly.

He swept his hand toward the brick road in front of the station. "My motives are nothing but noble. Shall we?"

She shrugged and turned again toward Station Road. Two carriages waited for hire. "Here, this one should do," he said, taking her by the elbow. He could feel her arm go rigid, even under the heavy cloak, but she did not pull it away. Motioning for the driver to keep his place, he helped her up into the seat.

"Thank you," she said primly, the cold pinking her cheeks and nose in a charming way.

"My pleasure." Sidney touched the brim of his bowler hat. "And may I ask what time you'll be returning?"

The eyes narrowed again. "Why?"

"I thought you could use some company on the train. I'll go back to the inn and wait."

"Wait all day? To accompany me for a ten-mile ride?"

"I've newspapers," Sidney said, lifting his satchel.

She stared at him, her face reflecting an inner battle of emotions. "What about Catherine?"

What about Catherine? He gave Miss Turner—and himself—the only answer he had. "I honestly don't know."

Their eyes locked again. At length she glanced away and said, "Half-past four."

Thirty-Two

You wish to found a *school?*" Fuller Sedgwick asked from behind his desk on the twenty-third of February. "Have you taken leave of your senses, son?"

It's possible, Hugh thought, smiling in spite of his nervousness. He sobered up quickly at the look his father was giving him.

"You should see the children of Whitechapel, Father. There's so little hope in their faces. They learn just enough at primary school to realize there's a better world out there, and that they have little hope of ever being part of it."

"Tragic, yes, but you'll find that in any slum in London. The poor will be with us always."

"That doesn't mean we haven't a responsibility to help them."

His father set his pencil down with a loud *snap*. "I do hope you're not lecturing me. I give quite liberally to charities."

"I know that, Father." Finally Hugh sat, and leaned forward. "I'm sure it's that very part of you inside of me that makes me feel such overwhelming pity every time I walk those streets. But I feel strongly that God is leading me to do more than send money away somewhere, when these children are practically in our shadow."

"And so what precisely do you propose to do?"

"There's a Wesleyan minister—Mr. Holland—who's directed me to an old meat tinning factory available to let on North Street. It has two large rooms on the ground floor, and a scullery of sorts that can be converted into a water closet. Just needs a few boards here and there, some patching on the roof." He wrinkled his nose. "A good scrubbing down and airing out. By spring, I'd like to hire a couple of schoolmasters."

"With what?"

Hugh cleared his throat. "My legacy from Grandfather." The five hundred pounds per annum, collecting interest since he was eighteen, was more than adequate, even for future growth.

"And what does Miss Henslow think of this?"

"I've . . . not told her yet." But he was certain that he could do right by Lillian, even if he spent every penny of the legacy. There was still his salary here. Lillian's father's position as vicar of Saint Mark's provided for middle-class comforts but not vast wealth, therefore she would not have to make an adjustment to a lower standard of living. And he would make it up to her when he and his siblings inherited Sedgwick Tea in the distant future—*very* distant, he hoped, looking across at his father.

Some of the tension left his father's face. "Then you're not planning to give up your position."

"Why, no, Sir. It never entered my mind." He was a tradesman, not a schoolmaster.

"I'm relieved. But I must ask, how do you propose to make certain this school is run according to your desires? That your teachers even appear on time? And sober? Sedgwick Tea wouldn't be all it is today if we didn't stay involved."

"I plan to nip over there every day at lunch. That's all I can do, besides try to hire staff who give evidence of dedication."

His father hesitated. "You're only twenty-three years old, Hugh. What happens if you grow bored with the whole project?"

That had not occurred to Hugh. He could not conceive of it happening, for this had almost consumed his thoughts since that first walk in the slum a month ago. The same energy he had applied to figuring out the best way to market Sedgwick Tea in the States burned even brighter when working out a plan for the school.

One of his ideas led him to obtain a list from the British Museum Library of addresses of philanthropists and business leaders. In the evenings he had started writing letters, asking in each for the sponsorship of one child. If the child could help out his family with the same pittance he had earned—or *would* earn at the factory—then the child would be free to pursue an education, and hence, some hope for a brighter future.

That was only one of his ideas. Still, it *had* taken only months for his interest in his studies at St. John's College to wane.

But when did you ever feel this strongly about your studies? he asked himself. Had he indeed found his passion, of which Mr. Billingford had spoken back in Cambridge? Or was he being delusional?

"I can't promise that I won't, Sir," he admitted. "But I hope with all my heart that I've gained enough maturity to keep my commitment, no matter what my mood."

"I hope so as well." His father stared across at him for a moment, then picked up his pencil again. Hugh took the hint and got to his feet.

"Thank you, Sir," he paused at the door to say.

"For what?"

Hugh smiled. "For not trying to talk me out of it."

"Fat lot of good that would do me," the man said gruffly. "I tried to talk you out of University."

An hour later his father appeared at his office door, looking almost sheepish. "Your school will need desks and chairs. If you're still determined to do this, come spring, I'll buy them."

"Please don't take offense," Peggy said to Catherine with arms linked as they trailed behind others on their way to Cambridge on the Sunday of the twenty-sixth of February. "I'm sorry that you miss Lord Holt. But it's nice—having you here on Sundays again. If Milly were here it would be perfect."

Catherine smiled. "Yes, perfect."

That said, if she could change circumstances with the snap of her fingers, she would be pulling off a glove to do so in a heartbeat. But what could she do? According to Sidney's letter of three weeks past—which she had practically committed to memory—it would be wise if he settled the affairs with his tenant farmers in Northamptonshire now, so that he would not have to send and receive wires at every stop of their honeymoon. She understood about as much of these affairs as she did the stock market, but appreciated that he wanted to devote his attention exclusively to her after their wedding. It was worth a little sacrifice.

As much as she sympathized with Mr. Turner for the mysterious ailment that baffled his doctors, she wished Milly did not have to spend every Sunday in St. Ives. Only four weeks remained of Lent Term, four more weeks to be with her two best friends before her life would change forever.

"If you had to be an animal, which one would you be?" Peggy asked as they neared the Great Bridge.

Catherine had to think about that one. "Cows seem to have pretty serene lives."

"Must you two dillydally?" Elizabeth Macleod called from the group some thirty paces ahead.

"Just enjoying the stroll!" Peggy called back.

Miss Bernard turned to send Elizabeth, and then Peggy, a warning look. The headmistress had lectured her students often about setting good examples, with so many of the University hierarchy still cold to the notion of women's higher education.

Peggy winced and then resumed the conversation with lowered voice. "Until they end up in someone's steak-and-kidney pie."

"Hmm. A house cat, then."

"You would eat mice? Raw?"

"No, I would have a little stove," Catherine said, elbowing her in the side. "What would you be?"

"A sea lion."

Catherine recalled the sea-lion exhibit at London's Zoological Gardens and nodded. The animals did appear to have a jolly time. "Then I would be one with you," she said.

It was nonsense chatter, but it felt as good to her soul as the chill breeze upon her cheeks. With Peggy she could relax. She did not have to watch her words for fear of being perceived as ignorant or uncultured. *He just wants what's best for me,* Catherine reminded herself.

She had yet to inform her friend that she would not be returning for Easter Term. In Peggy's eyes, quitting school would be almost as bad as excommunicating oneself from the Church. She could already hear the argument between them in her head. And clearly Peggy still had not accepted that Sidney was good enough for her.

She had not confided in Milly either, for Milly had enough troubles on her shoulders. She went about the corridors with a haunted expression, as if tormenting herself over every uncharitable word she had ever said about her father.

"You know what we should do?" Catherine said. "Meet Milly's train."

Peggy agreed. "But you'll have to be the one to ask Miss Bernard. I may not be in her good graces today."

After the service in the University Church, while they were having lunch in Mrs. Golden's Reading Room for Ladies, Catherine approached the headmistress and gained permission to accompany Mr. Willingham to the station. They did not have to be prodded into hurrying back to Girton after the choral service at King's College, and at half-past four were seated on the bench in the bed of the wagon behind the driver's seat.

"I just wait here, as she's got no luggage," Mr. Willingham turned to say after reining the team to a halt on Station Road in Histon.

"We'd like to meet the train," Peggy told him.

"Very well," he shrugged, and climbed down to unlatch the wagon bed and help them to Station Road. They were on the platform less than three minutes when a whistle sounded from the north, and less than a minute later the locomotive for the Midland Railway chugged in with belches of steam.

"I've always loved the smell of trains," Catherine said as the guard scurried from door to door. "Isn't that odd? All that oil and coal and steam."

"Probably because you have fond memories connected with traveling so much," Peggy analyzed, hazel eyes scanning the handful of people exiting the first-class compartments. "Do you see her?"

Catherine shook her head. "Not yet."

When the flow of exiting passengers ceased, Catherine looked down the line of coaches. "Could she have ridden second-class?"

"Can't imagine why. First-class had plenty of room." They walked closer to peer in every door, just in case. Their search fruitless, they left the platform.

"Why, there she is," Catherine said, returning Milly's wave. Their friend started walking toward them from the wagon, where she had stood near Mr. Willingham just a moment ago.

"Where were you?" Catherine asked when the gap between them closed.

"Why, aboard the train," Milly replied. "How good of you to meet me. But you shouldn't have gone to the trouble."

Peggy gave her a quick sideways embrace. "But we watched—"

"I didn't feel up to first-class."

She didn't explain, and Catherine wondered if it had to do with Milly's guilt over her earlier criticisms of her father. Perhaps she didn't feel she deserved first-class? *You're analyzing like Peggy now,* she told herself. But what other reason could there be?

When Peggy moved aside, Catherine stepped over to embrace Milly. Her friend smiled and put an arm around her shoulders, but her posture was stiff.

You poor dear, Catherine thought. Milly and her siblings had been practically exiled from the home they had loved, and still Milly blamed herself for feeling resentment over it. The uncharitable thought that Mr. Turner deserved his illness flitted through Catherine's mind. She pushed it away, glad that Milly could not read her thoughts.

"How is he?" Peggy asked as the trio walked again toward the wagon.

Milly shook her head. "The same."

———

Aunt Irene's parlor door closed with a muffled *click* the following Sunday. First laying his coat and her cloak over the back of the nearest chair, Sidney took Millicent's mink hat from her head and gathered her into his arms. Their kiss was long and intoxicating, until a sharp pain pinched his chest.

"Mmph?"

"What is it?" she said as he loosened his hold upon her.

He reached into his waistcoat pocket. "These," he said, and carefully tossed the smoked-glass spectacles onto his wool coat.

She smiled. "Why do you carry those about if you never wear them?"

"They bring me good luck," he said, reaching back to pull the comb from her silvery hair so that it tumbled down her shoulders. He did not explain himself—that the spectacles had brought Catherine into his life, thus eventually bringing *her*. Any mention of Catherine caused a pained look to her beautiful face, often tears, not to mention deepening his own feelings of guilt.

He folded Millicent into his arms again—he refused to address her as Milly, for it was too common a name. Today they would *have* to discuss Catherine. And he dreaded the thought immensely, for he would be revealing the cowardly side of himself that he despised. Would Millicent think less of him?

That would be unbearable. He pushed the thought from his mind. "Give me a poem," he murmured, drinking in the lavender scent of her silvery hair.

After a thoughtful silence, she quoted,

> *"Full well I know what love does mean,*
> *Full well its force and tyranny,*
> *And captive in love's chains have been*
> *Since first I set my eyes on thee."*

In the Henslow parlor in Bloomsbury on the evening of the ninth of March, Hugh stared at the ring box resting on the sofa space between them as his heart was battered in his chest.

"But we'll still have a comfortable living, Lillian," he said, looking up at her again. "A nice house, a couple of servants, even a carriage . . ."

She shook her head and wiped beneath her green eyes with a handkerchief. Crimson splotches stained her freckled cheeks and slightly upturned nose. Still, she was a beautiful young woman, with fine features and waves of shiny brown hair. "I've lived *comfortable* all my life, Hugh."

"And I stand to inherit a share of the business when my father passes on."

"Your father's a healthy man, Hugh. He could live another thirty years."

When he gave her a shocked look, Lillian sighed and shook her head. "I didn't mean it that way. I hope he lives forever. But I would like to have the things I've missed out on, and while I'm young enough to enjoy them."

The stab into his already bruised heart was almost unbearable. "I thought you didn't care about money."

"I thought so too," she replied, holding herself with her crossed arms. "I turned down Sir Jeffery's proposal after we met, and he's—"

"I know, I know," Hugh cut in bitterly. "Twice as rich as I am. Neville's already rubbed that in my face." He dug into his coat pocket for his handkerchief and blew his nose.

She blew her nose as well and turned watery eyes to him again. "I fear I would grow to resent you later, Hugh. But if I talked you into giving up this notion of a school, you would resent me."

I'll give it up sprang into Hugh's mind. He opened his mouth to say the four magic words that would bring everything back to the way it was, but they would not budge from his throat.

Already he had received two letters from people willing to sponsor children. His dream no longer stopped at the small school in an abandoned factory, but traveled on down the future to a vast facility that would accommodate hundreds of slum children. The vision even included two dormitories for those orphans who now slept in alleys and doorways. *They'll need housemasters too,* he thought.

Was it ego that made him relish the thought of being able to reverse the downward spiral of so many young lives? He hoped not. The difficult thing about being young was that one had to search one's motives so often. Older people seemed to know their own minds.

"Hugh?"

"Yes?" He blinked at her as the image of the school building dissolved in his mind.

She frowned as if aware that *she* was not the subject of his woolgathering. "I said . . . will you be all right?"

"Be all right?" A lump welled in his throat. How would he ever be all right? "Will you at least give this some more thought, Lillian?"

For one hope-filled second, she stared at the ring box between them as if battling temptation. But then she tightened her lips and shook her head. "I'm sorry, Hugh. I won't change my mind."

The sun doesn't rise and set according to your own happiness, Hugh told himself at his writing table two hours later. He blew his nose into a second handkerchief and looked at his bed. Heartache was a great robber of strength, he was discovering. How tempting to bury himself in the bedclothes and sleep for days. But he had set a goal of writing three letters per night, and this was only the first.

Thirty-Three

*C*atherine and Peggy traded sleepy smiles outside Milly's bedroom door on the morning of the twelfth of March. "Helping Milly dress to meet the train" had become a weekly project. But when Catherine's second series of light knocks went unanswered, they gave each other annoyed looks.

"She hasn't even bathed yet?" Peggy said, turning the knob.

It was going to be a pulse-racing rush. And to make matters worse, rain had set in last night, meaning Milly would have to leave even earlier than usual. Catherine followed Peggy into the room, washed with just enough diluted light from the rain-pelted window to allow her to see the lamp and matches on the bedside table.

"Milly?" Peggy said as Catherine took up the matches. Just as the light flared, Peggy turned to her. "She's not here."

"She wasn't in the bathroom," Catherine said, lighting the lamp. She held it up, looked at the rumpled bed, then scanned the room as if Milly were hiding in a corner.

"Do you think she went to breakfast?" Peggy asked.

Catherine drew in a calmer breath. That would mean that Milly had already dressed. Perhaps they would enjoy a leisurely Sunday breakfast after all.

But Milly was not in the dining room, nor could anyone they asked recall seeing her. "Did you check the infirmary?" Susan Martin asked.

"She was fine last night," Catherine said, for the three had studied at her table for end-of-term examinations that were to begin in one week. Milly had even borrowed a ribbon from Catherine's chest of drawers for the trip, so it was clear that she intended to go to St. Ives today.

But they could not leave that stone unturned, and fortunately the infirmary search proved fruitless. Unfortunately, so did another peek into the bathroom and Milly's apartment. Any minute Catherine expected their friend to appear, teasing them for their worries. But when she had not done so a half-hour later, she and Peggy talked it over and decided it was time to involve Miss Bernard. Soon the whole student body and faculty were looking for Milly. Mr. Willingham was even pressed into service, after he stated she had not reminded him yesterday that she would need transportation to Histon Station this morning.

No one went to church, and every face Catherine met in the corridor was anxious. By ten o'clock, Mrs. Bernard had sent Mr. Willingham to Cambridge for a policeman. Two arrived in blue uniforms with shiny brass buttons. They felt Milly's window ledges and carpet for dampness.

"No one broke in to carry her off," one said.

Catherine and Peggy, peering from the open sitting room door, gave each other identical relieved looks.

"Is there anything missing?" a policeman asked Miss Bernard.

The mistress turned to the doorway. "Misses Rayborn and Somerset here are her closest friends."

Peggy went through Milly's chest of drawers, and Catherine, her wardrobe. The portmanteau Milly kept stashed behind her shoes was missing, Catherine noticed. She was as familiar with Milly's wardrobe as her own, and moved through the gowns. Four were missing, along with two pairs of shoes, her mink hat, umbrella, and black cloak.

Peggy's report was similar. Two pairs of gloves, reticule, and two nightgowns and some undergarments were missing.

"Perhaps she was worried about her father, and decided to go early and stay a few days," Miss Welsh suggested.

"She didn't mention it to Catherine or me last night," Peggy said.

"And why would she have slipped out after dark," Miss Bernard said, "when no trains were running?"

Miss Welsh nodded thoughtfully. "And in the rain, yet."

Recalling Milly's reluctance to travel first-class when it was available last week forced Catherine to put concern over her friend's welfare above her reluctance to gossip about her. "She's not been herself lately," she told Misses Bernard and Welsh.

The policemen finally collected their umbrellas from the entrance hall and left to search the streets of Girton and Histon, promising Miss Bernard that more men would be recruited for a Cambridge search. At noon the rain cleared, but that did not lighten the somber atmosphere at the college. Peggy and Catherine spent most of the day in the entrance hall, hovering and anxious, trying to recall any overlooked scraps of last night's conversation that might give a clue.

When the original two policemen returned to report their progress—which was no progress as of yet, Miss Bernard herself caught the afternoon train to St. Ives.

At six, most students sat down to steak-and-kidney pudding and mashed potatoes in the dining hall, Catherine and Peggy included. They had skipped breakfast and lunch, and hunger had finally overtaken them.

"Look, she's back," Ann Purdy said, motioning toward the doorway.

Catherine's pulse jumped as she jerked her head to look. But it was Miss Bernard standing there, staring over the assemblage with an expression of infinite weariness.

"Ladies, may I have your attention?" she said, stepping into the dining hall.

Catherine and Peggy reached for each other's hands. Voices that were already hushed quieted to silence.

"I appreciate how concerned you are over Miss Turner's disappearance. I am relieved to inform you that she has not fallen victim to some misfortune, but sadly, I must add that she has decided to leave Girton and will not return."

"Just before exams?" someone said from another table.

"Yes. Now carry on with your meal, please. We must not allow this unhappy event to detour us from our goals."

In the buzz of conjecture going on in the room, Catherine and Peggy were pressed for answers from those at their table.

"We've already told you all we know," Peggy said.

Catherine pushed away her half-finished meal and longed for the comfort of Sidney's arms. He would know just the right words to console her. She could just hear him saying, *Surely they'll allow her to enroll again once her father is recovered—or passed on.*

As they left the dining hall, Miss Welsh advanced upon them as if she had been waiting for that purpose. "Miss Bernard wishes to see you."

In the mistress's office, Miss Welsh directed them to two chairs and closed the door to stand just inside.

"I do not indulge in gossip, particularly when it has to do with my students," Miss Bernard said, face still very grave. "But I'm compelled to ask if either or the both of you were aware that Miss Turner was not visiting her father for the past several Sundays."

For a second it seemed that Catherine was viewing all of them—herself included—from a distance. Nothing made sense. It was as if Milly and the young woman Miss Bernard was speaking of were two different people.

"But she was, Miss Bernard," Peggy said. "He's been ill."

Catherine, finally collecting her wits, added, "We even met her train two weeks ago."

"Miss Turner's father was surprised to learn of his ill health." Faint suspicion mingled with the gravity in the woman's face. "On your honor, you had no knowledge that Miss Turner was meeting a man?"

Catherine and Peggy traded stunned looks in the silence that fell. When she could speak, Catherine said, "Milly would never do such a thing." The irony hit her that she herself had done the very thing that sounded so unethical when attached to Milly.

"We would know if she were," Peggy insisted. "This can't be so."

"She did not get on with her stepmother," Catherine said as soon as a possible scenario popped into her head. "Is she the one who told you about this man, Mrs. Turner?"

The headmistress sighed and sat back in her chair. The suspicion had drained from her face, leaving just weariness. "I must insist that you are to keep this to yourselves, for we have the reputation of this school to protect. I'm only informing you because you were such good friends. But Miss Turner wired her family this morning that she has eloped. That was all the message said."

And there was nothing more to add to that. Miss Bernard counseled them not to allow this to detract them from their studies, and dismissed them. As they walked down the corridor in a stupor, Peggy wiped her eyes and said with low voice, "Why would she do such a thing?"

"I don't know," Catherine replied, while a little seed of fear took swift root inside her mind. Fellow students, privy only to half the story, gave them sympathetic looks. Some paused to murmur how dismayed they were.

Peggy was turning the knob to her sitting room door when Catherine looked down the corridor. They needed to talk this out, to try to make some sense of it all. But it was as if an invisible chain was pulling her to her own apartment, where the fear welling inside her would surely be squelched.

"Let's go to mine," she said.

"Very well," Peggy said, closing the door again.

"Who could he be?" Catherine whispered as they neared her door and no one was in hearing distance. To voice the question was to drown out the other question in her mind. *Just a coincidence,* she told herself.

Peggy had not replied. Catherine looked at her. Her friend was staring back with stricken expression.

"What is it?" Catherine said.

"Oh, Catherine! Don't you know?"

Suddenly Catherine could not draw enough air into her lungs. "No!" she cried, and pushed herself through her doorway. Inside her apartment she dropped into her upholstered chair and broke into sobs. She heard the door close. Peggy knelt in front of her and took her hands. *Not Sidney!* chorused though Catherine's mind over and over as Peggy stared up at her with red-rimmed eyes.

"There, there now." Peggy's voice was thick with emotion. A knock sounded, then the voice of Mary Dereham, Catherine's neighbor on the sitting room side.

"Is . . . there anything I can do?"

"No, thank you!" Peggy called.

Catherine's throat felt raw, and every cavity in her face felt packed. Still, a sliver of hope remained. She knew Sidney better than she knew anyone on earth, even better than she knew her own parents. At this moment he was in Northamptonshire, probably reading his newspapers, unaware of the torment she was going through.

Or perhaps he *was* aware, in some mysterious way. Weren't their hearts so much in tune that their silences even communicated? Why should distance make that any less so?

And Milly had met someone when she went home for her father's birthday. For some reason, she was not able to tell them. Perhaps she feared they would disapprove. But surely they would receive a letter this week, explaining all. They would shake their heads and say, with loving exasperation, "That Milly!"

"I'll get you a handkerchief," Peggy said, releasing her hands. She had just walked around the table when Catherine felt an overwhelming urge to have Sidney's ring in the palm of her hand. The proof of his devotion to her and the future they would begin in just two weeks. She rose and followed Peggy into the bedroom.

"What is it?" Peggy said, turning to look at her.

"My ring."

Peggy stood aside, and Catherine pulled out the top drawer. The jewelry pouch was there behind her ribbons and gloves, as usual. Just the feel of it in her hand reassured her. She untied the drawstring and dumped the contents on the top of the chest of drawers. The ring was missing.

"No . . . please . . . no!" she sobbed. She rifled through the jewelry to be sure, then started pulling out the contents of the drawer and heaping them on top.

"Are you sure it was in there?" Peggy said.

"Yes!" Catherine cried, and in her heart, she knew.

She went through the motions of being a student for the twelve days remaining in term, walking about as if in a vacuum from which all joy had been sucked out. She spent much of the time in bed in a lethargy born of exhaustion, and when hunger overpowered the appetite-killing ache, she filled her stomach until her senses were temporarily dulled.

A knock sounded at her sitting room while she was packing for Hampstead after exams. She walked from the bedroom and opened the door. Miss Sinclair stood in the corridor, looking atypically somber and more than a little uncomfortable. "Miss Bernard would like to see you in her office, Miss Rayborn."

The mistress was kind, but blunt. "One would almost suppose, by looking at the results of your examinations, that you ceased attending lectures halfway through this term. I can appreciate how your friend Miss Turner's leaving caused you grief, but life is a series of meetings and partings. One learns to adjust and press on. It's part of becoming an adult."

"Yes, Miss Bernard," Catherine said. The words did not hurt as much as they should. Not much got past the raw ache caused by Sidney and Milly's betrayal. Also, she was so deprived of sleep that she walked about as if in a fog, the people about her just players in a dimly lit theatre.

"I regret taking this action more than you can imagine," Miss Bernard said, "but when you return for Easter Term you will be on academic probation."

"Probation?"

"If your marks do not improve dramatically, you will have to sit out the following Michaelmas Term. This isn't a punishment, Miss Rayborn, but a warning I do hope you will heed. You're too bright to throw away your schooling over some personal disappointment."

"Yes, Miss Bernard."

The mistress gave her an odd look. "Have you nothing to say?"

Catherine thought for a second. What could she say? That in spite of lying about her whereabouts and filling pages with Sidney's name when she should have been studying, daydreaming of Sidney when she should have been listening to lectures, she somehow did not deserve this? "No, Miss Bernard," she replied dully.

"Very well then. I do hope you'll use this vacation to reexamine your motives for enrolling here in the first place."

What were they? Catherine asked herself, for the nervous soon-to-be fresher boarding the train seemed like a totally different person from who she was now. "Yes, Miss Bernard."

Laughter from one of the rooms fell upon her throbbing ears as her leaden feet carried her back up the corridor. She turned the corner and almost collided with Beatrice Lindsay.

"Catherine! I was just at your room. I'm serving as 'postman' today, with everyone busy packing." Beatrice flipped through several envelopes. "I know I saw—yes, here it is. Florence, eh? I wish I were there."

"But I don't know anyone in—" A pang stabbed her heart at the sight of the familiar script. She mumbled thanks, hurried to her room, and closed the door. There was nothing Milly could say that would make everything all right again, but still, Catherine tore into the envelope.

Dearest Catherine,

Catherine's eyes filled. How cruel, that Milly could use such sentiment after destroying her life!

> *By now I am sure you have learned that Sidney and I were wed on the twelfth of March. We are very happy, yet in the midst of that joy is a dark place that I cannot help but visit often. You are there, staring at me with so much hurt in your expression that I sometimes burst into tears.*

"You poor dear," Catherine muttered sarcastically, swiping beneath each eye with her fingertips. When she took hold of the letter again, the *twelfth* smudged beneath her thumb.

> *Please believe that we did not intend to fall in love. But once those feelings became realized, we were powerless to fight them. We beg your forgiveness for not informing you that we were seeing each other. Because you are so dear to both of us, neither Sidney nor I could bear to witness the grief this news surely caused you.*
> *One thing brings us consolation, and that is a gentleman waits in your future, perhaps just around the corner, who is your perfect soul mate. One day, when he has swept you off your feet, you will look back on this turn of events and thank God that His plans are so much more perfect than ours.*

I dare even to hope, dearest Catherine, that one day we shall all be friends.
I am,

Very truly yours,
Milly

"Maybe they'll name their first daughter after you," Peggy muttered two hours later, after stopping by the room to see why Catherine had not appeared at lunch. "She didn't even apologize for taking the ring."

A tiny thread of uncertainty worked its way into Catherine's hostility. "Are we really certain she's the one who—"

"She took it, Catherine. People want their heirlooms to stay in the family. Lord Holt would have asked for it by now if they didn't have it. Also, Milly and I were the only ones to know of it, and I wouldn't have touched that ring with a cane."

Catherine blew her nose. "You disliked him that much?"

"Yes," Peggy replied, hazel eyes frank. Her thumb savaged the flap of the envelope. "I didn't appreciate what he was doing to you."

But you didn't really know him, Catherine thought, eyes clouding again. The Sidney who took her arm protectively when they crossed streets, read the children's books his mother authored, and told her how just looking at her smile made him feel that all was right with the world.

The sorrow was so heavy in her heart that she thought it would choke her. She swallowed past the lump in her throat. How could he—and Milly—have changed so abruptly?

Or were those flaws in character there all along—hidden—perhaps not even realized by their owners? *A year ago you wouldn't have considered yourself a liar* came painfully to mind.

"What will you do with this?" Peggy's voice cut into her thoughts. Thumb and forefinger held the page by a corner as if it were contaminated.

"I don't know," Catherine replied. She could barely fathom which nightgown to pack, which was why her bed was still littered with heaps of folded clothing.

"May I offer a suggestion?"

"Yes."

Peggy sent a pointed look toward the fireplace. With a dark smile, she said, "Unfortunately I've had some experience with disposing of letters. But it would be an honor . . ."

Catherine nodded. "Go ahead."

She watched Peggy take three steps to the fireplace and lay letter and envelope over the smoldering coals.

For every waking minute of the past twelve days, Catherine's mind had harbored a hazy notion that this was all a big mistake, that she would wake one morning and life would somehow have reverted again to the happier days when Sidney loved her. That notion dissolved when the last black wisp disappeared up the chimney, and she had to press her hand to her mouth to stifle a sob.

Compassion filled Peggy's freckled face. "I'll be back," she said after a quick embrace. "I'm going to find you something to eat."

"But I'm not—"

"You will be later."

She returned with some bread and cheese and a cup of hot chocolate, which she had asked of Mrs. Hearn. Only because Peggy had gone through the effort, Catherine allowed herself to be coaxed to the study table. She used the hot chocolate to wash the food down her dry throat, while Peggy finished the packing. And in the morning before they set out for Cambridge Station, Peggy brought her breakfast, aware without it having been discussed that Catherine could not endure too many wishes in the dining hall for a lovely Easter.

In the train they held hands almost all the way to London, and the thought entered Catherine's dulled mind that, were it not for Peggy's little gestures of compassion, she would not have had the strength to get out of bed this morning.

They would be neighbors beginning next term, the only bright spot she could see in her future. Peggy had gained permission for the move from Miss Bernard. During vacation, Mr. Willingham and other school servants would be moving her belongings. "Thank you," Catherine managed to say as they embraced before parting at King's Cross.

Peggy kissed her cheek. "God will see you through this, Catherine."

The ache inside was so acute that it robbed Catherine's other senses. It was as if she were encased in glass like Snow White, able to see the reunions going on about her but unable to feel the joy radiating from them. As for feeling anything from God, the case might as well have been made of iron.

Thirty-Four

*I*t was all a misunderstanding," Sidney said. He stroked her hair as she rested her head upon his shoulder. "I've been busy in Northamptonshire. She's nothing to me."

"Then why is she here?" Catherine asked, one eye peering at Milly, smiling at her from Mrs. Fry's parlor chair. "And why is she wearing the ring?"

"Mother . . ." Milly said in a childish voice. "Danny took my dominos from my room."

"Danny, what have you been told about asking Sister's permission?"

"Aunt Naomi?" Catherine mumbled. The images in her mind evaporated. She opened one eye.

"But I couldn't find her!" Another childish voice came from just outside her door.

"Sh-h-h . . . you'll wake Catherine."

Catherine rubbed her face as footsteps faded in the corridor. Sunlight slanted through the gap in her curtains, and the chimneypiece clock revealed that it was almost nine o'clock. *You have to get up,* she told herself, fighting the temptation to close her eyes again and hope that Sidney's bittersweet presence would return. *You're not a guest at a hotel.*

Even though Sarah, William, Uncle Daniel, and Aunt Naomi had forgiven her when she confessed her duplicity three days ago, she knew that she still had to prove herself to them. It was one of the very few things that still mattered.

She drew on her dressing gown and went to the bathroom to freshen up. "Good morning, Mademoiselle," Marie said while on her way to Sarah and William's room with a stack of folded linens.

"Good morning, Marie." There was neither sight nor sound of Aunt Naomi and the children. Back in her room, Catherine dressed quickly. She was heading for the door when she noticed the letter to her parents she had started yesterday evening, but had not the energy to complete. Thinking of her family and Bombay brought Lieutenant Elham's face to mind.

You should have at least written and explained that you had a beau, she told herself. Instead, she had ignored his last two letters. Perhaps she should write an apology? Mention that she would be in Bombay again this summer?

A little wave of nausea came on the heels of that thought. No man could ever take Sidney's place. The emptiness inside screamed out at her, and she understood why Grandmother Lorimer had passed within weeks of her husband. Loneliness was as painful as any ailment she had ever suffered, and the curative was out of her reach.

Write Lieutenant Elham tonight, she told herself, ignoring another wave of queasiness. A stale crust was better than no bread, especially to a starving person.

"He signed?" Sarah said into the telephone mouthpiece. She reached for one of the sofa cushions and shoved it behind her lower back. With just two weeks remaining before her due date, she had discovered long ago that carrying the weight of a little one caused a strain upon other parts of the frame. "Very good! And when you speak with Mr. Sedgwick again, please do tell him that we enjoy his tea."

"Then we'll bring you some next time we visit," the elder Mr. Mitchell said through the telephone line. "They sent us a case here."

After replacing the earpiece, Sarah handed the telephone back to Avis to replace on the side table. She could have done it herself, but she had learned that any task that involved stretching or twisting brought admonishments from family members and servants. "Thank you, Avis."

"Good news?" Naomi said as the maid left the parlor. Bethia, bereft of Guy's company now that the boy went to the National School during the day, lay on her stomach on the carpet demonstrating to three-and-a-half-year-old Danny how to play dominoes.

"We'll start shipping Sedgwick Tea to the States in June," Sarah replied. She no longer went to the office, but kept abreast of the goings-on through Friday morning telephone conferences with one or the other of the Mitchells. The two also visited occasionally, just as the elder Mr. Mitchell had done with the late Mrs. Blake. However tempting it was to sit back and collect income, relying solely upon their proven expertise, she had to remind herself that Mr. and Mrs. Blake had sacrificed much to build Blake Shipping, and so she owed a duty to their benefactors. "Mr. Mitchell says they sent some tea out to the office."

"Yes?" Naomi said. "I do like it, but nothing can compare with the tea Mrs. Blake used to get from China."

"I would give my best gown for a cup of it right now," Sarah said, then sighed and looked down at her protruding stomach. "Even if it still fit."

"Good morning."

Sarah turned toward the doorway as much as possible without twisting. Catherine entered, leaned down to put a kiss upon her forehead, bent down to pat the children's heads, then kissed Naomi's forehead. However promising these displays of affection—the first since her arrival three days ago—Catherine still looked bleary-eyed and distant. Her hair hung down her back in strings, a section just behind her right ear was even creased from the pillow.

"I'm sorry I slept through breakfast," she said, lowering herself into the cushion beside Sarah.

"I asked Trudy to save you something. Why don't you ring, and we'll have a tray sent up?"

"I . . ." Catherine's eyes stared vacuously out into space, as if she had lost her train of thought, but at length she replied, "I'm not sure if I'm hungry."

You shouldn't be, after having thirds last night. The thought gave Sarah no pleasure. It seemed that food had become her cousin's solace. Food and sleep.

Sarah intercepted Naomi's little nod and looked at Catherine. Her cousin was leaning forward, wiping her eyes with the heels of her hands.

"I'm sorry," Catherine sniffed. "I just can't stop . . ."

"Why is Catherine crying?" Danny asked his mother.

Naomi rose from her chair and took his hand along with Bethia's. "Catherine is sad."

"Why is she—"

"I'll explain when we find Father. Let's go see what he's doing."

The children did not protest, and sent Catherine's weeping form shy looks of mingled curiosity and sympathy as they left with their mother.

Why did you bring this upon yourself, Catherine! Sarah knew the thought was uncharitable, but she could not help but remember how strongly she had warned her against Lord Holt.

But at least he was out of her life for good!

Sliding as close as her bulk would allow, she began rubbing her cousin's back. "Poor, dear Catherine. I know you can't see it now, but this was the best thing that could have happened to you."

"That's what Milly wrote in her letter," Catherine said with bitter voice.

She sat, still leaning forward, with arms folded and hands cupping opposite elbows.

"I fear she'll find out for herself just how true that is."

"She said they're very happy."

"Every woman is happy on her honeymoon," Sarah told her. "It's during the day-to-day living that she learns just how important integrity is in a man. It affects every part of their married life."

Catherine wiped a sleeve across her brimming eyes. It was frustrating to Sarah to witness the misery in the girl's expression, even in the way she held herself, as if fearful of coming apart if she let go. All this emotional agitation, and for a man without even the decency to inform her that his affections lay elsewhere?

"Oh, Catherine," Sarah groaned. "Do you value yourself so cheaply?"

Her cousin blinked dully at her.

"You have a good heart. Is it worth nothing to you?" Sarah said, resisting the urge to grab both her shoulders and shake her until all memory of that horrid man left her mind. "Will you hand it over again to the next lord or army officer who happens by, without even taking the time to discover if he's worthy of it?"

If Catherine absorbed anything from those words, it was impossible to tell, for she turned her face away again and drew her arms more tightly about herself. They sat in silence punctuated by the ticking of the long-case clock, Catherine's occasional sniff, and faint voices in the corridor—probably Mrs. Bacon's and Claire's. Still rubbing her cousin's back, Sarah prayed for just the right words to help restore her to wholeness.

But before her prayer was answered, Catherine unfolded her arms and pushed herself up to her feet.

"Thank you, Sarah," she said with glassy eyes and a pasted-on little smile. "I should go to the kitchen before Trudy puts everything away."

"We can ring—"

"Thank you, but I'd rather just go down there."

"She's just going to need some time," William told Sarah as she lay nestled in his arms that evening. "I remember how wretched I felt when I thought you were in love with Ethan Knight. No one could have reasoned away those feelings."

A little sadistic part of her, that Sarah did not know she possessed, rather enjoyed hearing that, now that this particular sadness was all in the past. "You were terribly wretched?"

"You know that I was. I think you rather enjoyed having that power over me."

"I didn't realize that I had it," she confessed. "And I probably wouldn't have known what to do with it, if I had."

They lay silent for a while, relishing the closeness. After a while Sarah murmured drowsily, "Pity you can't go to your lab and invent a pill for heartache."

"I'd be the wealthiest man in the world," he said, squeezing her shoulder. "I know you're concerned about Catherine. But it's not good for the baby, for you to get overwrought by her problems."

"I'm honestly trying not to, William. But I've never seen anyone so despondent."

"And again, I say time is what will help her. All you can do is make her comfortable while she waits it out. Fretting over a broken leg or a broken heart won't make either heal any faster." He yawned. "And you need to be devoting your mental energies to names for the baby."

"Names." Catherine sighed. "You're still adamant that a boy won't be William?"

"Yes," he murmured into her hair. "Or everyone will address him as Willie to differentiate between us. I'll not do that to our boy."

"And if she's a girl?"

"Hmm. No, Willie won't do for her either. So we'll have to put our brains to work." He yawned again, then sighed contentedly. "Tomorrow."

The yawn was infectious. After catching it, Sarah nodded against his shoulder. "Tomorrow."

At the lunch table the following day, after filling herself at lunch with two large servings of hashed mutton, boiled cabbage, three rolls, and a rhubarb tart, Catherine said uneasily, "Would anyone mind if I walked to the subscription library? I'm studying Plato next term, and Peggy advised that I should read *The Republic* during vacation. I wouldn't be gone long, just long enough to check it out."

She could not add that studying would give her an excuse to stay in her room for hours, away from everyone's efforts to cheer her.

"Of course not," Sarah said. "Would you like Stanley to drive you?"

"Thank you, but I've not been outside for any length of time for days." Surely some fresh air upon her face would quell some of the torment in her mind. Then it occurred to her that Sarah might wish to have someone else observe that she actually went where she said she was going. "But if you'd rather he drove me . . ."

Sarah gave her an understanding smile. "Whatever you wish."

"May I go too?" Bethia asked.

"Of course," Catherine replied. Having her young cousin along would destroy any tiny remnant of suspicion that might remain in anyone's mind. That was the trouble with having told so many lies, she was discovering. Her credibility had been so damaged that she felt guilty even when telling the truth.

"Me too?" Danny asked.

"Sorry, dear," Aunt Naomi said. "It's almost time for your nap."

Danny's face puckered—not as if he would cry, but with the resignation of a child who has learned that his nap is not negotiable.

"We'll take a turn about the garden before your nap," Uncle Daniel consoled. He turned to Catherine with green eyes narrowed thoughtfully. "You know . . . I hate to spoil your walk, but there's actually a copy of the book upstairs. We used it while I was tutoring Sarah."

Sarah nodded as if having forgotten. "That's so."

"I'll be in there doing some research in a little while," he said. "I'll look for it and set it out for you."

"Thank you." Catherine smiled at Bethia, whose narrow shoulders were slumped with disappointment. "But there's no hurry. Bethia and I need to take our walk first."

They strolled from one end of Cannonhall Road to the other, Bethia thankfully inclined more toward companionable silence than chattiness, though she did speak of her excitement over a trip she and Danny would be taking with their parents in the summer. The breezes sifting through the new leaves of the birches flanking the road were refreshing upon Catherine's face. If only a breeze could somehow waft through her mind, lift out all the sorrow and guilt and feelings of worthlessness.

". . . but Father says Guy can't come with us," Bethia went on in her breathy little voice.

Catherine smiled at her. "You're very fond of him, aren't you?"

"Well, I love Danny more because he's my brother, but Guy's my best friend."

As they passed Admiral Kirkpatrick's home on their return trip, Catherine wondered if his grandson was still considering visiting him for the summer. Perhaps he would be here before she left for Bombay, or at least when she returned. Not that she was interested in him romantically, but she did feel she might have been a little antisocial during Sarah and William's Christmas party, with her pointed comments about being away. It wouldn't hurt to be a little nicer, were they to meet again.

On the heels of that thought came the memory of Sarah's comment yesterday. She could almost hear her cousin's voice: *Will you hand your heart over again to the next lord or army officer who happens by, without even taking the time to discover if he's worthy of it?*

It wasn't fair for you to say that, Sarah, Catherine argued back mentally. *William loved you from the first and never stopped, so you've never felt what I'm feeling.*

"That was very kind of you to include her," Uncle Daniel said, rising from the table when Catherine entered the library an hour later, after Aunt Naomi had taken Bethia for her nap.

"She's pleasant company," Catherine told him.

He handed her Plato's *Republic* from atop a stack of a half dozen books upon the table. "You know, I've read this several times. If you've any questions, do be sure to come to me, and I'll answer them if I can."

"Thank you, Uncle Daniel." She tucked the book under her arm. The affection in his green eyes was as soothing as the air upon her face earlier. It was almost as if her father were there with her. Loathe just yet to leave the room, she asked, "What are you researching?"

"It's not a cheerful subject, but it is one that has always interested me. The Black Death."

"Thirteenth century?" she guessed, trying to recall her British history lessons with Miss Purtley.

"Close," he said. "Thirteen forty-eight, and it killed almost half of England. But are you aware that the plague struck approximately every decade for over three hundred years afterward?"

"Three hundred years?"

"Until the flea-bearing black rat was exterminated."

"And those books you have are about that?"

Touching the top of the stack, he replied, "They merely contain references to it. I'll be spending a lot of time at the British Museum Library when I've gleaned all I can from these. And now that the children are old enough to travel, Naomi and I will spend most of the summer researching the effects of the plague upon smaller communities."

"Bethia mentioned the trip."

He smiled. "And I'm sure she also mentioned not having Guy along."

"I believe she did," Catherine said, returning his smile. And she was keeping him from his work, however much she wished to stay. She thanked him again and turned for the door. As she crossed the room she heard the dull scrape of chair legs against the rug, the creak of his settling into the seat, the scratchings of pencil against paper. When she touched the doorknob her reluctance to leave this harbor of compassion—without judgment—was overwhelming. So she stood, and eventually pressed her forehead to the doorframe.

"Catherine?"

She heard the chair moving again and shortly afterward felt hands upon her shoulders. "Come sit with me," her uncle said.

She allowed herself to be guided back to the table. After he helped her into a chair he went around to the other side and closed his notebook. He regarded her with kind eyes while she dug into the pocket of her skirt, past a half dozen whole and broken cinnamon biscuits, withdrew her handkerchief, and blew her nose. The loose bits of cinnamon made her sneeze, but eventually she said, "I'm sorry, Uncle Daniel."

"There's no need to be sorry," her uncle said. "It's only natural to cry when we're hurt."

"Thank you."

He did not ask why she had thanked him. Perhaps he understood what a relief it was to be simply granted permission to weep, no matter that the person for whom she shed tears was not worthy of them.

But of course he understands, she thought. She had been so wrapped in her own misery that she had forgotten the story Mother had once told her, how Uncle Daniel's first wife had jumped off Waterloo Bridge. Uncle Daniel had even suffered the added grief over his infant daughter, Sarah, presumed to have drowned in her mother's arms. Surely, through it all, he had learned the secret of coping with loss.

"Would it help to talk about it?" he asked.

Catherine nodded, unsure of where to begin. She blew her nose again, while he waited patiently. At length she said, "Does it hurt to speak of your first wife, Uncle Daniel?"

"It doesn't hurt," he replied.

"Did you love her very much?"

The green eyes briefly closed, opened. "Very much."

"As much as Aunt Naomi?"

After a pause, he said, "Yes and no. I loved Deborah with my whole heart—as I do Naomi. But then, the quality of love I was able to feel as a young man was different from the kind I have now for Naomi."

"Still, you were very . . ." Her mind tried to supply tactful words.

"I was crushed when she died," Uncle Daniel said.

Catherine gave him a grateful look for making this easier for her. "Then, when did you reach the point where the hurt went away? When you married Aunt Naomi?"

He shook his head. "If that had happened, Catherine, then my love would have been an interchangeable, needy thing. As though with one recipient gone, I could merely attach it to another person and continue on my way. As if my heart were one large leech."

While she was absorbing that, he said gently, "You're wondering how you'll ever get over the young man."

"Yes," she replied, trying to control the trembling of her bottom lip.

"Before I tell you how you'll do it, I'll tell you first what *not* to do. I turned to gin, and for some years it took control of my life."

"I've never been tempted to drink, Uncle Daniel," she reassured him.

He leaned forward to brush a crumb from the tip of her nose. "I've lived long enough to see people do the same with food, Catherine."

They've noticed, she thought as warmth spread through her cheeks.

"But like gin," he went on, "it won't fill that hollow space in your heart."

"Fill that hollow space . . ." Catherine echoed, knowing what he meant. But she had assumed the hollow space to be unique to her own suffering.

"Neither will another romance," he added.

How does he know? she thought, recalling the letter she had finished just this morning to Lieutenant Elham, and her thoughts only minutes ago of Eric Kirkpatrick. "It hurts so badly, Uncle Daniel. I can hardly bear it."

"You poor child." He reached out to take her hand. "I'm afraid time is the only remedy for that sort of pain."

"Time," she murmured, disappointed. How many times had she heard that?

Uncle Daniel gave her an understanding smile. "But it's an effective remedy. Trust me. And you can help it along by keeping busy." Letting go of her hand, he nodded toward the book on the table in front of her. "It's good that you've something with which to occupy your mind."

"Yes." Absently Catherine ran her thumb along the gilt lettering. "Why is it so much harder to fall out of love than it is to fall in, Uncle Daniel?"

"I don't know the answer to that, Catherine. But that should warn us to be more judicious about deciding whom to love."

"No one decides to love," she told him. "It just happens."

He shook his head seriously. "Cupid with his arrows is a myth, Catherine. We have a great deal of choice in the matter. And again, it's essential to our future happiness that we choose the right person, taking time to learn all about his character *before* allowing our hearts to become so besotted that we can't see his or her shortcomings."

She braced herself, waiting for him to point out Sidney's character shortcomings and tell her how fortunate she was that he was out of her life.

Instead Uncle Daniel said, "May I suggest that you work on mending that hollow space, becoming a complete person, so that we aren't having this talk over some other young man six months from now?"

She had assumed herself to be a complete person, at least until Sidney walked out of her life. For the first time, she now questioned how she could have fallen in love with him so completely, so rapidly, if not for some lacking on her part. "How does one do that, Uncle Daniel?"

"By first understanding why that hollowness is there, Catherine. Have you heard of Blaise Pascal?"

"The mathematician," she replied.

"Also one of the most respected scientists of the seventeenth century. *And* a poet. He was researching the nature of the vacuum when he wrote that everyone is created with a 'God-shaped vacuum,' which we try in vain to fill with other things. But Pascal wrote that the infinite abyss could only be filled by an infinite, immutable Object, God Himself."

Infinite abyss, Catherine thought. An appropriate description. She wondered if Pascal had learned this from personal observation. *Surely he did,* she thought, for how did one explain to another how forcefully an emptiness inside could scream out to be filled?

"I learned that gin would not fill it," Uncle Daniel went on. "And I've seen others try it with money, fine things, and yes, romance. Saint Augustine understood that centuries before Pascal was born, when he wrote *Our hearts were made for you, O God, and they shall not rest until they find their rest in you.*"

"I've been a Christian since I was a girl, Uncle Daniel," she told him. Even though God seemed so far away lately.

Gently her uncle said, "The Scriptures say that God created us for His pleasure, Catherine. That means He desires to be a vital part of our lives. Not just for a couple of hours on Sundays, but in our daily walk."

She was about to tell him that she had said nightly prayers since a little girl, but on second thought did not think that was what was meant by a "daily walk."

When she asked exactly what it *did* mean, her uncle replied, "The key for me was thanksgiving, Catherine. When I began thanking God for every good thing that happened, I began to feel an incredible closeness over time—a friendship, if you will—that extended into all areas of my life."

"And God took away your emptiness?"

His lips formed a tender smile. "I won't deceive you into thinking that my grief vanished over losing Deborah—and Sarah, presumably. And that I was not terribly lonely for the companionship of family. But as I grew closer to God, more *complete*, the frantic daily need to fill that hollow space faded away."

"But you were still lonely."

"Not like before, Catherine. It's difficult to explain, but God gave me an assurance, a feeling deep down that one day things would be better. Friends remind each other of such things. By the time I met Naomi, I was able to love her as a whole person, caring for her needs ahead of my own."

She thanked him and left shortly afterward, promising to consider all he had said. That evening at bedtime, she stuck a ribbon between pages twenty-four and twenty-five of *Republic* and went to the window seat, parting the curtains. A light rain fell, blurring the outline of the three-quarter moon against the dark sky.

Thanksgiving.

Of course even *she* knew that there were so many things for which she could be thankful. The pain had overshadowed them, pressing them into small corners where she could not see them, even when every night from her pillow her lips murmured the routine thanks for home, family, and provision. She thought for a minute, then prayed, *Thank you that my Uncle Daniel was so generous with his time and counsel.*

She determined that, before turning in, she would think of other things for which she had never thanked God. They came easily . . . Peggy's loyal friendship, Sarah and William's forgiveness for her lies, that she was able to stay up all day today without having to nap, even that she was put on probation instead of being required to sit out a term.

The only one that did not come easily was the thanks she offered for discovering Sidney's true nature *outside* of marriage. Afterward she waited for the change that would follow, mindful that it would come in small doses. But the hollow ache inside was just as acute, and she crawled beneath the covers sorely disappointed.

The house quieted, the muffled footsteps of servants settling in above ceased, with just the ticking of the clock and soft patter of rain against the glass magnified in the darkness. Sleep would not visit for hours, she knew, for bittersweet memories of Sidney would taunt her.

Unless she refused to allow them access to her mind. Had she the strength to do that? She thought again of Uncle Daniel's assurance that healing would come with time. How much time? Instead of thinking of Sidney, she pictured herself on a dark road. Wholeness waited at the end, too far away for her eyes to see it, for her skin to feel its warmth, but as long as her feet kept moving, she would reach it eventually.

Thank you, Father, she prayed under her breath. Surely one could wait out anything if there was a glimmer of hope for the future.

Thirty-Five

I am thinking of dyeing my hair," Marie said as she braided Sarah's long hair on the eighth of April, the day before Easter.

Sarah looked up the mirror at the grey strands cropping up at Marie's temples, stark among the glossy black hairs. Marie was too proud to ask for advice, but obviously hoped some be offered.

"You still have beautiful hair," Sarah said. "So thick."

The lady's maid nodded, picked up a section of Sarah's to comb gingerly through a snarl. "Coarse too. But that is good. It hardly knots—not like your fine hair. The only bother is that it takes long to dry. I live with sniffles each winter. And now the grey."

Smiling to herself, Sarah wondered if a certain widowed Frenchman had something to do with this discussion. Every Sunday for the past month Marie had accepted the lunch invitation of Mr. Pierpont, master chef at Hampstead's Corinthian Hotel, and his three daughters, ages ten, thirteen, and fourteen.

"I wouldn't dye your hair if I were you," Sarah told her. She had heard enough horror stories from William regarding cosmetics of earlier centuries—lead in face powder and red sulfide of mercury in rouge. Even as recently as last century, women were swallowing complexion wafers made with arsenic to achieve a white pallor, lethally effective because they poisoned the blood so that fewer red hemoglobin cells and less oxygen were transported to the organs. "At least not until you ask William to analyze what's in it. You don't want to ruin your health for vanity's sake."

As soon as the last words slipped out, Sarah grimaced and wished she could snatch them back again.

"I am never vain, Madame," Marie informed her, twisting her hair into a coil.

Sarah sent her a benign look in the mirror. "But of course not."

A light rapping sounded. "You may come in," Marie said before Sarah could speak.

Naomi entered and said to Sarah, "Your father rang from the Museum library. He says Catherine made her train on time."

"Good," Sarah said, smiling at her stepmother's reflection. There was some worry over that, for Stanley had noticed a wheel wobbling on Heath Street and had to turn the coach and drive it back slowly, then hitch the horses to the phaeton. "It'll be good for her, staying busy."

"She did seem a little better last week," Naomi said. "At least she ate sensibly."

"I am glad I had no romances when I was young," Marie said, inserting a comb into Sarah's coiled braid.

"But you're making up for lost time, aren't you?" Naomi said.

Sarah held her breath. Not she or William, nor even Mrs. Bacon was bold enough to speak that way to Marie. But Naomi and Marie's relationship could only be described as "fondly abrasive," going back to the years they were both servants in Mrs. Blake's house.

And indeed, Marie laughed. "As you English say . . . it is better late than never."

That made Naomi laugh, and Sarah did the same. But only for a second, because her abdomen was seized in a mildly painful grip. She put both hands on the dressing table to wait it out.

"What is the matter, Madame?"

Sarah turned to look at both anxious faces. "I'm not sure."

Two hours later everyone was sure, for Doctor Lloyd had packed up his satchel and said he would return after having lunch with his wife. "Plenty of time," he reassured them. Still, he had ordered Sarah to bed, and agreed that it was not too early to ring William and Father.

John William Doyle entered the world at half-past five, red-faced and howling indignation at having to leave his warm cocoon. Once bathed by Mrs. Bacon and swaddled in a blanket, he quieted, his unfocused blue eyes staring up at Sarah as she held him close. When William was allowed into the bedroom he stood at the head of the bed, a hand resting upon Sarah's shoulder.

"Would you like to hold him?" Sarah asked. Already the memory of the pain was fading, replaced with a feeling of such protectiveness that she knew she would fight to the death for this little life in her arms, were it required of her.

"In a minute," he said thickly, dark eyes lustering. He wiped a tear from his cheek and smiled at Sarah. "I just want to look at you both for a little while."

———————

On the twenty-second of May, Hugh paced the pavement in front of what he simply called North Street Secondary School. The cannery was patched and scrubbed, the water closet installed, coat hooks lined in geometric order on the walls of the entrance hall, and two dozen desks ready to receive occupants in each downstairs classroom. The upstairs flat, where the factory manager must have resided, still needed work, but it had a serviceable kitchen where Hugh's staff could make tea and even warm up lunch on the iron stove.

He was more than pleased with his staff, even though Oswald Garrett and Kevin Madden were as different as chalk and cheese. Mr. Garrett was in his forties, married, short and thick, and the minister of a Baptist chapel on Leman Street. Mr. Madden, a bachelor, tall and loose limbed, was a recent graduate of the University of London. Having been raised at Saint Luke's Foundling Home in Spitalfields, he saw himself in every slum child. The two got along quite well, and had spent the past two months visiting tenements in the dark lanes and alleys spidering out from Whitechapel High Street.

They had even accompanied him on three occasions to a ragged school in nearby Limehouse, founded by philanthropist Dr. Thomas Barnado, to observe the routine and ask advice. Gracious that he was, Dr. Barnado was skeptical over Hugh's success in finding sponsors so that young factory workers could afford to leave their jobs. But by devoting almost every minute of his free time to letter writing and paying calls, Hugh had managed to enlist seventeen sponsors willing to pay the one-pound, twelve shillings monthly, and many more expressed a willingness to do so once the school proved itself.

In addition to former factory workers, there would be other students that Mr. Holland had helped ferret out, some too frail for factory work and some homeless. Hugh wasn't quite sure of their number yet—Mr. Holland had warned them that the one thing a person could count on in Whitechapel was that one could not count on everyone keeping his word.

More dreams had been added to those already stored away in Hugh's mind. One day every child, even those unfit for factory work, would receive a stipend. Not only as an incentive to attend faithfully, but as a motivation to study hard, and with a sense of pride for being able to help one's family.

Today Hugh's father had allowed another day off, with the warning that he expected his duty to Sedgwick Tea to remain his primary focus once the school was up and running smoothly. That would not be a problem, Hugh had assured him. But for now, his thoughts were miles away from the stack of work waiting on his desk.

"I've made tea, Mr. Sedgwick," Mrs. Garrett said from the front doorway. Of medium height and frame, she was plain of face but with a wealth of light brown waves swept loosely into a topknot. She and Mr. Garrett had no children. "It's still early. Won't you come in for a bit?"

Hugh turned to her. Saint Jude's bells chiming out a quarter of eight was to be the signal for all interested children to set out for school. That was twenty minutes from now, but what if some were to arrive early? "Thank you, but I should stay out here."

"Then I'll fetch you a cup. One lump and a slice of lemon, yes?"

"Why, yes," he said, smiling. "Thank you."

After she disappeared through the doorway, he stared up at the second-storey windows and wondered if a classroom could be squeezed in there at some future date. The thought of having to expand was immensely exciting. In the future, would some doctor or banker or even schoolmaster say that the knowledge he gleaned from this school gave him a glimpse of what could be?

"Big dreams," he muttered, and did not realize he had spoken aloud until the words fell upon his ears. He chuckled at himself. *Perhaps Father's right— you've taken leave of your senses.* Senses were a bore anyway, he thought.

He was halfway through the cup when he spotted two children approaching in the distance from Berner Street. A boy and girl with the same fair coloring, appearing to be about the ages of ten and eleven. They carried treacle tins for lunch pails and darted uncertain glances toward him and the facade of the school.

Hugh poured the rest of his tea into the gutter and darted inside to set his cup on the window ledge. "Two on the way!" he called. He could hear Mrs. Garrett giving word to the schoolmasters, who would stay inside. Dr. Barnado had advised that the students' first glances of their teachers should be in the schoolrooms, with study commencing precisely at eight. *Order is essential to maintaining discipline* was Dr. Barnado's proven philosophy, but he expressed no advice against Hugh standing outside with kindly Mrs. Garrett on the first day.

As they drew close he noticed the girl's scuffed, creased shoes, and that the boy's boots were coming apart at the toes. But their worn clothing looked clean. They stared shyly at the cobbled stones ahead.

"Good morning, Harold . . . good morning, Helen," Mrs. Garrett said, stepping forward.

Both pinched faces relaxed somewhat. They mumbled, "Good morning, Mrs. Garrett."

Hugh stared at the woman with wonder as she wrapped a maternal arm around each shoulder. With a glint in her eyes she told Hugh, "We met when I made calls with Mr. Garrett."

You need to pay this woman wages, was Hugh's first thought as Mrs. Garrett introduced him to the children. In the distance he could see a group of three coming from Grove Street, two more a few feet behind them. His second thought was, *How will you bear going back to work tomorrow?*

"You're just a little angel," Catherine cooed to the baby in her lap on Sunday afternoon of the eighteenth of June. "Yes . . . an angel."

Ten-week-old John wrapped both wee hands around Catherine's index fingers, opened his mouth in concentration and pulled slightly, so that his little head barely raised a scant fraction of an inch above her knees.

"He likes to stretch like that," Bethia said, seated on the right between Catherine and Naomi. The girl leaned toward her nephew to singsong, "Don't you, John?"

Uncle Daniel tinkered with his camera on the tripod, ducking behind the cloth, then coming out to move the legs to the side a bit. Danny watched with hands obediently clasped behind his back.

"Your Uncle James and Aunt Virginia would love to see you," Catherine said softly to the baby. "Wouldn't you like to come with me to Bombay?"

William, seated in the chair Uncle Daniel had pushed aside, smiled. "Sorry, Catherine . . . they'll have to settle for a photograph. We can't do without our little man."

But little John gave Catherine a sloppy grin as if delighted with the idea. Catherine laughed. She was surprised at how good it felt to do so.

"Yes, what would Mummy and Daddy do without our John?" Sarah said from Catherine's left, in the soothing voice everyone used when addressing the baby.

John blinked at his mother, released Catherine's fingers, and relaxed, shoving a fist into his mouth.

"Let's take our places, shall we?" Uncle Daniel said. Sarah helped prop the baby up in Catherine's lap while Naomi arranged the children at their feet so there would be room for William on the sofa.

"Will the light hurt John's eyes?" Bethia asked.

"No, Bethia." Uncle Daniel stepped forward to raise Danny up on his knees. "It'll only make spots for just a few seconds. Now, be very still, and let's have a smile."

He ducked under the cloth again. Two seconds later there was a flash. Everyone blinked at each other until the black spots faded. The baby let out a little squeak and started pumping his fists and kicking his feet. Smoothing the silken blond hair over his velvety scalp, Catherine realized that for the past half hour or so she had felt a measure of happiness. Thinking about the gaping ache in her chest made it return, but it was encouraging to know that even small doses of happiness could be found. A half hour today—perhaps a whole hour one day soon. The photograph would be a reminder, lest she start to doubt that it could happen.

Thank you for that nice time with my family, Father, she prayed as she rearranged some belongings in her trunk that evening. *And thank you that baby John is so healthy and sweet. And that my parents will be pleased over my marks.* Some days she had to strain to find things for which to be thankful, but she knew it was good for her. It forced her to look outside her own despondency at the things going on about her. And she was discovering that the gratitude that naturally grew from those thanksgivings opened up a new pathway of communication between God and herself, a closeness she had never felt before.

Peggy accompanied her, along with Uncle Daniel and Bethia, to Tilbury two days later. Peggy would not be staying at Girton all summer as last year, for William had gained permission for her to work for the Commission for the month of July. It was not a paying position, she said in the train's coach, but the experience would be so valuable that she would be willing to pay *them.* And she would still be able to study the months of August and September at Girton.

"Mr. Doyle said I may even accompany him to make an investigative call or two," Peggy was saying.

"The East Side deaths?" Catherine said.

"I hope so."

From her long acquaintance with William, Catherine understood that the glow in Peggy's eyes was not in anticipation of exploiting tragedy for excitement, but an eagerness to solve the puzzle and prevent more deaths. Yesterday evening William had mentioned the lack of progress in solving five mysterious deaths of the past three months. Because they had occurred in the slums—Spitafields, Wapping, Whitechapel—and with no common element yet to link them, they did not even receive newspaper space.

"Who died?" Bethia asked.

Catherine gave Uncle Daniel an apologetic look. She recalled now that William had waited until the children were in bed to discuss that particular investigation. The train to Tilbury was obviously her place to blurt out the wrong thing. It was just that Bethia conducted herself like a sober little lady in the company of adults, making it easy to forget about her tender ears.

"Some poor people," Uncle Daniel replied gently, his little smile signaling to Catherine that no apology was necessary. "We don't know their names."

"Did they take bad medicine?"

"That's what William is trying to find out."

"Will you tell me when he does?" she asked.

"We'll tell you."

The S.S. *Heron* waited at dockside with stevedores loading barrels and crates of supplies and passengers' trunks. Outside the Bursar's office, while Uncle Daniel was making arrangements for Catherine's trunk, Peggy said, "Do you still plan to come up to Girton early?"

"Late August," Catherine replied, and gave Bethia's hand a gentle squeeze. "After a couple of days in Hampstead. My walking partner and I will have some catching up to do."

Peggy smiled at the girl, then up again at Catherine. "I just know we're going to have a wonderful year."

Catherine had to laugh. When Peggy gave her an odd look, she explained. "That's what you said last year."

"Oh dear, did I?" Peggy laughed too, and Bethia joined in, though with the uncertain expression of someone who didn't quite follow the joke. That amused Catherine so much that she laughed again, not intimidated by the frowns sent her way by a couple of dowagers.

The lightheartedness lasted long after the coastline of England dipped into the water. When the ache pricked Catherine's chest again, she noticed that it did not hurt quite as much as before.

"Are you looking forward to seeing your family?" Mrs. Jennings asked, beside her at the deck railing. Having decided that seeing her daughter again was worth a repeat of last year's seasickness, she had gamely written months ago to see if Catherine would care to travel together again.

"Very much," Catherine replied. "And this time, it's our turn to have you and your family over."

"Oh, but you don't have to—"

Catherine waved away her protest. "Mother has already planned the menu."

"Then that would be lovely, thank you." But the older woman's smile seemed a little strained. After a hesitation she said, "Lieutenant Elham probably won't be accompanying us. He's . . . engaged to a young woman he was introduced to at Chapel. The new sergeant major's daughter."

"I see." Catherine had agreed with Uncle Daniel that she should not be thinking of romance until she could face life as a complete person. But until she reached that point, she knew she would be tempted to take shortcuts to fill the emptiness. She had abandoned the idea of writing Lieutenant Elham weeks ago, but lately had struggled with whether she should contact him once she reached Bombay. Now that the temptation was removed from her, she felt a surprising relief, a relaxing of an inner compulsion.

"Please give him my best wishes," she said, and meant it.

Thirty-Six

*D*earest Aunt Phyllis, Catherine penned the tenth of
July, one week after arriving in Bombay. She fol-
lowed the salutations with the usual wishes that the family were all enjoying
good health, told how Father and Mother and Jewel were enjoying good
health; and once everyone's health was established, got to her reason for
writing.

> *I have not seen Lord Holt for months now, neither do I expect or wish
> to, as he has married someone else.*

The identity of the "someone else" was irrelevant, at least where Aunt
Phyllis was concerned. She hoped that her aunt would read between her carefully scripted lines, for courtesy forbade her to put to ink the blunt words
moving across her mind:

> *Please stop pleading his case to Mother and Father! It's ancient his-
> tory, like the Punic Wars, and it only causes tension in the household.*

Instead she added her wishes that the children's experiences at their new
schools this coming fall would be rewarding. According to Mother, the tutor
had given notice last spring. She sealed the envelope and went over to her
window to peer out between the slats of the chick screen. The rains had
paused for an unusual two days in a row, though the sky was darkening with
the promise of a torrent. A handful of boys were tossing a ball back and forth
in the courtyard, their laughter and good-natured jeers floating along the sul-
try air.

What began almost four months ago as forcing herself to look for things
for which to be grateful had become a habit, so automatically she thanked
God that the schoolchildren were able to make occasions for laughter, even

though they could not join their families over the summer for various reasons. *If I ever have children, I'll never send them off to school,* she thought.

No matter that Father and the schoolmasters were kindly, they were no substitutes for parents, and she could only imagine the tears shed in cots during the night. She had never given thought to what it would be like to be a mother, but with the milestone of her twentieth birthday only three weeks away, she supposed some sort of reflection was in order.

She smiled at the memory of little John's smile, the scant weight of his body in her lap. Sarah and William were equally matched in their dedication to their son, in their determination to be good parents. That was important, she realized. She had seen in Aunt Phyllis's family how out of balance a household could become when one parent's devotion overspilled the limits of common sense in an effort to make up for the other parent's supposed failings.

Yet she had not given parenthood a thought when she fell so completely in love with Sidney. What sort of father would he have made, with his cowardice and cheapness? The way he treated those people he considered his social inferiors? Or how he paid lip service to integrity, but did not practice it? And the way his generosity only seemed to extend to occasions from which he could benefit?

Only now was she able to see those flaws, now that she was forced to step away from him. It sobered her to think she had come within weeks of joining her life with his. Would he have taken time to nurture their future children, to love them as much as she would love them? Or would the anxiety of constantly having to make up for their father's shortcomings turn her into someone like Aunt Phyllis, and their children into unhappy social misfits?

Birds did not lay eggs until their nests were complete and sturdy, yet she was so charmed by a pair of blue eyes and sharp wit that she had been willing to build a family upon such an unstable foundation.

"You stupid girl!" she muttered, tears clouding her eyes. For she still loved him—not as much as when they were courting, not even as much as last week, but enough still to hurt. *How long will this take, Father?* she asked. *Won't you just remove those feelings from me?*

An answer came from that part of her mind that heard God speak, not with words, but with impressions that stirred her emotions or helped her to see reason. *Look at what the pain has taught you.*

If the wounds from loving Sidney were so easily healed, she would never have learned what a fragile and precious thing the heart was, and how it must be guarded. Not locked away from all experiences, but protected, as best able, from those who would treat it callously.

And she never would have learned the folly of allowing sentiment to cloud her mind. She had a good mind, albeit a scattered one at times. Her mind would have noticed Sidney's character faults and served warning, especially if she had asked God's guidance in the matter.

Next time I'll be more circumspect, she promised God. If a *next time* ever came. For at twenty, most unmarried women were considered poised upon the brink of spinsterhood.

Better to be a spinster than in an unhappy marriage, she thought with all sincerity. And Sidney had occupied enough of her thoughts today. She rose and took book one of Virgil's *The Aeneid* from atop her chest of drawers. She had determined to finish translating books I through IV from Latin before the end of summer, so that she would have a head start on Michaelmas Term. The desire to teach had taken root within her again, increasing in the same minuscule degrees that her longing for Sidney decreased. *Inverse proportion,* she thought, smiling and settling into her chair. Peggy was not the only one with a talent for putting situations into mathematical formulas.

Two days later the *Times of India* reported that fifty Europeans were killed in Alexandria riots the previous day, leading to bombardments of the city's fortifications by British naval vessels. Tensions had been brewing in Egypt for seven years over the increasing European influence, particularly that of Britain and France and their support of the Turkish viceroyal government.

"This means war," her father told her. "You'll not be traveling back until we're sure the Canal is safe."

————

Whitechapel was not the worst of the many districts that William had visited in the course of his investigations. But it was dismal enough. "Are you sure you're up to this?" he asked Miss Somerset on the morning of the seventeenth of July. They stood halfway down an obscure passage leading off Batty Street. It was just one of the dozens of narrow avenues of closely packed nests, too narrow for a carriage and filled to overflowing with dirt and misery and rags. William carried his purse in his waistcoat packet to discourage pickpockets. The girl had followed his advice and dressed in a plain blue gown, carrying no reticule and wearing no jewelry.

"I'm up to this, Mr. Doyle," she said with shoulders squared.

He took a small notebook from his coat pocket, checked the address, and they continued down the lane. Groups of people idled about gin shops and squabbled in doorways, and every post and corner seemed to support an occupant leaning against it. "A Miss Arber died at an umbrella factory on

Commercial Road three days ago," William explained when they stopped outside the minuscule, gateless courtyard of a crumbling ground-floor tenement.

"She complained to co-workers of headaches, hearing loss, and blurred vision for several days, but she wouldn't stay home for fear of losing her position. We suspect lead poisoning. Her sister, a Mrs. Smith, allowed our investigator, Mr. Hinks, to collect the few open tins of food from the cupboard and the contents of the ash bin, but our tests have been negative. And she refuses to grant permission for a postmortem."

He had decided to bring Miss Somerset along, even though the stakes were high—or rather, because the stakes were high. Catherine's friend knew enough chemistry to ask the right questions, and yet she still looked like a schoolgirl. A very benign presence. He wished he had thought to ask her earlier.

But she balked at the courtyard entrance. "What should I say?"

"Anything that will gain us permission."

"What if—?"

"You'll do fine. Just relax."

Biting her lip, she took the arm he offered. They picked their way over the few remaining flagstones spaced between dried clumps of grass and worn patches of earth, passing a sagging clothesline upon which grey nappies hung to dry. The door opened a scant three inches after William's knock.

"What do yer want?" asked the woman on the other side, mistrust and annoyance evident on even the small portion of face she allowed them to see. Childish chatter came from behind, and the faint sound of a crying infant.

Miss Somerset gave her a wide-eyed stare, and William held his breath. *Come on,* he urged silently. *Just take charge.*

"Good morning, Mrs. . . . Smith?" she said.

"Who wants ter know?"

Miss Somerset nodded, the shoulders squaring again. "But . . . of course. It's not fair to ask your name when we haven't given you ours." She held out a gloved hand. "My name is Miss Somerset, and this is my assistant, Mr. Doyle."

Good for you! William thought, suppressing a smile as Mrs. Smith opened the door wide enough to accept Miss Somerset's handshake.

"We're from the Hassall Commission, and we've some concerns over the circumstances of Miss Arber's untimely passing. If we could come in for just a—"

The woman's hand shot back through the gap like a tortoise head withdrawing to its shell. "You can just turn yerselfs around. Just 'cause me sister took up with any bloke who'd buy her a bauble don't mean I have to allow you folk to go carvin' her up like she was a slab of mutton!"

Miss Somerset sent William a panicked look.

Don't back down! was the message he hoped she could read in his eyes.

"I understand," she said in a soothing voice. "A postmortem is not a pleasant thought. But just think. No matter how your sister lived, she has the opportunity to save some lives now. Don't you think she would wish that?"

The woman snorted, her grin revealing two dark gaps in her yellowed teeth. "My sister never gave a tinker's curse over anybody but herself. But you ain't gonter take a knife to her."

"But—"

"NO!" she exclaimed. William flinched as the door slammed with a splintering thud.

Miss Somerset turned to him, hazel eyes rimmed with red. "I'm so sorry."

"You tried your best," William told her. "I appreciate that."

They walked through the weed-choked courtyard in silence. They had gone twelve feet or so up the lane when Miss Somerset said, "Wait."

William looked at her.

"You said I should say *anything* that will get us the postmortem?" she asked.

"Absolutely."

She nodded, turned around, and beckoned him on. William's first series of four knocks was ignored, and was his second.

"Please try again," the girl asked.

He stifled a sigh and raised a fist. This time door flew open and narrowed again to a gap just wide enough for one eye.

"If I have to send fer the police . . ."

Miss Somerset raised a placating hand. "This is the last time we'll trouble you, Miss Smith, but please hear me."

The eye narrowed, but the gap in the doorway remained.

"Mr. Doyle, here, is very wealthy. And he'll give you ten pounds if you'll allow the postmortem."

The eye fastened upon William. "Twenty," said the mouth below it.

"Done," said William.

The door opened. "Won't you come inside?"

"You're a genius, Miss Somerset," William said, carefully folding the letter with Mrs. Smith's mark.

Miss Somerset blushed with pleasure. "Then you're not angry about the money?"

"Angry? Not one iota. I can't wait to tell everyone." He could not wait to call home either, for it was Sarah who had suggested William allow Miss Somerset to gain some experience there this summer.

Their cabby was waiting on Commercial Road, as instructed. William was giving him instructions to take them back to the Commission when Miss Somerset turned away from the hansom. "Mr. Sedgwick?"

William looked over his shoulder. A young man had halted on the pavement, brown eyes uncertain above his smile. "Miss . . ."

"Somerset," she said, extending a hand. "I first met you on the train to Cambridge, remember? *King Lear?*"

The young man grinned. "How could I have forgotten?"

William held out a hand as Miss Somerset beckoned him closer. The name had struck a chord, and once the introductions were made, he remembered from where. "Are you connected with the tea company?"

"I work there with my father and brother. But I've also founded a charity school nearby." Mr. Sedgwick had said the latter part with more enthusiasm than the first, and indeed, he was smiling as proudly as a father mentioning his children.

"How interesting," William said. "Please take no offense, but you're rather young to be founding a school. What prompted you to do so?"

He looked a little sheepish, but replied with conviction, "It was something I felt God was impressing me to do. And now opportunities are opening that I could scarcely imagine happening when we started."

"Yes?" William dipped into his pocket for notebook and pencil. "I'll give you my address. Do send my wife and me some information."

"Why, thank you, Mr. Doyle!" Mr. Sedgwick's eyebrows rose hopefully. "Perhaps you both would care to have a tour?"

"I'm afraid I have urgent business." William looked at Miss Somerset. He wasn't certain what her relationship was to this young man, but he seemed a decent sort. If she had hopes for a courtship, he was happy to help it along. "But Miss Somerset may wish to stay, if you'll see her to a carriage afterward."

"I would be delighted," he said.

"Oh, but I need to get back to the lab," said Miss Somerset.

"We'll not have the results of this until late this afternoon at the earliest," William said, patting the paper in his coat pocket. He didn't want to come out and say *postmortem* because it made people uncomfortable, plus Commission business was not something to be discussed out on the street. "Take an hour or two."

"We opened the doors two months ago," Hugh went on as they turned the corner from Berner to North Street. As soon as they passed the front of an old livery stable, he could see the building in the distance. Just the sight of it made him feel good. He was aware that he was babbling, but it was a relief to talk about the school to someone interested. While his family expressed pride in what he was doing—his father even sponsoring two students in addition to donating the desks—there was at home and in the office an almost palatable undercurrent of resentment that he should be so absorbed in something out of the realm of the family business.

"And we've now thirty-seven students. Most of them possess only rudimentary reading skills, so that's our strongest emphasis. We had thirty-nine students in the beginning, but unfortunately two enrolled only because they assumed it would be easier than factory work, and gave their schoolmasters grief until we made them leave."

He gave her a cautious look. "I'm aware of how that sounds, but we had given them fair warning, and we could not allow them to steal classroom time from the thirty-seven who are serious about education. Ironic, that *I* was never serious about it, but as Mr. Holland—he's a Wesleyan minister who helped us find students—says, life is hard here, and we pay the children no favors when we mollycoddle them."

"Thirty-seven students?" Miss Somerset said, hand resting in the crook of his arm.

But her smile seemed pasted on, her expression distracted, and Hugh wondered if Mr. Doyle had pressured her into accompanying him. "If this isn't a good time, Miss Somerset . . ."

She looked at him. "I beg your . . . oh, no, I'm very eager to see your school. You're conducting summer classes?"

"Just *this* summer—we started so late in the year, you see, and there is so much to do. We'll let out in August for a month's vacation."

"I see." They walked a mere three steps more when she looked at him again and blurted, "I burned the letter."

Now it was his turn to beg pardon. "The letter?"

"The one you sent Catherine—Miss Rayborn—at Girton. That's why she didn't answer it."

He had only scant memory of what he had written over a year ago. Still, he was relieved for the sake of his ego to learn that lack of interest had not prompted the young woman to ignore his letter.

"Why did you burn it?" he asked.

She glanced away as color spread to the roots of her red hair, and he knew. Perhaps that was why Miss Rayborn had asked him to wait until spring to write.

He patted the hand resting in the crook of his arm. "Water under the bridge, Miss Somerset."

"That's very kind of you," she murmured.

"How *is* Miss Rayborn?"

Worry entered the hazel eyes. "She's in Bombay with her immediate family."

"Ah," he said with a nod. "I remember her mentioning Bombay to you on the train that time. Her father is headmaster of a school, yes?"

"Yes. She's supposed to return on the twentieth of August, but her father wired her uncle that the date of her departure will depend on the conflict in Egypt."

"The Suez Canal." He realized the connection. "How unsettling. I'm glad she's acting with caution."

"And I. But I do hope she makes it back in time for Michaelmas Term."

They walked in silence for a moment, and then she said, "I could inform you when she does . . ."

"I beg your pardon?"

"In case you'd care to write again. I believe she'd like to hear from you. That is . . . you're not married, are you?"

"I'm not married." A picture came to his mind, Miss Rayborn exiting a coach in front of the Lyceum with an aristocratic-looking man. "Hasn't she a beau?"

"Not any more," Miss Somerset said in a hopeful tone.

They were approaching the entrance to his school. Mr. Madden's voice floated through the open window to their left. "*. . . give us an example of some action verbs?*"

A little part of Hugh wondered what might have been. But then, it probably wasn't meant to be. Not with so many obstacles. And his heart still ached for Lillian, though his duties at work and the school allowed him little time to brood.

"Thank you, but I'm really quite busy," he said politely. Holding open the door to the entrance hall for her, he returned to the subject that interested him most. "I was pleasantly surprised at how bright most of these children are . . ."

Thirty-Seven

*M*iss Arber's postmortem revealed definite lead poisoning. During the following week, William and fellow Commission investigator Frank Hinks interviewed a half dozen people showing early stages of the same symptoms of which Miss Arber complained—workers in the umbrella factory in Whitechapel, a brickworks in Spitafields, and a shipping warehouse in Wapping. Snuff turned out to be the common denominator, namely Rose of Lancaster Quality Snuff, packaged by Halliday Tobacconist on, of all places, Bond Street, safely removed from the victims of their hemlock.

"They were coloring their tobacco with lead chromate," William explained to Sarah on the twenty-fourth, between spoonfuls of the beef and vegetable soup Trudy had insisted on warming over for him. They sat together in the dining room, Sarah in nightgown, wrapper, and slippers, he in shirtsleeves with his coat hanging on the back of the chair. He had had a long day, between visiting shops with Mr. Hinks to remove the product from the shelves and consulting with the Hassall Commission's attorney to draw up a request for arrest warrants for the two Halliday brothers.

"Lead chromate . . ." Sarah said, and gave a little shudder. "Those poor people. Didn't you catch someone coloring mustard with it once?"

"Twice. And now and again we put someone out of business for adding minuscule amounts to snuff. But they obviously dumped too much in a batch and, not wanting to waste it, sold it to shops on the East side."

That was what galled him the most about those who would do such things. Nine times out of ten they pushed their poisons off on poor people because not much notice would be taken. Poison snuff in Mayfair or Kensington would have been front-page news. But at least the *Times* would be sending a reporter when he and the police went to Bond Street tomorrow morning to make the arrests.

"Why don't you bring Miss Somerset along too?" Sarah said, as William tore a piece of bread to dip into the soup. "She's leaving for Girton next week. Wouldn't it be satisfying for her to witness the end result?"

"To an arrest?" William had not invited Miss Somerset along to follow investigations, as certain areas of Spitalfields and Wapping were not safe for even an escorted woman. The girl was clearly disappointed when he consigned her to the laboratory with the three other chemists, but she had not protested. *Respects authority,* William thought. She would be a fine addition to the Commission one day.

But the Halliday brothers could come along meekly, or then, they could rail in language unfit for a lady's ears. When he mentioned that to Sarah, she said, "You could warn her to be prepared to step outside. But give her the choice of whether or not to go."

"Very well. I'll invite her just because you asked me."

"You're a dear," she said, putting a hand upon his arm.

William smiled. "I have my moments. Now, tell me what my son did today. Did you sing the Periodic Table to him as I asked?"

She laughed, and he touched a tendril of the blond hair spilling over her shoulder and felt almost sorry for the Halliday brothers, comfortable in their beds for the last time until who knew when? To lose the company of loved ones, and all for a few extra shillings?

He had lived poor longer than rich, worked longer as a servant than a respected chemist. Through poverty and wealth, he had discovered that the things that brought him the most pleasure cost him nothing materially. Gratitude overwhelmed him, that God would place shining examples of that lesson in his life: Aunt Naomi, Daniel, Vicar Sharp from Mayfair, and even Mr. Duffy. And that he would learn this lesson while young enough to avoid storing up regrets that would embitter his old age.

"What are you thinking?" Sarah asked.

He smiled and picked up his spoon again. "I'll tell you later." Such things were not meant to be discussed at a long table over a bowl of soup, but in the privacy of their chamber, with her resting against his shoulder while their son slept in his cradle nearby.

The weight of Hugh's father's stare was almost unbearable, not for any hostility in it, but for the disappointment.

"I anticipated as much," he said.

"You were correct. Being an absentee headmaster is too difficult," Hugh told him. "I've tried, but we've almost twenty additional students coming in September. I'm needed there."

"You're needed here too."

"But you have Brian now. And Lane next year. You got on just fine before I ever came."

Sadness lengthened his father's face, making him appear older than his forty-seven years. "I had such dreams, Hugh. My sons here at my side . . ."

It took all of Hugh's self-possession to hold back tears. "They weren't my dreams, Sir," he said in a soft voice. "And if I were born a daughter instead of a son, you wouldn't demand this of me."

Again, the stare. "Demand?"

"How else can I see it, when I'm not able to leave without this terrible guilt?"

His father's shoulders rose and fell with his sigh. "Are you absolutely positive this is what you want to do?"

"I was never more sure of anything, Father."

"Very well."

The words were said with such futility, as if his father had given up all hope in him. Getting to his feet, Hugh said, "Thank you, Sir."

"Umhmm." His father picked up a file from his desk.

Hugh swallowed, as the image of his father blurred. "I'll make you proud of me one day."

His father looked up again. The two stared across at each other. The older man's eyes reddened. "I'm proud of you already, son. Never forget that."

He rose from his chair and held out an arm. Hugh hurried around the desk. It was the first time that Hugh could recall his father embracing him. It made him feel honored, as if his father had just now accepted his adulthood, and yet at the same time he felt protected like a small boy. Hours later, after he had cleaned out his desk and left the office, he could still feel the strong arms about his shoulders.

————

On the twentieth of August, British troops arrived at Port Sa'id and closed the Suez Canal at both ends. The conflict ended a little over three weeks later when the British defeated the Egyptian Army at the Battle of Tel-el-Kebir, and the Canal was deemed safe for travel again. The next P & O Steamer to leave Bombay was on the fifteenth of September. Fortunately, the bookings Catherine and Mrs. Jennings had secured earlier were honored. The thirteen-day journey commenced without incident, other than Mrs. Jennings' seasickness and declarations that she would never travel this way again. On the twenty-eighth they arrived in Tilbury. Catherine was only able to spend the following day with her Hampstead relations, for she had to take the train to Girton on the thirtieth to prepare for the beginning of her third year, just days away.

Peggy met her on the platform at Cambridge Station. They embraced, and Catherine nodded toward a group of giggling female freshers.

"Were we ever that young and naive?"

"You know the answer to that," her friend replied. "Let's see to your trunk—I've a carriage waiting."

"Really? How did you know I would be here?"

"Mrs. Doyle wrote to me at Girton after your father wired that your ship had left. I simply added the days and figured you'd be here yesterday or today."

"Very astute of—" Catherine left the last word hanging and looked at her. "You weren't here yesterday too, were you?"

The sentiment in Peggy's smile canceled out the casualness of her shrug. "I happen to have missed you. We have so much catching up to do."

Twenty minutes later as the cab carried them up Regent Street, Peggy told her of the month spent at the Commission, particularly the "lead in snuff" case. "My name was even in the *Times*!"

"How exciting," Catherine said, smiling. She had read the article about the arrest, and William had already given her all the details. But then, Peggy had listened to her go on and on about Sidney, so a little *quid pro quo* was in order. "I'm very proud of you."

"Oh, Catherine . . ." Peggy's cheeks were ruddy with happiness. "I'm so sure this is what God wants me to do with my life. You can't imagine how good it felt to apply what I've learned toward helping people."

"Really?" Unable to resist the urge to tease, Catherine said, "And where did you learn bribery?"

"Bri—?" Her friend winced. "The postmortem. Mr. Doyle told you."

"The story will be chuckled over in the Rayborn-Doyle family for years to come. I wrote of it to my parents and Jewel last night."

"Oh dear," Peggy said, pressing hand to cheek. "And I've not even asked about your family, your summer, anything. And after all you've been through. Will you forgive me?"

"There's nothing to forgive. And I've really not been through anything other than having to spend an extra six weeks with my family. But it may be my last time, as my parents are seriously considering leaving Bombay after this school year."

"The trouble in Egypt?"

"Jewel and I think they miss England too, but they'll never admit it."

Peggy studied her face. "And how are you . . . ?"

"With regard to Sidney?" Catherine finished for her.

She looked relieved not to have to say it herself. "Yes."

"To be honest, there were some dark times. But I can see a light at the end of the tunnel now."

"I'm glad, Catherine."

A narrow boat of eight rowers with a coxswain in front to steer and shout *Pull! Pull! Pull!* shot by on the Cam beneath the Great Bridge, followed by two more boats abreast and one trailing behind them. Sunlight sparkled in their wakes.

"*And* . . . I translated the first six books of *The Aeneid*," Catherine told her when the River was behind them.

"*Six?*"

The incredulity upon Peggy's face was gratifying, as if Catherine also had accomplished a great feat—which, perhaps she had, considering how difficult it was to make her mind stay attached to anything written pre-nineteenth century. "I had all that unexpected extra time . . ."

After they stopped at Girton College, Catherine insisted on paying the driver. "You had to pay for a wasted trip yesterday," she told Peggy. She gave him an extra half crown to help Mr. Willingham carry in the trunk, then linked arms with Peggy and started toward the terra-cotta brick building that was beginning to feel like a second home. *Third home,* Catherine amended.

"I've two surprises for you," Peggy said as they passed through the main entrance.

"What are they?"

Peggy led her to the reading room, unlinked her arm, and took a step backwards. "Look around and you'll see the first one."

Catherine's eyes scanned the room, stopping at the Gower Bell telephone on the wall.

"A telephone!" she breathed.

"They moved the Queen over there," Peggy said with a nod toward the portrait hanging on the east wall. "We're only connected to Cambridge now, but Miss Welsh says the lines will extend to London by summer. Can you imagine?"

"Remarkable!"

Taking her arm again, Peggy said, "And now on to the second surprise."

"What is it?" Catherine asked.

The hazel eyes had a mysterious glint. "You'll have to stop by my apartment."

The *something* Peggy produced, after rustling papers in a drawer, turned out to be a square of paper. Catherine set her reticule upon the study table and took it from her. It was a photograph of an old brick building with a pair of windows on each side of an entryway, and four windows above. She squinted at the lettering on the signboard above the door. "Nord Streed Fhoot?"

"North Street School," Peggy corrected, folding her arms. "It's in Whitechapel."

Catherine lowered the photograph, looked at her friend. "And . . . ?"

"Hugh Sedgwick gave it to me. He mails them out with solicitation letters. He founded the school himself. Mr. Doyle and I happened upon him when I was working for the Commission."

"William never told me."

"Perhaps he didn't realize you two were acquainted." Peggy pointed to one of the top windows. "A grandmotherly sort of woman makes soup in the little kitchen for those who can't afford to bring lunches. Mrs. Garrett is her name."

Catherine looked at the photograph again and thought of Hugh Sedgwick's prank on the train almost two years ago. *You can never really know what's in a person's heart.* Or perhaps Mr. Sedgwick had not known himself at that time. Wasn't she just beginning to learn what was in hers? A little wave of regret washed over her, and she handed the photograph back. "That's very generous of him."

Peggy bit her lip, seeming to have something more to say.

"What is it?" Catherine asked, and realized after she spoke, *They're seeing each other.* It was perfectly within Peggy's rights, she reminded herself, for she had no claim to Mr. Sedgwick, especially after her engagement to Sidney.

She smiled at her friend. "I'm very happy for you, Peggy."

"Happy for me?" Peggy gave her a blank look. "Why?"

"Well, you and Mr. Sedgwick."

"You think I still—?" A smile flickered across Peggy's lips. "I'm not interested in him, Catherine. What I'm *trying* to tell you is that I confessed to him about burning the letter."

"But why?"

"Because it's haunted me for months." Her hazel eyes reddened. "If I hadn't burned the letter, perhaps you and Lord Holt never would have . . ."

Catherine set the photograph upon the study table and stepped up to wrap her arms around her friend. "I would have been trading one idol for another," she said. For she had worshipped Sidney, she could see now, placing him in the space in her heart reserved for God. She had no doubt that she would have done the same with Hugh Sedgwick, had there not been barriers in the way, or even Lieutenant Elham, had she stayed longer in Bombay last summer.

"There's still hope," Peggy said as if she had not heard. She took a step back, wiping her eyes with the heel of her hand. "When we're in London between terms, I'll ring him and ask for another tour, tell him I want to show you . . ."

The faint hope that rose in Catherine's mind alarmed her. Had she come so far, learned so much, only to slide back into neediness again? She shook her head for her own as well as Peggy's benefit. "I can't do that, Peggy."

"What do you mean?"

"You know how you feel that God's leading you to help others with your knowledge of chemistry?"

"Yes." Peggy gave her a wary look. "You're not thinking of changing to *Chemistry* . . ."

Catherine had to smile. "I believe He's telling me to concentrate on my studies and grow closer to Him for the time being."

"But that doesn't mean you can't—"

"That's exactly what it means." If romance was to be allowed into her life again, it would be after she had become a whole person, her mind not ruled by her heart.

At length Peggy shrugged. "Whatever you say, Catherine. But I had some marvelous daydreams of the both of you gushing thanks to me for bringing you together."

"You can bring me together with some lunch instead," Catherine told her, taking her arm. "I'm famished."

They ambled down the corridor, pausing to welcome freshers and to return the greetings of old friends. A tray of sandwiches—egg mayonnaise and roast beef—and a bowl of pears were set out in the dining hall. They took their plates to their usual table, now empty. Catherine pulled a bit of gristle from her roast beef. "I suppose you could tell me a little more about North Street School."

At Peggy's knowing little smile, Catherine rolled her eyes and said, "I wouldn't be studying to be a schoolmistress if I weren't interested in schools."

Thirty-Eight

As Catherine and Peggy began their third year on the second of October, Catherine discovered that the earlier in the day she began her studies, the less prone her mind was to wander, and thus her concentration was improved. And it helped that there was not the distraction of a personal life in turmoil. She was even able to pay the kindness Peggy had shown her toward someone else; she had happened upon fresher Daphne Myton weeping as she left Latin I, and began tutoring the girl in the evenings thrice weekly.

She surprised herself by sailing through Greek I, II, and III, which did not soothe the disappointment over below-average marks in Ancient and Medieval Topography during Lent Term. Still, she thought she did well on her examinations at the close of the school year. Until she was summoned to Miss Bernard's office, on the twenty-second of June, 1883.

"I would like to ask of your plans after graduation," Mrs. Bernard said, folding her hands atop her desk. "Will you move to Bombay?"

Tension eased out of Catherine's neck and shoulders. *After graduation* had a promising note, and surely meant she would not be starting Michaelmas Term in the fall with another probation. "My family will be moving back to England next month. My father is to become headmaster of a boys' boarding school outside Sheffield."

"Do you plan to move there?"

"No, Miss Bernard." While she was overjoyed to have her family only a four-hour railway journey away, she would be twenty-two years old when she graduated. She feared the maturity she had striven for during the past year would regress under her parents' protectiveness.

"I've recommended you to a personal friend in London. A Mrs. Whitmore, headmistress to the Ryle Day School for Young Ladies in Belgravia. Are you familiar with it?"

Stunned as she was that Miss Bernard would recommend her to *anyone,* she replied, "My cousin Muriel attended there until two years ago." When Miss Bernard did not fill in the silence that followed, Catherine realized that she might be wondering why her cousin had left the school, and hastened to add, "But they moved to Sheffield—my cousin's family."

"I see." Miss Bernard seemed satisfied with that. "If you're interested, Miss Whitmore asks that you ring her when you arrive back in Hampstead to schedule an appointment. It is in regard to a teaching position that will become available next year, when one of her teachers marries."

"Next year?"

"Female college graduates are, sadly, still in short supply in Britain. Those of you intending to teach will find yourselves in high demand by the better schools."

Catherine stared across at her. "But why me, Miss Bernard?"

The headmistress smiled. "I'm aware that you must struggle to maintain your marks. Your tenacity is commendable, Miss Rayborn, as is your empathy for others who struggle. You have been tutoring Miss Myton, and it was you who caused the others to accept Miss Turner when you were freshmen—as disappointing as the case turned out. As I said to Mrs. Whitmore, you'll make a fine schoolmistress."

"I shouldn't be long," Catherine told Stanley on the twenty-ninth of June, after stepping out of the coach on leafy Wilton Street in Belgravia, London.

Stanley walked over to open the cast-iron gate, beside a bronze plaque reading *Ryle Day School for Young Ladies, est. 1837.* "No hurry, Miss." He patted his pocket. "I've a book with me. Ever read *Tom Sawyer?*"

"Why, yes."

"If Guy got himself into half the scrapes that boy got into, my hair would turn white. But Tom's a funny little mite."

Catherine agreed that he was and walked the brick path toward the white three-storey building. A faint melancholy had come over her since the coach entered Belgravia, for Sidney's house would be but two blocks northwest, and Green Park just a stroll to the northeast. *You can't hide from him all your life,* she told herself. But she wondered if considering a position in an area so awash with memories was wise.

A maid answered and led her to the headmistress's office. Miss Bernard had obviously pressed Catherine's case strongly, for Mrs. Whitmore, a widow with hair and eyes the color of tea, offered her the position after asking a few questions about her interests and classes, and even family. "Contingent upon your graduation, please understand, but Miss Bernard assures me that you're committed to reaching that goal."

"I am, Mrs. Whitmore."

"Very good. You'll see that our wages cannot be matched in any school in London." The woman handed a sheet of paper across the desk. "That is one reason openings such as this rarely come about."

The figures on the paper were indeed impressive, though her legacy from Grandfather spared Catherine of having to make wages her main consideration. She asked, "May I see the classrooms?"

"But of course," Mrs. Whitmore replied, seeming pleased that she would ask. She led Catherine down polished oak floors reflecting the electric bulbs that were starting to illuminate sections of London. "I only wish classes were still in session, so that you could observe. Our students hail from the finest families in Britain. We've had a waiting list for the past decade."

She opened the first door. Empty desks were queued in precise rows, maps and charts adorned the paneled walls. Catherine could picture herself standing at the blackboard while well-scrubbed faces followed her lead in their French recitations.

"*Apropos,* to the purpose . . . *capapie,* from head to foot . . . *je ne sais quoi,* I know not what . . ."

It was all quite impressive, and the fact that she was *wanted* here added to the attraction. Still, she hoped she had learned her lesson about leaping ahead of God.

"When must you have an answer?" she asked.

Mrs. Whitmore nodded approval, as if Catherine had passed another sort of test by not appearing too eager. "By the end of August will allow me ample time to schedule other interviews, should you turn down the position."

They smiled at each other, the look in Mrs. Whitmore's eyes saying that she was aware that no aspiring schoolmistress in her right mind would turn down such an attractive position.

Catherine nodded and thanked her. "By late August."

That afternoon she sat out in the garden with Sarah and Aunt Naomi, while fourteen-month-old John dozed in his pram near Sarah. Ten feet away from the cast-iron benches, six-year-old Bethia and four-year-old Danny lay on their stomachs, admonishing each other to be quiet as they dangled blades of grass in the goldfish pond in the hope of attracting a curious nibble. Guy, now eight years old, sat cross-legged and picked softly at the three strings remaining on an old violin that Trudy had found in a secondhand shop. Peggy was coming for lunch tomorrow and had promised to restring it for him.

Catherine had her summer planned out. She would return to Girton on Monday, the second of July. The month of August was reserved for helping her parents and Jewel settle in Sheffield, then she planned to return to Girton the first of September for another month of studying ahead. Peggy would be joining her there only then, for William had gotten permission to hire her for two months this time.

"If you decide to accept, I do hope you'll plan to stay with us," Sarah said, after Catherine told her and Aunt Naomi of the Ryle school interview.

"It's so kind of you to offer," Catherine replied. "But there is a boarding house for ladies just across the street. Three of the schoolmistresses stay there. It would be most convenient."

"Bethia's school may possibly have a staff vacancy next year," Aunt Naomi said. The six-year-old had just completed her first year at the National School on Christ Church Road, where Guy attended. "Would you like me to ring the headmaster and ask?"

The children had seemed caught in their own little world, but Bethia jumped up from lying on her stomach and hurried over. "Oh, do say yes, Catherine! You could stay here then, and perhaps you would even be my teacher!"

Catherine smiled at her aunt. "I suppose it wouldn't hurt to ring him."

The following morning the headmaster, a Mr. Houghton, informed Aunt Naomi that he was not yet certain if he would have any teaching position available a year from now, but should one occur, he would contact her to arrange for an interview.

Peggy arrived at ten, having walked the short distance from the omnibus stop on Heath Street. The wood to Guy's violin did not seem warped, she said after looking it over. Along with violin strings and bow, she had brought her first lesson book, *The Violin for Small Fingers.* "You have the advantage of knowing how to read music from your piano lessons," Peggy told the boy as the family, minus William, gathered in the parlor. Guy mumbled a timid "Thank you, Miss," but his keen eyes watched her fingers knot strings and twist pegs.

"You'll play us something, won't you?" Sarah asked, after Peggy had tuned the instrument and pronounced it suitable for a beginner.

Peggy smiled and tucked the violin under her chin. "Hey Diddle Diddle" was her first tune, to the delight of the children, followed by "Baa, Baa, Black Sheep." For the adults—and Guy, who listened, motionless, with head cocked—she played Schubert's melancholy "Gretchen at the Spinning

Wheel," and then a more mood-lifting "The Hen" by Haydn.

After a lunch of fricasseed chicken and vegetables, Catherine asked if Sarah minded if she accepted Peggy's invitation to spend the night on Saville Row. "We would first make a side trip over to Ryle Day School," she added. Guilt no longer goaded her into listing her exact whereabouts, but she was simply motivated by the rules of courtesy befitting a houseguest. Sarah insisted they have Stanley drive them, and forty minutes later the carriage was carrying them down Belgravia's old elegant lanes.

"Austere, isn't it?" Peggy said hesitantly as they sat outside the gates.

"But Mrs. Whitmore was very pleasant," Catherine assured her. Still, she did not have the courage to proceed past the gates without the excuse of an interview.

The carriage was moving back up Grosvenor Place when Peggy's hand gripped Catherine's arm.

"What is it?" Catherine asked.

"Nothing," Peggy replied, removing her hand and staring straight ahead.

Catherine leaned forward to look past her. Sidney and Milly stood waiting to cross the intersection. They looked like elegant statues: Sidney in bowler hat and grey suit; Milly in a peach-colored gown and straw hat. As the carriage proceeded, Catherine twisted in her seat. It was then that her eyes met Milly's.

"Turn around, Catherine," Peggy said.

The distress that washed across Milly's face was obvious, even from the growing distance. Her lips were moving as Sidney leaned his head closer to listen.

"Turn *around*!"

This time Catherine obeyed, staring ahead while two sets of eyes burned into her back.

Peggy touched her arm again. "Are you all right?"

"I'm not sure." They rode in silence up Picadilly. To the right was Green Park, and Catherine could see the bench where she and Sidney had sat sharing a pear almost two years ago. Had he and Milly sat there just minutes ago?

"You knew it would happen eventually," Peggy said.

"Yes." After a moment's thought, Catherine realized something. She turned to Peggy. "I looked at Milly more than Sidney."

"I see." But Peggy's eyes glazed a bit as if she were trying to establish some point to that statement.

"It just struck me. It's the loss of Milly I feel more deeply now."

"More than Lord Holt?" Peggy said skeptically.

Catherine nodded. "Don't you see? Our friendships—yours, mine,

Milly's—grew into a love for each other. What I felt for Sidney was infatuation. It overshadowed everything else, but proves to have lasted the shortest time."

She had to laugh at the look Peggy gave her.

"The shortest time . . . *relatively* speaking," Catherine explained. Her heart felt lighter than it had in over a year. Sidney would probably lurk in the back of it for a while longer, but his presence was beginning to shrink. As for Milly, while Catherine could not yet bring herself to forgive her, she felt a tug of pity for the torment she must be going through, as evidenced by the look upon her face.

Catherine fought against that feeling. *She hurt me, Father,* she prayed.

Just as you hurt those who have now forgiven you, said a calm voice in her mind.

She had spent the night in the Somerset flat before, so the street noises coming through Peggy's open bedroom window did not surprise her. Patterns clicking upon the pavement, wheels and hooves on cobbled stones, and almost constant voices, some even discernible.

". . . said it'll be ready in short order . . ."

". . . chambermaid found it behind the armoire just when I feared . . ."

". . . stitched me 'ead up like mendin' a shirt . . ."

It was quite a change from Hampstead's and even Girton's after-dark calm. But she found it interesting. Every scrap of conversation represented a whole sphere of experience not connected with her own. It made her feel excluded from the flow of life, in a mild sort of way, yet she wondered if some of those passing by outside looked up at the windows and felt the same about the people above the shops.

Two sets of footsteps, belonging to male and female voices too low for any words to be discerned, passed across her field of hearing and faded. She pictured Milly and Sidney walking arm in arm. She had always assumed that one could not possibly forgive a person until the bitterness over that person's actions naturally dissipated with time. But if that were so, why would God be prompting her to forgive now? Could it be that forgiveness was an act of making the *will* perform contrary to its own desires and *conform* to what God desires?

With great effort, because she had to align her thoughts so that she meant it, she prayed under her breath, *I forgive her, Father.* She swallowed. *Sidney too. Please help me to squelch any bitterness that may arise in the future.*

She was surprised at how that simple prayer released a ton of weight from her conscience. So much so that she was tempted to wake Peggy to tell her. But her friend's steady, peaceful breathing changed her mind.

The toast, which Mrs. Somerset served with eggs and bacon at the breakfast table, had a thick, buttery, flaky crust and a smoky flavor from being held over the fireplace. Catherine had three pieces and talked herself out of a fourth. No longer was she compelled to fill her stomach to aching; it was her taste buds that begged to be pampered this morning.

After breakfast they went up to Peggy's room and braided each other's hair. "What would you like to do today?" Peggy asked as she pushed the final hairpin into Catherine's chignon.

"Aunt Naomi and Sarah plan to take me shopping for school clothes tomorrow," Catherine replied. "But I wouldn't mind walking over to Collins'." Collins' Booksellers was just six or seven shops down. The recently-published *Treasure Island* would make for refreshing breaks between classics.

Peggy combed her fingers through the fringe above Catherine's eyebrows. "I'm glad you're wearing your hair fringed again. Much prettier. After Collins', let's go have a look at Mr. Sedgwick's school."

The last part was slipped in with the same casual tone Catherine could imagine Augustus Caesar using while saying to Cleopatra, *"You've lovely eyes . . . by the way, Egypt belongs to Rome now."* She swiveled around on the bench. "Absolutely not."

"But—"

"I know what you're trying to do . . ."

"I'm trying to do nothing," Peggy protested, her hazel eyes wide with injured sincerity. "Honest. Besides, it's summer. He won't even be there."

"How can you be so certain?" Not that Catherine intended to go, but she could not help a little curiosity.

"He spends most days at the tea company—that's what he said last year. We wouldn't even have to go in. Aren't you even remotely interested in seeing the school?"

Catherine was more than remotely interested. She told herself it was simply because she had never known anyone to have founded a charity school, and would be just as interested if the founder were anyone else in her acquaintance. Grudgingly, she said, "But is it safe?"

Peggy pursed her lips in thought. "I didn't feel threatened, but then, I was either in the company of Mr. Doyle or Mr. Sedgwick. But I suppose it would be wise to take a hansom instead of the omnibus."

"We'll hire a coach," Catherine insisted. She realized she was committing herself only after the words left her mouth. But she did not take them back.

"Whitechapel?" said the driver at the coach stand. His nose was as red as a fall apple. "Why, I were born and reared there!"

Even standing two feet away, Catherine caught a whiff of his breath. "Will you excuse us for a minute?"

He gave her a hazy grin and began whistling "When You and I Were Young, Maggie," as he adjusted the bridle on one of his horses.

"He's potted," Catherine whispered when she had drawn Peggy a few paces apart. "Should we walk down to another stand?"

Peggy sent an unenthusiastic look down the street, then toward the team in the harness. "As long as the horses are sober . . ."

They returned to the driver, and Catherine asked, "You're quite certain you're familiar with Whitechapel?"

"Like the back of me hand, Miss."

"What about the old meat tinning factory on North Street?" Peggy asked doubtfully.

"There's a school there now," he said, and grinned at Catherine's and Peggy's surprised looks. "Me brother lives two streets down."

He started climbing up in his box, so Peggy opened the door herself. Catherine stepped toward the front and looked up. "We don't want to stop directly in front of the school, mind you. Just close enough to be able to see it from the window. Do you understand?"

He waved a hand and started whistling again.

Whitechapel did not shock Catherine as much as she supposed it would, for she had seen far worse in many areas of Bombay. Still, it was a place of intense depravation. Signs of the inner lives in the closely packed nests oozed out into the pavements and gutters, for the primary school children were out for summer. They darted about the roads with naked, muddy feet below their rags, playing in little groups with oyster shells and pieces of broken china, or using a stick and frayed ball to play something resembling rounders.

After they had turned down yet another dismal lane Peggy, who had insisted on taking the rear-facing seat, looked again through the window on Catherine's right. She tapped the glass and sat back so Catherine could see. "The brown brick building up ahead. But I wonder why those people are moving about."

Catherine looked. The people, older boys, were carrying bundles and stacking them on the pavement. As they drew closer she recognized the bundles as desks. And when they drew still closer, she gave Peggy a panicked look. "Isn't he going to stop here?"

"Oh dear," Peggy said. But she did not seem terribly disappointed.

The carriage halted directly in front of the school. Catherine turned to her window again and flinched. Hugh Sedgwick's face was on the other side of the glass, only inches away. Shielding his eyes with his hand, he peered at her curiously. She was about to ask Peggy to have the driver move on, when recognition flooded his brown eyes. He gave her the crooked smile she had forgotten.

Thirty-Nine

*C*atherine had to squelch the temptation to say, *We just happened to be passing by* as she took his proffered hand and exited the coach.

"How good to see you again, Miss Rayborn," he said, pushing back the wheat-colored hair from his forehead. He was hatless, his collar unfastened and shirtsleeves rolled to the elbows.

"Thank you," she said, still mortified. What must he be thinking? "We assumed your classes would be out for summer."

He smiled at her again. "Actually, your assumption was correct."

He offered a hand to Peggy, who came out saying breezily, "My fault that we're in your way, Mr. Sedgwick. I was so impressed with your school that I pressured Catherine to come have a look."

Bless you, Peggy! Catherine thought.

"I'm glad you did." Mr. Sedgwick motioned to indicate the half dozen boys carrying out desks and assorted items. "You've caught us on an exciting day. We're moving to larger quarters two blocks down. Our wagon should return any minute."

"Should we have our driver move?" Peggy said.

Catherine seized the legitimate excuse. "We really should leave them to their work."

"Better yet," Mr. Sedgwick said, "let's take your coach to the new place. I'll pay the fare. Have you time?"

"We have," Peggy said without looking at Catherine.

"Splendid!" He turned to one of the older boys. "Tom, please tell Mr. Garrett I'm going to the new building."

"Yes, Mr. Sedgwick."

"There's a good fellow." He walked over to look up at the driver. "Can you find Thomas Street?"

"Aye."

"Well, there's a big yellow stone building. It was once—"

"A cotton warehouse." The driver belched and scratched his stomach. "Well, are ye goin' to get in, or shall I drive meself there?"

"We'll triple our classroom space," Mr. Sedgwick said from the rear-facing seat as the coach began moving. His face was as animated as William's would become when speaking about his son—or about some recent chemistry discovery. "It was just one vast interior when we bought it six months ago. We've had to cut windows and add walls, a second storey with kitchen, dining hall, and bathrooms, and two more classrooms for future growth. But some sponsors kindly donated toward the mortgage, so we'll be paying less than our former rents."

To Peggy he said, "I had no idea, when I happened upon you and Mr. Doyle last summer, that he was connected with Blake Shipping. They transport shipments to the States for my father, and sponsor four of our students."

"Lovely." Peggy nodded at Catherine. "Are you aware that Miss Rayborn is related to the Doyles? She stays with them in Hampstead."

"What a small world," Hugh said. "Tell me, Miss Rayborn, will you be leaving soon for Bombay?"

She was surprised that he knew this about her. "Not any more. My family is moving to Sheffield in August."

He asked if last summer's situation in Egypt had anything to do with that, and she told him that it was a contributing factor. And Catherine had a question for him, one that genuinely interested her. "How did you come to begin a school?"

Settling back into his seat, he replied, "Back in January of last year, I was searching for a boy who had picked my pocket and fled into Whitechapel some days earlier. I happened upon a factory dismissing for lunch and was distressed to see so many children among the workers."

"Did you ever find the boy?" Peggy asked.

"No, Miss Somerset . . . or rather, not to my knowledge. It was dark. But I've prayed God would lead the boy to us, if he's not already one of our students." A smile quirked beneath the brown eyes. "My faculty know to keep their purses light. While we strive to teach morals as well as academics, it's best not to leave temptation about."

They stopped behind a wagon hitched to two horses. Two boys were unloading the last few desks, while others carried desks and chairs inside.

"The adults are working too," Mr. Sedgwick said as if he just realized

Catherine and Peggy could have the wrong idea. "We didn't hire laborers for the actual move because we want the children to understand that they're very much a part of the school. And we're taking them on a train down to the beach at Hastings as a reward next Wednesday."

"I think what you're doing is marvelous," Catherine told him. She felt no self-consciousness in saying so, for it was true.

"Why, thank you, Miss Rayborn."

"You must keep terribly busy," Peggy said as he reached for the door handle. "How do you manage running a school *and* working for your father? And have you a wife or fiancée also requiring some of your time?"

All Catherine could do was pretend an intense interest in the unloading going on outside her window, while she willed her cheeks not to betray her.

"I no longer work for my father," she heard him reply. "And there is no wife or fiancée. Shall we?"

The boys carrying desks and chairs paused to allow them entrance through the wide doorway. Once inside, Catherine was so caught up in the beehive of activity going on about her that she forgot her irritation at Peggy. The oak paneled walls smelled of fresh varnish. Classroom doors stood open. Boys and girls wielding brooms and mops and cleaning rags ceased chattering to send them curious looks or shy smiles.

"If we continue growing, we'll hire two or three more teachers next summer," Mr. Sedgwick said as they stepped inside a Mr. Madden's classroom. "We have an incredibly gifted and dedicated staff. They make this school what it is."

Mr. Madden, a young man, leaned on his mop handle and smiled. "Mr. Sedgwick gives himself far too little credit."

The sheer energy of the place was impressive, as if everyone was embarking upon a monumental project. *The students are out for vacation,* Catherine reminded herself when she unfairly compared the school to the staid academy in Belgravia.

Out in the corridor, a boy approached to tell Mr. Sedgwick that the driver of the wagon desired to have a word with him. Mr. Sedgwick introduced the boy as Harold Tanner and said, "Show Misses Rayborn and Somerset about until I return, will you?"

The boy blushed to the roots of his blond hair, but escorted them to another classroom where newly hired teacher Mrs. Thorn, who appeared to be about twenty-five years of age, asked Catherine and Peggy if the map of Britain she had just hung on her classroom wall was level from a distance.

In another classroom her husband, Mr. Thorn, was arranging books onto a shelf.

"Are you fond of school, Harold?" Catherine asked when they were back in the corridor.

"Oh, yes, Miss." Timidly, but proudly, he raised the collar of his patched blue shirt to show a bronze badge the size of a penny. "I won the mathematics medal for second form last year."

"Good for you!" Peggy said as Catherine leaned closer to admire it. When they were reunited with Mr. Sedgwick and the boy was gone, Peggy gave Catherine a pointed look and then opened her mouth.

Please . . . no more, Catherine thought.

"Miss Rayborn has been offered a teaching position at the Ryle Day School in Belgravia."

"Indeed?" Mr. Sedgwick seemed impressed. "I've a cousin once removed who taught there some years ago, before she married."

"She hasn't decided yet, though," Peggy said. "She has until late August to—"

"May we see upstairs?" Catherine cut in.

At a table in the dining hall, a Mrs. Garrett and Mrs. Beeby, mother of a student, were slapping together bread slices, mayonnaise, and ham and adding them to a mountain of sandwiches upon a tray. Mrs. Garrett said, "You'll stay for lunch, won't you?"

"Yes," Mr. Sedgwick said. "Do stay."

Catherine found herself wanting to do that very thing, and it alarmed her. Had she only deceived herself into believing she had grown past an infatuation with every eligible male who looked her way? Would she soon be scribbling Hugh Sedgwick's name in the margin of her notebooks?

"No, thank you," she said before Peggy could commit them to staying the whole day. "We really must leave now."

They had not even seen the whole upstairs yet. Though disappointed, Hugh did not press. He told himself he wasn't setting a good example for the students and staff anyway, by socializing while they worked. The half dozen boys outside had almost emptied the wagon of another load.

"The ladies' driver is asleep, Mr. Sedgwick," Mr. Madden told him.

They all turned to look. The coachman was slumped sideways in his box, head propped upon bent arm and sagging mouth sending out sonorous gusts.

"He's a bit tipsy," Miss Somerset explained.

"He is?" That worried Hugh. "You really shouldn't be in this neighborhood without a responsible male escort. I'll accompany you as far as—"

Miss Rayborn was shaking her head. "Thank you, Mr. Sedgwick. But he's done all right so far."

"And he's familiar with the neighborhood," Miss Somerset added with obvious reluctance.

Stepping over to the coach, Hugh reached up to give the toe of the man's boot a shake. "I say, Sir!"

The driver opened his eyes and sent him down a bleary smile. "Time to move on, is it?"

"As soon as the ladies are inside. But are you still able to drive?"

"Aye. Joost takin' a little nap."

Hugh paid the man, over the protests of his two guests. "Your visit was a tonic to me," he said, opening the coach's door. "We don't have many visitors. Please say you'll come again when we're settled."

Miss Somerset offered her hand. "We will, Mr. Sedgwick."

Miss Rayborn also extended her hand. But as Hugh took it in his own, she barely met his eyes, and replied with a less committal, "Thank you for the tour, Mr. Sedgwick."

She's aware that her friend's plotting, Hugh thought, restraining a smile. And her discomfort over it surely meant that she was not entirely disinterested in him. If she were, she would not care enough about his opinion to be embarrassed.

She was not so wide-eyed and naïve looking as when he sat across from her on the Express three years ago. That there was more of the woman and less of the schoolgirl made her more attractive in his eyes.

Lillian, happily wed to Sir Jeffery, seldom visited his thoughts any more. He had decided he did not need anyone. When loneliness crept up upon him, he simply plunged himself more deeply into work. But seeing Miss Rayborn again reawakened the interest he had had in her once before, and made him aware of how painfully out of balance his life was.

He wondered if Miss Somerset was not the only one attempting to initiate something. Could it be that God was involved in a little matchmaking Himself? *If you are, Father,* he prayed under his breath as he watched Miss Rayborn settle into the seat, *please give me some sign.*

"The dark-haired one likes you," Mrs. Garrett said when Hugh carried a couple of chairs up to the dining hall.

"And just how do you know that?"

"I could tell by the way she tried so hard not to look at you. Now, what young woman could avoid looking at your pretty face, unless it was to hide her affection?'"

Mrs. Beeby chuckled, and Hugh mugged a face at both women. He was beginning to lose the feelings in his arms from the elbows down. But recalling his prayer of just minutes ago, he stood studying Mrs. Garrett.

She cocked her chin at him. "Why are you looking at me that way?"

"I'm just wondering if you're my Gideon's fleece."

Instead of asking what he meant, Mrs. Garrett shook her head and resumed making sandwiches. "That I don't know, Mr. Sedgwick. I suppose you'll have to call on the young lady and find out for yourself."

"But why shouldn't he know you plan to teach?" Peggy argued as the coach rumbled up Fleet Street. "He owns a school."

"It was so obvious that you were hinting that he should offer me a job," Catherine replied.

"Well . . . I was."

"It made me seem desperate. Can't you see that?"

"No, I can't. Because I took care to mention the Ryle School wanting you."

"Not desperate for a *job*. Desperate that he should court me. Especially after that bit about the wife or fiancée."

Peggy's little smile was maddening. "I don't recall suggesting that he court you. But it's obviously on your mind."

"No, it's not," Catherine said automatically. At Peggy's disbelieving look, she shook her head. "Very well . . . it is. And that frightens me."

"But why? He's a very decent man."

"Because I was doing just fine. I don't know if I can trust myself yet."

"You're going to have to trust yourself sometime, Catherine," Peggy told her. "Or will you hide yourself from every eligible man who comes along?"

That was the trouble, Catherine thought. She did not *want* to hide from Mr. Sedgwick.

But the whole mental struggle could be moot, she realized. While Mr. Sedgwick had been nothing but hospitable, he had given no indication that courtship had even entered his mind. The thought both comforted and disturbed her.

"Just when I think I have my life in order, chaos," she told Uncle Daniel the following afternoon in the library, where his stack of manuscript pages on the bubonic plague now rose a good three inches above the writing table.

"And what brought this on?" he asked, folding his arms and rocking back in his chair.

She held up the envelope delivered only an hour ago. "A Mr. Sedgwick asks to visit Sunday afternoon to speak with me about my plans after graduation."

"Sedgwick? Like the tea company?"

"His father owns it. And Mr. Sedgwick owns the school Peggy and I toured yesterday. I was quite impressed with the place. But at this point I don't know if it would be wise to teach there."

"Why not?"

Realizing he knew nothing of their bumbling attempts at corresponding during her freshman year, she told him, even going back to the prank on the train.

"Interesting fellow," her uncle said with a little smile.

"I was glad to see him again, Uncle Daniel. That's the problem. What if I'm deceiving myself, and am only desiring a position there as an excuse to be near him?"

Uncle Daniel scratched his beard thoughtfully. "You're stronger than you think, Catherine, and God has matured you over the past year. Just ask Mr. Sedgwick for several months to pray over it."

"I agreed to give the Ryle School an answer by the end of August."

"Then you'll have two months. And you'll have greater clarity of thought being up at Girton, removed from the situation. Tell Mr. Sedgwick that, and then see how God leads. He's not failed you yet, has He?"

Her uncle was right, of course. God had not failed her, even when His answer was no. *Especially* not when His answer was no, she thought, recalling her frantic prayers that Sidney would stay in her life. Were God indulgent to every whim of His children, He would be like Aunt Phyllis, and His children as maladjusted as hers.

That evening she prayed earnestly, *Help me not to step ahead of you again, Father.* And then added, *And when Mr. Sedgwick calls, help me not to slip back into neediness.*

*T*he white-haired gentleman reading just on the other side of the low stone wall seemed a good candidate for directions. Hugh stepped closer. "Excuse me, Sir?"

"Yes?"

"Will you be so kind as to direct me to number five? I can't seem to locate any house numbers."

The man closed the copy of *Quarterly Review* over an index finger and rose from the wicker chair, despite Hugh's protest that he needn't. "Nonsense, young man," he said. "Rising from chairs is the only exercise I get these days. My doctor forbids me to tend my garden. Says the damp soil's bad for my rheumatic hands."

Hugh shook his head sympathetically and glanced about. Not a stray twig marred the uniformity of the shrubberies. Flowers in beds stood in precise rows from shortest to tallest; yellow pansies in the front and brilliant blue delphiniums bringing up the rear. "You've quite an orderly garden."

"Not as much as when I did it myself, but one learns to relax one's standards when he reaches my age, lest he drive everyone else insane." He extended a gnarled hand over the wall. "I'm Admiral Kirkpatrick."

"Hugh Sedgwick," Hugh said, shaking the hand with care.

"Yes? Any connection to the tea?"

"My grandfather founded the company."

"Well, what do you know! I prefer coffee myself, but my Martha—God rest her soul—was quite fond of Sedgwick Tea. She said she could always expect every cup to taste the same."

Hugh understood now the proximity of the wicker chair to the road. But what could he do? Interrupt the man's sentimental musings and hurry on? "I'm glad she liked it, Sir."

"She didn't put anything in it either. No milk or sugar, just tea." The gentleman smiled. "Look at me, holding you at attention like this. Number five is the next house. The Doyles—that's who you're looking for, yes?"

"Yes, thank you. And may you have a pleasant afternoon."

The old man saluted him and wished him the same before returning to his chair. Once an elm with low branches cleared his sight, the Doyles's house loomed ahead, grey and Gothic and interesting. At the door he straightened the collar of his tweed coat before ringing. An older women with spectacles and warm smile took his bowler hat and bade him wait in the hall. Seconds after she disappeared with his card, he heard footsteps on the staircase and looked up at Miss Rayborn and a bearded older gentleman.

"Good afternoon, Mr. Sedgwick," she said.

Hugh smiled. "Good afternoon, Miss Rayborn."

She was wearing her hair in a chignon, and looked very nice in a simple lavender gown with small embroidered violets. When they reached the ground floor she introduced him to her uncle, Daniel Rayborn.

"Have you horses that need watering, Mr. Sedgwick?" the man said as they shook hands.

"Thank you, but I walked from the omnibus stand."

"Good idea. The fresh air is most invigorating."

Hugh assumed Mr. Rayborn was to act as chaperone, but the man excused himself. "My son-in-law and I are concluding a chess match, and our wives are putting the children down for naps. But do come up and meet everyone later."

"I would be delighted, Sir." He would certainly like to thank the Doyles for their support of the school.

"Do you mind if we sit outside?" Miss Rayborn asked as her uncle turned again for the stairs.

Hugh didn't mind at all. In fact it suited him fine, given what he wished to discuss. They walked down the corridor and out past a terrace into a breathtakingly lovely garden. Not as precisely trimmed as the one next door, but he preferred the organized disorder of it, the stray vines clinging to the wall, the beds overspilling with flowers of all heights and hue.

When they reached some benches near a small pond, he walked over to marvel at the trout-sized goldfish. He was used to his sister Claire's succession of goldfish in bowls, and never realized that they adjusted their size according to their containers. "Do you think they would grow even larger in a lake?"

"It has never occurred to me to wonder," Miss Rayborn confessed, staring down at the glints of orange-gold. "But I'll ask my uncle when we go back inside. He once wrote a biology text. Surely he would know."

"A biology text? Indeed?"

She smiled. "Uncle Daniel has a wide range of interests. He's writing a book about the bubonic plague now."

"Tell me about everyone else," he said as they settled at either end of a nearby cast-iron bench. With his encouragement, she described them all, even down to the coachman's son—which would explain the faint, sometimes off-key, sounds of a bow being drawn against violin strings coming from a window over the stable.

How odd, Hugh thought. His contact with Miss Rayborn over the past three years had been so scant as to be almost nonexistent. Yet he felt as if she had been a part of his life those years, though in the most tenuous way. Was it simply because she was beautiful? He hoped he was not so shallow, but then, he had only to look at Neville for proof that young men generally cared more about the fairness of the cheeks than the quality of the mind.

A maid with auburn hair came from the house with a tray. There was room on the seat between them for cups and saucers. After the maid, whom Miss Rayborn called Avis, was gone, Miss Rayborn raised her cup and looked at him with grey-green eyes merry. "I do hope you like *Sedgwick*."

"It's tolerable," he replied, smiling as he squeezed his lemon slice into his cup. And he realized that, as much as he was enjoying himself, he should move on to his reason for coming, for the members of her family could possibly decide to join them at any minute.

He has nice eyes, Catherine told herself as she took a sip of tea. It was not so much the thick lashes or amber flecks that brought on the observation, but the openness and amiability of them. She was silly enough to be flattered back when Sidney's blue eyes were so intense upon her. Now she thought that having a man devour her with his eyes would be unnerving and even insulting. She was aware that she looked nice, had groomed herself to that end. But she desired also to be appreciated for her mind and character and life experiences. She was a person, not a bauble to dazzle the eyes, or worse, a meal to whet the appetite.

Perhaps Uncle Daniel was right; she had gained some maturity after all. She hoped so.

Mr. Sedgwick took another drink from his cup and replaced it on its saucer. "Miss Rayborn . . . do you recall my mentioning a cousin once removed who taught a number of years at Ryle School? Geneva Lewis is her name."

"I do," Catherine replied while attempting to establish the connection between his cousin and the school in Whitechapel.

"I do hope you'll forgive my meddling, but I took it upon myself to ring her Thursday evening. She told me that her experiences were favorable, that Mrs. Whitmore was a supportive and considerate headmistress. I wasn't sure if you had any information beyond your interview, so assumed Geneva's insight might be helpful."

It was as if Catherine's taste buds were prepared for tea, but the contents of her cup had suddenly changed to hot chocolate. Her mind, prepared for one thing, had some difficulty making the transition. Through it all she had to maintain a smile, so that he would not notice her disappointment.

And she was not successful at that, for a little dent appeared between his brows. "Forgive me, Miss Rayborn," he said. "Should I not have meddled?"

"No. It was very considerate of you." The strain of the smile was too great, so she allowed it to slip from her face. "Your cousin's recommendation will be most helpful."

He stared at her for a moment and then cuffed his forehead with the heel of his hand. "What a dolt I am! It never even occurred to me . . . did you think I was here to offer you a position at my school?"

Why did you have to give up lying? Catherine asked herself sourly. But she could not bring herself to admit the truth, so she simply turned her face from him.

She felt his hand upon her sleeve.

"Miss Rayborn, please hear me out. While I'm sure you're immensely qualified, or you wouldn't be pursued by Ryle School, I can't even offer to interview you because you're a woman."

Now she had no difficulty looking at him. Did he not realize she had met Mrs. Thorn while he was out chatting with the wagon driver only three days ago? "Mr. Sedgwick, there is a woman preparing a classroom at your school now."

"As is her *husband*," he said. "I have to consider the safety of my staff, Miss Rayborn, and Whitechapel is no place for a woman without a reliable daily escort."

Catherine recalled his concern over Peggy and her leaving in the care of the inebriated driver, and realized he was being forthright with her. There was nothing to do but admit her humiliation, for he could surely read it upon her face. "I can't tell you how embarrassed I am, Mr. Sedgwick."

"Embarrassed? Whatever for?"

"You came all the way out here to pay me the courtesy of sharing your cousin's experiences, and I leapt to conclusions."

"I should have worded my note more clearly, Miss Rayborn." His lips quirked into their smile. "But I must admit that I felt awkward all the way here, so it's a comfort to know I'm not the only one suffering."

"But why should you feel awkward?"

"Because I didn't come out here only to share Geneva's experiences. I could have done that over the telephone."

"Then why else are you here?" she asked, truly puzzled.

He blew out his cheeks and started tapping the sides of his thumbs together, while the toe of his boot jiggled from side to side like a runaway metronome. "It's unfair that men have an easier go at most things, Miss Rayborn. Such as passing through Whitechapel without being overly concerned about safety. But we also have to take the initial steps in courting, and that can be a terrifying thing. I may appear all calm and collected, but you must remember I've had acting experience. My insides are quivering like that boy's violin strings."

Catherine was too amused to become nervous. "I've witnessed your acting talent firsthand, Mr. Sedgwick. But you don't seem calm and collected to me at all."

"I don't?" He chuckled, and the shared humor clearly relaxed him, for the thumb tapping and toe swaying ceased. "Well, without further bumbling preamble, may I ask permission to call upon you now and again?"

"I'm flattered, Mr. Sedgwick." *It's fine to be so,* she told herself when panic attempted to strike. *As long as you remember to guard your heart until you're absolutely sure.* And one could not become absolutely sure in one fine afternoon in a garden, or even over the course of a summer. "But I'm returning to Girton tomorrow."

"Oh. I didn't realize. Then of course, I understand."

His acting talent had failed him again, for she could see the disappointment in his brown eyes. The temptation came, urging her to offer to delay her return. Or to give some reason for returning to London in a week or so. But as she had learned through painful experience, impulse was a child who simply wanted what it wanted, with no thought to what was best in the long run.

"But may we have another try at corresponding?" It would even be best, she realized. Through letters, they could learn more of each other without emotions intruding upon reason. She could concentrate on her studies without pining over a pair of brown eyes or crooked smile.

He gave her a wary look. "You're not just being kind, are you?"

"It wouldn't be kind to ask, if I really didn't want to hear from you. But will you have time, with all your responsibilities?"

"You'd be surprised at how a person can squeeze in time for letter writing," he said, smiling again. "I'd like very much to correspond with you. Just please stay on good terms with Miss Somerset this time."

Their earliest letters touched upon superficial things, descriptions of the events of their days; Catherine's family's move to the school near Sheffield, Mr. Sedgwick's visit by some philanthropists seeking advice for a school they desired to build in the Bethnal Green slums, Catherine's lecture schedule, a copy of a poem about the River Thames that Mr. Sedgwick's sister Noelle had written.

Catherine penned in one letter: *We have grown used to the constant sounds of hammering while another wing is being built and the dining hall doubled in length.*

And from Mr. Sedgwick: *Hammering is a very familiar sound to us here, as the September rains revealed to us that our roof is but one wide sieve.*

Later letters delved a bit deeper and included consolations for each other's disappointments, such as Catherine's low mark on a *Judio-Claudian Emperors* composition, and Mr. Sedgwick overhearing his father praise his brother Brian's accomplishments in the office with not a word for Hugh's school. They also shared each other's joys over such things as the successful surprise birthday party Catherine arranged for Peggy, and the offer of the Charitable Organizational Society to provide uniforms and shoes for Hugh's students.

By December, the salutations of Miss Rayborn and Mr. Sedgwick were discarded in favor of "Dear Catherine" and "Dear Hugh." They were able to be transparent with each other, to pen things they would have had a difficult time voicing.

Catherine wrote: *When I finally understood that it was not Lord Holt whom I had loved, but the intoxication of love itself, the very last traces of his presence left my heart. I have no more doubts over having accepted the position at Ryle Day School. The possibility of happening upon Lord Holt again does not worry me. The opposite of love is not hate, I believe. It's simply no longer caring.*

And from Hugh: *I realize now that Lillian was wise to call off our engagement. I would have allowed work to consume even the time that should be set apart for family. I have since learned balance from watching the Garretts. While they are dedicated to the school, they do not allow the urgent things to overshadow the important things.*

What Catherine appreciated most about their correspondence was that they had become friends. A courtship built upon friendship was far more comfortable, she had discovered, than one built upon flatteries and flirtations and seesawing emotions.

What lay in her future? She could not see beyond that curtain. When she prayed for a peek, the answer she received was *In due time.*

Forty-One

*I*n 1826 Ralph Bradshaw founded Sutton School in Derbyshire's beautiful Hope Valley because he did not wish to send his eight sons away for a quality education. Mr. Bradshaw, an illiterate who made his fortune from his needle and pin factory in Sheffield, gave the institution his wife's maiden name lest those sons expect privileges not extended to the remainder of the student body.

The grey gritstone buildings were arranged about a quadrangle. On the east was the three-storey building housing dormitories and classrooms. On the north stood the kitchen and dining hall. Tennis courts and stables faced the south, and to the west were the chapel and library. Cricket matches took place in the field behind the dining hall, and a gap in a hedge beyond led to the headmaster's cottage.

Catherine's father had replaced a Mr. Parry, whose five-year tenure ended after a student's hand was broken during a caning. James Rayborn's first act was to abolish corporal punishment. His long-held philosophy was that he had no biblical mandate to strike another man's child, and he preferred to weed out those few who could not be motivated toward good behavior by a reward and demerit system. He proved the seriousness of his edict nine days into term by expelling a six-former for bullying younger students. His strictness was tempered by a calm, pleasant demeanor, which won him the respect and admiration of students and staff.

The respect was reciprocal. However, Catherine's father still maintained a distance between school and family—or rather, between school and eleven-year-old Jewel. She sat between her parents during chapel services and took lessons at home from Miss Purtley, along with the grounds keeper's nine-year-old daughter, Florence. Muriel was her only other playfellow, whom she saw only once or twice monthly when she accompanied Mother the eight miles to Sheffield or when Aunt Phyllis paid a call.

"I'm afraid you're doing her a grave disservice," Catherine gathered the nerve to say on the seventeenth of December, two days after arriving from Girton. She had waited until her sister was abed, Father was relaxing in his parlor chair, and she and Mother were wrapping gifts to ship to Hampstead via railway.

"Disservice?" Father turned half-closed eyes toward her. "What do you mean?"

Her mother paused from wrapping Bethia's jigsaw puzzle. "We raised you the same way, and I daresay you've turned out just fine."

"And I'm very grateful for all you've taught me." Catherine wanted to qualify that right away. "To be generous to those less fortunate . . . to set goals . . . and to have no prejudices. I always knew I was loved." Her fingers worried the ends of the ribbon around the box containing Aunt Naomi's bracelet of Blue John stones from the Castleton caverns nearby. Why was it so much easier to bare one's heart to friends than to parents?

"But even with your best intentions," she went on after a quick prayer for just the right words, "there were two things lacking in my childhood. I didn't realize this until I left home and suffered some pains for the lack of them."

At the phrase "suffered some pains," a dent had appeared between her mother's brows, and her father's eyes widened a fraction.

"Two things," he said when she was finished. "Well, what were they?"

Catherine gave him a look that begged understanding. "The most important was a close relationship with God. Because we never discussed our Christianity, I assumed God's part in my life was consigned to bedtime prayers and church."

During the silence that followed, snowflakes pelted the windowpanes with muffled little *pings,* and the fire snapped and sputtered in the gate. At length Mother set Bethia's wrapped gift aside and said, "I wasn't brought up in households where such personal matters were discussed, Catherine. But you knew you could come to us with any question."

Her father nodded. "Any."

"And I'm grateful for that," Catherine said. "Only, even with both of you there for me, I didn't even realize there was a void in my life. It was when I went away to school that I started trying to fill it with other things."

"What other things?" Mother asked, paling a bit.

Father looked uneasy. "You didn't take up smoking cigarettes, did you?"

Were the moment not so serious, Catherine would have laughed. God help her if she were inclined to smoke, with the family she had!

"No, Father. I'm speaking of romance. My happiness became determined solely by whether or not I had a suitor. And I came very close to marrying a terrible man."

The dent in Mother's forehead deepened, and a frown tugged at Father's lips. Catherine had confessed her slipping about to see Lord Holt, but not *why* she had been so consumed with him. She, like her mother, was brought up in a household where such matters were not easily discussed.

But she forced herself to press on. "Had I the security of a close relationship with God, I don't believe I would have fallen in love with Lord Holt . . . and practically every other young man who crossed my path. You don't want that to happen to Jewel, do you?"

The latter was effective strategy, for Jewel was the light of their lives. Catherine's parents looked at each other. Eventually Father blew out his cheeks. "The blame must be laid at my feet. I *was* brought up in that sort of home and have forgotten what a comfort it was. I fear I've devoted more attention to my work than my children's spiritual growth."

"You're a *good* father," Catherine reminded him. "And it's not too late. She's only eleven."

His eyes glistened, but he gave her a little smile. "I'll try, Catherine."

"You said two things, Catherine," Mother said quietly. "What else was lacking?"

Catherine drew in a breath. "Boys."

She had to smile at how quickly both sets of parental eyebrows raised. "It's not what you think," she said. "Because I was so shielded from their association, they were a mystery, and I assumed the only relationship possible between males and females was one of romance. I'm only now learning how to form friendships with them."

"Boys," Father muttered.

"Are they such horrible beasts, Father?"

"No, of course not. But around my little girl?"

"You have to prepare her for when she's no longer your little girl."

"That's something to consider, James," Mother said. "And I have fond memories of playing with the three Douton boys next door."

"Really, Mother?" Dear as she was, Catherine could not imagine her participating in something as unproductive as frolic, even as a girl. "What did you play?"

Her mother waved a casual hand. "Pretend games for the most part, because your Aunt Phyllis and I couldn't bully them into playing with dolls, even though two were younger. Robin Hood was the favorite."

"Robin Hood?"

Sentiment softened her grey eyes. "Phyllis and I took turns as Maid Marian. Whoever lost out had to be one of the merry men. Neither one of us ever got to be Robin Hood, though. The Douton boys could ignore our gender for Little John or Friar Tuck, but not their leader."

"I would have allowed you to be Robin Hood," Father said.

She inclined her head toward him. "Thank you, James."

Father wove his fingers together upon his chest, pressing the tips of his thumbs into his chin. "While what you're saying is reasonable, Catherine, I certainly can't send Jewel out to the playgrounds with a hundred and forty male students. What would you suggest?"

Having invested considerable energy in determining how to approach them with the problem, she had not thought to save some for the solution. But Mother surprised her again.

"How many students are staying over Christmas, James?"

"Five," Father replied. As in India, there were families either unable by circumstances beyond their control, or more sadly, unwilling to be inconvenienced by children too old to be pawned off on nursemaids. Father maintained daily contact with the students, but it was the housekeeping staff who looked after them.

"They could come here for lunch," Mother said. "Mrs. Chapman cooks such huge quantities anyway. I should have thought of that days ago. The poor boys—set aside from their families."

Father looked doubtful. "Five? With Jewel?"

"Under our supervision, of course."

When he stared musingly into the fireplace, Mother gave Catherine a victorious little smile and handed her the spinning-top intended for John to wrap.

The boys, ranging in ages from eight to thirteen, sat with watered-down hair and somber faces at their table the following day. Catherine could appreciate their abashment, for even now she could not imagine herself dining comfortably with Miss Bernard's family.

She wrote the gist of the table conversation to Hugh.

Father: "Mr. Robyns here constructed the papier-mâché model of the solar system that hangs from the science classroom ceiling."

Mother (giving the boy her brightest smile): "Indeed? I shall have to go and have a look at it very soon."

Mr. Robyns (blushing and staring down at his mulligatawny soup): "Thank you, Mrs. Rayborn."

Catherine was happy to report in her next letter that the awkwardness lessened considerably when Father and some of the school staff took sleds out to the hill beyond the stables, and the five boys were naturally included with the rest of the children. *And Father read aloud from Saint Luke in the parlor this evening,* she wrote on Christmas night. *It's a good start, don't you think?*

On the fourth of January, Catherine's last evening home, Father had the stable master hitch a team of Clydesdales to the school sleigh and drove the family to nearby Hathersage. Savory aromas met them outside The Millstone Inn, famous locally for their fish and chips. For a little while Catherine's family devoted more attention to the plates of perch, fried potatoes, and stewed carrots than to conversation. But when the edges of appetite were satisfied, Father turned to Catherine and said, "This young man with whom you've been corresponding . . . ."

Catherine swallowed a half-chewed bit of potato with a gulp that thundered in her ears. Mother and Jewel seemed to be holding their breath. Father held fork poised between plate and mouth, a carrot segment impaled upon the tines, and regarded Catherine expectantly.

"Mr. Sedgwick?" she supplied uneasily.

Propelling the carrot into his mouth, he chewed and swallowed. "Why don't you invite him up for Easter vacation so we may meet him?"

She looked at her mother, intercepted her nod, and turned again to her father. "Are you quite sure, Father?"

"Quite." He doused the fish remaining on his plate with vinegar, as if unaware of the quiet stir he had caused. "We should come here more often, Virginia. It's very good."

"You didn't even inform him you'll be in town?" Peggy asked on the morning of Saturday, the sixteenth of February.

Catherine threaded the leather strap through the clasp of the portmanteau upon her bed. She had just finished saying that Dr. Precor had excused her in advance from this afternoon's lecture on Advanced Mythology, but she knew that it was not Dr. Precor of whom Peggy spoke.

"It's Marie's wedding day. I couldn't presume upon her to invite someone she hasn't even met."

"But he could at least see you off at the station Sunday. Why don't you ring him when you arrive?"

"I couldn't possibly." Catherine tugged at the second strap. "He lives with his family. What would they think?"

"Granted," Peggy said at length. "But you've not even invited him for Easter yet . . . have you?"

With no more straps to fasten, Catherine looked up at her friend standing at the foot of the bed. "Easter's still two months away."

"Why are you afraid to see him?"

It was no use denying it, when Peggy could read her as easily as a chemistry text. She sighed. "I've had one failed romance already."

"And so the letters are safer."

"Yes." How could she explain? She could so easily pour out her thoughts to Hugh in her letters, as he obviously could to her. However much she desired to see him again, what if they discovered that the bond forged by ink and paper just could not be maintained in person? She was so fond of him. Could she bear the disappointment?

When she had not elaborated, Peggy shrugged and said, "If he ever proposes, perhaps you should look into marriage via post. The vicar—no, the postmaster general—could hold up your two envelopes and proclaim you husband and wife."

Catherine picked up her portmanteau by the handle. "Now you're being silly."

"You're the silly one," Peggy shot back with an affectionate smirk. "But who can tell? People are busy. Perhaps you'll set a trend. Though how you'll manage the children part of it is beyond me."

"Peggy!" Shocked as she was, Catherine could not restrain a smile. "I'll mention Easter in my next letter."

When her friend folded her arms and gave her a skeptical look, Catherine rolled her eyes. "As *soon* as I return."

Mr. Pierpont's three dark-haired daughters fluttered about Marie, fussing with her satin train, arranging the folds of her long tulle veil, as if she had become *Mother* in their minds long ago. The wedding was an intimate affair, conducted by Rev. Troughton of Christ Church and held in the parlor of 5 Cannonhall Road. Guests besides the Doyles and Rayborns and their servants were Marie's sisters and brother-in-law and the elder Mr. and Mrs. Mitchell. Marie would be introduced to the remainder of her husband's family in Reims this summer, when the girls could accompany them, Aunt Naomi had informed Catherine.

Dearly Beloved, we are gathered here in the sight of God and in the face of

this company, to join together this man and this woman in holy matrimony;
which is an honorable estate, instituted of God in the time of man's innocency,
signifying unto us the mystical union that is betwixt Christ and His church . . .

After the ceremony and vicar's blessing, wedding party and guests left the
sitting room for the hall downstairs, where chairs and tables with white linens
were arranged. Caterers from the Corinthian Hotel served a supper of mock
turtle soup and roast guinea-fowls, crimped cod and fried oysters, and vegetables in various sauces. The wedding cake was Trudy's loving handiwork, a
two-tiered concoction of flour, butter, currants, candied citron, and spices
under almond icing.

"We thank you each for helping to make our day joyful," a glowing Marie
said on her husband's arm before leaving with her new family. "You must
please come to visit us soon."

After the last guest had left and the children were tucked into beds, the
adults of the family ended up in the parlor to savor the occasion a little longer.

"Mistress of her own home, after serving in others' for so many years,"
said Aunt Naomi, the one person in the room who knew exactly how that felt.
"She deserves this happiness."

"Who'll take her place?" Catherine asked. As able as her cousin was in
many ways, the deformed hand made getting dressed difficult without the
help of a lady's maid.

"Avis," Sarah replied. "She's thrilled over the promotion."

"She'll do a good job." Aunt Naomi sighed. "But I'll miss having Marie
about."

William chuckled, stockinged feet propped upon an ottoman, and Hector
dozing in his lap. "You'll miss sparring with her, you mean."

"Yes, that too," she admitted readily.

High spirits from the enchantment of the occasion kept the adults awake
for another hour. Inertia caused by comfortable chairs and a warm fire
accounted for a second hour. As conversation eddied about her ears, Catherine's thoughts returned again to Hugh. She had not been so geographically
near him since their correspondence began last June.

How she now wished that she had informed him that she would be here!
A simple line in one of her letters would have done it. Yes, there was an element of risk—as there had been in leaving her family in India to set out for
college at eighteen. Could anything worthwhile be accomplished without
incurring some risks? Would she prefer a life of bland, safe, lonely mediocrity?

"You young people may sit up all night if you wish . . ." Uncle Daniel's
voice broke into her haze of thought. He was on his feet, assisting Aunt

Naomi to hers, ". . . but we old folks require sleep." That stirred everyone into sluggish motion, and good-nights were traded about between yawns.

A soft knock sounded at Catherine's door minutes after she had extinguished her lamp and slid under the covers. "Come in?"

Sarah opened the door in an aura of corridor light. "You're still awake?"

"Yes," Catherine said, pushing aside the covers. "Come in."

"Do stay in bed." The glowing coals in the grate illuminated Sarah's nightgown-clad form like an apparition as she padded across the carpet. At the bedside she took Catherine's hand and said, "Marie was so pleased that you would take time from school to come."

"I was touched that she would invite me."

Semidarkness did not conceal the worry in Sarah's expression. "You seemed a little melancholy in the parlor. The wedding didn't bring on some sad memories, did it?"

"Sad?" When the meaning of the question sank in, Catherine shook her head. "I hardly even think of those days any more. It's as if they happened to another person."

"Then you've forgiven me for sending you away that time?"

Catherine wrapped her other hand about their clasped hands. "You should have locked me in the attic until I came to my senses."

Sarah smiled. "Will Mr. Sedgwick come by before you leave?"

"No. He isn't aware I'm here."

"But why?"

"Because Peggy's right." Catherine sighed. "*I'm* the silly one."

"Beg pardon?"

She confessed her cowardice and regret. "But I'm going to invite him up to Sheffield for Easter. You'll hardly believe this, but it was Father's idea."

"Will wonders ever cease?" Sarah leaned forward to kiss her forehead. "Now go to sleep."

Forty-Two

*S*unday afternoon Catherine planted farewell kisses upon the foreheads of her three cousins settling down for naps, and then changed from her church dress into a traveling ensemble of navy-blue cashmere. Once Stanley had collected her portmanteau, she folded her cloak over her arm, took up her reticule, and walked down the corridor to the staircase. Her feet had just touched the landing above the ground floor when Sarah's hushed voice drifted up to her.

"Surely another ten minutes won't matter."

"Only if traffic is light." Uncle Daniel's voice this time.

And from William, "That's the trouble, Sarah. You can never predict—"

"William . . ." Aunt Naomi interrupted.

As Catherine descended, all four faces stared up at her. But her curiosity had no time to ripen, for she was caught up in farewell embraces, admonished to take care, and helped into her cloak.

Outside Stanley was adjusting the horses' traces in the damp chill air. He gave Comet a sociable slap on the flank on his way to the coach's door. That was when the meaning of the conversation struck Catherine. She glanced back at the house. "Sarah rang Mr. Sedgwick, didn't she?"

Uncle Daniel gave her a regretful look. "He wasn't certain if he could come. She shouldn't ha—"

But he paused, cocked his head at the sound of approaching hooves, and stepped around to the back of the coach. Catherine moved beside him. A coach pulled by two horses turned from Cannonhall Road into the carriage drive. Her uncle smiled. "But then again . . ."

The ruddy-cheeked driver reined the team to a stop and tipped his hat at Catherine and Uncle Daniel. Hugh, clad in topcoat, scarf, and bowler hat, emerged from the coach and advanced with hand outstretched.

"Good afternoon, Miss Rayborn, Mr. Rayborn. I wonder if I might have permission to escort Miss Rayborn to King's Cross?" His brown eyes met Catherine's. "That is, if you have no objection, Miss Rayborn."

Catherine nodded dumbfounded assent to her uncle's questioning look.

"Very well, Mr. Sedgwick," Uncle Daniel said as the two shook hands. Stanley, grinning from either sentiment or relief over not having to make the trip—or both—handed her portmanteau up to the other coachman. A minute later Catherine was seated on Hugh's right while gravel snapped beneath them.

"My father's coach," Hugh explained.

"Oh. Very nice."

"How are you keeping?"

"Very well, thank you," Catherine said. "And you?"

"Well. Thank you."

When he did not fill in the awkward silence that followed, Catherine said, "Has your mother recovered from her cold?"

"Yes, thank you," he replied.

"I'm glad."

Another silence hung between them. Catherine stared blankly at the facing seat, realizing with sinking heart that her fears had been well founded. The ease and intimacy of their correspondence could not carry over into face-to-face conversation.

"Catherine?"

When she turned toward him, his brown eyes were filled with sadness. "You weren't going to inform me you were here?"

"I couldn't ring your house," she said feebly.

"May I ask why you didn't write of it beforehand? Did you not wish to see me? Have I been laboring under a false assumption?"

"I wanted to see you. But I was afraid."

A hand went to his chest. "Afraid of me?"

She shook her head. "That something would change."

"Change . . ." Another tense second or two passed. His eyes narrowed, but a hint of a smile quirked beneath them. "Does this mean you're fond of me, Catherine?"

She shifted her gaze down to her hands folded in her lap. "Hugh . . ."

"Well, does it?"

"Surely you can tell from my letters."

Her arm felt the light nudge of his elbow. "Then, how about you saying it?"

"Saying what?" she asked.

Another nudge. "You know . . ."

She still stared downward, but had to smile. "The man's supposed to say it first."

"Where is that written?"

"I don't know. Somewhere."

"Ah, but you're a modern woman of the eighties."

Finally Catherine looked up at him. "I'm also my father's daughter."

Hugh chuckled appreciatively, eyes shining. "I'm very fond of you, Catherine."

"And I you," she said softly.

"You can't imagine how I've treasured your letters." He scooped up her gloved left hand. "How overjoyed . . . and distressed I was when Mrs. Doyle rang that you were here."

"I'm glad she did," Catherine said.

"Truthfully? Then you're not sorry I came?"

Just the thought of how close she had come to not seeing him caused her breath to catch in her throat. "I'm glad you came."

They chatted with the ease their correspondence had established. She told him of the wedding, and he of the piano a Presbyterian chapel had donated to the school. When she mentioned Easter vacation, he said he would be happy to come.

"Can you spare the time away from Whitechapel?" she asked.

"I'll make the time," he said, squeezing her hand. Too soon the coach halted at King's Cross Station. As the boarding whistle sounded on the locomotive of the Great Northern Railway, Hugh stashed the portmanteau beneath the padded seat of an empty first-class coach. Settling into the seat by the far window, Catherine held out her hand. "Good-bye, Hugh."

"Good-bye, Catherine."

He still held her hand, brown eyes warm upon her. A woman's voice came from the platform behind him. "Here is one, Alice."

With obvious reluctance he released Catherine's hand. "Do watch out for the men students," he said just before stepping out to make way for two women. "Some are notorious pranksters."

She smiled. "So I've heard."

On the seventh of April, Catherine, accompanied by her father and Jewel, saw Miss Purtley off at Sheffield Station on her way to visit her family in Devonshire, browsed in a bookshop, then took lunch at Royal Victoria Hotel. They walked back out on Victoria Station Road with over an hour to spare before Hugh's half-past-three train was due.

"We could visit Aunt Phyllis," Jewel suggested.

"Not without your mother," Father replied.

Catherine smiled to herself. He spent most of his time in the company of children, but could not bear the commotion of the Pearce clan without Mother to act as a buffer. Unable to resist a wicked impulse, she said, "What will you do if Aunt Phyllis decides to enroll the twins at Sutton, Father?"

"It would probably improve their behavior." He touched the parcel under his arm. "We'll sit and read while we wait."

They found a secluded bench at the station; Father seating himself in the middle with *Roderick Hudson* by Henry James, Jewel to his left with Anna Sewell's *Black Beauty,* and on his right, Catherine divided her attention between Robert Louis Stevenson's *Treasure Island* and the station clock. When the hands pointed to twenty-past three, she knew she could no longer delay voicing the concern which had occupied her mind for days.

She tore a bit of brown paper for a book marker and closed her novel.

"Father?"

"Mmm?"

"You do recall that you were the one who suggested inviting Hugh here?"

He moved his eyes from the page to her. "Why would I forget?"

"I just would appreciate your remembering—and not making any sort of negative hints."

"She doesn't want to be embarrassed, Father," Jewel explained from his other side.

"Or for Mr. Sedgwick to be embarrassed," Catherine added.

Father let out an injured sigh. "I'll be the soul of hospitality."

He not only lived up to his promise, but went the second and third miles. He practically monopolized Hugh's company, leading him about every square foot of the school. And Hugh seemed more than willing to be led about.

"Well, they're both headmasters," Mother reminded her on Thursday. "Mr. Sedgwick can learn much from your father. And your father enjoys having someone ask his advice."

They had taken advantage of a rare fifty-five-degree early spring afternoon by carrying wicker chairs to the far side of the hedge to watch the croquet game between Jewel, Florence, and three boys remaining at school over the Easter vacation. Until Mr. Rumboll, the grounds keeper, came to inform Father that a crate of newly published geometry texts had just arrived.

Even though the texts would not be used until fall, Father had to go give them a look. Naturally he invited Hugh, who had popped up from his chair like a cork in water. At least he had had the courtesy to ask if she and Mother minded.

"You had your chance then," Mother reminded her above the youthful banter and clicks of wood against wood.

"I couldn't very well ask him not to leave."

"Another peg point!" a boy crowed, raising a mallet over his blond head in a self-congratulatory salute. "You may as well concede defeat."

"Pride comes before a fall, Andrew!" Florence shot back.

Catherine and her mother traded smiles. And beyond the field the men were approaching, Father speaking with his hands making motions for emphasis, and Hugh listening intently.

Mother nodded in their direction. "Would you rather they be at odds, Catherine?"

"No, I'm happy Father likes him." It was just that in the three days since Hugh's arrival, they had not spent one minute alone together. But that was something even a woman of twenty-one could not admit to her mother, no matter that she desired nothing less innocuous than having her beau's sole attention for just a little while.

". . . discovered that if mathematics is the first subject of the day, the students fare better in grammar," Father was saying as they came within earshot.

"Why is that, Sir?"

"Because the mind is still in the habit of logical, orderly thinking. A student who has spent an hour balancing equations will more easily recognize when a sentence is not balanced . . . for example, the subject and verb are not in agreement."

"Was the shipment complete?" Mother asked.

"Yes." Father took to his chair again, smiling out toward the young people. "Who is winning?"

"Andrew, it appears." Mother turned to Hugh, standing beside the chair he had abandoned. "Do have a seat, Mr. Sedgwick."

But Hugh smiled and said, "Mr. and Mrs. Rayborn, I wonder if Catherine and I might have permission to take a stroll."

"A stroll?" Father said.

Catherine wondered if the discomfort in his expression had to do with the notion of their being unchaperoned, or that he would lose his disciple for a little while.

But Father was still Father, and so she was not surprised when he said, "Unchaperoned, Mr. Sedgwick?"

"Just to Hathersage, Mr. Rayborn. We would return well before dark. How far is it . . . two miles?"

Forcing herself not to appear too eager, Catherine said, "It's a pleasant day for a walk, Father."

"I could do with a bottle of Glycerole," Mother said. "The girls' Easter shoes will need oiling."

"Very well." The smile Father gave Hugh did not mask the effect of his pointed words. "You'll not stray from Sheffield Road, Mr. Sedgwick. Agreed?"

"Yes, Sir," Hugh said. "Thank you, Mr. Rayborn."

"Are you sure you want to tear yourself away from my father?" Catherine teased when the school and its buildings were behind them. They walked just to the side of the roadway, for new grass was kinder to the soles of their shoes than crushed stone. The moors and hillsides ahead were frosted white with anemone, the first flowers to burst forth after the rigors of winter.

He took her hand. "Would he have allowed us to walk, had he and I not spent so much time together?"

Catherine could not help but feel a dull disappointment. After all, her father was her father, and the idea of even Hugh flattering him was disturbing, even for her sake. "You weren't actually interested?" she asked.

"Not interested?" Hugh gave her sidelong look of surprise. "I'm still a novice and cannot begin to tell you the mistakes my inexperience has caused. The knowledge I've gleaned over the past three days is priceless. But yes, to be quite honest, if your father were a bricklayer, I would have developed a genuine interest in laying bricks. Anything to be allowed to court his daughter."

A picture developed in her mind; Hugh, pausing from slapping mortar on bricks to wipe the sweat from his brow with a shirt sleeve. Like the biblical Jacob laboring for Rachel. She rather liked that.

"But now that we're alone," he went on, "you'll have to teach me how to win your mother's approval."

"Oh, but you already have it."

"Really? She said that?"

"Well, not in so many words." Catherine smiled at him. "But I happen to know she bought Glycerole last week."

They knew not to ask to walk after Good Friday service at chapel, for the shops would be closed. Besides, it did not seem fitting to engage in courtship

on such a significant day. Mother woke Saturday morning claiming a stuffy
nose and sent them for peppermints. On Sunday the family joined the proces-
sion of carriages and wagons bearing school staff, school and house servants,
and the three boys to Hathersage for the Divine Liturgy at Saint Michael and
All Angels Church.

*Christ being raised from the dead dieth no more: death hath no more domin-
ion over him. For in that he died, he died unto sin once: but in that he liveth, he
liveth unto God. Likewise reckon ye also yourselves to be dead indeed unto sin but
alive unto God through Jesus Christ our Lord.*

Hugh read the Anthem with the familiarity of one who has attended such
services for years, and yet the reverence of one who has not lost his awe over
the miracle of new birth. During hymns, his clear quiet baritone touched
every note on key.

Thank you for new beginnings, Father, Catherine prayed beside him. *In our
temporal as well as spiritual lives.*

Father and Hugh spent all Monday morning compiling next year's calendar for Sedgwick School. After lunch, when Mother faltered at thinking of
something she required from Hathersage, Father just waved a hand and said
not to linger. But he gave no such order on Tuesday, Hugh's last full day, and
so they dawdled, sharing a bench outside the sweet shop to share a parcel of
sweetmeats, stretching out their time alone.

"Will you spend the summer here or in London?" Hugh asked as they set
out for the school again.

"Both," Catherine replied. "After a fortnight here, I plan to move into
the boarding house across from Ryle's. I'd like to be fully prepared when classes begin. If I'm allowed to graduate, that is."

"If? Your marks are very good."

"Thank you. But having spent the first two years practically hanging on
by my fingernails, I'll breathe easier when the certificate is in my hand."

"As it will be." With a cautious look, he said, "I'd like to introduce you
to my family. You wouldn't mind that, would you?"

"I'd like that," Catherine said.

"Excellent."

"But I warn you . . . I'll be a little nervous."

"Oh, but you've no need to be." He gave her a wry smile. "But then, I
was more than a little nervous over meeting yours. Perhaps its one of the
universal trials of falling in love . . . fear of the other's parents."

Falling in love? Yet they continued on as if he had simply commented on the weather. Five times her heels struck the new grass between them, six, seven. And still he said nothing.

Dourly Catherine recalled their conversation in the garden on Cannonhall Road. While Hugh may have rightly complained that men had the more difficult role in courtship because they were expected to take the initial steps, the women's role was just as difficult. Women were constrained from expressing any feelings from the heart until the man had done so.

"Did I just say what I think I said?" Hugh said at length.

A heaviness settled in Catherine's chest. Was there regret in his voice? With affected casualness she replied, "That you were afraid of my parents?"

"No, the latter." He stopped walking, and because he still held her hand, Catherine stopped too, though she did not allow herself to look at him. But oddly, she could sense his smile.

"This is rich, Catherine," he said, stepping around to face her. "I hardly slept last night, laboring over just the right words to say—and then to have it slip out like 'how do you do?' "

Perhaps the men have the most difficult role after all, she thought, raising her eyes to meet his. "You could try again."

His eyes shone. "Yes, I could do that." He took her other hand. "I love you, Catherine. You're the most wonderful person I've ever met. The fact that you're in the world makes it a better place."

"You thought that up last night?" was all she could say for the lightheadedness.

He shook his head, raised her folded hand to kiss a knuckle. "Just now."

"It was lovely," she murmured. "Shame you wasted all that wakefulness."

"It wasn't wasted."

He still smiled, but a bit of anxiety had crept into his brown eyes. Somehow in her hazy state of mind, Catherine realized he was waiting to learn if her feelings matched his.

"I love you, Hugh," she said softly.

There was a mutual moving together, his arms going about her, their lips meeting. "Nice," he said when they drew apart a bit for air.

"Nice," she echoed, but with quickened pulse, for she could hear hooves, see the little cloud of dust billowing about a horse and rider in the east. Hugh dropped his arms, and they resumed their walk two feet apart, as if they were no more than acquaintances traveling in the same direction by happenstance.

Mr. Jakes, stable master of Sutton School, touched the brim of his hat as his horse cantered past.

"That could have been my father," Catherine said. "We should hurry."

They continued on at faster pace, but stopping every several paces for another kiss. That ceased when they crossed a rising and the school came into their sight.

Hugh sighed. "I'm a happy man," he said, and began whistling to match their steps.

A scene from the past struck Catherine's mind like lightning.

The whistling stopped abruptly. "Is something the matter, Catherine?"

She blinked at him. "Matter?"

"You were frowning." With a worried look, he said, "Have I been too forward?"

"No." Self-consciously, for it was humiliating to admit even to Hugh how she had allowed someone to demean her so, Catherine explained. "It's that song. Lord Holt once chided me strongly for knowing it. He said it was low-class tripe."

"Low-class tripe? Indeed?"

She shrugged. "He had refined tastes."

"I beg to differ," Hugh said, touching the tip of her nose. "But I'll never whistle it again, if it makes you sad."

"Actually . . ." Catherine smiled. "It reminds me of how fortunate I am."

"Yes?" He grinned back at her and took her hand again. "Well then, it has just become my favorite song."

And as if to prove it, he started singing as they resumed their walk, his clear baritone floating in the fine spring air.

> *"He'd fly through the air with the greatest of ease,*
> *That daring young man on the flying trapeze.*
> *His movements were graceful, all girls he did please*
> *And my love he has stolen away . . ."*

Forty-Three

As slow our ship her foamy track
Against the wind was cleaving
Her trembling pennant still look'd back
To that dear isle 'twas leaving."

On the last day in June, 1884, random sniffs came from the occupants of the chairs arranged on the ground of Emily Davies Court, as well as from the fourteen young women seated upon the platform as Miss Bernard read from Thomas Moore's "The Journey Onwards."

> *"So loth we part from all we love,*
> *From all the links that bind us;*
> *So turn our hearts, as on we rove,*
> *To those we've left behind us."*

The University of Cambridge still refused to confer degrees upon students from the two women's colleges. But to students and faculty, the certificates soon to be awarded represented as much industry and tenacity as if they were diplomas. The women on the platform had passed the finish line, even though they had been forced to run outside the track.

Founder Miss Emily Davies stepped up to the podium to deliver the address.

"Miss Bernard, Miss Welsh, Distinguished Professors and Lecturers . . ."

On wings of reverie Catherine soared away from her place in the second row, to King's Cross Station, where she stood shivering with excitement. Graduation had seemed as distant as old age, those four years ago. Now she realized that the wind of which the poet spoke had been there all along; gently, almost imperceptibly filling her sails to carry her on toward ports that could not even yet be seen.

She looked out through the gap between two mortarboards at the familiar faces on the second row, just behind the professors and assistant lecturers. Mother and Father and Jewel. Sarah and William. Uncle Daniel and Aunt Naomi, Bethia and Danny. Aunt Phyllis, Uncle Norman, and their children. Catherine could not stop the wind, but God and family would always be the mainmast that supported her sails.

"*. . . we end one journey together and begin a new one . . .*"

She blinked and forced herself to pay attention to the address. It wasn't that she did not admire Miss Davies profoundly, but her brain was over-stimulated from the intense activities of the past several days; finishing up compositions, packing, singing around the piano for hours last night with soon-to-be-former schoolmates.

"*. . . this momentous occasion, we forge the fourteenth link in an unbroken chain of education, initiative, and industriousness . . .*"

Hugh smiled at her from the sixth row, as the front rows were reserved for family members. His letters were tied with a ribbon in her packed trunk. The one that had arrived two days ago said, *While I hope your tenure next year at the Ryle School is fulfilling, I cannot but hope you will not grow too attached to the place.*

She would have no memories of the ceremony if she did not pay attention, she told herself. Reluctantly she shifted her eyes from Hugh to the podium.

"*. . . support and guidance of your families, you took the first tenuous steps toward a commitment to lifelong learning, which will prepare . . .*"

She felt Peggy's hand touch hers. How pleased she was, that her friend would soon be the first woman chemist employed by the Hassall Commission. As they clasped hands, Catherine's mind took another flight, this time to a table at the Nave and Felly Inn, where Sarah was counseling her to put her friendship with Peggy before her desire to correspond with a certain young man. How right she had been! For Catherine was fully convinced that, had she sacrificed Peggy's friendship for Hugh in those days, she would have neither in her life at this moment. Peggy would have rightly felt betrayed, and Hugh would have eventually been frightened off by her neediness.

"*. . . challenges of this industrial era require women with keen minds, yet not at the expense of faith and integrity . . .*"

Pay attention! she ordered herself again. But her eyes soon fastened upon a woman in the very last row. Catherine had overlooked her before, for the wide-brimmed hat and dark spectacles did not allow for a lasting impression. In fact, the only thing distinct about her was her height. And on second look, the familiar set of her shoulders.

Milly!

Even though the eyes were shielded, Catherine could tell *she* was the focus of her stare. On the heels of that realization came the thought, *She doesn't even realize you've forgiven her.*

Of course, she had a good excuse for not informing Milly. But for that one sighting last summer, their paths had not crossed. And did God even expect that of her?

Applause brought Catherine back to the ceremony. Miss Bernard had the podium again, and one by one, called each graduate from the first row, then the second. Catherine sent a quick smile to her parents when her own name was called. All certificates awarded, the assemblage rose to its collective feet for the benediction, delivered by one of the professors, Reverend Starling.

"May the Lord bless you and keep you. As we walk life's pathway, may we ever keep our eyes trained upon His holy light, so that our feet are ever pointed in the direction of righteousness, and mercy toward others."

Mercy toward others echoed through Catherine's mind. While forgiving Milly and Sidney had been an act of obedience, *mercy* would be the act of easing Milly's obvious torment.

"Amen."

After a respectful moment of silence, graduates stepped down from the platform into the arms and congratulations of family members and friends. Catherine's cheeks were kissed, her back patted, her certificate passed about— until Mother took it, saying it would never frame properly if it became too wrinkled. Father stepped away and returned with a hand upon Hugh's shoulder. In all the activity Catherine noticed that Aunt Phyllis kept her distance from Sarah, but there was nothing she could do about that.

As groups began drifting toward the dining hall entrance for refreshments, those with cameras gathered themselves in small groups for photographs. Uncle Daniel began setting up his camera on the tripod. Several feet away Mr. Somerset did the same.

"Children in front, now," Uncle Daniel ordered, motioning. "Women on either side of Catherine, men in back."

Catherine spotted Milly again, standing just to the side of the gate, looking again in her direction. But Uncle Daniel became a benign despot whenever the camera was in his hands, so she submitted herself to standing in the center of the group, smiled when directed, and waited for the flash. Blinking at black spots, she looked again toward the gate. Milly was moving toward a carriage.

"What is it, Catherine?" Hugh asked.

"Milly." She nodded toward the gate. "I think I need to go to her."

"Then why don't you?"

"I will," she said, giving him a quick smile. To everyone within earshot she said, "I'll join you for refreshments in a few minutes."

"Catherine?" Jewel said, but there was no time to explain. Holding mortarboard clamped to her head with one hand, hefting her gown up a couple of inches with the other, Catherine hurried out the gate. A cabby was helping Milly into the carriage.

"Milly!"

Milly turned. The cabby sent a curious look over his shoulder.

Catherine closed the remaining twelve feet to stand at the side of the carriage. "I'm glad you came, Milly." As the words left her lips, wonder of wonders, she discovered she sincerely meant them.

With a shrug, the cabby climbed up into his box. Milly removed the spectacles to reveal indigo eyes that were red-rimmed and shadowed. "How can you say that?" she said thickly.

"Because I truly am. I forgive you. I only want your happiness."

"Happiness," Milly whispered as if no longer acquainted with the word.

"Milly?"

Milly blinked at her. Tears quivered from her lashes. She dabbed a handkerchief at them and rose from her seat. "Oh, Catherine!"

When she stepped onto the pavement they fell into each other's arms, Milly weeping and saying over and over how sorry she was, and Catherine patting her back and insisting she was forgiven.

"Are these hysterics by invitation only?"

Peggy's voice. It was then that Catherine realized she should have pointed Milly out to her friend before leaving the platform, for Milly's elopement had hurt Peggy almost as much as it had hurt her. She stepped aside so that the two could embrace. The weeping began anew.

"You'll join us, won't you?" Catherine asked when the tears subsided and the two finally drew apart.

"Yes, please, Milly." Peggy blew her nose into a handkerchief. "Everyone will be so happy to see you."

Milly sent the brick building an uneasy glance. "No . . . I can't. It took every bit of my nerve just to come to the ceremony."

Catherine nodded. "We understand."

With reddened eyes wide Milly looked at her. "But please tell your Aunt Naomi I will always have fond memories of the macaroons she used to send you."

"I will," Catherine promised. Suddenly the request struck her as oddly funny, in spite of the gravity of the moment. She snorted through her nose in an effort to hold back a laugh.

Both looked at her.

"What is it?" Peggy asked.

"I don't know, it's just—" Another snort escaped her. Catherine covered her mouth and nose with a hand, but could not stop her shoulders from shaking nor tears from forming in her eyes.

Milly smiled. Peggy let out a little chuckle that rolled into a laugh. A fraction of a second later Milly caught the same affliction. The three laughed until Catherine's sides ached, Peggy began hiccuping, and Milly was wiping her cheeks again. This time with a smile, though the levity had not driven away the sadness lurking behind her eyes.

They said their farewells. Catherine and Peggy watched Milly's carriage until it turned out of sight.

"That felt good, didn't it?" Peggy said as they linked arms and started toward the school building.

"Very good," Catherine replied.

They parted to join their families inside the dining hall. Father and Uncle Daniel, William, Uncle Norman, and Hugh were engaged in a friendly argument over whether Cambridge or Oxford would win the Henley Regatta next month. Jewel and Bethia and Muriel were discussing whatever interested seven-through-twelve-year-old girls. Six-year-old Danny watched, fascinated, as a boy his age demonstrated how to crack his knuckles. One twin—Catherine wasn't sure which—sat making fork rows through the icing on his cake as if bored to tears, while the other listened to the men's discussion as if mildly interested. Amazingly, Aunt Phyllis was admiring Sarah's photograph of John, as Aunt Naomi and Mother looked on.

Mother glanced her way and moved apart from the women to hand her a fork and dish of butter cake with pineapple glazing. "I know you like pineapple. This is delicious."

Catherine tasted it. "Mmm. Very good."

"Do be sure to thank Miss Davies for such a moving speech."

"Was it?" Catherine said before thinking.

The grey eyes filled with disbelief. "Catherine. You *didn't* daydream during your own graduation."

"Well . . ."

"For four years you've looked forward to this day," Mother said with a longsuffering sigh. "And you won't even remember the most important part of it."

Catherine leaned forward to kiss her soft cheek. "I'll never forget the most important part."

GET SWEPT AWAY
in Kristen Heitzmann's
Gold Rush Romance!

SHE ARRIVED *with little more than*
what she could hold in her heart.

Crystal, Colorado, is known as the diamond of the Rockies, but to Carina
Maria DiGratia, newly arrived from California, it is more like a lump of
coal—dirty and rough, its worth masked. Still, she resolves to forge her way
as best she can, determined never to return home.

Quillan Shepard then enters her life, both strangely protective and mysterious. Discerning the truth behind his haunted past will open Carina's eyes in
new ways, test her courage and faith as never before, and make her heart
yearn for a love she's never known.

◈ BETHANY HOUSE

11400 Hampshire Ave. S. • Minneapolis, MN 55438
www.bethanyhouse.com • www.kristenheitzmann.com